LOVING THE WICKED

ALSO BY REBECCA JOHNPEE

The Wicked

LOVING THE WICKED

REBECCA JOHNPEE

TOR PUBLISHING GROUP
NEW YORK

This is a work of fiction. All of the names, characters, organizations, places, and events portrayed in this work are either products of the author's imagination or used fictitiously.

LOVING THE WICKED

A Bramble Book
Published by Tom Doherty Associates / Tor Publishing Group
120 Broadway
New York, NY 10271

www.torpublishinggroup.com

Bramble™ is a trademark of Macmillan Publishing Group, LLC.

EU Representative: Macmillan Publishers Ireland Ltd., 1st Floor, The Liffey Trust Centre, 117–126 Sheriff Street Upper, Dublin 1, D01 YC43

The Library of Congress Cataloging-in-Publication Data is available upon request.

ISBN 978-1-250-38583-3 (trade paperback)
ISBN 978-1-250-38584-0 (ebook)

First Edition: 2026

Printed in the United States of America

10 9 8 7 6 5 4 3 2 1

For those who battle in silence,
your strength is louder than you think.

Caution

Zahra: Oh, hi again, we'd love to say—

Zahra and Elio: Welcome back to our world.

Zahra: If you're here, I'm guessing you survived the first book. Congratulations.

Elio: Or condolences. Depending on how attached you got.

Zahra: This story still deals with criminals, but this time, it digs deeper into the mind. We want to make sure you're well informed and prepared before you dive in.

Elio: Yes, we're talking guilt, trauma, obsession. The kind of things you can't shoot your way out of.

Zahra: (softly) Or escape from by running.

Elio: To make sure we have all grounds covered, here are lists of trigger and content warnings to look out for.

Zahra: Violence, murder, and gore—still a part of the package.

Elio: Mentions of past child sexual assault. Not graphic.

Zahra: Depression, trauma, suicidal ideation—

Elio: And a touch of psychosis—hallucination, paranoia . . .

Zahra: Overdose, too.

Elio: (dryly) Always something to look forward to.

Zahra: Oh—and explicit sexual content. One scene in particular explores BDSM dynamics.

Elio: (sighs)

Zahra: (laughs) What? We have to be very clear about these things.

Elio: Anyway . . .

Zahra: If any of this sounds heavy, please take care of yourself first.

Elio: But if you're ready—

Zahra: (grins) Welcome back to the chaos.

LOVING THE WICKED

Prologue

Fourteen years ago

ELIO

From what I wore to how I talked and walked, to the first time I had sex and tasted alcohol, and down to my first cigar, my father had been the voice that decided who I became.

I told myself I didn't mind. He was my father, and I was his shadow. His merciless soldier. His machine. I was to follow in his footsteps. Never make mistakes. Remember his advice and implement his instructions.

That was me, three hundred and sixty-four days of my life.

The day of my birth was the exception, which made sense because it was the only day I got to be me. Twenty-four privileged hours where I got to live outside myself, rearrange my thoughts and my previous experiences if I could.

But that all changed on my nineteenth birthday.

My father had forgotten, which meant I ought to have forgotten, too, but December 1st had been permanently etched into my memory.

The first thing I did that day was visit the church in our compound. I knelt and prayed for the salvation of my soul, just like my mother had taught me.

After that, I left the premises, but unlike the other times, I didn't feel lighter; I felt . . . heavier.

Pushing down the feeling, I went to get food and drinks for my brother, Elia. He had no idea it was my birthday; I never once told him; he just knew I stayed longer on this particular day. But unlike the last time, I didn't join him to eat; I just watched. When he asked why, I told him I had no appetite.

He was ten and old enough to pick out my lie, but he didn't ask any further questions.

When I finally left, I went to a private bar, got myself a beer, sat alone at a booth, and drank on an empty stomach.

It was the first birthday I celebrated with . . . sadness.

I was about to take on another year of being Elio Marino. Of living in this skin, in this time, in this face, of talking with this voice, wearing these clothes . . . another circle of ups and downs, of *yes, sirs* and turning a blind eye, another round of living a lie that was programmed to be my truth.

I was about to do it all over again, and the feeling was downright . . . draining.

The bar was dimly lit, and the music was nothing more than a dull hum in the background. I was on my fourth bottle of beer, my hand on my chin, my eyes closed, drowsy but alert enough to know I was still sober.

At the very back of my mind, a distant thought haunted me. For the past four years, since the day after I almost killed Elia to please my father, I'd caught myself doing the same things my mother once did. The same silence. The same way she'd stare at nothing for hours, as if she could see the end of everything. It terrified me to recognize her silence in my own.

I was slowly becoming a shell of myself. But I hid the cracks well; I willed them to leave, for me to sleep better, for the dark thoughts to let me be . . . but the more lives I took, the more I fell deeper and deeper into that shell, the more my mind failed me, breaking piece by piece.

At least I'd always had December 1st to pull me back out of the shell. But my dark thoughts had now tainted my one day of freedom, and I knew there was no coming back from that.

I knew my nineteenth birthday would mark the day I felt the heaviest because there was nothing to celebrate. I could only mourn the next year to come. I could only hate the thought of taking in my first breath when I woke up the following day.

My birthdays would now be the worst days of my life. Constant reminders that I was still living.

I shook my head, pushing those thoughts away, and took another swig of beer, looking around and catching the eyes of a pair of women sitting at the far end, one of them waving at me, the other twirling the ends of her blond hair.

Discomfort settled inside me, and I looked away.

Seventeen had been the first and last time I had sex.

I had been at one of my father's private clubs. He'd been celebrating a successful shipment for whatever the fuck he did outside the business. I knew it was a huge shipment because 75 percent of his capos were present. They were so rowdy, and I was not too fond of the crowd, but I endured as they conversed in cheers and slurred words.

My father had put a drink in my hand. It wasn't my first taste of alcohol. I'd had lite beers with Casmiro occasionally, but nothing this strong.

When I finished it, he pushed another, and then another, and then another, until feeling my toes began to seem like a struggle between life and death.

Everything that happened from that point blurred into flashes and short clips—the raw and thick smell of cigars in the air that night, the gruffness of his voice when he called two women over . . . two women with barely any clothing; he was grinning when they both leaned into me, but his face zoomed in and out of focus.

Then I'd felt hands touching my thigh, disappearing into my shirt to rub against my chest, lips on my neck.

I think I was trying to protest the idea, but my father's voice had climbed on top of my own. "Take him up and show him a good time; his signature gave us this." He raised his glass like he was doing me a huge favor. "Enjoy, Marino."

I remember being led somewhere. And then falling on a soft mattress. I remember one of them trying to kiss me, but I remember stopping her and the chuckle she gave afterward when she whispered in my ear, "No kissing, got it."

And then I remember waking up naked, next to two sleeping, *naked* women. The headache afterward, the lipstick marks on my skin, the first minute of panic, and then the long shower I had taken. I hated it. I hated it all. I tried to tell myself later that I'd consented, that the alcohol had been a choice, but the facts were simple: I was seventeen, he had supplied the drink, and he had handed my body over.

That night, I stood in front of my father's bedroom door, a gun in my hand, imagining myself entering and emptying my bullets into him.

But I couldn't do it. He was my father, my mother's husband, and my siblings' guardian. I couldn't kill him, so I slipped my gun behind me and walked away.

To this day, I wondered if I'd made the right decision. Walking away.

I knew if I didn't leave now, the girls currently watching me would find their way to my table, and I didn't need that.

Not today.

So, I finished my beer, paid my tab, and left the bar.

Reaching the compound an hour later, my phone buzzed in my pocket, and I fished it out, seeing my sister's name on the screen with a text message that had my stomach jumping.

Mari:
SOS

I rushed into the house. The sound of glass shattering, coupled with screaming and crying, had me running toward my mother's room.

I skidded down the hallway, my heart in my throat as I spotted Mariana on her knees, holding a crying Lorenzo in her arms, right in front of my mother's room. Mariana was crying, too, and I caught the sight of blood on Lorenzo's arm; the seven-year-old had his head buried in my sister's chest.

Mariana looked up, her eyes burning with anger upon seeing me. "Where were you!" she screamed at me. "She fucking hurt him!"

I heard loud mumblings, glass shattering, thuds, and incoherent screams from behind the closed door.

I swallowed the lump in my throat. "Go—get up, go stitch him up; I'll be with you both soon."

She shot me a confused look, her gray eyes blinking as if she hadn't heard me right. She got to her feet, and Lorenzo refused to look up. He never did. Never looked at me. I was on Papà's side, not theirs. Never theirs.

"Soon? You want to go in there? She's—God, she's out of touch with reality! She hurt Enzo!"

"Please, Mariana, go to your room, lock your door—"

"What if she hurts you? Mamá isn't here anymore!"

"No, don't say that, she's just—she's fine, she's just going through something."

"I'm seventeen, I'm not a fucking child, Marino! She needs medical attention!"

"Mari, please, take Enzo away; I'll handle it."

"But she's—"

"Enzo's hurt, go help him—clean his wound—"

"What if she—"

"Fucking go! Go to your damn room and lock the fucking door, Mariana!" I bellowed.

She flinched; fear clouded her eyes, a look I'd seen her wear whenever our father was around. Enzo's crying grew louder, and he hugged Mariana tighter.

I calmed, reaching for them. "Mari—"

She drew back in haste. "I hate you!" she yelled shakily, pulling Enzo away with her.

I watched them disappear down the hallway, biting my tongue and silently cursing myself for losing control like that.

Sighing, I pulled off my shoes and socks, knowing Mamá didn't like it when you entered her room wearing them.

I pushed open the door, my heart melting the moment I spotted my mother pacing back and forth, biting her fingers as she mumbled. Tears were streaming down her face, her feet were bare, and she left bloodstains on the ground as she stepped on the shattered glass, almost like she didn't feel the pain.

"Mamá," I whispered as I entered the room. I didn't care about the pain that bit at my feet as I rushed toward her; I didn't care that I was cutting myself; I just knew I had to get to her, to bring her back here. To me. To reality. "Mamá," I called louder this time, stopping before her as she tried to step past me.

I blocked her path, and she moved to my other side, which I blocked again. Her eyes were unseeing.

"Mamá, look at me." I tried to catch her gaze.

She shook her head, trying to get around me, but I wouldn't let her, and then she screamed. She threw slaps and blows at me.

"Get out! Get out, you bastard!"

I tried to grab ahold of her hands as she screamed. "Mamá, it's me. It's Elio, look at me!"

"No! Elio's dead! You killed my baby! You drowned my only child, you bastard! Get out! Get out of my life! Leave me alone!"

"No. Mamá, I'm okay! I'm alive, Elio's here, I'm here!" I caught her hands, and she tried kicking me. "Mamá, please, stop—" She drove her head right into my jaw, and I tasted blood on my lip, but I still tried to subdue her.

"Leave me alone!" she screamed.

"No, look at me! I'm here now! I'm here—"

She fought me. I didn't want to hurt her; she was so fragile that I feared I'd bruise her wrist if I tightened my grip.

I loosened my hand, not letting her go because I knew she would turn to find the nearest object to hurl at me, and when she did turn to reach for a vase, I wrapped my arms around her from behind, holding her tight, locking her back to my chest.

"No!" A scream tore out of her. "Let me go, Ricardo!"

"Mamá, it's Elio! Try to listen to me, please!" The desperation in my voice rumbled from my chest.

"Fuck off! I will murder you, you son of a bitch! I will fucking kill you for killing my baby!" As she screamed, she forcefully tried to squirm her way out of my hold, but I held firm, even though my head was a bit foggy from the alcohol.

We both staggered on our feet, and I must have stepped on something because I was falling to the ground, still holding her.

To shield her head from hitting the bedpost, I swirled us around and took her position. My elbow landed on a shard of glass, and the back of my head connected forcefully with the iron pole.

I saw fucking stars for about two minutes, but I still held her firm, even as she kicked her feet, jabbing her elbows into my stomach.

Sweating with the effort, I tried to keep her steady. I tightened my hold around her, her back pressed to my chest as I locked her legs with mine, ceasing her movements.

"Please let me go! Don't hurt me!" she cried out in panic.

"I will never hurt you," I told her calmly, feeling warm liquid slide down my scalp to my neck; I knew it was blood. The sharp pain at the back of my head was almost blinding. "Never, Mamá."

"Then let me go, Ricardo."

"It's Elio. I'm Elio. *Por favor*, come back to me." I rocked her back and forth gently. "Por favor," I whispered.

My grip tightened.

"You killed him. You killed my only child."

My chest tightened. "Mamá, you're scaring me. I'm not your only child, and I'm here, goddamn it."

"You killed my Elio."

I dropped my head to the crook of her neck from behind. "I'm alive, Mamá. I'm okay. Listen to my voice."

She calmed as she mumbled, "He's dead."

"No, he's very much alive. He's holding you. You gave birth to him on this day, nineteen years ago; you said he smiled at you even if he couldn't see you; you said he refused to let go of your hand. You said you sang him a lullaby in Spanish every night. You said he was priceless."

"Priceless," she whispered.

"Yes." I held her tighter, kissing her hair. "I'm here."

"Here." It was barely above a whisper, and I knew she was passing out.

"I'm never leaving you. Ever." I rocked her back and forth, looking around at the mess in the room, knowing it would freak her out when she woke up.

I stayed that way for five more minutes before laying her on the bed and proceeding to clean the room. When I was done, I went to her bathroom to grab a medical kit before cleaning her wounds and tucking her in.

I watched her for a few seconds and then exited the room.

I forgot my shoes, my bruises, and that I needed to calm myself down as I charged down the hallway, aiming for my father's study.

I didn't bother knocking; I just barged in. The fury swirling in my veins was fucking blinding. My chest heaved as I watched the two men sitting opposite him stare up at me with frowns while my father looked at me with disappointment.

"Elio, what is the meaning of—"

"Out!" I bellowed at the men.

They looked baffled, and my father gasped.

When no one moved, I sneered. "If you make me repeat myself, I will make sure the both of you regret ever fucking leaving your homes. Try me."

A second passed before they hastily got to their feet, and from the pinned castle emblem on their suits, I could tell they were two of my father's highly respected capos, and I still didn't fucking care.

When they left, my father shot up from his seat.

"You do not disrespect—"

"Quiet!"

His mouth clamped shut; surprise and caution filling his wide eyes.

"My mother's sick. You will not turn a blind eye to it anymore."

"Elio—"

"It was not a fucking request, Father."

I was running on adrenaline. I couldn't—on an average day—speak to this man like this. But I was done keeping quiet.

"She's getting worse," I said.

"*It doesn't matter*," he said in Italian.

I gawked. "She hurt Enzo. She hurt me! Don't you fucking see it!" I responded in English because I realized he was trying to take control.

"Your mother is fine! And you will not speak to me this way, boy!"

I walked over to him, got in his face, gripped the collar of his shirt, and yelled, "My mother needs help! She needs help, you bastard! Help! It can only get worse! What if she hurts herself? Hm? What do we do then? What the fuck do we do? She dies, then what, hm? Speak, you fucking bastard!"

His eyes searched mine. Twitching. "You sound more like her than yourself."

I frowned in confusion. "What—"

"*Are you sure you're feeling all right, son?*" he asked also in Italian.

I paused, realizing how my breathing came in short gasps. My gaze flicked to my tight grip on his shirt, and I instantly let him go, stepping back.

"I'm fine."

He shook his head. "No. No. I am not taking any chances. Get some shoes, boy; we're getting a diagnosis."

Fear clamped my gut. "I said I'm fine!"

He shot me a glare. "Do you want me to use force? I will."

There was no countering that, and in a few minutes, we were on our way to the family hospital.

"If we can get Mamá—"

"I don't want to hear nothing of your mother," he snapped.

We arrived at the hospital, and the process started. They ran tests, did bloodwork, a scan to rule out anything neurologic. The doctors asked a hundred questions. It took time. I remember the antiseptic smell and a nurse's high voice, not her exact words. I remember how the late night bled into morning, how the processes were expediated, how when the sun came up, I sat in a room where a psychiatrist told us I had major depressive disorder alongside some other brain things I'd blocked out because I felt the shift in my father's demeanor, and his eyes had darkened in the way they did when he was looking for quick solutions.

A few minutes later, we were driving back home; the car was silent until he spoke.

"You're joining the army," he announced.

I snapped my head to him. "What?"

"You're joining the fucking army."

"Why?" I asked, baffled.

He was wise enough to pull over to the side of the road but left the engine on as he responded. "Didn't you hear the diagnosis? You're crazy, and I promise that I will work it out of you."

"I'm not crazy."

"You are."

"I'm not fucking crazy!"

"You are!" he yelled back.

"I can't even get into the army. You think they'd let me in, knowing my health conditions?"

"I will get you in. There's a more private and secret base for people like you. I'll make the calls."

"This is insane. You can't just—"

"Look at you!" he yelled suddenly, the vein on his forehead throbbing. "A fucking disappointment. Despicable and weak like your fucking mother."

"I'm not weak. Depression isn't weakness," I gritted out.

"Oh, it is, and you *are* weak."

"You don't know what you're saying."

"I know exact—"

"No!" I glared at him with disbelief, my heart hammering. "No, I carry this fucking family on my back while you fuck and cheat your way through Italy. I am there for your wife and your children; I'm there for you! I'm there for fucking everyone but myself! Why the *fuck* wouldn't I be depressed!"

He looked at me like I was a stranger. "This. This right here, this despicable behavior, is why you need to get your head re-arranged."

"I don't need anything—"

"If I say you need something, then you fucking need it! Do not counter me."

"You're the one who's crazy. If you send me away, who's gonna look after them? Who's gonna hold Mamá when she forgets who she is again or what year this is? You can't do that to them, to me."

"You are joining the army, and you are getting your head on straight."

I shook my head, looking ahead, my breathing ragged as I said, "How can you not see that you're ruining my life?"

"I am making you better."

Looking back at him, I ignored the anger in his eyes and

focused on his ignorance and fear. "No, Papà, you're making me worse."

That seemed to shut him up. He cleared his throat. "I am your father. You are to listen to me and do what I say. I know what's best for you. Leave the family to me; that is not your job. Getting better is your job. You will take my place someday, and I won't have you ruin my name, Elio. You are a Marino. No Marino is a weak fuck. The private base will remind you of that. Am I clear?"

I rested my back on the leather seat, clenching my jaw hard.

"Am I fucking clear, boy."

"Yes, sir."

"Good." And then he started driving again. "You leave the day after tomorrow."

I looked out the window, thinking of the promises I was about to break.

I did it all mechanically.

We reached home, and I was out of the car before he could call me back. I went straight to Mariana's room, unlocking the door with the master key.

She and Enzo were on her bed, fast asleep. A book rested on her chest, almost slipping off.

I walked in, took the book from her body, dropped it beside her, and turned off the reading lamp.

I raised the duvet, covering them before leaning down to kiss both their foreheads. "I'm sorry," I whispered. "I'm so sorry."

I left the room and didn't sleep that night. When morning slowly crept in, I went to Elia. Told him I was sending him away. He broke my fucking heart, crying and begging me not to separate us.

I didn't tell him the reason. It was better if he hated me. Knowing my father had other plans for me in that army, I wouldn't be able to reach out.

I was going to be cut off. I was going to be tortured. This was his play.

Elia held me tight and made me promise I wouldn't leave. I knew he wouldn't drop it; I'd been prepared for that. That was why I suddenly remembered a drink I had gotten for him on my way here; it was why I walked to my car, brought out the chilled juice box, walked back into the safe house, and watched him drink while he told me what his homeschool teacher had said about whales.

It was why I watched him fall asleep suddenly, drove him to the airport, and handed him to the people who would take him to Los Angeles. It was why I stood there till the plane took off and disappeared from view.

I crouched down, covered my face with my palms, and let out a guttural yell that made my chest ache throughout my drive home.

I made sure I didn't see Mariana, Lorenzo, or my mother that day.

The next day, I was on my way to the army.

The whole process was a blur.

They shaved my head.

Gave me the uniform. And took me to a different facility.

And throughout my stay there, I received very special treatment.

A year later, my father came to take me home. He was impressed by my progress. He gave me a hug that I didn't return. I didn't even look him in the eye once. The horrors I'd gone through, the things they'd done to me, the dark thoughts multiplying in my head with every second that passed.

The numbness churning in my gut.

I had been right. He'd made me worse.

But I knew my anchor was back home. Back at the compound, my family.

They were the only reason I was even remotely eager to return to that compound.

My father had taken me straight to the meeting house. We were there for about three hours before I was free, and I raced to my room to change out of the uniform my father had forced me to wear to the meeting with his capos.

But the moment I walked out of the room, and the building, all I saw was chaos, soldiers running helter-skelter—barking orders.

"Water . . . hurry up . . . they're inside . . . fire . . . church . . . burning . . . stop the fire . . . quick!"

The voices filtered in and out of my head.

I will never forget the rage of the massive plumes of smoke erupting from the building, the overwhelming smell of gasoline that clogged my throat, the smell of burning wood, and the heat of the fire warming my skin from where I stood. For a second, I couldn't make sense of it. Then the screams started, and my mind caught up. My heart tightening and dropping.

I ran—God—I'd never run as fast as I did in that moment, my aim was to burst through the flames as though that were possible. At that moment it felt possible, at that moment I wanted to cut off the hands clawing at my skin, holding me back from reaching them, saving them.

I watched the fire claim everything. My mother. My siblings. The church.

And I was too late.

I hadn't been there.

I watched the footage from the church multiple times right after my father had gotten rid of everyone who'd witnessed or seen what had really happened so that he could create a narrative in his favor.

I watched and watched repeatedly—my mother bathing the church in gasoline, tying my siblings up. My mother's delusion as she kissed each of their foreheads while they cried, the flick of a lighter, and then, nothing. I let every single detail of that video sew itself into my head.

Because I would need it.

I would need it for when I burned it all down, with my father and me as the victims of our own demise.

CHAPTER ONE

Elio

"There you are." Casmiro's gruff voice cut through the quiet hum of the afternoon. I hesitantly tore my eyes from the page in the *Politics Today* magazine I was reading, raising my head to find him walking toward the gazebo. The air smelled faintly of chlorine, courtesy of the pool beside me which had just been cleaned, its surface still rippling under the sunlight. Casmiro's steps were careful, hand pressed against his torso, while he climbed the two steps before settling into the chair opposite me. "I went to your house to find you."

I looked down at the magazine, not deeming his state severe enough to check for complications. "You should not be out. You need to heal properly."

"I'm fine," the man offered with a grunt as he relaxed back into the chair. I could feel his stare, but I didn't want to talk, nor did I want to entertain any human company. His presence irritated me, and indulging him was not advisable, seeing as I didn't want to say something he wouldn't like to hear. "It's awfully quiet lately," he said.

I didn't respond as I reread a line for the third time.

He cleared his throat. "You never got back to me on how your interrogation went with the man you caught from the gang that attacked me at Turin—"

"He is dead."

There were a few seconds of silence before he spoke again. "How did it go?"

A mind-video of me slashing a throat, scanning a file, traveling three regions away from Milan, slashing more throats, painting walls red, muffling screams, and carving out flesh filled my vision but vanished with a blink.

"Unsuccessfully."

"And you killed him just like that?"

"Yes."

"So . . . How do you suppose we find the people responsible for the shooting at my racing company?"

"Word has been sent to our associates in Sicily. They will handle it. You need not bother."

I heard him sigh. "I have been . . . meaning to ask," he started, taking my silence as a cue to continue. "It has been two weeks since Street left. I asked my people, and they say you haven't properly addressed our search for the painting. May I know if they left because of the media chaos after the bus incident?"

"What other reason is there?"

"We sorted out the media alongside some of our associates in America, and the painting is no longer of interest to the masses." I saw him shift in my periphery. "I think we should bring Street back in. I still communicate with one of them, Upper. And he says they are close to—"

"Casmiro."

"Yes?"

"Your presence is a bother to me," I said, raising my head to regard him. "Do you mind leaving." It was not a question.

He blinked at me, a frown pulling down his brows. "Did something happen?"

"Casmiro." I closed the magazine. "Leave."

"Why?"

"Does my command mean nothing now. Have we grown too familiar that you do not understand a simple statement." Those were also not questions.

His frown remained, and he didn't make any move to leave. "Now I know why nobody dared say a word when I asked about you. You're in a mood. But we don't have time for your moods. The stakes are higher; we need to get moving if we—"

"We leave for Mexico next week."

His frown deepened. "Why am I just hearing this?"

"Because I am just deciding it. Now leave."

"Tell me what happened. Who pissed you off?"

I groaned, regretting not bringing a cigar or a drink with me. "You are not going to leave me alone, are you?"

"No. You're acting worse than you usually do. Everyone is waiting for you to snap, so they're working extra hard, making sure you'll see no reason to snap and—"

"I made a mistake." I cut him off, watching how his frown morphed slowly into surprise. I knew that statement might have sounded foreign to him.

"You . . ." he drawled, not comprehending, "made a mistake."

"Yes."

"Can you elaborate?"

"How comfortable are you with discussing matters regarding my brother?"

His eyes searched mine before he asked, "Why would you assume I'm uncomfortable talking about your brother?"

I dropped the magazine onto the table between us. "You have not exactly been forthcoming since you learned of his existence; I believe before your accident, we weren't on speaking terms."

He shook his head, sighing. "I was angry you didn't tell me."

"I did not tell anyone."

"I'm not anyone," he snapped. "I thought we were trusting each other now; I mean, all those years ago? Did you think I would hurt him if I found out?"

"No. I didn't want you to know because I never planned on seeing him again."

"Would you have told me if I didn't find out?"

"No."

He was clearly displeased with my response. "All right. Let's get back on topic. Who pissed you off?"

Going silent, I thought about it.

Telling him what had bothered me 24/7 for the last two weeks would make it seem real. It would force me to admit that I have been thinking about it . . . about *her*, and I didn't want to because my gut told me I'd made the right decision, but my head, mind, and whole being wanted to seek her out.

It was unhealthy.

I was aching to once again be in her presence, know what she was doing at all times, keep her attention on me. I was longing for the only woman I couldn't have. My addiction wasn't fading. This wasn't withdrawal; this was a full-bodied denial of my feelings and what I truly wanted.

Zahra had left a gaping hole inside me, and I was to blame for it.

"Elio?"

Casmiro's careful tone of voice shoved me out of my thoughts.

"I was involved with Zahra. Romantically."

I expected the silence that followed.

Casmiro's stare was blank for about a minute before, haltingly, his brows drew together, and he frowned, his lips thinning.

"You were what?"

"I knew beforehand that she was involved with my brother, but she told me she wasn't, and I believed her because I thought she was telling the—"

"Hold on, hold on." Casmiro sat up, his hand supporting his torso. "Just double back for me. You fucked . . . you fucked that cunt?"

The flare of withheld anger that smeared the walls of my chest had me pinning him with a glower. "Call her that again, and I will shoot you and make sure you die this time," I warned. "That's not a threat. I will kill you if you repeat what you just said."

He waved his hands dismissively, a tight frown on his face. "You fucked her?"

"Don't put it like that."

His eyes widened as he gestured wildly with his hand. "How the fuck do you want me to put it?" he exclaimed.

"It's not—" I stopped, clearing my throat. "It *was* not just the sex. There was something else."

Casmiro frowned, blinking as if trying to understand what I was saying but failing to. "Something else, like . . . you had her sign an NDA or some sort of—"

"No, nothing like that. I meant, it wasn't just physical."

He backed up. "Wait . . . emotional? Feelings? You . . ." The confusion on his face morphed into concern, a grimace, and then disbelief. "You *like* Zahra?"

I frowned. "You speak of it like it is some sort of fatal illness to like her."

"I'm sorry, I just don't see it. In my head—trying to picture you and—what—no—you're joking."

Annoyance brewed, and my chest tightened. "Why would I joke about this?"

"I don't know, to fuck with me? Make me think I'm in some coma hell . . . Are you my fucking subconscious? Am I dying?"

"Do not be unnecessarily dramatic about this. You were the one who wanted to know why I was in a mood."

He nodded. "Right, yes. I wanted to know, but I didn't think you would tell me you've been fucking—hold on, when did this start?"

"Months . . ." Her face flashed in my head, the carefreeness in her smile that always made her brown eyes look like a good coffee, the sweet smell of vanilla and amber always coming from her hair, the softness of her skin—

"Elio," Casmiro snapped and I blinked.

"A few months now," I continued. "Although it was a little back and forth at first." I sighed. "I won't disrespect her by telling you any details; all you need to know is that we were involved until recently."

"I thought you didn't like her? You tried to drown her, for fuck's sake."

"That was before I got to know her. I could not understand why she made me feel things. I could not predict her. I still can't, nor do I want to. I only seem to know her better now."

"Just because you fucked her."

"Before then," I corrected. "She has this . . . charisma, very much like mine, and I was interested, and one thing led to another, and we . . ."

"Right." Casmiro shook his head. "I am way too sober for this conversation, and—"

"You are not drinking."

"No, I think I am—"

"The doctor clearly stated you cannot drink alcohol until you've fully recovered," I told him. "Banish that thought this instant."

He sighed. "How am I supposed to digest all you're telling me with a clear mind? For God's sake, it's just impossible. I thought you were celibate."

I raised a brow. "Was I?"

"I haven't seen you with a woman in so long—like, years, and—just—of all the women out there, you choose the one who personifies suspicion."

"I cannot help who I like."

"I don't know, E . . . I've never trusted that woman. I don't like her at all. I don't know why, I just don't."

"Hm." I nodded, averting my gaze. "I can imagine why."

"No, no, you don't get me. I told you the day I was attacked, she threatened me. She told me to stay out of her business. The look in her eyes, her whole demeanor? Everything changed in that one second I glanced her way. If I could read minds,

I would have definitely caught her plotting something." He pinned me with a stare that begged me to see reason. "Think about it, E, she threatened me, and then I'm being shot at, hours later? Can't be a coincidence."

"I see the sense in what you are saying. But I asked her, she denied it, and I decided to give her the benefit of the doubt. Besides, there was no concrete proof to show she was indeed behind your attack."

He worked his jaw, shaking his head. "She's using you. I am one hundred percent sure she doesn't feel anything you're feeling for her."

My chest tightened at the truth in his statement. "I know that. But all of this was not why I told you about our temporary involvement in the first place. It concerns my brother—"

"Right, she just randomly has the *only* living Marinos wrapped around her fingers."

"Ignoring that observation, the mistake I made was getting involved with her without checking to see if my brother still held feelings for her."

Casmiro's lips thinned. "So you messed up your relationship with your brother by sleeping with his girlfriend."

"She told me they weren't together."

"She's a liar, E. A skillful one. There's a possibility she was even trained to lie."

"I am aware," I said, my tone flat, refusing to rise to the bait.

He sighed. "That's why you had them off the case? Because you both—ended your, uh . . . temporary involvement?"

"No. I needed Elia out of the compound. I needed Zahra out too. She was complicating things, messing with my goal, and I wouldn't say I liked that she had kissed my brother. I didn't want to entertain the way it made me feel. It distracted me. It made me . . . angry at him. I am never angry at him." I frowned, realizing I still carried that anger.

"Wow." Casmiro breathed out, scoffing and shaking his

head in disbelief. "I've never heard you speak of a woman like this; it shows you're not only saying this because the sex was good. You really do like her, don't you?"

I sighed. "It is now in the past. None of it matters," I said. "That is why I am in a mood. You wanted to know, now you know."

Casmiro watched me for a long time before he gave a very loud sigh. "Maybe it's for the best. Nothing good will come out of you attaching yourself to that woman."

"Maybe," I murmured, shifting my gaze back to the pool.

It would be easier if everything around me didn't remind me of her—this gazebo, that pool, my house, the casino, the office, even the torture rooms. It would be easier if when I smelled food spices, or vanilla, or even hear someone speak in Spanish, my mind didn't drag back to her. It would be easier if when I closed my eyes, I didn't see the look on her face when I told her she was a mistake.

It was a cruel thing to say. Knowing all that I knew about her, that meaning would have run deeper than what I wanted to convey.

But Casmiro was right. Nothing good would come out of it. Not just because Zahra had her many secrets, but because I didn't plan to be here long. There was no use in starting something I wouldn't finish, especially not when I was this close to getting all I wanted.

CHAPTER TWO

Zahra

I was certain the man patted my chest twice.

He also did the same to my ass, and I'm pretty sure I didn't imagine how he squeezed a little.

I kept my eyes on him, raising a brow when he finally lifted his head to look at me. He cleared his throat and stepped back before speaking into his earpiece. "She's clean, just a phone. I'm sending her up."

He swiped a key card in the slot beside the elevator and I watched it slide open.

"Get in, someone will take you to him when you reach the top floor."

Without saying a word, I stepped into the elevator, keeping my face straight as the doors closed.

I was alone.

I let out a breath, then I started coughing, covering my mouth with my hand and discreetly taking the small device from my tongue, stylishly brushing my vest, then my hair, which had grown out quite a bit. I tucked my hair behind my ear while fixing the device in my ear and clearing my throat.

"Zahra's online." Upper's voice reached me first.

"Great, let's get this show on the road," Dog said.

"Okay, Z. I'm in position, anything goes sideways, send the signal and I'll fall in," Devil said, voice a little breathy.

"Hopefully nothing goes sideways. We're just here for information, not to pick a fight," Milk said.

"That building is armed to the teeth, and considering how

wonderful all our missions have been going of late, we can't be too sure of anything," Upper said.

I knew it would be fine because I had it under control. The man I was going to meet was someone I'd conducted business with before I met Street. They didn't know that, and I planned to keep it that way.

I planned to keep a lot of things in places where I could control them, namely, my past and the man who had plagued every one of my waking thoughts since we left Milan, the man who was responsible for the shit mood I'd been in since the moment I left that interrogation room and he told me we were free to go.

I shook my head, mentally erasing the thoughts of him as I stood straighter, squaring my jaw, and entering into the likeness of the Zahra I'd been before Street. I needed everything about that version of myself if I wanted to get information about the manor.

"According to your intel, Daniels should be done with his prior meetings so this is your best window to speak with him," Milk said.

"I'm landing on zeroes, Zahra. Can't access any live footage from beyond the elevators, so we won't have eyes on you in there," Upper said.

Good.

"That's not good but you'll be in our ears so everything should still pan out the same," Dog said.

"Find him, charm him, get the info about the manor, and get out," Milk said.

I looked up at the camera in the elevator to show I understood.

We'd clocked that the painting was here in Mexico, but we needed an in that wouldn't result in innocents being caught in the crossfire, or word getting out that something suspicious was happening in the manor. I knew the news had calmed down after the school bus disaster, and the heist going live. Everyone knew who Arturo Garza was, so I suspected it was just a matter of time before people started to put two and two together, hence why the man who bought the manor had found it necessary to hide his name for his own safety.

The quest just got a lot deadlier, and to play a deadly game, one needed the help of deadly people. And now that we didn't have the backing of the Marino empire, we were completely on our own.

Street didn't know it, but I was fully responsible for them now, and I'd be damned ten times over if I let them get stuck in the crossfire of this whole shit.

The elevator stopped and the doors slid apart.

As expected, someone was there to usher me to where I'd be meeting the man whose help I needed.

Yaroslav Yegorov.

A very popular Russian transporter—*smuggler*—of anything. Drugs, contraband, and, most times, important people. He was also privy to high-level-clearance information, which was exactly what I wanted from him.

Street, in all their goodness, thought I was going to meet someone named Enrique Daniels, a man involved in underground real estate dealings, but it was for their safety that I hid the truth. They didn't need to be messing with someone like Yaroslav. At least not when they knew absolutely nothing about my past.

The second we turned a corner of the hallway, approaching the door at the end, I turned off my comm, knowing they'd probably be freaking out, so I pulled out my phone and shot Upper a quick text.

Me:

Very armed inside. Can't risk them finding the comm, plan still the same. Will give signal if things don't go well.

I slipped my phone into my pocket without waiting for a response, schooling my features into a frown as the man who'd been escorting me pushed open the door and gestured for me to walk in.

I stepped into the cold office, the door shutting behind me.

My gaze was fixed on the bald man standing by the window, a familiar tatted face turning to regard me as a smile broke out on his lips, eyes shining in surprise. "My, my, my . . ." he said, his accent as thick as I remembered it. He stepped closer to me. "So is true then . . . you really are the one who requested an audience . . ."

I deepened my frown. "Why would you believe otherwise?"

"Why, because . . ." He walked behind the desk to take his seat, gesturing for me to do the same. "I know you never do business in person, you see . . . unless is important."

I took the seat opposite him. "You hear correctly. I need some information I think you ha—"

"Straight to the point?" he asked, relaxing in his seat. "That's not fair. I hear you disappeared from Sicily . . . If my source is right, this is the first time anyone has seen you in what, six years? Seven?"

I locked my jaw. "I don't see how that concerns you, Yaroslav."

"No?"

"No."

He sighed, raising his hand in surrender. "You don't want to chat."

"Exactly."

"Fine." He blew out a breath. "Tell me how you found me. I only arrived in Mexico three days ago."

I got comfortable, smiling. "You know I have my own sources, Yaroslav. I might have left Sicily, but the city did not leave me."

Amusement filled his dull blue eyes. "Ah, I see," he said, then sat up. "I have other business to attend to. Tell me what you think I can do for you."

I didn't need to beat around the bush with this. The faster I was out of here, the less damage control I had to take care of. "Are you familiar with the name Arturo Garza?"

Recognition flashed in his eyes, followed by a sigh. "Yes, I am, and no, I don't know where the painting is. Is that all?"

Shit. Of course several others had gotten to him about this.

We really didn't have much time.

"I'm not here about the painting," I said, which had the man frowning. "I'm here about the manor."

His brows shot up. "Ah . . ."

"Yes. I heard there was a sale recently . . . I need to know who the buyer was."

He watched me for a few seconds before asking, "What makes you think I'd know?"

"Because you wouldn't have asked me that question if you didn't know anything."

His lips tugged up at one corner. "Well, I don't know the name of the person who bought the manor, but I know the name of the man who was in charge of the manor prior to the sale. I also know that he'll be coming to Mexico next week to finalize things with the anonymous buyer."

I nodded. "What's the name of the man in charge?"

Yaroslav's smile widened. "Do you think I'll just hand you that information for free? Come on, Faizan."

I ground my teeth, glaring at him. "What do you want? Money?"

He rolled his eyes. "Please, don't insult me."

My phone buzzed in my pocket. I ignored it, keeping my eyes on Yaroslav. "Then tell me what you want and I'll have it delivered."

"No need for the trouble. I need intel. An address."

I blinked. "For who?"

"E2. You've heard of the assassin, yes?"

I frowned, recognizing the name, having heard it from Manuel several times.

Even *I* have been in close contact with that name.

E2 was a private, faceless assassin who worked jobs for people in the Mafia, or cartel lords who wanted to get a job done, clean, smooth, and quiet. E2 was also the best assassin in the underground business for three reasons. One, they were efficient and always got the job done without mistakes; two, nobody knew who they were, if they were male or female; and three, because you cannot find a killer that doesn't exist.

E2 came at a very high price, meaning you would have to be ready to pay for them to get the job done. Sometimes, the pay wasn't money; it was information. Valuable information that made it difficult for them to be targeted or even traced.

"I have heard of them, yes," I said.

"Good. I have been trying to get ahold of the assassin for years, but is like they dropped off the face of the earth. I know you have done business with them in the past; do you know where to find them now?"

I shook my head. "No. When I hired the assassin we didn't talk long enough to help me determine their whereabouts. When they got my job done, I never heard from them again."

Yaroslav deflated. "I suspected as much . . . Maybe you can help me with something else then?"

"I—"

"There's someone I need you to meet. I owe her a favor and she's cashing it in by wanting to meet you."

This got my attention. "Who?"

Yaroslav pulled out a small card and a pen, quickly scribbling something on the card.

"Kareem Fadel."

"What?"

"The man in charge of the manor, Kareem Fadel," he said, slipping the card toward me. "Go to that address tonight at nine o'clock. You'll find the woman who wants to meet with you. She'll also have some intel on this Kareem fellow."

I watched him carefully. "Are you playing a game, Yaroslav? I'm pretty sure you know better than to mess with me."

"That I do, is why the intel she has on Kareem is another small favor I owe her." His lips curled. "You're welcome."

I didn't take my eyes off him as I got to my feet, swiping the card from the table. "If I find out this is a trap, you won't live to see ten o'clock."

He scoffed. "Always with the threats, this one. Is why is never a pleasure doing business with you, Faizan."

Ignoring his comment, I turned away from him and walked out of the office, wondering who the hell this woman was, and why she wanted to see me.

My phone buzzed again, and I pulled it out, checking the text I'd received.

Upper:
Um . . . Zahra? Why the fuck did my system just log a facial-recognition hit on Enrique Daniels currently stepping out of a hotel in North Macedonia?

Shit.

Upper:
Who the hell are you meeting?

For fuck's sake.

I started typing the lie as my brain spat it at me. Sending it quickly.

Me:
I was shocked too. He sent his associate, I guess. I'm out though, and I've got a name. Kareem Fadel. Run it through ur systems. Be with u soon.

CHAPTER THREE

Zahra

"So the man is an Arab philanthropist," Upper said, reading from his tablet. "And he takes it to the next level. This guy participates in, like, twelve to fifteen volunteer projects a month. People love him."

The short let was warm, the ceiling fan creaking as it rolled, doing little more than stirring the smell of burgers and beer around.

Dog snorted. "Let's hope he loves people, too, because now that Marino has booted us out, he's our only in for getting into that manor, and getting that cursed painting," he said, biting into his burger, half listening to us and half concentrating on the telenovela currently playing on the TV at a low volume.

I was no better, my mind was split between the card burning a hole in my pocket, and the man I refused to think about.

Milk let out a sigh from her position on the couch as she swallowed the burger she'd taken a bite of. "It still baffles me to think that we've been traveling the world looking for this painting, and it never even left the mansion. It's like the most obvious place it could have been, and we didn't even think of it."

"Bloody quest twists. They're never fun," Upper said.

Who could the woman be? How does she know me? Why did she want to meet? Why am I trying so hard to block off thoughts of Elio? Why am I upset?

"Zahra."

Should I have said more in that interrogation room? Tried to explain to him that what he thought happened wasn't what happened? What would have changed if I had done that? Would we still be in Milan?

"Zahra?"

And why should I even try to explain it to him? He could think whatever the hell he wanted to think, we weren't even serious or exclusive or . . . whatever it is people are when they casually fuck . . . Why should I care?

Why do I care?

"Z!"

I flinched, raising my head to see everyone staring at me. "Yeah?"

Devil's gaze was filled with concern. "Are you okay?"

I blinked, forcing down a swallow. "Yeah . . . yeah, I'm fine. Did you ask me something?"

The room went quiet. Even Dog had stopped watching his telenovela, staring at me with that same concerned look.

Milk broke the silence. "Upper asked if Enrique's associate gave you a specific date for Kareem's arrival to Mexico."

"Oh." I shook my head. "No, he didn't. He just said next week."

"Got ya," Upper said. "I'll keep an eye on the airports, flight records, hotel bookings, and travel itinerary bookings, so we don't miss him."

I nodded. "I'll ask around too. I actually spent some time in Mexico years back—"

"You did?" Milk interrupted with a frown.

"Yeah, but not for a long time. I worked at this tattoo parlor for a few weeks, and it'll shock you how much these people pick up on words from the street. If a man like Kareem is arriving, they should have heard something useful."

Devil nodded. "Okay, that should help, too . . . Tomorrow we'll—"

"I plan to go today."

There was a pause.

"It's late already; wouldn't it be best to go when you're well rested from today's job?" Milk asked, but I shook my head.

"I'm good to go today," I said.

Nodding, Devil rose from his position on the bed, discarding his nearly finished burger. "I'll come with you, just—"

"Oh no, I've got it." I managed a tight smile, leaning off the wall. "In fact, I should get going, I, um . . . need to clear my head a bit, so I'll walk for a while and head down there later."

"You didn't even eat your burger . . ." Dog trailed off, then frowned. "Have you eaten at all today?" he asked.

I looked down at the table where my burger lay untouched. "I don't really have the appetite."

Silence followed as they all continued to stare at me.

"I'll be back later," I said, exiting the hotel room without another glance their way.

It was still an hour until the meeting time, which was perfect because while I'd lied about wanting to visit the tattoo place, I didn't lie about needing to clear my head.

So I walked for a while, stopped at a small store to get a pack of cigarettes because it was cold out and we were meeting at the port of Manzanillo, and also because I didn't think to take a thicker jacket or a coat.

Elio would have definitely thought of that.

I grumbled at the thought, and a few minutes later, rented myself a motorcycle before driving to the meeting point.

I arrived about ten minutes early, parking the motorcycle far from the port and finding my way in. I fished for the card in the pocket of my jacket, following the directions, and stealthily walking between the maze of containers. The air was sharp with salt and machine oil, ground slick from the rain that had fell earlier. I shuddered as the cold air from the ocean nearby sneaked through the excuse of a jacket I wore.

Reaching the container I was meant to wait at, I wasn't surprised when I found the area empty.

"¡Muévelo más rápido, cabrón!" someone shouted in the

distance, the rough voice carrying over the clang of metal and hum of cranes.

Other voices reached me from all around but they belonged to the people who worked there. I nodded to myself, turning a corner and stopping two containers away from the one where I was supposed to meet the woman. From this angle, I could spot anyone approaching and avoid whatever trap this might turn out to be.

A chill ran down my spine as I leaned on a container, fishing in my pocket for the pack of cigarettes, and lit one up. For warmth, I dragged in the smoke and let it out just as my phone vibrated in my pocket.

I pulled it out while looking around, brought the device to my view, and caught a text from Milk.

> *Milk:*
> **Can you please grab something to eat while you're out?**

Another text popped in.

> *Milk:*
> **I worry.**

I smiled, letting the cigarette hang between my lips as I typed and sent a response.

> ***Me:***
> **Ok mom.**

I probably wouldn't. I didn't have the appetite, and I wasn't feeling hungry. Exiting her message box, I scrolled down to *his* message box. The nickname "Dad" was still saved as his contact.

I clicked on the name, my stomach clenching when I saw

the last conversation . . . or lack thereof. It was the night before the school bus incident. I'd just left his house and told him to text me when he woke up. He didn't respond to the text because he'd called instead.

God, it seemed like a long time ago.

Should I text him now? Would he respond? Do I want *to text him?*

"Oh for God's sake, this is driving me nuts," I mumbled, because how the fuck did I go and fuck things up by catching feelings for someone like him? I was always careful . . . hell, I fucked around with Devil way longer than I did with Elio and it didn't get me this worked up. How did this happen to me?

Why do I want to fix it? I shouldn't want that.

But dammit, I do, and I need to stop denying it or it'll drive me crazy.

I took another drag from the cigarette, let it out, and started typing. I sent it before I could chicken out.

Me:
Hey, it's me

I stared at the message with a frown. "Of course he's gonna know it's me . . ." *Assuming he still has my number.* Fuck. I typed and sent another message.

Me:
Zahra, it's Zahra. How are u doin?

Delivered.

He still has my number then. Which is a good sign.

Fidgeting, I flicked the cigarette away, feeling warm enough from the knots in my stomach as I waited for the message to indicate *read*. It didn't.

I waited . . . but nothing came.

Quickly, I started typing another message, sending it without a second thought.

Me:
I've been think about u

Delivered.

I reread the message, my frown deepening. "Oh God." My fingers moved fast.

Me:
***thinking**

"Jesus fuck, what am I doing?" I muttered.

"Yeah, even I think that's a little too desperate."

I jerked away from the container, my hand slipping behind me to whip out my Glock, pointing it right at the shadowed figure who was also quick to pull out their weapon, pointing it right at me.

"Drop the gun," we both said at the same time.

I frowned, squinting to see who the person was. If she could just step into the light a smidge.

"Jinx," she said. "Just like when we were kids."

"Darling, I don't know who the fuck you are, and I won't hesitate to pull this trigger if you don't drop the gun."

"Not until you drop yours first."

"Awesome, we're both gonna die then. Take a few steps back. Let's make it a good old duel."

She laughed, which made my caution falter a bit. The sound of her gun clattering to the ground was all I heard as her silhouette raised both hands and she stepped into the light.

Jesus fu—

"Hi, Zahra." She smiled softly.

Long black hair, pale skin, and a familiar smile that brought back memories from when I was twelve had me lowering my gun. "Daiyu?"

She grinned. "In the flesh."

I didn't wait to check my surroundings as I rushed to throw my arms around her. "Oh my God," I said, hugging her tight. "I never thought I'd see you again."

Daiyu and I had only spent two years together, but during those two years, she was the closest thing to a friend I'd ever had. We'd met when I was moved to different Handlers at the age of twelve, after I was almost hurt by a drunk Manuel. She was ten when I moved in, and we had hit it off immediately, too mature for our age with everything we'd both been through. When I was fourteen and about to be moved to a different level, I knew I'd never see her again . . . but now . . .

I pulled away, my wide eyes searching hers. "You're out." I smiled, shaking her shoulders. "You got out . . . How?"

She shrugged. "I was claimed at seventeen, and the person who paid for me turned out to be an idiot. He's dead now, and all his properties belong to me."

I let out a relieved breath, slipping my gun back behind me. "When did this happen?"

"Four years ago . . . still fresh."

"Yeah," I said. "But you're out, and you're alive and—God, I'm so happy to see you, Daiyu, you have no idea."

Her lips curved, her eyes softening. "I think I do because I'm so happy to see you too. When I heard you were claimed, I was so sad, and then I heard he came for you—Manuel. Then the Contis took you in and I thought we would never see each other again, but when I heard you were in Mexico? I knew we had to meet."

"Yeah, I'm glad you reached out," I said, then frowned. "What the hell were you thinking getting yourself involved with the likes of Yaroslav?"

She sighed. "It's a long story, but to keep it short, I needed ammo for me and my people, and he was the only one who could get it done."

At that, I stepped back a bit, frowning. "You and your people? What are you talking about?"

Her gaze stayed on me. "That's why I wanted to see you. I started a secret op about a year ago. My team and I hunt down Handler houses around Europe, and we save as many lives as we can."

I swallowed. "That's amazing, Daiyu . . . I—That's dangerous, but amazing."

She shrugged. "I saw no other purpose for me after I got out. It was a no-brainer."

Yeah, for me too. But I couldn't tell her that.

"So . . . you need my help with something?" I asked instead, knowing we couldn't be here long, and we couldn't risk having this conversation over dinner.

"Yes," she said, her gaze darting around quickly before focusing on me. "I know you can't get mixed up because of your involvement with the Contis and I totally understand that. I don't want you to get caught in the crossfire, but we've been tracking a major shipment for the last few months and I'm talking about thirty level-two Plants."

My stomach dropped. "What?"

Level-two Plants, meaning fourteen-year-olds who had just finished level one with their Handlers and were about to be trafficked to different parts of the world for sex work. Just like I was when I turned fourteen, just like *she* was.

"Apparently, they're going to be passing through here in about two months," she said.

I nodded. "Okay, go on."

"There's going to be a three-month cruise with this new ship called *Celestial.*"

"*Celestial*? Not conspicuous at all."

She snorted. "Well, it's a huge deal. There's so much noise

about it on the internet. People are calling it *Titanic II*, but safer."

"Way to jinx the ship," I said.

"You know how people are, but get this, they call it a 'cruise from home,' meaning it's not traveling around the globe, it's just basically circling a particular territory, not too far from the city and not too close that you couldn't explore a small island. It's super exclusive for basically only rich people."

I scoffed. "Of course."

She smiled, understanding my snark. "It's going to be heavily guarded because of the big names that are going to be present. There will be smaller boats in case people want to leave, or go to the city for one thing or another. It's just a waste of time and money, if you ask me, but, here's where it gets interesting. The people who are going to be in charge of trafficking the level twos are going to be on the cruise in about two months, after it begins."

A chill ran down my spine. "They're passing through the ship?"

"With the smaller boats at the ready, no one is going to ask questions. They'd probably be in disguise, slipping right under the nose of authorities."

"And that's where you come in," I noted.

"Yes, save the kids before their lives are basically destroyed forever."

I nodded. "Okay, what do you need from me?"

"Access to the cruise. I don't know how Yaroslav did it, but he somehow made sure the guy you're hunting down is going to be one of the big names on that ship."

Which was obviously the other favor Yaroslav had granted her.

"My people and I don't have that kind of money," she said. "I was hoping since the guy you're looking for is on that ship, you'd be going as well, and you can help us get in?"

I crossed my arms over my chest, nodding. "It's possible. I

have a couple of people I'll need to take care of first before we do this, but I can get you in when it's time," I said.

She frowned. "Are you sure?"

"I'm positive," I said, knowing there was no way in hell I'd let her do this on her own. "Leave it to me."

Relief flooded her face. "Thank you, Zahra. Truly."

"No need to thank me." *Thirty freaking children* . . . My stomach turned as I met her gaze. "Come rain or shine, we're getting on the *Celestial*," I said, my brain already formulating a plan, "and we're going to get those sons of bitches."

CHAPTER FOUR

Elio

I'd contemplated asking to speak to Casmiro before leaving for Mexico. I didn't want him getting suspicious, but I needed to at least talk to him before we went after that map and those flash drives.

I sighed, taking a long drag from the cigar as I watched him approach the gazebo. The ember glowed faintly in the dark, and I flicked off the ash, my gaze following the steady rhythm of his stride. He looked less pale than he did the other day, but he still moved with caution, one hand brushing his side like he was mindful of an ache he would never admit.

The bright moon and the lights around the pool cast shadows on his face, highlighting the tight line of his mouth as he climbed up the stairs to the gazebo. We hadn't spoken since I told him about my involvement with Zahra. He was probably still trying to wrap his mind around it.

I didn't blame him.

Casmiro took the chair across from me like he'd done the last time, the faint scrape of wood against tile echoing under the hum of night.

"What's this about?" he asked.

I leaned back, the cigar balanced between my fingers, watching the smoke twist upward before I finally spoke. "I wanted to tell you this in person. Kareem Fadel. You heard of him?"

Casmiro's gaze narrowed, his brows dropping. "Yeah, here and there."

"Great, I received intel a while ago. He's a main piece in the puzzle to getting the original painting. I already have things in the works. I'll be at a cruise ship called *Celestial* with him—just to finalize a couple of things. It might take a few months, but that isn't why I called you here."

His frown deepened. "Okay . . . I'm listening."

"Before I leave for Mexico next week, I would like to discuss something with you, regarding Elia, and some other minor things."

He nodded slowly. "Before you leave . . ." he drawled, confusion in his eyes. "Why not discuss it now?"

I focused on the warmth of the cigar. "I want to be certain of my situation before I do. It is nothing to worry about, just . . ." I shrugged lightly. "Future planning for yourself."

"Okay . . ." He eyed me with suspicion. "Why would we discuss my future, though?"

I frowned. "Why wouldn't we? Do you want to be second to me all your life?"

"I have never complained; this job and this family are my blood."

"I know." I sat up, placing the lit cigar on the ashtray. "I do, but I also know you have been capitalizing on your racing business, and the cars you haven't had the chance to work on because of the family business. I can help you draft out a starting plan, expand it into—"

"What's happening?"

I blinked. "We are talking."

"I know we are talking, but why are we talking about this?"

"I have been doing . . ." I rubbed my jaw absentmindedly. "A lot of thinking lately. Every individual has something they are very passionate about. But you were born into the family, so automatically, you have had to put your passions second. Let us change that."

"I am completely content with my passions being second." He eyed me. "This is random."

The sound of familiar footsteps approaching had me backtracking.

"We will discuss it later," I said, looking up to see Angelo dressed in a sharp, dark blue blazer and slacks, with a file in his hand, looking like he'd just left his home and was heading out to a meeting.

"Evening, Marino," he greeted me before looking over at Cas, who had gone stiff. "They cleared you for movement?"

Casmiro blinked. "What?"

"The doctors, did they clear you?"

Casmiro cleared his throat, caught off guard by Angelo's presence. I knew he always liked to be prepared. "Yes. A few days ago. I'm good."

Angelo nodded before turning to me again, oblivious. "I got the information you requested," he said, taking the chair by my side as he handed me the file. "Did a lot of digging. It was buried in the archives; somebody went to a great deal of effort to hide it."

"My father wasn't the best at hiding things. If it were me, you would never have found it," I said, opening it and reading through. My chest tightened with each word I read, realizing how detestable my situation was.

"What is it?" Casmiro asked, sensing the shift in my demeanor.

I could tell Angelo waited for my answer, too, as he had been dying to know why I'd asked him to dig out my military admission file. The one my father never showed me.

"It's information from my time in the army, or lack thereof," I said, closing the file. "About a month ago, I had some flashbacks to my time in *camp*. It was a memory of me and my—well, the person I thought was my commander. I was in some sort of trance. Hypnotized, I suspected. I have only now confirmed it."

"Why would they do that?" Angelo asked. "Hypnotism is usually reserved for soldiers who suffer from mental breakdowns after a war; you were okay."

"Hm. It started before any real mission was put in place. My father asked for some private training for me when he found out—" I glanced at Casmiro, realizing my slipup.

"Found out what?" Casmiro asked.

Angelo looked at me, probably wondering if I would say anything.

I sighed. "He found out I had inherited my mother's mental illness."

Casmiro's eyes widened. "What?"

"It is hard to remember what exactly the full diagnosis was. I think I was made to forget some of it. But it was clinical depression, with some other hereditary things."

Casmiro frowned. "What the hell—"

"Which is not the case anymore," I lied, and caught Angelo looking away from me. "I am okay. I have just been concerned about this hypnosis issue. I have no idea what memories are real, or fake, or if some of my thoughts are my own. It is concerning."

Casmiro sat up straighter, worry in his eyes. "We can undo it, right? Seek professional help—"

"Hm. No. I don't have time for all of that."

Angelo sat up. "I think Casmiro's right. You should undo it, get help, get ahold of your mind, and own your thoughts."

"I am fine. All I wanted was confirmation."

Angelo's frown turned personal. "Why are you so hell-bent on never getting professional help with literally anything?"

My response was right on the tip of my tongue. "I am undeserving of it."

Angelo made a strained noise. "I am tired of hearing you repeat that every time you're told to get help. Honestly, I'm beginning to wonder if you were made to think you don't need help." He shook his head before getting to his feet. "It's almost time for one of my meetings . . ."

My eyes didn't leave his face, which was etched with a frown. "We will leave for Mexico next week."

"Noted." He straightened his blazer. "I will arrive when I can. Have a safe flight," he said, nodding curtly to Casmiro and me before walking away.

"He knew about it, didn't he?" Casmiro's voice had me looking back at him. "You told him."

"He found out."

"But he knew," he pressed, "and I didn't."

"It was not important, Casmiro. Do not make an issue of it."

He sat up. "An issue? You're not seeking medical help for something that could be detrimental to your health. I didn't know about it. I am your shadow; I should know everything about you."

"You do."

"But I didn't know *this*."

"Now you do," I answered. "Besides, it is not of any importance. I am the same person you have always known."

"You are not." He clarified, "At first, when you came back from the army, I assumed your change was because of all you had had to do there; people are never the same when they return. But something else changed."

"This conversation is irrelevant."

"It's not. You don't realize it, but you became so much like Ricardo. The beliefs you once swore against were now your motto. You trusted no one; you had these new methods of torture that at first scared the shit out of me. The way you talked, the words you used. You just weren't the same."

"How does your new lightbulb moment help our current predicament?"

"It doesn't, because we are not talking about that; we are talking about you, how to undo whatever those people did to you."

I tilted my head, watching him. "What if I don't want to?"

"What?"

"What if I like what they did to me?"

"What if you were made to think that you like it?"

"What if I like that I was made to think I like it?"

Casmiro shook his head. "I hate that there is no winning with you."

"There is nothing to be won, just like there is no issue here. Hm? I do not need help, nor do I have the desire to get any—nor the time, for that matter. I am almost at the finish line, finding that painting, getting the ultimate power over everyone with power." I straightened in my chair. "That should be your focus right now, Casmiro. That and trying your best not to be obvious about your interest toward my ex-consigliere."

His lips lifted in a snarl. "Keep your voice down."

I looked around. "He's long gone."

"There are soldiers around, for fuck's sake."

"We both know they won't talk." I leveled him with a taunting stare. "We both know you want me to keep my voice down so you don't have to hear me say it."

I knew I had successfully taken his attention off my health when he glared at me and said, "You are wrong."

"Ah . . . am I?"

"Yes. It's not what you think. I just wasn't prepared for his arrival."

I shook my head.

Angelo's family had been with the Marinos for decades, although Angelo himself was never around when we were young. He'd lived predominantly in America where he was schooled all his life, but he visited the compound at least five times a year.

Casmiro had been irrationally obsessed with him. But he never talked to him. He just stalked from afar. When Angelo took over for his father as the consigliere, Casmiro made sure to keep his distance, and Angelo, well, didn't suspect anything.

Now, they conversed when necessary. They weren't friends, nor were they enemies; they were like coworkers in the same department. Except one was obsessed with the other, who was oblivious and probably didn't care if the obsessed one existed or not.

I didn't care. I could politely ignore it as long as I wasn't put in the middle and affected by it.

"Your helpless pining is beginning to move into pathetic territory. How long has it been? Since we were, like, fourteen, and he was twelve?"

"Says the guy who slept with his brother's girlfriend."

"Is that supposed to make me . . . back off?"

"You know what? You were right the other day; we are not supposed to be on speaking terms." He got to his feet with a grunt. "I will leave you now."

"Don't forget our discussion earlier."

"I'll be sure to," he said before making his way out of the gazebo, careful of his injury.

I sighed, watching him until he was out of sight, carrying the amusement from our back-and-forth with him.

"Evening, sir," greeted the receptionist at the motel when I reached her. "We had the room cleaned as usual; everything is in place."

I nodded, slipping her a bundle of banknotes. "Thank you," I said. "Did you, by chance, happen to feed him this morning?"

The woman frowned. "What?"

I sighed. "Never mind," I told her before walking away, knowing she had cleaned, meaning he had been fed.

When I reached the room I shrugged off my coat, seeing his quiet figure in the chair, staring out the window like he usually did.

I walked over to him. "Do you ever use the bed?" I asked, settling on the windowsill, watching his frail form, looking as sickly as ever.

My father sighed. "The cars keep me company."

"There's a TV in the room to keep you company," I reminded him, but he didn't seem to acknowledge that. His gaze was focused solely outside the window. "I would have come by sooner. But there was a little chaos; I had to handle it," I said, but he remained quiet. "You won't ask what it was about?"

"You will tell me anyway."

"Not really. I don't think I want to revisit it. But there is one thing I think you should know, though."

He dragged his droopy eyes up to look at me. "What."

"I know where the painting is, and soon, I will have those flash drives. Soon you will be out of here; you'll get the death wish you so badly long for."

His face tried to form a frown. "You still want to burn down my empire; you are still vengeful."

I scoffed. "After all these years, one would think you would register the fact that burning it all down is how we will end. Did you think your wife burned down that church with her and your other children for a show? She was showing us how it would all end. Your thirst for power, money, and status. The fire can take it all away. It's a cleansing we both need, unfortunately."

He was quiet for a stretch of minutes. "I am disappointed," he finally said.

"Why?"

"This was not what I wished for you, Elio."

I dragged in a deep breath and let it out as I spoke. "You did this with your own hands."

He shook his head. "No. *You* did this. Your head was never going to be fixed. You want to end up like your mother only because you are just like her. Crazy. Delusional. Pathe—"

My backhand connected with his cheek in a hard slap that had his head swinging to the side at the impact. The sting bit at the back of my hand as I stood upright, my anger simmering. "You won't be seeing me for a while. Hope that will teach you a lesson on how to control that godforsaken tongue of yours."

"You won't succeed." He wheezed. "You don't have the spine to do it. To burn it. You are too weak; you would have done it if you really wanted to do it. That is why I am not worried. It won't work. You will *fail*."

I clenched my jaw so hard that I felt pain.

Slowly, tentatively, I leaned down, looking him right in the eye, reveling in the hate and fear I spotted there as I spoke.

"Why don't we wait and see."

CHAPTER FIVE

Zahra

A week later

Slipping my hand underneath my pillow, I pulled out the gun that had taken up permanent residence there. I had contemplated leaving it behind, but couldn't.

I slowly traced his initials with my thumb. EM.

Fuck.

I miss him.

If pathetic were a person, it would be me.

Elio wasn't responding to my texts.

I sure as hell didn't predict it would affect me this way, but it did. It left me with my thoughts, and those thoughts slowly transformed into guilt . . . and then regret.

At first, I packed up the guilt, and ignored the heaviness in my chest, which had been—to be honest—there since I left that cell at his compound.

I knew I'd been compromised, but I didn't think it had gotten to the extent where I would be so tucked into myself, sinking into feelings I had no business feeling, especially at a time like this, a time when I needed my focus on the job I had to do.

My headphones firmly covered my ears, music playing, song after song starting and ending. I wasn't really listening to the lyrics.

I turned on my side on the bed, facing the window; it was a floor-to-ceiling window showcasing the vast dark blue of the sea. Even with my headphones on, I could still hear the dull hum of the ship. I was missing out on all the fun just because I couldn't get out of my head.

I never miss anyone. I shouldn't miss *him*. It made no sense that I did, did it?

How could I miss someone who ignored me half the time? Someone who told me I was a mistake? I knew I was a mistake, but did he really have to *say* it like that? Like he didn't mean it but had to say it so we would have no reason to see each other again?

Couldn't he just say, "Fuck off, we are nothing. You are better than me, and you messed up but made the right choice. I don't want to see you because whatever tension between us is just too much, and I think you are better off without me"?

I sighed, knowing Elio would never say words like that.

I might have hurt him, but I probably should have been more honest. I should have made him listen to me. I talked him out of turning his lights off; why couldn't I talk him into listening to me?

Three weeks of these thoughts filtering in and out of my mind, taking my focus away from everything else around me. God, it was driving me crazy.

I knew I messed up, but I didn't need my mind reminding me of it every waking second.

It was funny because weeks ago, I hadn't realized that I'd missed hearing his voice or that I liked his accent. Or his different facial expressions when explaining something to me while being a smart-ass. I knew he had a beautiful smile, but I was only just realizing how addictive it was.

Now I knew why I liked to say things to get on his nerves. It was so he would scowl in that gorgeous way of his.

And there was the way he furrowed his brows when thinking.

There was also the fact that he liked looking at me—specifically at my hair. It was the first thing his eyes always latched onto before he drank in my face.

Odd how just a few weeks were all it took to make me admit that maybe it wasn't just his touch, or the sex. Maybe it was just . . . him. Maybe I was so high on him that I became insufferable to everyone around me. I knew I had to fix it.

But before I could make Elio listen, I would have to tell Devil. He was one of the reasons Elio turned a one-eighty and ended everything before anything really happened.

I groaned and turned on my back, staring up at the ceiling. Maybe I just needed to get Elio out of my system. I had had a taste that wasn't enough, a taste that had me thirsting for more. I longed to have a meaningful or a stupid conversation with him where he'd try to prove me wrong by stating silly facts that I didn't give a shit about. Things had been quiet on his end, and I wasn't even wondering why he wasn't making any moves to get the painting or if he knew where it was. I only cared about him . . . what he was doing, *how* he was doing.

Had he given up on setting things right with Devil because of me? Did he really think I had purposefully tried to take away hopes of reconciliation between them?

I closed my eyes and sighed.

When had I lost control of my feelings? When we made love in the bathtub? When he took me to his house in Turin?

I slipped the gun right back underneath my pillow just as the door to my room opened.

We'd booked the silver suite on the *Celestial* cruise, which included five bedrooms and a lounge.

I removed my headphones and looked at Milk, who stood by the door, dressed casually. "Hey, we're heading out of the suite to eat; you coming?" she asked.

I plastered a small smile on my lips. "No, I'm good."

Her shoulders dropped, eyes filling with concern. "Oh . . . you want us to get you anything?"

"I'm good, thanks."

"It's food, Zahra."

I let out a small laugh. "Yeah, I know, I don't think I have an appetite. You guys go ahead." I sank farther into the bed.

"Have fun." I tried to sound cheerful, but it came out half-assed.

She threw her head back and yelled, "You guys go on without me and Zahra! Get us food, we'll hang back!"

"Got it!" Upper yelled from somewhere in the suite.

"You don't have to do that," I told her as she entered the room, closing the door behind her. She kicked off her sneakers, walked over, and climbed into bed with me. "Seriously, go have fun," I said as she got under the covers, scooted closer, spooning from behind.

"It won't be fun without you there," she murmured against my hair.

I groaned, but my appreciation for her staying behind caused a swirl of warmth in my chest.

"I don't like sappy shit like this," I murmured back, relaxing into her hold as her chin rested on my shoulder.

"I do; deal with it."

I couldn't fight off my smile.

"You've been sad since we left Milan, don't think we haven't noticed. I gave you time and space to tell me or any one of us yourself, but it seems you won't do that on your own."

"I haven't been sad," I said, trying to sound nonchalant.

"You've barely been eating for the past three weeks."

I chuckled, falling deeper into her body. "Just because I am barely eating doesn't mean I'm sad."

Milk scoffed. "You never say no to food."

I managed a shrug. "I guess I'm just having a bad month."

"You can tell me, Zahra," she said softly, genuinely. "Whatever it is, I'll try to help you sort it out. Anything to get you out of your funk." She hugged me tighter, intertwining our fingers.

Telling her didn't ultimately seem out of the question. If I were going to tell Devil, there was no way all of Street wouldn't find out.

Besides, I needed some of Milk's unhinged and unfiltered

advice. I was contemplating whether now was the best time to tell Devil or not. I needed a boost of confidence, a vote to go ahead.

I took a deep breath and turned so we could face each other.

"Promise you won't freak out," I said softly.

She pressed her lips together, eyes searching mine. After a few beats of silence, she said, "Honestly, it depends."

"Come on, Milk."

"Fine, okay . . . I won't freak out," she said reluctantly.

I let out a breath. "I think I like someone I shouldn't like."

Her eyes widened instantly. "Devil? I thought it was over with—"

"No, not Devil—"

Her nose scrunched up. "Dog?"

"God, no." I laughed. "Why the fuck would you think that?"

She shrugged. "I know it can't be Upper, so—oh my God . . . *Me?*"

I shook my head. "No, it's not you."

Now she looked confused. "Then who?"

I swallowed. "Devil's brother."

Her brows drew farther down. "Devil's . . ." She trailed off, but then her brows shot up in surprise. "Oh," she said as realization brightened her eyes. "Oh . . ." But then confusion took over again. "Oh?"

"Yeah. Shocker," I said, pressing my head farther into the pillow as Milk got on her elbow so she could look down at me.

"You like Elio," she stated.

"I think I do."

"You think? You've been moping around for *weeks* because of him! There is nothing to thi—Oh my God, you like Elio? Wha—How? Why the hell do you like him? What has been happening? Why didn't I notice? Wait—That one time I came to your room and found only pillows arranged in your body shape on your bed, were you—*with him*?"

I frowned. "What time?"

She sat upright. "Dog said you were probably on the roof, but I didn't—"

I sat up. "Dog?"

She huffed out a breath. "I don't know when exactly this was, I can't really remember, but I came to your room, and you weren't there. Instead, there were pillows. So I brought Dog in because I thought he might know why you snuck out, but he told me you were on the rooftop right after he made me search for your stash of weed—obviously, we didn't find it. But damn—" A grin split across her face. "You're smooth."

I blinked at her. "Wow," I said, raking my hair back from my face. "Why didn't you ask me about it afterward?"

She shrugged. "There wasn't really anything to ask—But hell, Zahra, that is not the point right now. How did it start? Do you think he likes you too? Why did it end?"

I sighed. "It was harmless flirting at first, but then, well— Hey . . . Wipe that fucking smile off your face."

She held up both hands in defense. "I'm just surprised," she cooed, shifting closer to me. "I mean, you like someone . . . I don't know why I like that you like someone, I just do. And hell—Elio Marino? That's huge! He's so fucking hot. Are you joking?"

"I wish I was."

An excited, goofy grin spread across her lips. "So, did you guys, like . . ." She wiggled her brows. "How was the sex?"

I groaned. "It was . . ." I trailed off and closed my eyes. I could still smell him, feel his touch, feel him . . . I didn't know when a sigh left my lips. "It was elite. So fucking elite." I opened my eyes. "I didn't remember my name for the first few minutes; I felt so soft afterward. You know when you have sex with someone, and you just feel soft everywhere when you finish?"

"Cum high," she said with a dreamy sigh.

"There, that's the phrase," I said with a laugh.

She did a little excited jump. "I had a feeling after that art exhibit. I could feel the tension from the other end of our comm. I should have paid more attention."

I shrugged.

She must have sensed my sudden resignation. She tucked her hair behind her ear. "So, what happened?"

"He called it off."

She frowned sadly. "Why?"

"I shared a kiss with Devil. On the bus."

She sucked in a breath. "I didn't know that," she said. "Upper doesn't know that; Upper *cannot* know that. He and Devil just started acting like friends again."

"I know, but it wasn't anything serious; he was just trying to help me. Elio found out, and he thought I was messing with him this whole time."

She sighed. "Did you explain?"

"I tried to. He didn't wanna hear . . ." I stopped and shook my head. "I'll fix it though. I need to know how to tell Devil before I fix it. I don't want anything to come back and bite me in the ass."

"Yeah, that's true. He should know. If you plan to take things seriously with Elio, then . . . you have to. No secrets. Secrets ruin relationships."

I nodded. "He might get mad. Like, really pissed because he told me to stay away from Elio, and I did the opposite."

"Devil's gone for Upper, Zahra. He might not care."

"But he—"

She held my hand in hers. "Why are you acting like a fucking chicken? The Zahra I know wouldn't give two fucks about what Devil would think. He doesn't own you, and you do not owe him anything. No friendship rule said you couldn't bone his brother. If you like someone, you should be with them."

An odd kind of nervousness took over me. It was so out of character, so fucking stupid. "What if I don't know if I should be with them? Fuck, I sound so pathetic, like a girl who likes a boy. I hate this. I don't want this."

She laughed. "It's normal, Zahra. You're blooming now."

I scowled. "Fuck off."

"Right, right, do you want to be with Elio? You really want to fix it?"

"I think so . . ."

"Give it to me straight."

"I do."

Her hand squeezed mine. "Then put a sock in it. Tell Devil, give him the middle finger if he tries to fault you for liking someone, and then we strategize on how you can get your man." She poked my rib.

"Don't get ahead of yourself; Elio is *not* my man."

"Sorry, just the high from the pep talk," she said. "But hey, I'm sure it'll be fine."

"Yeah . . ." I nodded. "Yeah . . . I'm overthinking it."

"Exactly." She continued, "I still can't believe we are having an actual conversation about a guy . . . We never do this."

I smiled softly. "Yeah, I've never liked a guy before so . . ."

"Did you call or text him since we left?"

I nodded, reaching for my phone and pulling up my chat box for Elio's contact. "I texted several times, no response," I said as Milk took the phone from me, scrolling down, her eyes widening as she kept on scrolling. "He hasn't blocked me yet, it's on *delivered*, but he never checks it. Do you know what that means?"

"Uh . . ." She kept on scrolling.

"What is it?"

"First off, why is his contact name saved as . . . 'Dad'?"

I smiled. "It's an inside thing. You wouldn't get it."

"Right, well . . . I'm wondering why he hasn't blocked you."

"What? Why?" I inched my head forward to peer at the screen of my phone.

She dropped the phone in her lap, looking up at me and shaking her head. "You spammed him, Zahra; you keep spamming him. The last message you sent was from a few minutes ago."

"But he didn't respond, and I got anxious, okay? When I text someone, and they don't reply, it just makes me all itchy, and it has been a week, and he hasn't blocked me, so that means there is still room for me to explain . . . or does it mean he doesn't find me worthy enough to block?"

"You're overthinking it again. Maybe he's just busy?"

"For a week?"

"Maybe he doesn't check his phone, see? He hasn't opened them yet. So, I don't think there's anything much to worry about; you're good."

"But I—"

The door burst open and Dog rushed in. "He's here."

"Who's here?" Milk asked.

"The man who is in charge of Arturo's manor, our golden ticket to Chihuahua paradise, the philanthropist who is—"

"We get it," I said. "Shit. How are his surroundings looking?"

"He got a platinum suite." Dog scowled, clearly jealous.

"That's not what I asked," I said.

"He's not alone, some family members maybe? Fellow philanthropists in the big seats, hot-as-fuck dancers. I think there's gonna be a dance performance at some private event in his suite, I don't know, but it's pretty elite. We need an in."

"Zahra can go in as one of the dancers," Milk said, and I looked at her in surprise.

I smiled sweetly. "That's awesome, Milk. It's totally okay to speak for me. I love you so much; you're the best."

She rolled her eyes. "I've seen you dance. You rock, and it'll get you out of your funk."

"You saw me drunk, dancing on a table once."

"It was sexy as fuck," Dog said, leaning against the door. "I think I got a boner that time. You do that with the target, and bam, you get an invite to tour the manor. Then you introduce us as your adoptive siblings because your father loved helping people. Man charmed, painting ours, map collected, gold ours. Easy as pie."

Milk nodded excitedly.

"How do we get into the private event?" I asked.

"Devil is working his magic, and Upper is assisting," Dog said.

"How long do we have till the performance?" Milk asked.

"About an hour, two, tops?" Dog answered.

Milk smiled creepily at me, her hand rising to stroke my cheek as I inched back warily. "That's enough time to turn you into a dancer."

It took Dog getting rid of one of the dancers to get me into the back room as a replacement from another dance crew. Milk did my makeup and got me into the missing dancer's dress and jewelry while the other dancers filled me in on what they had planned.

There was no time to practice. They assured me it wasn't that hard; they even showed me a video of their choreography and told me we would be more like background noise because everyone would be paying attention to all the other things going on.

I don't like dancing. It wasn't a skill I learned out of personal preference. The times I had to do this were because I had to draw people's attention to my body and fetch money.

I stopped my thoughts there as I stared at my reflection in the mirror. The chain veil covered half of my face and my forehead. Only my eyes were on display, and my makeup was a little on the heavy side, but appropriate enough for the costume.

"Hey." Milk's hand fell on my shoulder. "Are you okay?"

I nodded, getting to my feet, ignoring how my stomach twisted. "I'm good."

"No one will be paying attention. I took a sneak peek at the event; people are packed in, and I don't think anyone is listening to the band playing. This is just a background thing."

"Okay, I'm ready." I turned to the other dancers, two girls who looked about my age, fixing each other's jewelry pieces. "You guys good?"

"Yes," one of them answered.

"I was hoping Fatima's stomachache would subside before it was time," the smaller one said. "She practiced so hard for this."

"Yes, poor Fatima," I said distractedly, picking up my phone and sending another *Can we talk? Text me back* message to Elio. It was delivered.

I waited a few seconds for a response, but nothing came.

Milk snatched the phone from my hand with a glare. "I never expected you to be a clingy girlfriend," she said. "It's pathetic."

"I know. I'm just stressed. It might be more from the fact that he thinks that I'm trying to sabotage his relationship with Devil."

"I understand, but let's get through this first, okay?"

I nodded. "Right, yeah, you're right, okay."

The place was packed, as Milk had said. I was grateful for the dim lighting and the chatter of people around.

When we got onstage, I allowed my body to get familiar with the environment, let my eyes roam the crowd: the men and women were all in casual clothing, and the air was chill. You could tell only rich people were here, the smell of expensive perfumes, calculating smiles, old costly wine in elite-looking wineglasses.

My eyes zeroed in on the target.

Kareem Fadel. Late fifties. Wealthy, the philanthropist of all philanthropists. According to everything else we'd dug up, this man sought perfection, enchantment, and orderliness. He saw people for who they were, hence why he was who he was and still breathing.

Word from the people was that he was kindhearted; he shared his things as if the people he helped were family. It was admirable.

And I had to ace this right out the gate.

"Hey," I called to the two girls. "I'll give you ten thousand dollars each if you get off this stage and leave this to me."

They frowned, eyes filling with confusion.

"You have that kind of money?" one asked.

"And more, if you want. Quick decisions. We don't have time."

"You're not some . . . assassin, are you?"

"Do I look like I carry a fucking gun with me?"

One of them nodded. The other shook her head.

"Great, then. Are you leaving or not? It's either ten thousand each, or I fuck up this dance and have you both on Kareem's bad side. Time is ticking."

They looked uncertain at first but then hopped quietly off the stage. I spotted the DJ frowning at them and then at me with confusion. I nodded for him to carry on.

My eyes settled on Kareem again as the lights started to dim. I swallowed my nerves. Then something silver glinted beside Kareem.

Rings.

Familiar rings.

My head snapped up, and I caught his gaze across the short distance; just when the lights around the room turned a dark red, and a bright white spotlight centered on me, the intro to the Arabian song started playing.

Elio Marino was sitting there, right beside Kareem, frowning in suspicion, confusion, and surprise.

Shit.

I collected myself with great difficulty, getting my head back on track as my body responded to the music and I tore my gaze from him.

Background fucking noise, my ass. I could hear the chattering die down, heads turning my way, the music and I the only things catching people's attention.

If I got out of this alive and unscathed, I would kill Milk. And I would enjoy it thoroughly.

My foul thoughts calmed me as I let the music own my body, becoming a partner with every rising and falling note.

The woman who'd taught us this technique had said the waist movement was the power of the dance, but most important, you had to let the music talk to your body. I worked on my hand placement, twirling my wrists with the beat of the traditional goblet drums, the echoes of the flute, mixed with the luring of the oud, and then attuned my body until it became one and the same with the enchanting secrets of the music.

I twirled my waist and lifted my hips to the language of the instruments, freed the muscles around my hands and neck, letting my ankles and the pads of my feet get familiar with the ground.

I was no Milk, but a dance like this could break any tension in a room, seduce any man or woman who bore witness; it could touch souls that never bargained to be touched.

The eyes on me had doubled in number, and I made eye contact with several people, loving the way wineglasses were stopped an inch before lips, too distracted by the dance.

Sensual hypnotism was real, and it was a weapon I didn't wield often. But now I had Kareem's undivided attention and knew I had gotten us that invite.

My gaze shifted to Elio, once again catching his stare. This time, I didn't look away as I put on a show for him, going extra soft with my movements, my hands moving up my hips to the deep indent of my waist, where he liked to touch me, then I dragged my gentle caress to the sides of my breasts before moving up to my neck where his lips had once made a home.

His eyes followed my hands, and I felt my skin heat up under his lustful scrutiny.

A smile curled onto my lips as I flattened my palm, dragging it up my neck to my chin as I twirled my head around, moving my waist in the other direction when we neared the end of the performance.

The dancers had informed me that we were never to go near Kareem, but I knew my mission would be successful if he called me right after.

With the way he watched me like one would watch a piece of art, I should have absolutely no problem.

The finishing lure of the music had my legs taking me around in a sensual twirl, aligning my hip movements with my wrist, stomach, and waist, slow and steady at first before I increased the pace.

It felt like I was falling into the music. A possession I knew was contagious, contagious to the point that I wasn't ultimately surprised when my last move after the music came to a drum-and-abrupt stop, and left the room in a graveyard silence.

My gaze shifted to the entrance of the back room to catch Milk standing there, jaw hanging as she looked at me, unblinking, entirely still.

A single hard clap had my attention snapping back to Kareem, who was on his feet, clapping with a massive smile on his face, shaking his head as his eyes gleamed with astonishment. His clapping brought everyone out of their daze as they joined in with chants of appreciation.

Kareem made his way over, extending his hand toward me as I removed my veil.

I placed my hand on top of his too-soft one, the wrinkles by his eyes pronounced as he kissed my knuckles. "You were *beautiful*. It was an honor to watch you," he said as he helped me off the stage, and another band started setting up.

"It was an honor to dance for you, Kareem."

He laughed boisterously, hand to his stomach as he sat down and ushered me onto his lap. I draped my arm over his shoulders. The game was on.

My gaze slipped to Elio, who was purposefully looking away, his jaw clenched hard as he lit a thick cigar, placing it between his lips, cheeks hollowing when he pulled hard on it. He didn't look as frustrated as I kind of hoped he'd look, no, he looked like he didn't have any worries, dressed in a short-sleeved black shirt that showcased his arm tattoo, his hair a little wet and roughly slicked back, no stubble on his face—he looked better than he did when I was around him.

"You flatter me," the man said with a grin, drawing my notice when his hand moved up my hip, an action that seemed to grab Elio's attention. Those eyes finally rose to catch my gaze as he let the smoke out of his mouth—thick and white, mixed with the atmosphere, it was the same color as his eyes right now. "What is your name, beautiful?"

"Zahra," I said, looking away from the man who I felt was seconds away from yanking me away. To kill me? Kiss me? Fuck me? His eyes said it all.

All hope wasn't lost.

"Zahra," Kareem pronounced slowly, "I must say, you rival my wives. What would it take to wed you so you can dance like that for me every day? I have never seen a performance that spoke directly to my soul."

I flattened my hand on his chest and smiled. "It would be most desirable to wed a man as generous as you are and a sin to deny such a proposal, but I already have someone who speaks to my soul, just like the music did."

Elio looked away.

Kareem smiled. "It is a shame. Your someone is fortunate; they should kiss the ground you walk on. If they don't, you should leave them."

I laughed wistfully. "If only that were possible, Kareem. The man in question complements my being. You can't leave someone like that."

Elio looked back, locking eyes with me from underneath his lashes. His face still wore no expression, but those eyes . . . the way he looked at me . . . My body flushed with heat.

He turned his face away again.

"Allow me to introduce you to my companion today," Kareem said, gesturing to Elio. "This is Elio Marino, the most genuine and generous man I have ever met."

"It's a pleasure to meet you, Mr. Marino."

"Hm." Elio gave what could be considered a nod if you looked close enough.

Kareem regarded him with a smile. "What did you think of the performance, Marino?"

"Good."

This mother—

Kareem laughed, looking back at me. "A 'good' from him is like heaven's blessing. He is a man of few words."

"I can see that." I smiled, lowering my tone. "Thank you for your very kind word, *sir.*"

He stiffened, hesitated, then gave another infuriating "Hm."

He put the cigar between his lips, indicating he was done talking.

Kareem indulged me in a conversation about how he was excited to be on the cruise; he also invited me to all his events here and within Mexico until the end of the cruise.

I knew I had him wrapped around my finger.

Mission accomplished—for that part.

Elio didn't speak again, acting as if I were nonexistent.

He only looked at me when I rose to get myself a strong drink at the bar.

It irked me that he was pretending I wasn't there.

I took the shot the bartender placed in front of me and threw it down my throat. The tension in my muscles relaxed almost immediately at the burn.

"Zahra Faizan."

The drink almost came back up my throat as I snapped my head to the side, and the burn became hotter when my eyes took in the person the voice belonged to.

Bright, almost blue eyes stared back at me, a small crooked smile on his lips as he leaned against the bar, gloved hands, like his cousin's, holding a whiskey glass. He wore a dark gray long-sleeved shirt that broadcast his biceps, and black slacks over solid thighs, a familiar form I had not expected to see here.

A form I should *not* be seeing here.

"Vitale Conti," I stated.

His eyes twinkled. "That was quite a performance. To think you were holding out on me all those times."

Almost like I could feel his eyes on me, I turned in Elio's direction, and yeah, he was watching.

This is not good.

I looked back at Vitale. He was Manuel's distant cousin, a year older than I was, intelligent, relentless, and not so fucking foolish. Which had me trying to figure out why the *fuck* he was here.

"How's the Conti estate these days?" I asked, even though I couldn't hide my discomfort.

"Surviving," Vitale said, bringing the glass to his lips without looking away from me as he took a sip. "How are *you* these days?" He swirled the contents of his glass.

"Surviving," I responded as he watched me with those calculating eyes. I looked around before settling my focus on him again. "What the fuck are you doing here?"

"What is everybody doing here? I'm having a good time."

"Vitale," I ground out.

"I wanted to see you," he stated, setting the glass on the table and moving closer to me. I inched back instinctively; the resemblance he bore to Manuel always had a way of making me raise my guard. I usually managed it well but it had been a while since I'd seen him. "I see some things never change," he said softly.

"You shouldn't be here."

"You shouldn't be here either. It has been years, Faizan. My patience is growing very thin."

"Your statement has a tone that I do *not* like," I said.

His hand wrapped around my arm suddenly, yanking me closer to him. "I am not your *puppet*."

"I didn't me—"

His grip tightened into a painful grasp, cutting me off as

he spoke through clenched teeth. "I hold the other end of this fucking string, Faizan."

"What are you doing?" I whispered.

"I am at my wit's end with you. We had a deal."

"And it's still standing."

"Is it?"

"Vitale—"

"Problem?" Elio's voice had my heart almost flying out of my throat as Vitale let go of my arm suddenly but didn't take his eyes off me.

I took a few steps back from him as I swallowed, looking up at Elio. "N-no problem."

Vitale picked up his glass and then looked at Elio, the taunting smile back on his face. "We were just having a friendly catch-up."

Elio's gaze dropped to the reddening bruise on my arm and then to me; something cold and vacant reflected in his eyes as he looked back at Vitale, the whiskey glass in his hand, the sharp edge of the counter, and then Vitale's neck.

How could one speak and show without speaking and showing?

The smile on Vitale's face faltered.

Vitale did not do well with threats. They were merely a challenge to him.

But this challenge might very well get him killed, and that would not happen. Not on my watch.

I stepped closer to Elio. "It's fine. We were just catching up. We haven't seen each other in years." It wasn't a lie, but Elio didn't budge or take his eyes off Vitale.

Then I focused on the foolish one who couldn't see his own life flashing before his eyes. "Vitale, *please*."

Vitale reluctantly stood straighter. "I'll go explore the party. Nice seeing you here again, Zahra." And then he raised his glass to Elio with a slight nod and that damn smile. "Marino."

He brushed past us after giving me one last pointed stare before saying, "Call me sometime."

Elio's eyes followed him until he was out of sight.

I let out a breath. "He was Manu—"

Elio raised a finger, stopping my statement without looking at me. "Do not . . . speak to me," he said then turned to leave, but I reached out to grab his arm, moving to stand before him.

"I want to speak to you."

"I gave you a chance. Multiple times."

"I know, but just give me another one. I'll clear everything up," I said, my eyes searching his vacant ones. "Please? The benefit of the doubt?"

He looked away from me, his jaw clenching like this request was the last thing he wanted to grant.

"If you still don't want to speak to me after I explain everything that went on in that bus, I promise I'll back off," I pressed.

After a few seconds, his gaze met mine again and the silence stretched between us, increasing my doubts, drawing in defeat before he surprisingly nodded. "Okay," he said, gesturing with his head toward the entrance. "Come with me."

CHAPTER SIX

Elio

Social gatherings and I were like enemies that would never, under any circumstance, find common ground.

It was why I'd asked Gemma to accompany me when we arrived at the cruise ship a day ago.

Angelo had joined me the day after I arrived to give me the intel on Kareem, and to take care of other affairs he had on board. He'd dropped off his bags in one of the rooms, along with his furry, wide-eyed black cat, Mimi, whom he left in my care due to his mother's unavailability.

He'd returned to Milan and then to Turin for in-house business but promised to hurry it up because, he said, and I quote, "The last thing I want to return to is a cat with a bullet in its stomach."

I wouldn't actually shoot an animal, but still that was a wise decision. He wasn't aware Gemma was an expert in taking care of cats. He wasn't aware of Gemma at all, or Sailor, whom she had brought along and dropped in my suite the following day, so Mimi wouldn't be "sad and alone."

I did not understand her logic, but she seemed to believe what she was saying, so I let it go.

Gemma had been a little wary when I told her about the trip and asked her to accompany me. She also said, and I quote, "You're rich?" to which I responded, "I am comfortable."

After which, she interrogated me about my job, and I supplied her with, "I am into business politics." And then I had to prove it to her by showing catalog upon catalog where my name had been mentioned under various business strategies for Milan. She had stared at me wide-eyed and asked, "Why the hell are you friends with me?" I ignored her statement politely, and we eventually ended up traveling together.

Casmiro had wanted to come as well, but I asked him to stay back due to his health issues. I wanted to remove his watchful eye from my actions, now that he knew about *my* health issues. The stubborn man fought me on it until I decided that if I needed him, he would be the first person I would call. Although he told me he would arrive either way if that call took longer than he liked. "Damn compound affairs, I would have my right hand hold down the fort," he said.

I agreed because if things went as planned with Kareem, I would not need to stay in Mexico for an extended period. If I was lucky enough, I might not get to mourn through the first morning in December.

For the first time in years, I could taste the achievement of my goal. I could touch, see, and feel it. The thought satisfied me; it satisfied a need I didn't know I had. It made me feel lighter.

No distractions.

No Street.

No Elia.

No . . . *Zahra.*

My thoughts slammed into a wall on that one.

No Zahra.

I finished the bourbon in the glass, pouring myself another. The event room was filled with strangers, all drinking and mingling. The air was heavy with the smell of sea salt, mixtures of expensive perfumes, and the familiar scent of Cuban cigars. The low golden lights around were warm and inviting enough to tame my irritation from being surrounded by so many people. I could feel Kareem's stare, but I didn't look over. Gemma hadn't accompanied me to this event; she was at the other end of the ship at some party she'd been invited to by strangers she claimed were her people. So, I had to live through this gathering with alcohol and cigars.

The things I had to do to get what I wanted. It would only make the final moment worth it. Endurance built anticipation, after all.

"I must say," Kareem started, rolling his vowels, and clipping endings like he was in a rush to reach the point, "when I invited you, I didn't think you would show."

"Hm."

"Why did you show up?" he asked, curious.

I swirled the contents of the glass. "There are two cats in my suite; it was either me throwing them into the ocean or coming here."

Kareem laughed like my words were coated in pink fluff. "You have pets."

"No. My . . . friends have pets."

"The things we do for friendship," he mused aloud. "Are your friends here tonight?"

"No."

"Why didn't you bring them? This party might be elite, but it is open to friends of my friends."

I finally looked at him. "I will bring them to the next one," I said, even though I had no intention of coming to the next one . . . or any other one. Ever.

Kareem sighed with satisfaction, and I watched him look around with a big smile on his face, taking in the crowd of people all gathered around, carefree like the rest of the world didn't matter—only this moment.

I had felt that way several times, but the scenario always featured a book or the woman I never hoped to see again. Once this deal with Kareem is implemented, I will ensure no one else gets to the painting before me, and after I have completed my goal, I will arrange for the gold to be sent to Street on my behalf.

"Mexico," Kareem said. "There's always this air of liberty in it. The night is always alive, and the people's smiles are so contagious it could make any sad man smile," he said, a wistful look in his eyes. "I am glad I came. Thank you for approaching me with this deal."

"It benefits the both of us."

"Yes." Kareem grinned. "The Garza manor is not inviting because it is grand and ancient. It was the man who lived there, the people who cared for it. The love and the smiles on their faces when they maintain it, the children who wander the halls and get awed by the artworks and sculptures, family portraits and endless stories."

"Indeed."

"When I reviewed your plans, I was filled with joy. I knew I had to look into it. I knew Arturo would want that. And coming from you, whom he spoke highly of; who was I to turn down your proposal?"

I nodded.

Kareem's grin turned into a small smile. "I see a brightness in you, Elio."

I blinked at him. The sudden change in the conversation's direction caught me off guard.

"You look surprised." He chuckled richly. "I know a good person when I see one. I am not blindsided by what you do or what your business truly entails. Politics is a dangerous field, and you would have to do equally dangerous things, but I see past that. Just the same way Arturo had."

I wondered what that man had told this one about me. But I didn't want to ask. I did not truly desire to know.

"You are set for great things, Marino. Your name should be more than what it is," he said, looking at me like he was looking through my soul, seeing the person I barely recognized anymore. "You should be setting paces, examples; if you can just touch upon that part of yourself, you will do good work."

I indulged him by nodding, hoping he was finished talking.

He watched me as though he was seeing things I couldn't.

"Ignore the rumors here and there about you. Only you know who you truly are."

I nodded yet again.

"If there is anything you need, even if it is my prayers, or a cleansing, give me a call, or an email, I will answer."

"Of course."

He grinned at me, refilling his glass as I looked around, his words playing inside my head, clashing with every intention I had for myself. It made me feel open, uncomfortable . . . I did not like it, and the reason was still a blur to me.

I noticed the change in lighting. The music that had been playing got quieter as my gaze sought something new to focus on, some form of distraction. I stopped my search when my attention settled on the stage where three people climbed on, dressed in traditional belly-dancing attire . . .

Nobody was paying attention, not even Kareem, as he spoke to someone who had managed to catch his attention.

My focus was drawn to the stage, my mind a haze as I studied the women getting into formation, the atmosphere already beginning to change.

A tether somewhere in my body stretched and then grew taut as I focused on the dancer in the middle. That height. That skin tone. That waist. That aura. *It couldn't be possible . . .* I frowned, watching closely . . . *It couldn't be her.* I knew my mind was prone to playing tricks on me, supplying false images and troubling memories, but it wasn't too late into the night. I wasn't trying to sleep naturally; I was awake, barely intoxicated.

She was here.

Her deeply accentuated eyes scanned the room like it was an opponent she wanted to conquer.

How I recognized her with that veil was proof enough that I had been lying to myself that the last I saw of her was actually the last I would *ever* see of her.

Why was I surprised? I couldn't precisely pinpoint it. There was this curl of excitement and wariness in my stomach, so tight that I had to battle with the expression I showed to anyone who could see me.

I watched the way she took a step back, her exposed, thin but curvy waist swaying with her movements as she summoned the attention of the women behind her. I could tell she was saying something, and the frowns on the faces of her companions spoke volumes of their discomfort with what she was saying.

It didn't last long because they seemed to agree to whatever she had proposed, and they were getting off the stage.

I watched how she slowly gathered her confidence, looking in my direction but not at me. Kareem was her target for the night. Not me. She didn't realize I was here.

The urge to get up and silently leave pulled firmly at my gut. However, my curiosity and my barely controlled obsession with watching this woman do remotely anything had my grip clenching around the glass. I remained seated.

I was confused as to why she was here and surprised as to why she was on that stage, dressed in a way that brought a different kind of heat to the room.

It took only a slight shift in her gaze to catch my stare. The way those bright brown eyes took me in with shock affirmed my assumptions about her not knowing I was there.

The light around us dimmed, and a bright spotlight was placed on her, giving me one of the most beguiling sights my eyes had ever gotten the pleasure to see.

Wow.

Zahra was standing there, glowing, in all the glories known to be bestowed onto a human being . . .

No.

That word seemed too small to describe what I was seeing . . . She was otherworldly; she deserved to breathe the same oxygen as gods and deities alike.

The woman before me was too good to be in this room full of undeserving parasites.

Anger bloomed within me.

The moment she took her eyes off me, I looked around to see she had not only caught my attention but everyone else's, women and men, young and old, and she had barely even moved yet, barely even blinked; her presence was enough to demand the attention of all.

When the song started to play, I focused on her once more. I watched, astonished and taken with the way she seemed to blend in with the music, the stage, the instruments. She owned every bit of this moment, and it felt like my lungs had finally succumbed to my ill will.

Her hands moved in perfect sync with her waist, like the music lived in her veins.

My mind, at this very moment, registered the fact that underestimating Zahra was a sin one shouldn't ever commit. I was convinced she could do . . . anything.

The way she moved. *The way this woman moved*—seducing the music, teasing everyone in this room without touching them.

I was amazed, dazed, proud . . . aroused.

I didn't have the luxury of looking anywhere else. I felt missing a second of this would seem like cutting off the air I needed to breathe.

Her body spoke languages my mind's reasoning failed to comprehend.

My lust was mixed with admiration and jealousy at the realization that I was not the only one she was seducing.

She was deadly. Like poison.

The poison—*God*—the poison was in the way she danced. One hip lift echoed in waves like a siren sound, a blessing, and a curse . . . My little witch didn't come to bewitch; she came to speak, and listen, I did.

Almost like she had sensed my thoughts—those eyes locked with mine, taking her time with her movements, adding a bit of fervor that increased my need for her. Those beautiful fingers felt up her hips to her waist, a silent message for me as she subtly reminded me how it felt to touch her like that, but her cruelty was a crime I was more than willing to forgive.

My eyes followed her movements, and my fingers ached to touch her; my body burned with need, and my cock hardened with obscene arousal, one I wanted to abolish but, at the same time, sate.

I was buried deep in lust for this woman, and I didn't care.

My eyes didn't leave her even after the dance finished, and Kareem, alongside everyone else, clapped like they had just witnessed and experienced the same thing I did.

I watched as Kareem walked over to her, taking her hand as he led her toward me.

The man's grand laughter over something Zahra might have said had me turning my head away. If I didn't look away, I might have stabbed him in the neck with a butter knife out of jealousy alone.

My growing rage flared when Zahra sat on his lap . . . in front of me.

The utter disrespect.

I ground my teeth, holding myself back from the vivid thoughts trying to dig their way into my brain as I proceeded to light a cigar, place it between my lips, and suck in the warm smoke until I felt the heat inside me. I knew I had no reason to feel this way. I knew I put a stop on our agreement to be sexual partners, but it didn't erase how attached I had grown to her or the jealousy biting at my reserve inconveniently.

I should leave.

But I couldn't. Not with her still here. Unprotected with different eyes turning our way, intentions clear in their gaze. I knew she could protect herself, but that did not erase the fact that she was the most careless person I'd ever met.

"You flatter me." At the sound of Kareem's voice and a movement from the corner of my eye, I turned to see his hand settling on her hip. She made no move indicating the touch unsettled her, and I couldn't help but look up, finding those eyes already on me, taking in my reaction as I blew out the smoke I had sucked in, detesting every second of my stay here. "What is your name, beautiful?"

"Zahra." That voice I hadn't heard for two weeks met my ears in a caress—the urge to grab her off his lap, pull her out of this damn event, and forget why I'd called it quits, tugged at me, but I kept silent.

"Zahra, I must say, you rival my wives. What would it take to wed you so you can dance like that for me every day? I have never seen a performance that spoke directly to my soul."

This conversation was beginning to make my anger evident on my face. Who in their right mind would make a proposal like that? More so to someone they don't know?

Kareem was careless.

I watched Zahra flatten her hand against his chest, and I had to remind myself that Kareem was old enough to be her father, and I needed him for other business.

But then Zahra responded to his proposal: "It would be most desirable to wed a man as generous as you are and a sin to deny such a proposal, but I already have someone who speaks to my soul, just like the music did."

I was quickly reminded of how easily she'd had me fooled by her relationship with my brother. I remembered why I broke things off, and I looked away from them, already deciding to leave; her safety wasn't—

"It is a shame. Your someone is fortunate. They should kiss the ground you walk on. If they don't, you should leave them."

She laughed like she was thinking of that someone. "If only that were possible, Kareem. The man in question complements my being; you can't leave someone like that."

And then there was a subtle tightness in my chest, remembering how I'd said those exact words to her. I looked toward them again and found her gaze on me, her eyes for the first time showing a little bit of vulnerability, a silent plea that showed she was talking about me . . . but this was the last thing I wanted; everything was going as planned.

This was a distraction; one I couldn't afford. Not right now.

I looked down, blinking back my focus onto what mattered. It wasn't my heart; it wasn't my need. It wasn't my lust. It wasn't her smile. It wasn't her voice. It wasn't her presence. It wasn't *her*.

"It's a pleasure to meet you, Mr. Marino."

My focus zeroed in on their conversation, and I realized I had been introduced.

"Hm," I said, barely lifting my head or reaching her gaze.

"What did you think of the performance, Marino?" Kareem asked.

"Good," I devalued.

I tuned out the rest of their conversation, only muttering an acknowledgment when Zahra spoke to me, and ignoring the use of the word "sir" from her lips.

When she stood up to leave, I watched to see if any of the Street members were around the area to stay with her, but the woman had gone to the bar to get a drink. I loathed how eyes tracked her movements like she was a specimen they couldn't wait to get their hands on. I could do things to those violating eyes belonging to men and women. The gore the results would bring. Food to my deranged soul.

When I turned my eyes away from people looking at her, I found one of them already making a move to talk to her . . . They exchanged a few words . . . but her stance, her composure . . . Something was off.

When she glanced my way, it wasn't a plea for help, but a glance saying, *This can't be happening.*

Whoever that man was, she knew him.

She looked away from me and then back to him; I watched them for a few seconds before breaking contact when Kareem moved to shake my hand and thank me for coming to the event. And then, after a few exchanges, his attention was needed in another area of the room, and he left.

When I turned back in Zahra's direction, what I saw had me frowning. The man was grabbing her arm with a gloved hand, and she looked uncomfortable.

I didn't know how I'd been sitting watching them one second and was already halfway toward them the next.

"Is it?" The man bit the question at her.

"Vitale—"

"Problem?" My voice cut into whatever conversation they had been having, making Zahra flinch. The man dropped her arm. But his eyes were still locked on hers while she stepped back, looking as uncomfortable as I felt with this man still breathing.

"N-no problem," she *stuttered*, her cheeks flushed, her previous composure completely deformed.

I watched the man pick up his drink. He was about two inches shorter than me, but when he removed his gaze from her and looked at me, his stare was leveled, unflinching, unafraid, like he had been expecting my arrival. "We were just having a friendly catch-up."

I tore my gaze from him and looked at the arm of the woman beside me, the bruise from his hold tainting her skin, tainting my control, tainting the shred of humanity I had brought into this event. I didn't hear or see anything or anyone; my focus returned to the man.

There were a thousand ways—*more* than a thousand ways I could kill him here and now—something quick, something sharp, something *painful*. The image slashing through my head tickled my brain; the anger flowing through my veins removed all rational thought.

Suddenly Arturo's manor didn't matter, suddenly I didn't care about burning it all down, suddenly my goal in life was to kill this man, and I wouldn't be okay until I did it.

I didn't know what was happening; I knew Zahra was

saying something to me and then to Vitale, who unfortunately turned his gaze from me. When I didn't get out of my head, even after he raised his glass in mock salute, said my name, and walked away, I knew the deed had been done.

I watched him walk away, knowing there was no way he was getting out of this cruise alive.

When he was out of sight, I got out of my head just in time for Zahra's voice to reach my head.

"He was Manu—"

I raised a finger, not bothering to regard her. "Do not . . ." I forced out, "speak to me," I finished, turning to leave, but she reached out to grip my arm, and she was in front of me.

Regretful but determined eyes searched mine. "I want to speak to you."

"I gave you a chance," I reminded her. "Multiple times."

A small breath left her parted lips. "I know, but just give me another one; I'll clear everything up," she said, sincerity lingering in her stare. "Please?" Her voice softened, getting straight into my head. "The benefit of the doubt?"

I looked away, fighting my head, my gut, my heart, and my damn mind at the same time. It was always a battle with this woman.

"If you still don't want to speak to me after I explain everything that went on in that bus, I promise I'll back off," she added.

I knew I wasn't strong enough to deny her this. All I had to do was remain passive; no matter what she said or revealed, I wouldn't acknowledge it. I couldn't afford any form of distraction for what I had planned.

I nodded. "Okay, come with me."

When we got to my suite, I looked around for the cats but couldn't find them. It appeared they were tucked somewhere around, and I appreciated that. I was in no mood to acknowledge their presence or answer questions from Zahra.

The woman in question walked in, and I closed the door behind us.

"Well—fuck, the platinum suite is fire," Zahra said, and I watched her take in our surroundings with awe, the large crystal chandelier hanging above, the pool table by the side, the soft cream couches, the eighty-inch smart TV, a balcony overseeing the large ocean below. "Rich people do get away with everything—"

"I don't have all night," I said.

She turned around, startled at the sharpness in my voice as she sucked in a breath, and shifted on her feet, showing nervousness. "Wouldn't you, um—want to sit down first?"

"No."

"Awesome, we're *doing it* standing." She grinned like she had just made a joke I was supposed to understand.

I stared blankly.

"Get it?" Her grin faltered. "Doing it . . . standing? Like doing . . . *it*."

Blank stare.

"No?" Her smile died as she cleared her throat. "Okay."

I waited for her to speak.

She sighed, fingers going through her hair. "Right, okay . . . um, first off. That guy from before was Vitale . . . Conti. We sort of grew up together back in Sicily. Not like grew up, *grew up*—he was the only person close to my age who didn't treat me differently after Manuel rescued me. He was the only one I could relate to. I haven't seen him in a long time."

"I did not ask about him."

"No, I—I know you didn't. I was just . . . telling you."

When I didn't respond, she swallowed, shifting on her feet again.

"You got it all wrong the other day. I wasn't playing with you, messing with you, or trying to ruin your relationship with Devil. I was even supposed to talk to him before this, but you were here so . . ." Her teeth clamped down on her bottom lip as she stumbled over her words. "Devil and I kissed, yes, but it didn't mean anything romantic at all. I had a—I had a panic attack, and he did it so I would calm down. If he hadn't, I wouldn't be here today."

Well . . . that wasn't a lie.

She squared her shoulders, looking away from me like she didn't like any bit of this conversation. "I was . . . *wrong*. I made a mistake, a temporary lapse in judgment, and . . . and I'm sorry for putting Devil's life in danger, and . . . and for making you worry," she said, sneaking a careful glance at me.

The sincerity in her eyes shook me. She was being honest; she was apologizing. She was doing all I'd wanted since the moment I started growing interested in her.

To disregard this just for my goal felt . . . wrong.

When I didn't respond yet again, I could see a twinge of defeat in her eyes, but with the breath she let out, I knew she was about to reveal more information she had never disclosed to anyone.

"I've been put to the test before. When I was younger, a year after living with Manuel." She swallowed. "There was a bomb, and he—he put people there in the—in a building. He, um—he asked me to defuse the bomb." She paused, looking as though she was contemplating whether to continue or not. Her hand moved to her cheek to rub away an itch I was sure wasn't there. "I thought it was just regular training, until—until I saw the bomb and the people . . . they were scared, crying. It was . . . it was terrible.

"Manuel was behind me, trying to guide me, but I was too scared. A lot was riding on it. If I failed, I would—I would kill them; if I didn't, I would save them. I *wanted* to save them. But—I was too scared, too slow, too weak. And the bomb went off. I didn't hear their cries anymore but the sm—the smell afterward . . . I couldn't sleep for days, I couldn't eat or think, I had nightmares, and Manuel, he . . . he didn't really care that I wasn't okay."

She let out an unsteady breath, looking at me with a strained smile. "You want me to be very honest with you, Elio?" she asked, taking two steps closer to me until we were just a step away from each other. "I am terrified. I am constantly fucking terrified. I put up this strong and impenetrable wall around myself; I make it so hard for anyone to trust me. I have these issues so fucking deep inside me, this anger that makes me a stranger to myself, and I hate it. I just want a make-believe life with my team. I really *truly* want to leave all this behind me; I want to go where nobody knows me, or my name, or the things I've done, but . . ." She gulped.

"I might have left Manuel, but he never left me. He's here"—she gestured to her head—"he's in my head, in every fucking action I take. I am often reminded that I am who I am today because of him, and it messes me up. That man took—he took, he took, and he took so much from me, and now I'm just . . ." She lifted her shoulder, dropped it. "Empty. Filled with so much hate, so much inferiority, so much malice."

She was so sincere that her words didn't have to be deciphered before they made sense to me.

"You want me to tell you why I always want control, why I never bend?"

I didn't respond.

"It's because I'm not allowed to. I don't have the . . . luxury of being *free* with my emotions. They've been used against me before, so I try as much as possible to stop that from happening again. I protect myself and my heart." Her gaze pierced mine. "This thing I'm doing, telling you all of this . . . I don't . . . I don't do it. I don't want to do it, but . . ." She shrugged with a cautious smile. "You're worth it."

My resolve melted, but I didn't speak.

She sighed. "Just tell me how I can fix this."

"Why do you want to fix it?"

"I don't know? Because—I thought aside from us . . . aside

from the physical aspect of our relationship, I thought we were friends?"

Friends. I didn't want that.

I nodded. "I have heard all you've said, I understand the position you might have been put in on that bus, and I apologize for the mental stress I might have caused afterward, but I still fail to understand what you want from me."

She blew out a breath like I had been making her work out for hours, and then she took the final step closer to me, and I could feel her warmth.

"You," she stated. "I want you; I want your body, your fucking weirdness, just you . . . all of you."

A warm, gentle glow settled inside me, but I locked my jaw as I said, "At this point, you're picking out my own words and throwing them back at me."

"Oh, come on, Elio!" she snapped, and it took all my resolve not to smile. "I am doing the best I can here; I want to swallow my own fucking tongue for even saying all of this shit to you! You're a fucking asshole who looks like he wants to kill me half the time, but I've known you for months, and you have wanted to kill me for months, but you ended up fucking me instead and telling me you like me but still want to slit my throat, and here we are!" She breathed out. "Here I am, doing the same while trying not to decapitate you for making me talk too much."

"Thought you liked talking."

"You know what? Fuck you, and fuck this." She walked around me quickly, already opening the door to leave, but I was faster, my front pressed to her back as my hand rose to slam the door shut before she could even open it fully.

With my palm still pressing on the door, a few spaces above and beside her head, and my body still locking hers between me and the door, I gave her a tiny space, and she turned around sharply with a murderous glare. "If you know what's fucking good for you, you would let me o—"

I caught her remaining words with my lips.

And it took the warmth from her mouth on mine, the thundering hard gripping and tightness in my chest, the nerve-tingling feeling up my spine to my stomach, and the goose bumps arising on my skin for me to realize the mind-rocking clarity of what I'd just done.

I had broken my last rule.

CHAPTER SEVEN

Zahra

I am in trouble.

Elio was kissing me, and my limbs, my fight, all my fucking resolve had melted with that single buzzing connection. I was standing, but it didn't feel like I was standing; my brain cells felt nonexistent, my bones were no longer erect, and breathing . . . *what even is that?*

Was I breathing before he pressed his lips to mine?

When was the last time I was conscious? Where the fuck am I?

I felt his hand come up to hold the side of my face—gently—as if he was afraid he would break me—and then, he pulled away, and I couldn't see; I could breathe air back into my lungs, even with how rapidly my heart was racing, but for some reason, I couldn't see—

Oh, wait.

I opened my eyes, catching the intense gray of his stare, now dark and filled with so much emotion that it had my stomach flipping without warning, watching me like I was his most prized possession—like I was the reason for his existence.

I might be exaggerating it, but goddamn, if that wasn't the message his eyes sent, I didn't know what it was. It was too much for me to handle; it was contagious—so contagious that I wanted to push him away and bolt out of this room, off of this cruise ship, out of fucking Mexico.

But my feet were pinned to the ground, my heart was beating in the same rhythm as his, my body was warm all over, and I was a fucking goner.

If my disgusting behavior with texting him didn't show me

how bad I had it for this man, this kiss just ripped the veil from my eyes.

"I vowed never to do that," he said, his thumb stroking down my chin to the pulsing vein in my neck. "I vowed to never kiss you or anyone ever again."

"Why?" I asked, my voice barely a whisper.

"You didn't like it the first time I did it."

That was enough to bring a frown to my face. "I never said that—"

"Your actions afterward spelled it."

Watching him carefully, I brought my hands to his firm chest, feeling his heart slam against his ribs and then my palm, so fast, so strong, so alive. I got onto my toes and snaked my arms around his shoulders and neck, my eyes searching his. "Did you lose your ability to spell?"

"I do—"

I lifted myself with a small jump, his shoulders supporting my movement as my legs went around his waist, and on reflex, his strong arms caught me in a secure grip.

"I loved it, Elio," I confessed, my hold tightening around him. "I loved it so much it scared the hell out of me."

His grip on my hips tightened. "*You* scare the hell out of me," he whispered against my lips.

"I know"—I gulped—"this is not good."

He nodded in agreement. "Is it bad that I want it anyway?" he asked.

My gaze flickered from his eyes to his lips. "No . . . because I want it too."

There was a silent agreement between us that made me feel like I was levitating. I wasn't the only one feeling these all-consuming emotions; I wasn't the only one confused by them; we were in it together, so I joined our lips, and he kissed me back, indulging me by parting his lips while my tongue found his—I knew there was no way in hell I was denying myself the bliss that seemed to come with him.

My fingers softly moved into his hair. One of his hands held me steady, and the other rubbed up my back to the back of my head, inside my hair, keeping me in place as he moved.

I didn't look, too riled by every tingle from places our bodies brushed together, but I knew he was carrying us away from the living room.

Without breaking the kiss, he opened a door and closed it, setting me on my feet while my hands left him, and he broke away; I was removing the costume I wore until I was bare-chested, while he was pulling his shirt over his head, and within seconds he was kissing me again, his hands exploring, touching, feeling, supplying me with a feverish effect I never thought my body could produce.

His lips left mine to go to my chin, kissing down my neck. I closed my eyes at the warmth of his kisses, baring my neck for him as his hands helped me out of the thin material of the skirt, leaving the chains around my waist; while I undid his fly, his need for me was prominent against his slacks.

"You almost killed me out there." He breathed against my ear, his voice a fever's whisper away from sounding like he was shivering. "I have never felt so many emotions at once; it was exhilarating."

I smiled, opening my eyes. "So it wasn't . . . 'good'?" I repeated his word from earlier.

"No. It was brilliant. I wish you could see how I feel, Zahra." His hand fell to my waist and then over my hand on his fly as his eyes locked with mine. "Words are too little to describe it."

While I was still lost, staring at him, he helped me by zipping down and taking off his pants before following through with his briefs and giving me a view of his thick, veiny length. This man was perfect in every sense of the word: sexy, charming, dark . . . I didn't know I had a type until him, but would I even consider him a type? He was a rarity, someone I was lucky enough to have this effect on.

He stepped back slowly, watching me like he was trying

to soak in the view of me, like he was trying to plaster every curve, every scar, and every imperfection onto his memory.

"Go bare for me," he rasped. "I want to see you."

I would have never done that. Given him control. But I've always had it all my life; one night, letting go wouldn't hurt to try.

I didn't take my eyes off him when I took off my underwear, which was my last piece of clothing, save for the chains around my waist; a chill traveled down my spine as he slowly looked at me, from my calves to my thighs to my stomach, my shoulders, and my face.

I wouldn't lie and say I wasn't vulnerable in this moment. Everything was on display for him, every pain I'd received, every memory I had held with a tight fist, every fear I'd felt, every slap, every blow, every cut, and every burn.

But there was no judgment in his eyes; nothing changed into a negative light; he just looked at me like he always had, but this time, it carried a more profound weight, like he was reading me, affirming to himself that this body—*my* body—would be it for him.

Maybe I was reading him wrong or in over my head, but there was nothing unserious about this moment—and *scared* didn't come close to describing how I felt; *terrified* was more like the word I would use.

"Come here," he said softly. I shifted a little on my feet, and the moment I started stepping forward and into his reach, his arm curled around my waist, pulling me to his body, his cock pressing against my stomach as he took a kiss, shutting my airway, stopping my heartbeat, igniting my need.

The wetness between my legs gave way to the aching thump from my clit to torture me; my nipples were hard against his body, my piercings intensifying the painful pleasure. A moan left my lips when he lifted me and carried me to the bed, his teeth biting my bottom lip as he laid me down, with him atop me, his cock right at my entrance; a little teasing brush of him against my slit pulled another moan from my throat, and a groan from his.

He was driving me crazy, but he was still kissing me, his tongue rubbing, lips sucking; he was taking his time, wanting us to taste alike. His hand went down to lift my left leg while I took the liberty to lift my right, giving him enough room to rub his cock against my slit up to my clit—it felt so good my heart was about to burst out of my chest. He didn't enter me; it was almost as if he was trying to coat his length with my wetness while he kissed me.

Sucking and licking and rubbing and teasing, building up my anticipation, leaving me a wet, needy, and moaning mess; the buildup around my clit was criminal. The room wasn't overly warm—the man wasn't fucking me, but I was sweating, I was delirious, not existing as myself; he was owning me now, pushing me to the edge but not letting me go.

His lips left mine, traveling down my chin to my throat, but he didn't stop his hips' movement; the sound of my wetness getting familiar with his cock was setting my stomach ablaze. It was dirty, it was intimate, and I was feral with a need for him to be inside me.

"I won't tell you you're beautiful," he whispered against my burning skin. "I won't tell you you're perfect; you already know that." He licked and kissed back up my throat. His eyes, a sexy smoky gray, filled with lust and admiration, stared at me. "You already know that I know that," he whispered, swallowing, his Adam's apple bobbing up and down. "What I will tell you, though, is that I see you, and I appreciate you sharing this part of yourself with me." He kissed the left side of my lips. "I will cherish it." He moved his lips to the other side. "Keep it." He kissed my nose. "Adore it." He placed a lingering kiss on my lips before breaking it and finishing, "And worship it."

He didn't let me digest his words before he pushed into me with a hard thrust that shoved a breath of his name from my lips.

He kissed me as he pulled out and gave another hard thrust,

and my hips lifted with it, my back arching at the sensation that traveled through every vein in my body, every hair on my skin rising to attention. Without seeing myself, I knew I was flush with need, just like the man above me, a fucking painting of pleasure.

He fucked me like he was trying to stamp in every word he had just let out of his mouth, like he wanted me to believe him. His pace increased from hard, slow paces to hard, fast paces.

I was a mess of moans, his name a chant upon my lips, his grunts and little deep moans a drive to my ego; I memorized each sound, how low his tone was—like he could barely contain himself, like he was on the brink.

The sound of his cock pumping into me was my official damnation. I would never want anything or anyone else like him or this.

A slow build formed in my stomach, and I wanted to drag this out. I didn't want to come, but it was apparent he had something different in mind because his lips covered a nipple, and his hand went to my clit, rubbing at the swollen bud. At the same time, he fucked me at a pace that could be considered inhumane—and I was coming, writhing, fucking convulsing as the feeling blinded me, took my senses, and threw them out into the ocean; the orgasm could have lasted forever because while his pace slowed, his hand still worked on my clit, the silver coldness of his rings making my thighs quiver.

My trembling fingers went around his wrist to stop him from further stimulating me, but his other hand removed my hand, intertwining our fingers and pinning them to the space above my head.

"You disrespected me," he breathed, slipping out of me.

"What?"

"Earlier tonight?" His eyes searched mine. "Sitting on another man's lap in front of me, letting him touch you . . ." Two ringless fingers drove into me in a violent thrust, and my walls clamped tightly around them immediately. "In front of me."

"K-Kareem?"

"And Vit-idiot," he whispered against my lips, his fingers thrusting harshly in and out of me, sending overwhelming sensations to my nerve endings, my toes curling. "Kareem will be spared, but the other one . . ."

"Hm . . . fuck," I moaned, clamping my teeth down on my bottom lip, my head pressing farther into the pillow, back arching from the bed as his fingers found my G-spot, and he made sure to hit me there with each thrust, curling around it, brushing and rubbing.

His thumb flicked my clit in pace with the thrust of his index and middle fingers, his hand squeezing mine against the mattress in a firm hold. "I will skin him alive and make it last the exact hour, minute, and second that bruise lasts on your arm."

He pumped faster, wilder, the sloshing sound of my wetness filling up the space between us.

Dirty, so fucking dirty.

My breathing came out in a gasp of moans, my stomach clenching, my thighs twitching open and closed around his body, which he somehow used to maneuver my thighs to remain open. My eyes rolled to the back of my head, and I was coming, and coming and squirting all over his fingers, my thighs, his body, his forearm. There was no biting my tongue to stop the short scream that left me as the wave took over my body, so suddenly; my other hand dug fingers into his shoulder. I was trying to push him off and, at the same time, pull him in.

It felt so good; I didn't want it to stop. His thumb rolled against my clit, and my hips twitched in pleasured shock.

I was coming down from my high when he removed his fingers, pressing himself down to whisper in my ear, "I like the way you come undone, querida." He softly kissed my earlobe. "But we're not close to being done," he said, and there was a wickedness to his voice that made my stomach jump. "You touched Kareem on his chest. In front of me," he said. "You danced like that in front of everyone, strangers and acquaintances alike."

"That wasn't my fault," I managed, but didn't recognize my own voice.

"I know . . ." he said, raising his body so he could look at me. "You're free to enchant people with your charm and aura all you want, but you do not do it in front of me."

My lips tilted upward. "Why? You get jealous?"

"Hm." He nodded, brushing the head of his cock against the sensitive flesh of my clit; I shivered. "I find the feeling of jealousy . . . inconvenient."

"De verdad?" *Really?*

"*Sí*, Zahra," he responded, pronouncing my name with its actual traditional intonation. "On your stomach, now."

He lifted himself, and though I was fucking done, and my thighs were weak and aching, I couldn't do away with the excitement inside me, and I also wanted him to experience his existence shattering around him just like mine had a few minutes ago.

So I turned over, brushing my hair back from my face, getting on my knees when his hands came around the globes of my ass and up my waist as he pushed me down, one of his hands going to the back of my head, pushing it down against the pillow, not too hard, but just enough so I couldn't move or look at him.

My heart thundered, my body buzzed, and I was anticipating. Waiting.

Both his legs came beside my knees as he supported me, relieving me of the stress of keeping myself up with half my stomach, my whole chest, and my head pressed to the bed, and my ass in the air, my back arched perfectly.

I felt him behind me, his length between my ass cheeks while his hand rubbed up and down my slit, tantalizing me, making me forget that this was the first time in a really long time that I was going into this position for any man, that this was the first time doing this of my own free will.

My hands gripped the sheets as he positioned his cock at my entrance—Fuck, I wasn't sure I still had another orgasm in me to give, but I could feel a dull throbbing in my clit, a tiny flipping in my stomach; I was still getting wet, glistening for him, aroused by him, his grip on my hair, the hotness of his skin on my thighs. When he slowly entered me, I pressed my eyes closed, a whimper falling from my lips as I clenched around him. He was so damn deep inside me, so fucking thick and warm, so good; he felt so good I wanted to cry.

His hand caressed my waist before holding me firm, pulling back a bit and thrusting into me again, dragging out another moan and a grunt. His pace was fast and slow at first, his pelvis slapping against my ass, the sound making the pleasure feel erotically painful.

I wanted to come, but I knew I couldn't. I cried out moans as his pace grew faster, his cock stretching my walls, going deep, hitting me where I always came undone, sending waves of pleasure up and down my spine, causing a small tear to fall from my eye, which fought to stay open.

His cock was like sugar, too fucking sweet to comprehend. He was too much but I couldn't bring myself to complain because I liked it; I liked him, I liked the pleasure and the pain that he supplied me, I liked the way he handled me and owned me, I liked it too fucking much.

His grip tightened on my hair, and my nipples brushed against the mattress, a stimulation of its own making.

"Oh fuck, oh fuck . . ." Words like sobs were leaving my lips, and his name was falling from my tongue like water. I was pulsing, my eyes filling up, my heart racing as I felt it, another orgasm tightening my stomach, driving in a shiver.

"*Zahra.*" He breathed my name like he was worshipping every syllable with a moan. Drawled to show how much he loved being inside me.

I was falling deeper and deeper as his pace grew harder and faster, falling sloppy and shorter. I knew he was close—and after four hard thrusts, hot cum coated my walls, triggering another orgasm from me, the third one tonight. Even with his support, my thighs gave out, and my breathing became gasps; I was weak everywhere, my bones were no longer bones, and sleep clouded my vision as he slipped out of me.

I felt his lips on my neck. He turned me over, his palm running up my stomach, past the swell of my breast, and then to the side of my face as he brought his lips down to mine.

I kissed him back just as softly as he kissed me.

When we broke away, his eyes searched mine as he said softly, "Hello."

I smiled. "Hi."

His thumb tenderly brushed the corner of my lips. "You did very good," he said, wiping the sides of my eyes.

"I think you broke me," I said with a lazy but sated grin.

His thumb moved to my bottom lip, brushing softly. "A good kind of break?"

I nodded.

He smiled—or I think he did; sleep was within my reach.

He dropped to my side, but his elbow remained on the bed, propping himself up, his fist to the side of his head while his other hand came to my stomach; he dragged his knuckles slowly to the side. The softness in his touch gave me goose bumps.

When his fingers settled on a scar I knew all too well, I shut my eyes.

"Who did this?" he asked. "Someone cut you?"

"Yes, training. Vitale. I was sixteen, and it hurt like a bitch." I chuckled softly, and his fingers trailed to another one; I knew what it looked like, a small round scar from a burn. It mainly looked like my skin now, but odd.

"What about this?"

"Fifteen, the man I was sold to . . . I didn't really last long as a sex worker before I was sold . . . roughly two years."

"How did it happen?"

I kept my eyes closed. "He only arrived on certain nights—mostly he would just want me to blow him; he didn't have sex with me—well, until that night . . . When he was done, he lit a cigarette, asked me to stay there while he blew it into my face for some sick reason, and then he pressed the lit end to my skin and said it was a mistake, he'd thought he kept the ashtray somewhere close. I only winced, even though it burned."

"And this man, what was his name?"

I managed a shrug. "It doesn't matter," I said. "Manuel killed him the day he rescued me." I sighed. "It was my first time seeing a massacre of that magnitude."

Elio's hand brushed the surface of my skin. "Did Manuel cause any of these scars?"

A sad laugh took over me. "He would never hurt me . . . at least not physically. He's mostly responsible for the emotional and mental scars no one can see . . . well, except you, for some weird reason." I opened my eyes a little, watching him stare at me with a serene gaze. I smiled and added, "Some weird, supernatural, gut reason."

Elio raised a brow, going silent but still teasing my skin with his fingers; I closed my eyes, relaxing into the feeling as he spoke again, voice deep and soft.

"Do you want to know something?"

"Yeah, I can't be the only one doing the revealing thing," I said with a smile.

"It is not much of a revelation, just an observation."

"I'm all ears."

"Do you recall when you assumed I had the genes that do not exist? The serial killer ones?"

"Yup, when you proceeded to say words I've never heard before?"

"Hm. I figured if there were genes like that, I would have them."

I frowned slightly but didn't open my eyes. "Why do you think that?"

"I have peculiar thoughts on occasions when I shouldn't have peculiar thoughts. It sometimes shocks me, and sometimes it makes me feel . . . more alive. Sometimes I have a strong urge to go through with them, to hurt someone because I like something about . . . them."

I opened my eyes slightly, just enough to see him; his face was still relaxed, no frown, no smile, just calm.

"Like a serial killer's victim type?" I asked.

He nodded.

I didn't know why I asked what I asked next, but I wanted to understand what he was saying. "What would yours be?"

"Mostly women," he stated. "With good hair. I feel like they would be my target." His gaze met mine and held. He didn't say anything for a while, and I didn't say anything either; his hand lifted, and his fingers fell into my hair, gently feeling the texture, his voice softening as he said, "Does that scare you, Zahra?"

"To be honest, yeah. A little . . . bit," I answered.

He removed his hand from my hair and swallowed, and I could see that he was blocking whatever made him feel like he could reveal that to me. "That was not my intention; I won't repeat it."

"No, no, it's—it's, uh . . . it's okay; I want to know what goes on in that head of yours, even though it's weird—but as long as you haven't—you know . . ."

"Killed a woman because of her hair?"

"Yeah . . ."

"No, I haven't. I won't. I will never. It's just that sometimes the thought—comes and goes."

I nodded. "Have you ever had that thought with me?"

"No," he said. "I didn't like your hair at first. But your friend, though . . ."

"Milk?"

"Hm. She has beautiful hair."

I didn't know why I laughed. "Noted; I'll ask her to stay away from you."

His hand fell to my stomach again, rubbing with the pad of his fingers and grazing with his knuckles. "You do not have to do that; I won't hurt her."

I closed my eyes again, trying to snuggle into him. "I know. I'll hurt you first before you think twice about it."

And then it went comfortably quiet between us for a few minutes; I was already drifting off before he broke the silence.

"Shower?" he asked.

"Hm, no," I mumbled.

"Hm, yes," he countered.

I groaned in protest.

"Don't worry, I will hold you."

I gave a weak snort. "I can hold myself."

"Oh yeah?"

My heart skipped a beat at how his voice dropped with those two words; I raised my head a little and peeked at him to see him hovering, lips curled slightly upward.

My head fell back on the pillow. "Fuck me, you really are something, Elio."

"Come on."

But my eyes were already closing; even as I was lifted from the bed a moment later and he took us to the bathroom, I still held onto him . . . I felt so fucking sore, and I wasn't sure my legs were ready to start working again.

All through the process of cleaning up, with him making me brush my teeth and dry my hair, I was in a half-dazed state. When I was back on the bed, with fresh clothes that were sizes too big for me and smelled like him, I felt like heaven was within my reach; I snuggled into the pillow with a contented smile.

He joined me without a shirt on, just sweatpants. He didn't make a move to lie down entirely. It was as if he wasn't planning on sleeping.

"I'm just gonna . . ." I started with a mumble. "I'm just gonna sleep for like . . . two hours . . . and then . . . I'll go . . . no spending . . . night."

His hand brushed my hair from my face, his warm knuckles brushing my cheek. "Want me to wake you?" he asked softly.

"Yeah . . . sure."

"Okay."

His *okay* sounded so far away . . . very far into a dark, echoing place . . . and I was out in seconds.

CHAPTER EIGHT

Zahra

Louis Armstrong was singing "What a Wonderful World" when I opened my eyes. I yawned and stretched my hands above my head, my legs taking that cue to stretch too.

Blinking my vision clear, my hand went under the white duvet and underneath the white shirt I wore; I rubbed my stomach and looked to the side at the open window. I caught the bright day, the clear and blue water, and the sky brightened by the sun.

I frowned, looking away and above me. I stared for a full minute before looking around the empty room.

The sounds of the music echoed against the walls, relaxing jazz, dreamy and soft—it made my thinking slow, gave the atmosphere a smooth edge that had me feeling like I was in the first scene of a mystery thriller, and I was that character who opened the film by dying.

The first meaningless victim.

Goose bumps traveled up my skin as I looked at the other side of the bed. Clearly, I was the only one who had slept here last night. Elio had probably stayed till I was deep in sleep and then left. I didn't want to think about why I felt a sting at that tiny detail.

I looked out the window again.

"Shit." I sat up.

He didn't wake me.

I threw the covers off myself and got off his bed and out of the room. My legs felt weak, like jelly, and I rubbed my eyes as another yawn left me. The music grew less muffled when I reached the living area, stopping short after I spotted Elio at the bar, sitting on a stool, the side of his head leaning on his fist, while he stared blankly at the half-filled whiskey glass he held.

His shoulders were slumped in a way that showed tiredness. He hadn't slept all through the night. Obviously, he hadn't taken anything to help him either.

I suppressed a sigh and then started walking over to him. He didn't look my way once; even when I reached his line of vision, his eyes didn't leave the glass.

"Hey," I greeted, seeing the slight dark circles underneath his eyes and a white bandage around his knuckles like he had sustained some injury.

"Hm," he responded, still not looking at me. Body here, mind elsewhere.

"You didn't wake me like I asked."

"Hm."

I stared at him for a bit, my head still asleep, and I was still sore between my legs from last night's . . . activities.

"Right," I said with a firm nod. "I need coffee to deal with this." I gestured to him. "Whatever this is. Where's the kitchen—"

"Left." He cut me off, still not looking at me. It was like he wanted me out of sight so he could stare peacefully at the whiskey glass.

"Why are—"

A knock on the door cut me off as my gaze moved to its closed frame. "You expecting someone?"

He raised his head and then glanced at the door before responding, "No."

The knock came again. "You're not gonna answer it?" I asked.

He looked away from the door and then to me before his gaze moved to the door and back to me again.

"Answer it," he said, pressing a button on a small remote beside him, stopping the music.

I frowned. "Do I look like your fucking butler?"

"With your hair like that, you wouldn't pass as room service, so, no, you do not look like my butler."

I gave him the middle finger with a sweet smile before walking past him toward the door and swinging it open with one hand while the other pushed my hair back from my face.

I frowned at the stranger I locked eyes with.

A frown had her brows dropping as she looked at me, too; bright blue eyes shone with confusion.

"May I help you?" I asked.

"Uh . . ." Her gaze darted to a space behind me, her eyes widening a bit in question, and I snapped my head back to see Elio watching, his face pointedly expressionless.

Looking back at the blond girl, I shifted to block her view of him, giving her a pointed stare. "Yes?" I pressed.

She was . . . uncomfortably pretty. There was a shine to her that made me want to frown. Barely clothed, she wore bright blue shorts, unbuttoned and unzipped, showcasing her bright blue bikini thong, which matched the bra that barely covered the swell of her breasts. Her blond hair was tied up in a ponytail, curly strands falling around her face like she woke up with the word PERFECT tattooed to her aura.

"Um . . . I'm sorry?" she squeaked out. "I think I got the wrong door; I was—"

"Wrong door?" I stated, confused. "You're just allowed to wander into a platinum suite reserved for private use, and you got the wrong door?"

She blinked at me, but my frown didn't let up. "Um . . . well, I—I have—uh—uh, topographical disorientation." She stopped, probably seeing the confusion in my eyes. "I have directional issues; it would shock you how many times I end up somewhere that I—you know, didn't initially want to go? I—I don't even know why the guards at the front didn't stop me—um . . . dumbblondmoment?" She rushed out the last three words, supplying me a half-assed laugh, and taking a step back while I squinted at her. "I will leave you now, and um—go . . . go find the right door."

And then she bolted out of sight. I tilted my head as I closed the door slowly before turning to regard Elio, who was finishing the last of his drink, completely unbothered.

"That was weird?" I voiced. "Is there really such a thing as topo-whatever she said?"

He glanced my way for a brief moment before going to pour himself another round, ignoring me.

Not wanting to acknowledge that or the girl with a screwed-up sense of direction, I made my way in the direction he had gestured to, another yawn leaving me as I padded barefoot into the large kitchen, grabbing a mug without really looking around, and then proceeded to the coffee—

My soul left my body alongside the scream that escaped my throat. It was so loud as I jumped and kicked something warm and soft that had brushed my feet.

It only took a glance for me to catch the black furry animal by my side, very still with a low warning growl, its fur standing erect all over.

My instincts told me to remain in place, but my legs were already working ahead of me; I bolted right out of the kitchen with the creature hot on my tail.

I think I was still screaming, still in flight mode, as I spotted Elio on his feet, approaching with a frown on his face.

"What happened—" He didn't complete that statement because I was on him in the next instant, my hands falling around his shoulders, my legs around his waist, inching up as he stumbled back with the impact of me jumping on him.

His arms came around me protectively.

"There's a fucking cat, a fucking panther. I don't fucking know, but it's—"

"Stopped."

My heart beat five times per second as I turned my head slowly backward to see the cat standing still in front of us, swollen with anger. It was too still, bright eyes watching, waiting for a movement, an excuse to attack, to chase, and I was breaking out in a sweat even though I was clinging to him in panic.

"Relax." He gently rubbed my back. "Your heart is beating so fast. Are you really that scared?"

I looked away, dropping my head onto his shoulder. "No—I mean—yes, b-but just don't fucking let go of me."

"I will have to let go eventually—"

I tightened my hold around him, knowing if it were possible, I would climb up onto his head just to—His grip loosened, and he moved to put me down; the deep purring sound grew a little louder.

I gripped his shirt, tightening my legs around his waist, refusing to let go. "Please, please, please don't let me go, I beg you."

"You'll be fine."

"No, no, no, *fuck* no, I swear to God, Elio, if you let me go, I will stab you until I hit a vital fucking organ; I am not bluffing."

He chuckled, bringing his lips to my ear. "This is a surprise," he said, his tone low.

"How do we get rid of it—"

"You can't; she lives here, for now."

I frowned, scared to even move. "What the fuck? You have a fucking cat? Why do you have a fucking cat?"

"She is not mine; that is Mimi. She's Angelo's."

My grip was still tight around him. "I don't give a fuck who her owner is; I just need her to stop looking at me like that."

"Hold on." Amusement laced his voice. "You can shoot people in the face, enchant a whole room filled with strangers, make me your subject, stop a bomb on a moving school bus, and the thing that scares you is a . . . cat?"

I gritted my teeth. "Gloat all you want; just don't drop me."

He patted my back reassuringly. "I am not gloating; I am just surprised. You keep surprising me at every turn."

"Glad I serve as your constant element of surprise, but that cat is not backing down from wanting to attack me."

Elio shifted slightly. "We just need to distract her, that's all."

I swallowed. "How do you suppose we—"

He made a *tst-tst-tst* sound, and something furry came running out of the kitchen storeroom, ginger and huge.

I inched farther up into his hold. "Oh my God, there's another one. There's another one!"

I couldn't see him, but I could hear the smile in his voice. "They are harmless, Sport."

"It chased me."

"That's because you ran from her, screamed, and scared her."

Elio stepped to the side, his arms still strong around me. I watched as the ginger cat came behind the black one, watching us too.

Surprisingly, the black cat—Mimi—had stopped growling, but it still watched us as Elio moved toward the kitchen until we were completely out of sight of both cats.

I released the breath I'd been holding, willing the pace of my heart to calm.

"Am I free to let you go now?" Elio asked.

I cleared my throat, releasing my hold on him as I managed a slight nod, unable to meet his gaze when he settled me atop the kitchen counter, his focus entirely on my face.

Pressing my lips together, I succumbed, and looked at him because I wanted to get the shame over with once and for all. "What? You don't have your own embarrassing fears?"

"If I have an embarrassing fear, I am yet to be acquainted with it."

"Yeah, whatever. I'm only human."

"A human who fears cats."

"So do a lot of people in the fucking world; get over it. And it's not like I fear-*fear* them. It's just—they're too soft, and there's just something about their eyes and—and how they just look at you like they can see your fucking soul. This one scared me; that's why I ran. Otherwise, I stay clear, even if I'm in the same environment as them."

Elio nodded. "Good to know. I will make note of that," he said. "Although, I must admit, seeing you in that state was amusing."

"I know you get pleasure from my suffering; that's an unspoken fact."

He nodded. "Yes. I do derive pleasure from your suffering," he agreed with a serious expression. "But this particular action of yours was pretty entertaining and cute. I never thought I would associate you with that word."

I blinked at him and opened my mouth to supply a comeback, but nothing came out, so I just sat there and squirmed.

"You said you wanted coffee?" he asked.

"Yeah, I did, but this little incident has done the job. I'm wide awake."

"I see," he stated. "Would you still like me to make you one?"

I raised a brow at him and laughed. "You know how to make coffee?"

"Yes," he said, and he didn't appreciate my underestimating him. "I do."

"Okay . . . sure, go ahead."

He turned to the coffeemaker, and I saw the ginger cat approach, leaning against the wall while it licked its fur.

"Is there any other animal you do not like?" Elio asked as he worked his way around the coffee machine.

"No . . . I don't know; I haven't seen a lot."

"Hm."

"What about you?" I asked, watching his back muscles work as he placed my mug under the coffeemaker.

"I haven't seen a lot either. But I suppose I would neither like nor hate them if I saw them. It is always neutral with me."

"Everything is neutral with you."

"Hm."

There was silence after that, just the sound of the machine working. He glanced my way at some point, asking me how I preferred to have my coffee. When I supplied him with the answer, he turned back to continue.

When he was done and had placed the mug beside me, he leaned against the oven opposite the counter, watching me as I took a sip.

It was . . . good. Not as great as Upper's, but good.

"Is it okay?"

I gave him a thumbs-up as I drank while he watched me.

Feeling calmer after the shock of the earlier events, I put down the almost-empty mug. I decided to break the silence, trying to understand why he didn't take his eyes off me, not even once.

They were calculating, assessing, like he wanted to broach a topic, but he wasn't sure how to proceed.

"So . . . why didn't you wake me?"

His gaze dropped to my lips. "I was about to," he said, meeting my eyes again, "but then I entered the room and saw you were sleeping soundly; I didn't want to wake you. Sleep is vital."

"Says the guy who didn't get any."

"Hm. You know why I can't go to sleep. I want to, I get tired and sleepy, but then I try to sleep, and it doesn't come. It's too loud in my head some nights."

I sighed, concern enveloping me. "I thought you had pills that you can take?"

"I wasn't in the right mind to take them."

My gaze fell to his bandaged hand. "How'd you get that?"

He looked down and managed to take it out of my view. "An . . . accident," he supplied.

"An accident from . . ."

"An accident," he repeated, straightening suddenly as he walked toward me. His hands separated my thighs and he stepped between my legs, placing his hands on either side of me. I sucked in a breath at his sudden proximity. "I want to discuss something with you," he said, eyes searching mine.

My throat went dry. "What?"

"I assume you are well aware that I am very straightforward, and I do not like being unclear with something this important to me."

I felt a new brick in my walls come up. "Yeah?"

"Good," he stated, ignoring the way my voice had sounded. "I have never been with any woman intimately more than once. You are aware that you're an exception, yes?"

"Uh . . . I mean, it's not a—it's not a big deal."

He frowned slightly. "It is. I have broken my rules and laws for you, I have gone back on my word, I have changed plans for you."

I shrugged. "The pussy is good, you gotta admit."

"Zahra."

"Fine. I'm listening."

"As I said, I do not like being unclear with something this important to me." His throat worked, and his eyes fell to my mouth for a brief moment before looking back at me again.

My chest constricted.

"I would like to start a relationship with you," he stated.

My lips parted, jaw hanging—I knew it was coming, I knew the kind of person he was, but I didn't . . . Ah, fuck . . . This isn't going to be pretty.

"You want . . ." I trailed off a bit, discomfort turning my stomach. "To . . . to date me . . ." I stated before adding "me" again, for clarification.

"Yes."

"Wh—" I stopped. Breathing became a bit . . . not so flowy as I tried to grasp how the conversation had gone from manageable to this. "Elio—"

"This affair won't continue if there is no title to tie it to, Zahra. I do not do affairs and secret rendezvous."

"And I don't do relationships; I have never done relationships, Elio."

"It would be a first for me too."

"Why would you want a relationship with me? What would you gain from it? I don't understand why you would—"

"Because I like you, ver—a lot. And just yesterday, you said you returned my feelings, so . . . Two people with a connection like ours can either grow or dismiss it. I'm asking to grow it."

I watched him for a moment, sighed, and shook my head. "I—This is—I'm not—"

"All I want is to title what we're already doing; I am not asking for something new or something we're not already doing, in case you misinterpreted."

"I know what you're talking about; it's just—I can't—There's no easy way to put it—"

Something dimmed in his eyes as he pulled back slightly from me. "You're rejecting me."

"No." I closed my eyes, opened them. "No . . . just, um, I mean, I don't—I am not into labels and commitment and all of that serious shit."

He drew away from me. "So you plan to be with other people while with me?"

I got down from the counter. "That's not—" I swallowed. "I don't know."

He frowned in disappointment. "You don't know? What—What do you mean, you don't know?"

I was saying all the wrong fucking things.

"Elio, this is sudden, okay? I know you don't do unlabeled things, but I've done unlabeled things *all* my life, and I can't—I don't know yet what I would be getting into if I said yes."

There was silence after that.

He nodded slowly. "What you would be 'getting into,'" he

repeated under his breath as if he were digesting my words. I could see the gears turning in his head. "With me? Or in general?"

"In general." My eyes took him in, because why would he even consider this with me? "Can we just . . . revisit this, at a later time? I need—I need time to think, okay? That's all. Time to think about it."

"I understand if you want to reject my proposal, Zahra," he stated. "It is probably for the best that you reject it. That was forward of me."

"No, it wasn't. At all. This is very new territory for me, and I really like you, a lot. You're everything I never thought I would ever have . . . in a way, if that makes sense, so I don't want to give you an answer now when my mind is . . . not functioning properly."

He nodded.

I sighed. "Hey," I said, cupping the side of his face. I inched higher to kiss him before pulling away and searching his eyes. "I already clarified that I wanted this, and I won't let a label thing ruin it. I just need to understand it. That's all."

"Hm."

"Don't fucking 'hm' me right now. Communicate with actual words."

"I don't know what to say," he responded.

He had told me on the rooftop how all his meaningless encounters had only lasted the one time they happened. I knew somewhere in the back of my mind that I wasn't a meaningless encounter; he showed me that last night—hell, he'd been showing me in a lot of ways.

I've known this man for months. I've hated and been irritated by him half the time. Even now, he still irritated me a bit, and he was not above a straight punch to the nose if he misbehaved, but—the only difference between then and now was that I understood the way that brain of his worked.

Right now, he was probably thinking he should have left things the way they were, but then again, even if he had left things the way they were, I already knew—he had told me when we were high out of our minds on that rooftop—how much he respects women, and the reasons he'd never been with anyone more than once.

I was an exception, and I knew him wanting to make things extra serious was a given, but I didn't think it would feel so overwhelming, so scary to the point that I wouldn't know what to do or say to avoid hurting his feelings or make him think I didn't care enough. I did.

It wasn't just the sex. But I needed time. At least to talk to Devil, clear things up, and tell him all that had been going on. Hell—I'd be willing to tell all of Street if necessary.

"I should go," I said. "I'll come by later after I think it through. You should try to get some rest."

"Okay."

I offered a smile, about to sidestep him, when I saw the two cats just by the entrance, watching us.

I looked back at him. "On second thought . . . Would you mind walking me back to your room to change into my own clothes and then to the door, please?"

CHAPTER NINE

Zahra

"Where the bloody hell have *you* been?" Upper asked the moment I walked into our suite, a coffee cup in his hand, his voice groggy, eyes dark from lack of sleep.

"Why do you look like you didn't get any sleep?" I asked, closing the suite door. He was wearing an oversized sky-blue hoodie with sweatpants, hair all angles of messed up, nose a different shade of red.

"I fell overboard, drank too much, had a mini fever all through the night, almost puked my intestines out, and—"

"Made out with a *girl,*" Dog said with a smug smile, appearing from around the corner as he grabbed a cup of coffee from the coffeemaker.

"What?" I asked as Milk walked out of her room, wearing a bathing suit and sending a wave my way.

"It was nothing." Upper sent a glare Dog's way, but Dog didn't see it because his eyes were on Milk, who looked like she was getting ready to head out. "The girl wanted to make her boyfriend jealous; she walked up to me and asked me to kiss her; I told her I was gay, and she said, 'Even better,' and then she was sucking my face."

"Oh . . ."

"And where are you off to?" Dog asked Milk with a frown as he leaned against a wall.

She was tying her hair up in a ponytail as she glanced his way with a grin. "While you guys were whoring away, I got invited to a pool party by some cool guys I met last night," she said. "They're staying in a gold suite, and it is *incredible*."

Dog's frown deepened. "So . . . you're just gonna fuck off to a stranger's space because 'Oh, hey, they think I'm pretty, and they're pretty, too; why not go to the pool party hosted by people I don't know just because I have great tits and I think they're cool.'"

Milk's brows shot up. "You think I have great tits?"

"Somebody shoot me," Dog said with an exasperated sigh.

Milk snickered as Devil came out of his room, freshly showered, looking more responsible than anyone else. "Z," he said with a frown, eyeing me from head to toe. "Where the hell have you been?"

I blew out a breath. It was now or never. "Okay, before Milk leaves for the cool people's party, can we all gather for a mini briefing?"

Milk's brows furrowed in confusion, and I knew she was curious about what this briefing meant. She would have told them the mission had succeeded, and Kareem had invited me to join his table.

They settled around the lounge area, Milk and Upper on a beanbag, Devil on the arm of the couch Dog had taken. I stood before them like I was about to give a speech. "As far as yesterday went, I think we already got that invite from Kareem. We talked, and he invited me and anyone I wanted to bring to events here and outside the cruise . . . So, we can score ourselves a private tour of the Arturo manor with a little talking."

"Yes," Upper said. "Milk told us how you fucked everyone without fucking them."

I glanced at Milk, who shrugged.

"That's a . . . really odd way of putting it, but yes, the dance was a success. It got us what we wanted, at least . . . it got us on the right path to what we want."

"That's a good thing, yeah?" Milk asked.

"Yes . . . except we're not the only ones after Kareem's attention," I said.

"There's always a bloody obstacle," Upper complained. "Again, can't we just break into the manor, a clean sweep?"

"Again, we already registered that would come with a twenty percent success rate. It is heavily guarded with several civilians that could be caught in the crossfire, and our best way is through a tour, undercover," I told him.

"So, who's the fucking obstacle?" Dog asked

I cleared my throat. "Marino's people. It appears since we stopped working for them, and decided to find the painting and the gold on our own, they upped their game. They know about the manor. Also, Elio was seated right next to Kareem, and they seemed to be close, so, yeah, we have big competition."

"Right." Devil nodded, a confused look in his eyes. "That doesn't answer the question about where you were; we were worried. Did you go with Kareem?" Devil asked with a frown. "You know you didn't have to—"

I shook my head. "No . . . I, uh . . . I didn't go with Kareem."

Milk's eyes widened in realization.

Dog's gaze narrowed on me.

Upper raised his brow.

Devil was confused.

I blew out a sharp breath, bracing myself as I blurted, "I went with Elio."

The silence after I said that was palpable.

Upper's coffee cup stopped midway to his lips.

Milk's lips formed an O.

Dog's eyes widened as he whistled.

Devil . . . was confused.

"I beg your pardon?" Devil asked.

"I was with Elio; I spent the night in his suite. Not that

it's any of your business. I just wanted to let you know that I still want that gold, just as much as any of you, so I might be sleeping with the enemy, but it doesn't mean I am compromised."

Milk shook her head slowly.

"Jesus Christ," Dog breathed out.

"I knew it . . . back in Turin. The matching outfits," Upper said.

I blinked. "That was pure coincidence, but yeah."

"What the fuck?" Devil voiced, his face scrunched in confusion and disbelief.

I sighed. "I didn't see the need to tell any of you because it wasn't serious then, but now—"

"Are you fucking serious, Z?" he snapped, cutting me off. I could feel the anger vibrating off of him. "My brother?"

"Devil—"

He shot to his feet, rushing toward the door as he gritted out, "I'm gonna fucking kill him."

Before he could pull the door open, I rushed past him to stand between him and the doorframe. "Devil—"

"Get out of my way."

"Give me a minute to explain."

"Explain what?" he fumed. "He always manages to fucking step on my toes; now he's done it with you? And you—"

"He didn't do anything I didn't want, Devil."

That made him stop, his eyes searching mine. "What?" He breathed out the question.

"Let's talk in my room, okay?"

"Z—"

"I promise I'll explain everything."

When he didn't respond, I cautiously took his wrist and led him toward my bedroom, shooting the rest of Street an apologetic tight smile before we disappeared behind the door.

I would deal with Dog and Upper later; Devil was the priority right now.

He removed his wrist from my hold, watching me with apprehension.

"I didn't know it would get serious between Elio and me . . . it was just supposed to be a onetime thing—"

"You promised you would stay away from him. You fucking promised me."

"I know."

He shook his head. "No, you don't," he said. "You don't fucking know. He could hurt you, Z."

"I know . . . but I also know he wouldn't . . . you know that, too, but for some reason, you're choosing to hate him and blame him for something he's not completely at fault for. I started it. He was very reluctant because of you—"

"Apparently, that didn't last."

I sighed. "Where exactly is your anger coming from? Is this because you don't like him or because you love me—which can't be the case since Upper?"

"Leave Upper out of this."

"I need to understand you, Devil."

He went silent, confusion in his eyes as he heaved a breath and looked up like he was trying to find the answer to my question.

After a while, he walked past me to sit on the edge of the bed, his hands brushing down his face.

I took the space beside him, angling my body toward his. "I didn't do it on purpose. I wanted to stay away; I did. I just couldn't," I told him. "You and I are not together like that anymore, and fuck it, if I were a bitch, I would point out the fact that you fucked around with Upper when we were together."

He looked at me with a confused frown. "You *literally* just pointed it out."

"Yeah, well . . . maybe I *am* a bitch."

He scoffed, looking away from me while shaking his head. "I don't know, Zahra, this is just so fucking weird. I mean, Elio?" He looked at me again. "How did it start?"

"Do you really wanna know?"

He blinked. "No. No, please don't tell me. I just—What did you mean by *serious*? What exactly is going on?"

I shrugged. "Half the time, I don't know what's going on. It just happened, and I was too deep before I could back away. But I promise he didn't hold a gun to my head and force me to like him or something. It's mutual, actually."

"You like him?"

"Yeah . . ."

"But you're not the kind to do commitment. And Elio, if I remember correctly, he doesn't do your kind."

"No, he doesn't."

"So . . ." He trailed off, shaking his head. "I can't believe we're having this conversation now. It's unbelievable."

"Trust me; I feel the whiplash every day," I said. "It's kind of like you said with Upper, how you felt whenever you saw him; it's kind of the same way I feel . . . not that intense but it's there nonetheless."

He shook his head. "I don't think I'll ever be able to forgive him for what he did to you. How can you like someone like that? He's not a—He's a lost cause, Zahra. You ought to know that."

I frowned. "Don't say shit like that, D. He broke things off with me because of you. He cares about you more than anything in this fucking world. I know you have your differences, but if you would just talk to him for a change—"

"You're fucking brainwashed," he said.

I frowned. "So that's it, you've given up on him because he tried to drown me?"

"Not just that. He's hurt you on multiple occasions, he—Can't you see that this is some part of his fucking ploy? How can he just turn a one-fucking-eighty from wanting to kill you to fucking you?"

"It wasn't a one-eighty. There's a lot you don't know about us or how this started. I only told you guys because it's not something I want to hide and because I respect you as my best friend. I don't need your approval to be with who I want to be with."

"I know you don't need my approval. But he's my brother. He's not a good person for you. He might be all nice now, but once you fuck up, there will be a bullet in your head. He's just like his fucking father."

Exasperated, I sighed. "Devil . . . I think you should talk to him."

His eyes searched mine. "What?"

"I think you should talk to Elio. You blame him for a lot, and you're wrong about literally everything. The longer you two keep walking on eggshells around each other, the more you continue to hurt each other unnecessarily."

The look in his eyes could define reluctance and confusion. "I don't understand."

I leveled him with a stare. "Remove me from the equation, remove my relationship with him . . . remove the fact that you're angry at him for hurting me all those times. And focus on your actual relationship with him. Focus on how you felt before he tried to drown me."

He looked away with a tight frown, his jaw clenching and unclenching.

"You don't hate him, Devil. You're just angry at him. You're angry that you pushed him away, and he didn't try to fix it. You think he doesn't care because he never shows it, and just like him, you left it that way. You're stubborn, he's stubborn, but at some point, one of you has to be the bigger person," I said and then added, "Personally, I think you should be the bigger person; then you get bragging rights."

His head dropped in a small laugh, and then he looked at me. "Why are you like this?"

"Because I will always root for you, D. I might like him, but you still come first to me."

"Really?"

"Yes, really—really, as in if a house was on fire and the two of you were stuck inside, and I could only save one person, it would be you, no questions asked."

"And you're certain his intentions with you are genuine?"

"Yes."

"What about yours?"

My stomach dipped. "What?"

"Your intentions. I know there's always something up your sleeve." He watched me. "I'm trying to make sure this is not one of them because if it is and—"

"I don't have ill intentions."

His eyes watched, brows furrowed, stare intense, and just like that, it felt like I was staring at Elio; this very moment took me to the times when it felt like Elio was trying to look into my soul to fish out a lie from my truth.

After he found what he was looking for, he nodded. "I don't know if—if I'll stop finding it weird . . . ever. You'll have to give me time, Z. This is not what I thought I would hear today."

"Of course." I swallowed. "Will you talk to him, though?"

"I don't know. I—I need time to think. To digest this."

I nodded, watching him rake his fingers through his hair, wondering what was going through his head, what kind of assurance he had seen in my eyes . . .

While somewhere in the back of my mind, I was fighting a battle with myself. Confirming all this and telling Street of my involvement with Elio meant I had accepted his proposal to give us a fucked-up and very unnecessary label—mentally.

And I shouldn't . . .

I really fucking shouldn't.

While not having ill intentions with him, there was no way I wouldn't end up hurting him at the end of the day. I shouldn't be selfish; I shouldn't have my cake and fucking eat it.

But I had never been known to be selfless when it came to something I really wanted.

So . . . selfish it is.

CHAPTER TEN

Elio

I started seeing my mother thirteen hours ago.

At first, I was aghast. She was so real, indubitably present. She carried along the feeling of being in an environment with another person. When she looked up at me from her position on the couch, my world stopped, rotated, and stood in place. The black dress she wore was the same one I'd seen in that video footage before she bathed herself in gasoline and set the whole church on fire.

I had closed my eyes for about five minutes, standing utterly still. When I opened them again, she was gone.

That was the first time I'd seen her.

That was the second time I realized I was no longer in control of my mind.

That was the thousandth time I'd told myself I shouldn't be here. I should hurry up. Finish this once and for all. Stop wasting time.

But it was also in that moment, and at that single thought, that I realized I wasn't as focused on that idea as I once was. It was the first time I acknowledged that I was stalling, not because I hadn't finished what I wanted to do, but because I thought I had a lot to look forward to. To anticipate. I thought there was enough reason to want to live, to change my mind.

I spent the entire night after being with Zahra battling with my own mind, mumbling pros and cons that refused to keep themselves inside my mind, slamming my fist into a mirror because I hated what my reflection showed.

A confused man. Unfocused nonsense. An indecisive entity. A man who couldn't even do what he truly wanted. A man who couldn't end the life he'd been craving to end since he had watched his family burn. A man who hated himself because he had these thoughts, this weakness, eating at him from the inside out. A self-inflicted parasite. Abnormal. Wrong.

My depression had arrived with a vengeance after seeing the woman who birthed me.

I needed to sleep.

Four days of sleepless nights was not something I let fester. But four days of sleepless nights with depression and hallucinations? I knew I needed a total knockout—a shutdown, something that would take me out for days on end. But I couldn't do that—I didn't trust myself enough to proceed with it, so wearing myself out was the most appealing option.

I brought out alcohol. Cigars didn't wear me out; they made me active.

So I drank, put on feel-good music, and waited.

That was until Zahra had woken up, and I had tried my best to block out her presence because I could already feel my body relaxing into the atmosphere, the alcohol, and the music.

But I should have known better.

Her scream from the kitchen had erased my hours of progress to find solace.

Suddenly I was more in tune with my environment. The alcohol stopped making me tired; it made me active.

The interruption, though, didn't irritate me. It surprised me. I was amused. My mood was lifted, and for those moments, holding her close to me while she asked me not to let her go, I forgot exactly why I couldn't sleep, why I was depressed. It felt good, *she* felt good, and I felt the instant regret of not wrapping my arms around her while she slept, of not tapping from that peace that seemed to make her body sink into the bed in sleep.

I wanted to. I really did. But I also didn't want to overstep my boundaries; she'd once said she was opposed to . . . cuddling.

And before I took a dive for the worse, I had been thinking of ways to change that opposition, to make the idea more acceptable to her.

Asking her to be in a relationship became the best solution. But seeing the way that question had brought forth a negative response, how uncomfortable she had been with the mere thought of committing to me—I felt angry—wanted to tell her she had no choice because she made me fall for her, she made me question everything I wanted for myself; the least she could do was indulge me, and not dismiss me.

But then, I saw how she fought for words, how her eyes had shined in discomfort and horror like being with me that way was as atrocious as signing a death sentence. I realized I had been too forward. I didn't think it through; of course she wouldn't want that.

Who in their right mind would want that?

After she left, I continued my drinking and put on some music again—I turned it off an hour later when my head started to pound—and I stopped drinking soon after when my stomach started to reject it. I felt the alcohol trying to come back out of my throat, and suddenly the room became too cold.

I turned off the air conditioner, turned on the heater, and then realized I didn't reasonably need the heat because my skin began to burn.

I was hot, cold, and uncomfortable.

The pounding in my head was worse than before.

I felt like I could sleep now, but I couldn't help the discomfort I felt; despite having changed the temperature in the room to something bearable, I was still so cold.

I decided to have another warm shower—after I did, I opted to find something heavy to ward off the cold—a thick black hoodie with thick sweatpants.

I dried my hair thoroughly because the wet strands irritated my eyes and neck, a clear sign that it was due for another cut.

My mind drew a blank when I tried to remember the last time I had cut it.

After I was all done, I settled on the bed, but with a tiny sniff of the pillow, my mind took me back to last night—to Zahra, who had rejected me and was now thinking about it so she could twist the knife further in by rejecting me again.

I pressed my nose into the pillow and breathed in like the creep she once referred to me as.

I lay there for a few minutes and then grew uncomfortable with the view of the vast ocean; the pillow became as hot as my skin.

I sat up with a groan, my hand falling to my side to keep me steady upon the sudden lightness in my head.

I grabbed the pillow, left the bed, walked to the dresser, pulled it open, picked up my phone, and turned it on as I walked out of the bedroom to the living room.

I settled the pillow on one of the long couches and lay there instead, pressing a remote to reduce the room's lighting.

My body felt too heavy to carry when I tried to move.

I needed medicine, something to dull the headache. I couldn't administer it myself.

Bringing the phone to my view, I squinted with a wince at the light, and I quickly moved to reduce the brightness before going to my contacts list.

Five names.

I clicked on Angelo's name, which immediately went to voicemail. Unavailable to answer the phone. I tried again . . . and again . . . same result.

My throat grew too dry, and my head ached. My breathing was getting loud, my breath as hot as my skin.

I clicked on Casmiro's name next, but it immediately said *unavailable*. There was no point in trying it again because he wasn't here to provide immediate aid—but then again, he could help alert someone nearby—I tried calling again. Unavailable.

I closed my eyes with a tired groan before reopening them. My gaze fell on Zahra's name . . . I contemplated it . . . thoroughly. She'd left here a couple of hours ago . . . She was on the cruise. She was close, and I wanted her here. Although she'd taken away my first chance to relax, I did not want her to leave.

I clicked on her contact, and it was silent for a few seconds before an automated voice came on. *"Sorry, you are not allowed to call this number."*

The line cut immediately. I frowned at the phone, redialing it. The same automated voice came on, repeating the same sentence.

I clicked on the message icon next to the call button, which brought me to her numerous messages that I'd ignored.

I sent her a *hello,* and instead of a *Delivered* notification to pop up under the text, it was *Not delivered*, with a bright red exclamation mark.

She . . . blocked me.

I pressed my lips together, biting my tongue. My fingers trembled on the phone as another wave of coldness hit me.

I shouldn't have said anything.

I left the message page and swiped right on her contact, my thumb hovering over the delete button. I didn't want to click it. But it was the right thing to do. She had made it clear with this action where she truly stood.

I felt sicker than before.

Was the thought of being committed to me really that scary? Had I been mistaken when she confessed to me the day before?

But she was so sincere . . .

I sighed, swiping back.

I dialed Gemma's number, and it didn't ring before it said *busy*, which meant she was on another call. I waited a bit before trying again, and it clearly stated, *"The person you are trying to reach is on another call at the moment; please try again later."*

I closed my eyes, releasing a hot breath from my heavy chest, a wave of dizziness taking over my head.

"Why are you surprised, my love?"

I froze.

The voice was right beside me, stressed and winded, soft and warm, familiar, too daringly familiar.

I opened my eyes and turned my heavy head to the side. She was seated at the center table, facing me.

My mother. Again.

My stomach turned, and I clenched my jaw.

"You thought they would answer?" A soft laugh left her. "They never answer, Elio, and nor will they ever. Not everyone is like you." She smiled. "You have to know that the only people who ever truly loved you are just an action away if you would just take that step."

I frowned. It was pained; I knew that because I felt it in my chest. Tight and choking.

I looked away.

"You don't like seeing me," she stated, and her voice sounded sad. "It shows in your beautiful eyes that you don't. Is that why you won't come to me? Because you hate me?"

I closed my eyes.

Not real.

She was not real.

"I am sorry, Elio. I know it will take you forever and more to get over what I did. But you have to understand . . . no . . . I *know* you understand. You want to do it, too, burn it all, just like I did. You know exactly how I felt. I had to do it, just like you must."

"Please leave me alone," I said softly. "Please."

"I was never there for you, Elio. You were always there for me; you never left me alone; why would I leave you now that you need me the most? Look at this place; it is empty. You're so alone in this world. It saddens me to see you suffering; I want to be here for you."

"No," I croaked out. "You're not real."

"I am as real as you want me to be, Elio. You have no idea how long I have been waiting for you to let me see you like this," she said, sounding so pleased. "There's something I have always wanted to tell you."

"Please go away." I could barely hear my own voice.

"But you wanted me here."

"Mamá, por favor, déjame en paz." I breathed. "Por favor."

"You called me here; I am the only one who answered."

I was being tortured; her voice was torture; her presence was torture. This was so unfair.

"Elio, I am here."

I pressed my eyelids tightly together. "I'm not crazy. It's just in my head. I'm not crazy," I chanted.

"Elio."

"I'm not cra—"

I felt a shadow over me, her hand on my cheek, so soft, so cold, so tender.

"My love, open your eyes."

When I did, I flinched sharply with a gasp at the melting face above me. Her face was burning; her smile was slipping, her skin was falling, eyes drooping. I couldn't breathe, I couldn't move, I couldn't—

My eyes snapped open, my breathing hard, my phone gripped against my chest.

I had dozed off after trying to call Gemma . . . That was a dream.

I slowly looked around me. The living room was empty. Too empty. Too quiet. Too eerie. Too lonely.

For a sliver of a moment, I felt . . . scared.

Sinking farther into the couch, I brought my phone to my view again, and without thinking, I clicked Elia's name, the last one on the list. It started ringing.

I knew he wouldn't answer; he didn't know the number after all, and it was careless to accept calls from unknown numbers; he should be—

"Hola."

His voice filled my ear . . . It was carefree, like he had been laughing and picked it up while distracted. He sounded familiar and unfamiliar. There was a bit of noise in the background: water, music, laughter.

"Hello, who is this?" his voice came in again.

I swallowed, trying to clear my throat, but it felt like a brick was on my chest, stopping my airflow.

"Hey! Make your fucking shot!" a male voice yelled at him.

"Who's that?" A female voice that sounded much like the one who'd rejected me hours ago came through.

"Don't know, wrong number, I think, where were—" The line disconnected.

I drew in a breath, fighting to keep my eyes open as I dialed the number again.

It rang three times, and he picked up.

"Yes?" he drawled. Irritated.

I opened my mouth to speak, but his voice cut me off.

"Breathing at the end of the line is not on trend anymore, so whoever you are—"

"Elia."

He went quiet. And all I could hear was the noise and music in the background.

After a good minute that felt like an hour, he spoke.

"Y-yeah? What do you want?"

"I'm sorry to bother you. I did not mean to call, but I—I don't have anyone else."

There was nothing from him in the first few seconds, but then he spoke. *"What happened?"* His voice had a new edge, one that sounded urgent, and the other end of the line was shaky like someone was running or walking fast with the phone. I was too disoriented to decipher it.

"I need . . . help."

The line disconnected the moment I spoke.

I groaned out a sigh, giving up as my phone dropped from my hand. I relieved my eyes of their stress and closed them again, allowing my body to succumb to the tiredness.

I was brought back into mild consciousness when I felt a hand on my forehead. The hand was soft, small, and warm, and a familiar smell—like my pillow, but stronger, nearer—filled my senses.

"Fuck, get some ice, D. He's burning up."

The sound of fast-retreating footsteps was what I heard next.

"I thought you said he was okay." A female voice cut into the silence, and I heard some other footsteps.

"He was when I left this morning. He was perfect, in fact." The hand—Zahra's hand came to my cheek. "Elio?" she called softly. "I think he can hear us; he's frowning."

"So, not dying then." Another voice cut in.

Her finger stroked my cheek, a shadow over me. "Hey, can you hear me?" she asked like she didn't want anyone else in the room to hear her.

"Well, do you think he took something?" the female voice asked again, soft, concerned.

"No, Milk, he had been drinking . . . whiskey, and he looked tired, too, but he wasn't this hot."

"He still looks hot to me."

"Jesus, Dog, I didn't mean that kind of hot—I meant hot as in sick hot—like, temperature over-the-roof hot—"

"I know what you meant; just messing with ya."

Someone touched my feet like they were feeling for something. "I think he has a fever, a bloody strong one; he's cold on his feet."

Zahra's hand covered mine. "His hands too."

Someone clapped, and my head banged. "It's nothing that can't be cured with fever soup."

"What's fever soup?"

"It's soup that cures fever; it goes without saying, Milk."

"The way you put it sounded like it's a soup that causes fever, not cures it," Milk responded.

"Why the fuck would I imply that? He's already playing catch with a fucking fever, so when I say fever soup, it should have automatically clicked in that pink brain of yours that I meant one that cures it."

"Is there one for causing it?" the one with the British accent spoke.

"Fucking hell, I'm friends with idiots."

"No, actually," Zahra spoke up, "with the way you put it, it just sounded like you have one for curing fever and one for causing it . . ."

"You're also a fucking idiot, Zahra; you just know how to package it." Dog groaned. "Anyway, it's one of my father's secret recipes; his grandfather passed it down to him. It was created when my great-grans Olga was on the brink of death from fever, and he made a soup and brought her back to life, fever gone. Then he made people from the church buy it for an outrageous amount of money. My great-grans died two weeks later."

I didn't hear anything else after that. The silence stretched into seconds, entering a minute before . . .

"I really hope Marino didn't hear that," Upper said.

"Me too," Milk seconded.

I squeezed Zahra's hand in mine, and she squeezed back before saying, "Nah, he didn't; he's passed out."

"I found ice and a small towel." Elia's voice entered the room again.

"Permission to use the kitchen, Devil?"

"Why the fuck do you need my permission?" His voice was

closer now, and right after he spoke, I heard a squeeze of water, and something cold and soothing was on my forehead.

"Uh, you're the brother?"

"Dog, will the soup help?" Zahra spoke up, stroking my forearm through the hoodie sleeve.

"Guaranteed, tested, and five percent trusted, but he's young, so . . . I don't think he'll die in two weeks."

"What?" Elia snapped.

"You have Elio's permission," Zahra cut in.

There was a slight snorting sound. "*Girlfriend* speaks for *boyfriend*, I see."

"It's not like he can speak for himself; get to the fucking kitchen and stop fucking around." Elia groaned.

"Or maybe I could just leave and fuck my way around this cruise because someone can't seem to appreciate when a friend is doing something for their sudden brother who he doesn't like, but has to help, because he doesn't want him to die like my great-grans Olga, bless her soul," Dog muttered.

There was a second of silence before Elia cleared his throat.

"Please. Dog. Help. Me."

"Maybe a little less strained, something forthcoming, from the heart—"

"Dog, for the love of God," Zahra gritted out.

"Fine, just because Zahra mentioned God, and I love God, so, yeah, I'll help," he said, and I could hear the smugness. "Milk, you want to be useful?"

"Yeah, coming."

"What about ingredients?" Upper asked.

"I'm sure it's all there. I checked the catalog for the platinum suite, and the stocked ingredients I saw will do the trick."

"Good."

Footsteps were retreating.

"Oh my God, there are cats!" That came from Milk. "Awww, he has cats?"

"Shit," Zahra cursed.

Elia sighed with a small laugh. "Wanna get off the floor?"

"Yes, please, help me lift him."

There were shuffles, shadows shifting, hands on my shoulders as half my body was lifted off the couch, but I was back down soon after, except this time, my head wasn't on the pillow; it was on soft thighs—Zahra's thighs.

"Thanks, the black cat almost clawed my eye out, and I'm not exaggerating. They hate me."

"You give off anti-cat pheromones. And . . . they sense bad energy."

"Well, thank you, Upper, that's an accurate observation nobody needed."

"I am delighted to have been the one to provide the observation," Upper responded. "Anyway, I know a little about the kind of medicine one can take to ward off a fever, and the mad headache the poor lad must be experiencing."

"You do?" Elia asked, hopeful.

"Yes, I took care of myself for a couple years before, uh . . . well, yeah, and there were some medicines left for me should I suffer a fever; I could stop by the medical wing and see if they have some of those things?"

"I'll come with," Elia said. "Fuck, I don't want to leave—"

"It's okay; I'm here," Zahra reassured him.

A shuffling. "Okay, you'll call me if anything happens or changes—"

"Sure, hurry before Dog is done in the kitchen."

Footsteps were descending. A door opened and closed.

Zahra sighed, and the cloth left my head.

A moment later, it was back, but colder. Her fingers entered my hair, stroking softly.

I let out a much steadier breath.

"You're not sick because I didn't give you a response earlier, are you? Because that's just fucking embarrassing on your part, and I might just change my mind and say no. I'm not about to be dealing with this shit every time we fight." She said for only our ears, "And we're going to fight every time; I'm a fucking handful. I'm not above stabbing or shooting you in the foot even though you make me feel all mushy inside; I'm a crazy bitch."

I groaned.

"Yeah, that's right, groan all you fucking want; you're stuck with me now, Dad."

"Please . . ." I fought out of my dry throat. "Shut up."

"You know exactly what to do to get me to shut up. Get well right now and go back to being healthy because you scared the shit out of Devil, and I do not like a panicked Devil; it makes me panic, and I hate panicking. Why the fuck didn't you call me?"

I cracked my eyes open slowly, catching her frown almost immediately. "You blocked me," I told her.

"I didn't—" She stopped, then her brows went up, eyes widening. "Oh, shit, yeah. I did that a while ago because, you know . . . I wanted to be the one to do it first before you did it. You know? Always get the upper hand, which by the way, I have the upper hand in this relationship, and I have all the control, and you don't have shit. I am running this whole game, this whole fucking show, me. You don't get a say, you get bupkis out of this, zero, nada."

I slowly blinked at her.

"Hold on." She lifted herself a little but held the side of my head steady as she settled back down, her phone in her hand.

Her fingers worked the screen.

"There, unblocked. Not sorry. I can be petty sometimes, and I own my pettiness." She cleared her throat. "That's also something you'll have to get used to."

"Just say no . . . it's okay."

"I already said yes. And I told Street. Too late to back out. If anyone is backing out of this relationship, it's me; you don't get to call things off, only I have that right; if you ever feel like you're tired of me, tell me subtly, and I will end the relationship. For now, I'll just give you a set of things you should look out for."

"Zahra—"

"Hide your credit cards . . . just hide them . . . No matter what you do, keep them away from me. I'm a thief, and Aladdin has nothing on me. Also, you should always respond to my texts to avoid me blocking your number again in the future. Always pick up my calls, and be kind to me, or I might just end up killing you . . . by mistake, and I won't regret it because let's be honest, I don't really like you that much."

"Okay."

"I'm not done. You can't fall sick; you can't ignore me or whatever that shit you did this morning was. You should talk to Devil; you should make Cassie stay away from me; you should keep Angelo's fucking cat away from me; you should—"

"Kiss me."

"That . . . was not what I was gonna say."

"I know. I'm asking you to kiss me."

"Oh."

"Hm."

She shook her head, turning it briefly toward the kitchen before looking back down at me, bringing a hand to the side of my face as she leaned down and softly pressed her lips to mine, her hair tickling my ear, falling on either side to frame my face.

The life force in my chest responded almost immediately when her lips closed around mine. I felt her somewhat panicked breathing calm down; I didn't know she was on edge before her whole body relaxed. She was giving in to me, to this.

She broke away. "Fuck—I think we would need a written agreement on this control shit."

"If that's what you want, I'll arrange it."

She kissed me again, letting it linger a moment, but then broke away. "You taste like alcohol." Her finger brushed my chin. "How much did you have to drink?" she asked, concern lining her brows.

"A lot."

"Why?"

"I wanted to sleep. It's getting so hard to . . . to sleep these days."

She nodded, her hand feeling my neck. "Hopefully, whatever Upper gets is strong enough to knock you out, or I could just . . . knock you out. A quick blow to the side of your head, you'll be out like a sack of—"

I raised my hand, palmed her face, and pushed her head back away from me, closing my eyes and muttering, "You are terrible at this."

She chuckled, removing the cloth from my forehead and pressing it back again.

"Hey," I called, my eyes still closed.

"Yeah?"

"You told my brother about us."

"Yup, I told everyone."

"Then why is he here?"

"You called him."

"I know. He doesn't . . . hate me enough not to answer?"

She sighed. "He came running here as soon as the call dropped and had us all panicked for a minute. Had me worried 'cause I thought someone had tried to kill you or something—with the way he reacted . . . and well, maybe I, uh—asked him to talk to you?"

That had me opening my eyes to regard her. "Why?"

"There was so much unnecessary animosity between you two. And I had a part to play in that, but aside from that, you're all each other has. I would kill to have my own family, like blood relatives who are actually related to me by blood in a not-so-fucked-up way. You two have that; I just tried to open his eyes a little so it wouldn't be hard for you to . . . to talk to him. I was going to come back here after some party we were at and try to talk to you, too, even though I know it's not my place to do that—"

"Thank you."

She nodded slowly. "Yeah, sure."

"No," I said, feeling a calm wash over me. "Elia is the most important person in my life . . . I will forever be indebted to you, Zahra, for talking to him, for being there for him when I wasn't."

Her lips thinned in a close-lipped smile. "Yeah . . . of course."

I stared at her for much longer, unable to shift my gaze.

Barely satisfied, I closed my eyes again, relaxing into her warmth before letting drowsiness retake me.

I was woken up a moment later, my state of mind a blur, as I was forced to sit up and drink whatever concoction Dog had prepared. It had me sweating, even after I had taken the drugs Upper and Elia had brought.

Elia had spoken directly to me, asking how I felt, and I responded with a nod, to which he let out a relieved breath.

A moment later, someone suggested putting on a movie.

Something called *Titanic*, and there was a little argument about it. I didn't really pay any heed to it; I was trying to relax and sink into the feeling of Zahra distractedly and discreetly drawing circles inside my palm while she hurled insults at Dog, insults that sounded so crude I wanted to shield my ears.

"How the fuck do you watch *Titanic* while you're kind of in the middle of the ocean?"

"It makes it feel more real."

"No, that shit is scary."

They were all bringing back my headache with their back-and-forth, but I kept quiet.

There was junk everywhere, the room wasn't empty; I could no longer hear the loud quiet. It was no longer lonely, and when they all agreed to watch the movie, it was quiet again but comfortable.

I don't know how long it was, but it was a long time because the big screen began to display a sinking ship; everyone had a solemn look on their face, including Zahra, who had a sad frown on her face.

Me, I did not like what I was watching on the screen. I did not like the chaos or the screams from the actors; I did not like the music in the background. I did not like the death and the hysteria.

My vision blurred, and in my head, all I could hear, all I could see, was the fire, the screams from my siblings and my mother, the chaos.

I closed my eyes, relaxing back on the couch and letting my head rest on Zahra's shoulder, begging for sleep.

But for once, I didn't really have to beg; it came . . . though it took its precious time; but with the quiet noise in the background, the warmth from Zahra's shoulder and her hold against my hand, I drifted off to sleep, and allowed the day's trauma to slip out of me.

CHAPTER ELEVEN

Elio

"You are foolish, boy! How do you go to ocean and not take blood test first! You want to die? You want to be fish food?" Gran Louisa exclaimed, her face zoomed in on the screen of Gemma's phone, and her eyes filled with worry and concern for me.

This thing called *genuine care* . . . it felt strange, different, and overwhelming.

I'd utterly neglected and underestimated the progression of things after Street came into my life. It used to be Casmiro and Angelo I worried about because I was satisfied with Elia's hatred for me, but now it wasn't just them; now it was Elia, Zahra, Gemma, Gran Louisa, Casmiro, Angelo, and maybe even Street if I were to give it a stretch.

"I never knew I would catch a fever, Gran Louisa," I told her with an apologetic look.

"Yes, Nonna, he was so healthy when we got here," Gemma said from her position on the couch beside me, Sailor against her chest, Mimi sleeping by my side.

"Can you tell when death will come? No. You have to prepare to make it go before it come. Fever is bad. Fever kill Gaida child at age sixteen. Remember Gaida from church, the Gaida who wear black lipstick every day?" she said, her lips pursed as if to drive her point home.

"Yeah, Nonna, but Elio is better now. He had some friends over, and they took care of him. His new girlfriend was here too!"

Gran Louisa's eyes widened, a shocked gasp leaving her. "You have girlfriend now, Elio?"

I turned my head to pin Gemma with a stare, and she beamed at me.

"Answer now!" Gran Louisa yelled.

"Yes, that is . . . hm"—I cleared my throat—"correct."

"Let me see! I need to know if she deserve pretty man like you."

I don't deserve her.

"She left," I told her. "They had an *event* to attend on the cruise."

Gran Louisa nodded. "Okay, bring girlfriend home when you leave ocean; I will cook for her and ask her important question."

Home.

I almost smiled as I nodded. "Okay."

"I will go now; I have church. Gaida is making cookies for us—it will not be good—but I have to prepare for lie. Poor Gaida."

Gemma laughed, shaking her head. "Okay, Nonna, talk to you later."

"Bye-bye," she responded with a wave while her hand came close to the screen as the call ended.

Gemma sighed as I handed her the phone and let my head fall back.

"Now I have to contrive a way to tell her my *girlfriend* would never be available to see her."

The culprit angled her body to face mine, but I didn't turn my head to look at her. "'Never Say Never,' Justin Bieber knew what he was talking about when he sang that song."

"I do not know who that is."

"I know you don't; I'd be surprised if you did," she said, laughter in her voice. "My main focus now is when and how you'll reintroduce us. The first time we met, it wasn't really great, and now she knows my face but doesn't know who I am; so before she sees me again with you and jumps to a conclusion, you—"

"I will introduce you both." I cut her off, turning my head to her. "When I am positive she won't kill you, and then me."

Gemma blinked at me. "Wh-what?"

"Zahra is . . . quick-tempered. I made a mistake not telling her who you were when she first saw you."

Gemma nodded, her teeth closing on her bottom lip. "Right, you're right. You might need to lay it on slowly so she doesn't misunderstand." She blew out a breath. "God, she was—she was intimidating. Not at all welcoming, but I know there's a softie in there." She grinned, poking my arm and wiggling her brows. "She likes you."

I sighed, narrowing my eyes and looking away. "Nothing special."

"Oh please . . ." Her tone turned sharp. "Spare me the false modesty and self-degradation. You are the most likable person I know."

I watched her. "You are naïve, Gemma."

"Probably, but I have that good-people tingle. I know when I see a good person."

"I suggest that you check the tingle. Might be broken."

She laughed, and I shook my head. Appreciating the fact that I could carry out that movement without getting a headache.

Zahra and Street had stayed till the morning, but then they had to leave for some casino bet they made . . . I did not want to know more or indulge them in their thieving activities, but Zahra had stayed an hour longer, and Elia had told me he would stop by later for a talk.

Since then, I'd been pretending that I wasn't overthinking what that talk would entail.

At this point, I didn't know what I wanted or where I stood with everything I wanted to do. My goal was not to settle with Elia; it was the opposite. But that didn't excuse the inconvenient fact that I wanted to talk to him, rebuild our relationship, and have him look at me like I was his family, his brother, his protector, his friend. I missed that . . .

But . . .

Right and wrong; tennis balls swung back and forth in my head.

Settle or ruin.

Happy or sad.

Peace or chaos.

Build a heart or break one.

"Hey." Gemma's voice brought me out of my head. "On a serious note, I'm happy for you. First relationships are always tough, but they're the most amazing; it all feels new, and the person looks like the sun when you see them." She spoke like she remembered her experience. "But I know you'll be great. She's very lucky; you're a really good guy."

I turned my head to her again and gave an appreciative nod. "Thank you, Gemma."

"Of course." She grinned. "How do you feel now?"

"Good. A lot stronger than I did yesterday."

Gemma had arrived after Zahra left, although she had texted to ensure the coast was clear first.

She'd been worried when I informed her via text to avoid my suite because I had company due to a fever. When she arrived, she told me she must have been on the phone with Luigi when I called.

And then she told me how Luigi had been sending her pictures of himself in a penthouse—to brag—according to her.

When she showed me the pictures, it was with a scowl on her face.

She and Luigi had a brother-sister relationship, constantly bickering and teasing. Apparently, just as Gran Louisa had named me a family member, she did the same with Luigi. Although I didn't care and probably wouldn't like to know about anything regarding Luigi or anyone else if I was being honest, I now had some obligation to listen.

My father would have hated this, me associating with people outside of the family and the business. But they made me feel almost normal; I would not change that for anything.

Being with Gemma and hearing Gran Louisa say, *Bring girlfriend home*, like I had every right to be there, warmed my chest and broke my heart—this was a helpless situation.

A situation where help was within reach, within grasp, where everyone wanted the same thing for me . . .

Get some help, Elio. See a doctor, Elio. Consult a specialist, Marino. I think you need a therapist. I think you need help.

Absolutely delightful. I knew I needed help; I knew I would get worse. This was how it started with my mother, the little mumblings, loud thoughts, hallucinations, lucid dreams, repetitive movements, repetitive words, self-harm . . . How she would claim to hear voices, how she lost interest in the things she loved doing, her lack of emotions—the total apathy, the fear—the same as I felt yesterday.

That fear had been small but so deep, so meaningful that it sent a chill down my spine, although I couldn't be sure if it was the fever or if it was my body showing me symptoms—I honestly couldn't be sure of anything these days.

It was even worse that I knew this—I knew I needed help, but that voice—those words . . . *I am undeserving of it. I don't need help.* They kept playing in my head whenever I even dared to consider the idea.

I wanted it, but that want had never been strong enough to bring forth a need.

When Angelo pointed out that I might have been made to think I didn't deserve the help, I began to look at things in a different light.

My father had been so against me getting professional and proper help. He didn't want to hear it or think about it.

I had always been yelling at my father, telling him my

mother needed help, and getting that for her was the right thing to do . . . but suddenly, I couldn't apply that same rigorousness to myself.

I don't know if I want to.

I don't know what I want.

I don't know who I am.

I don't know why my thoughts are breaking up or why the urge to speak them out loud seems like the most relieving thing in the world—

"Marino!" Angelo's voice from the entrance, and the door closing behind me, broke my thoughts and got Gemma's attention. "I got your text; I brought in all your pills and—oh—" I turned to see Angelo standing a few feet away, a surprised frown on his face. "Uh . . . fuck, I didn't mean to interrupt, but if you could give me a heads-up next time so I don't barge in and interrupt you with . . . someone else?" Confusion dragged his brows down even farther.

"Hello, Angelo, meet Gemma; Gemma, meet Angelo. We work together."

Gemma's eyes were wide, her jaw was hanging open, and she had wholly loosened her hold on Sailor as she bent slowly toward me, taking her eyes off Angelo. "You didn't tell me he was hot," she rushed out.

I frowned. "What?"

"You didn't tell me he was freaking hot; you didn't tell me he was swimming with hotness. Are you insane not to have prepared me for that?" she whispered loudly enough for both me and Angelo to hear.

"I didn't think it was important."

"You evil being! I am about to make a complete fool out of myself in front of probably the hottest man I have ever seen—"

"I can—I can hear everything," Angelo pointed out, and Gemma snapped up straight with a broad smile that almost made her ears fall off.

I watched her get off the couch, standing like she couldn't

bear to sit down when he was in the room. "Hi, yes—I knew you could hear me, and I know my face is a tomato, ketchup? Depending on the level of redness, it could be a strawberry milkshake—those pinkish-red ones with the cute little ice cubes inside and the beautiful straw that comes with the cup. And I don't know why I am talking about strawberry milkshakes or milkshakes at all because there is no milkshake here. I tend to embarrass myself a lot . . ." Silence stretched until she added "Ha!" for good measure or a closing statement. I couldn't tell.

Angelo blinked, flustered. "Hi, Gemma; a pleasure to meet you. I'm sorry about barging in—"

"Oh no, no, no, nothing like that; Elio and I are buddies. We roll with the flow of friendship, and, uh . . . there's nothing—you didn't interrupt anything at all, we were just talking about friend things, you see."

Angelo nodded. "Friends . . ." His gaze shifted to me. "Oh . . ." And then he looked back at Gemma. "He has mentioned you."

I have?

"He has?"

"Yeah . . . a long time ago." Then his gaze fell back to me. "This is Gemma, yeah, the one you got the phone for?"

Gemma's lips fell open. "What? You bought your phone because of me?"

"You wanted me to text you," I stated.

"Awww." Gemma's face softened. "That is so cute and sweet. I will forever treasure this information."

I allowed a stretch of seconds to go by, unsure of what to say before I settled on "Okay."

She beamed, looking back at Angelo. "Nice to meet you, too, Angelo; Elio has said so much about you, and Mimi, God, she's such a doll."

I watched a smile come onto Angelo's lips. "Isn't she? Is that yours?" He gestured to Sailor.

"Yup, she's mine." Gemma quickly picked her up with a

grin as Angelo approached, dropping the bag he'd brought in front of me before collecting Gemma's cat, cooing.

"Oh, she's heavy and soft, wow."

"She loves to be spoiled, and my nonna made it a habit to take extra good care of her."

Mimi perked up from beside me before she started meowing loudly.

"Attention seeker one minute and a stranger the next," Angelo said, handing Sailor to Gemma as he bent to pick up Mimi, kissing her head.

"Good. Now that we are done with meeting the cats and the people, can you explain to me why there are so many pill bottles?"

Angelo dropped his cat down again. "There are only four. Two of them are just the dosage you need to take before bed tonight; I'll hold on to the rest until I get back."

"Thank you," I said, but then I frowned. "Where are you going again?"

"Oh, I heard there were some mountains not far off. I booked a boat from the cruise with some others who wanted to check it out, just sightseeing. Are you interested?"

"No. I'm expecting someone."

He frowned. "Who?"

"My brother."

His brows rose up. "Oh. That's good." He looked pleased. "That's great," he said, nodding the same way Gemma was nodding now.

"Yes, I suppose."

"And I suppose she knows too?" He gestured to Gemma.

"Yes."

Angelo nodded. "Just how close are you both again?"

"Met-the-grandma close," Gemma supplied. "But like, not in a seek-her-hand-in-marriage kinda way . . . more in a *friends* kinda way."

"That's great." Angelo looked at me, surprised but happy. "Glad you took my advice."

I nodded. "Hm."

"Oh, uh . . ." Gemma spoke up. "If you need company to check out the mountain, I'd love to go."

Angelo smiled at her. "Of course, but we have to go now. We have just minutes to prepare."

Gemma dropped Sailor with an enthusiastic nod. After Angelo took the rest of my pills with him and Gemma kissed my cheek goodbye, they left the apartment.

I was alone again, but it didn't feel as distant as yesterday.

Pulling out my phone, I went to Zahra's message space, seeing the failed message still alight.

I blinked, and a sound went off on my phone, a message from her popping up in the chat box.

Zahra:
Hey, what's up?

Almost like my mind had called her into texting me. I responded.

Me:
Hello.

Her response came after a few seconds.

Zahra:
How are u feeling? Do u need anything?

I frowned. Confused.

Me:
Who is this?

Zahra:
Some random dude who kidnapped this phone's owner and tied her up below

deck because I have a nasty grudge to
pick with her.

Me:
Okay. Good luck.

Zahra:
It's me, u fucking asshole. Wtf?
Good luck?
Who the fuck says that?

The messages popped in three consecutive times, with no break.

Me:
Hello, Zahra.
I replied based on your earlier response. Regarding your question about how I am doing, yes, I am all right. Thank you for checking in, and no, I do not need anything.

I sent that and waited for her response, but nothing came afterward. I sat there in silence, waiting . . . waiting—I scrolled back to her first message and read them through, and then through my own responses.

Did I miss something? Should I add one of the yellow round faces? Was my response too formal? How do I make it informal? What—

Zahra:
Ok.

I frowned . . . tempted to ask who this was again. Instead, I typed out something else.

Me:
Where are you?

Her response took two minutes, thirty-nine seconds.

Zahra:
Room.

Me:
Have you returned from the casino?

This time it took longer, three minutes, forty-eight seconds.

Zahra:
Yh.

Guessing that was supposed to mean yes, I sent another response.

Me:
All right.
Are you occupied at the moment?

Six minutes, twenty seconds.

Zahra:
Yh.

I sighed, knowing I had probably said something wrong along the way. Then again, I wasn't well versed in starting or maintaining conversations and did not know how to turn off formalities.

I also saw no reason to apologize for doing nothing wrong,

so I reacted with a thumbs-up and left her chat box, getting the unspoken message that she didn't want to talk to me.

Maybe she was indeed busy.

Or maybe I was making excuses. Perhaps I should go to Angelo for advice on what to say and what not to say. I needed to be more knowledgeable. This was new. This was fragile. This was another first I knew nothing about.

This is me overthinking it.

I released a breath, looking around the space slowly, my feet tapping the ground repeatedly, my fingers tapping my thigh, the quietness growing too loud, the emptiness swallowing me whole, my hearing becoming dull . . . and suddenly, I was on my feet. I walked to the bar table, opened a cabinet, and removed a cigar box.

I placed a cigar between my lips, lit the end, and took a long drag, long enough that I could not drag in any more smoke.

I let the toxic cloud circulate through my system and—

Someone knocked, and I flinched in a startle, forgetting I wasn't breathing.

On cue, I entered into a fit of coughing, dropping the cigar in the ashtray as I pounded my chest with my fist, coughing with a wheezy sound, barely registering the smoke escaping my nose and mouth. My vision blurred as I tried calming down, taming the cough, and taking proper breaths.

The knock came again.

I inhaled little by little, gasp after gasp. The coughs calmed. I blinked my vision clear, making my way toward the door, clearing my throat, and getting a bit of control of myself again.

I opened the door, and Elia stood there, looking up from his shoes and directly at me; his expression morphed into instant concern. "What is . . . why are your eyes red?"

"Cigar. Coughing," I clarified, opening the door wider before turning and returning to the living room. The sound of the door closing and his footsteps following me were what filled the silence. "Want anything to drink? You can help yourself,"

I said, settling on a single couch while he settled on another with Sailor.

"No, I'm good," he said, his finger grazing his jaw as he looked around.

"I—"

"You should quit."

I stopped short, frowning. "What?"

He raised his gaze. "Smoking. It's getting to you. You should quit."

I did not take my eyes off him as I said, "It helps me."

"Killing you while it's at it."

I cleared my throat, uncomfortable. "You said you wanted to talk."

He brought his palms together, intertwining his hands. "Yeah, I do," he answered. "Listen, I don't wanna revisit the past and dredge up old wounds." He swallowed. "I know things have been rocky, and all our conversations have ended with me hitting and disrespecting you and saying shit that I don't mean . . . I'm sorry if my words hurt you; I was angry."

My brain picked apart his words.

"Was?" I stated in question. "Does this mean you're not angry anymore?"

He pressed his lips together. "I don't know," he stated plainly. "But I know I don't want to fight anymore."

"You don't want to know why I broke my promise?"

"It's not going to change anything if I do."

I tilted my head. "You don't want to confirm if I am indeed responsible for the death of my mother and siblings?"

He paused, watching me with a battle in his eyes. "Are you?"

Silence stretched into minutes, and then I shrugged, leaning back. "Might not have started the fire, but it doesn't mean I'm not to blame for it."

"What does that mean?"

My eyes searched his. "When I let you go, Elia, I let everyone go. When I let you down, I also let everyone down. My mother, Mariana, Lorenzo," I said, looking away from him. "I let myself down. I lost my purpose; I lost a lot . . . but I had hope that I would come back and see them again. I would meet you again, apologize, and get on my knees if I had to. But then I got out, got back . . . and it was all ashes. Hours too late. Minutes too long, doing absolutely nothing while standing by my father's side. If I had done things differently, if I had stood up to my father, put a bullet in his head, and told him I didn't need to join the army to keep my mind in check, maybe things would have been different.

"Days after they died I . . . I replayed possible scenarios on how things could have gone differently, how I could have kept them alive." I looked back at him. "Kept you here. I have regretted my actions every day until now. I deserve to pay for the pain that I caused you, my mother, Mari, and Enzo.

"It feels wrong to be respected, loved, and praised, since I did nothing worthy of respect, especially by you. So, you do not have to apologize for that. I deserve it and worse."

"No, it's—"

"Let me finish," I told him. "I am happy that you decided to talk to me and give me a chance. But I also want to let you know that it is completely okay if you do not want to give me a chance; you don't have to. If you are angry, be angry; if you feel like hitting me, do not hesitate. Feel what you want to feel. Do not spare my feelings."

He shook his head. "That's not what I'm trying to do," he said. "I meant it when I said I didn't want to fight anymore, Elio. I want—I know everything can't automatically go back to how it used to be, but—we can try to fix what we can. You're my only family, and regardless of the past, I still worry and care about you. Just the same way you do for me."

"Hm." I nodded. "And if I'm not mentally available at all times?"

"You don't have to be. I'm a grown-up; I have my own shit to deal with now. I just want to clear the air."

I nodded. "And Zahra? Am I to assume you have no concerns with our . . . recent relationship?"

His mouth opened and closed, and his hand moved to his neck as he spoke. "It is weird, I'm not gonna lie, but—I see it. You care about her, and she surprisingly cares about you. As long as you're both in check with each other, then it's none of my business."

"Hm." I nodded again. "You harbor no feelings for her? If you do, please tell me."

"I love Zahra; she's my best friend, always has been, but—things aren't like that. I thought they were at some point until I realized that wasn't the kind of love that you share with someone you want to be with."

He was picking his words, but I didn't have a right to call him out on it.

"This was good; I appreciate you making the effort, Elia."

"Zahra says I need bragging rights. Had to snag it," he said, looking around. "Do you just stay here? Only you? Doing nothing?"

"Yes."

He looked at me. "Wanna come over to our suite? Upper and Dog are setting up a game in the lounge, and Milk ordered too much food."

"And Zahra?"

"Uh . . . in her room? She went in after going to the casino and never came out; I don't know about now . . . Why?"

"Nothing."

Elia prepared to get up. "Would you like to join?" he asked, sounding hopeful. "Or if you have work and things to do, I understand—"

"I will join you."

He couldn't mask the surprise on his face. "All right," he said.

"The cats."

His gaze dropped to them. "We can take them if you want. Milk loves them, so she'll be glad."

I nodded. "Okay."

Honestly, I agreed to this for three reasons. One was because Elia asked, and after our conversation, I needed to cement my decision with this; number two was because the idea of staying here alone wasn't appealing, I knew I would start seeing and hearing things, thanks to paranoia; and number three—three was because of Zahra. Either I had offended her through my texts, or something else had happened.

If something else had happened, then I wanted to know. I hated texting, hated the fact that I couldn't see her face to know what changed, why it changed, how it changed, when it changed.

I needed to see her. The need was like a thirst on my tongue that I had to sate. I needed this. It. Her.

She took the quietness and my urges away. She was my new habit.

Unhealthy, I know.

But then again, I have never been one to cut off unhealthy habits; why would I start now?

CHAPTER TWELVE

Elio

I mean, it's normal to get tired of the hustle and bustle," Milk said, chewing on the slice of pizza she was eating. "You just want to settle down and have a comfortable life." She swallowed, picking up her drink. "Live your dream, have everything you want, be able to afford every need without having to steal or cheat or kidnap someone, you know?"

I responded to her ideology with a firm nod, unsure how the easy conversation had turned into what they would desire to do with their lives after they quit the criminal activities they were known for.

Their suite wasn't as large as mine, but it was still classy. The same couch that was in my suite was here, but the living room area was smaller, cozier. The windows didn't exactly overlook the ocean like it did mine, but while you could still see people on deck, the ocean wasn't too far away.

Sucking on the straw of her drink and gulping down its contents, Milk dropped it back beside her when she was satisfied. "If I could have had my way with life, I would have wanted something peaceful . . . like finishing college, designing a fashion line, having a salon that's like paradise, a spa place, a good husband, and a perfect family, living in some perfect house somewhere in New York . . ." She sighed. "I still plan to do it if we get that gold . . . I want to be normal."

Upper nodded, relaxing on the ground, his back leaning against the couch Dog sat on. "If I could have a do-over, I would have fought more for what I deserved."

"You should have," Dog muttered after taking a drink from

the beer bottle he held. "You came from money . . . If I were you, no one is booting me out that easy."

I wasn't certain what precisely they were talking about. But reading the room, it had to do with Upper's past.

I had been here for two hours. I wasn't bored, but I was supremely out of place; though this bunch didn't point out any oddity, they probably did not find anything bugging about my presence. Usually, I would call this careless, but I was 78 percent sure they were cordial because Zahra and Elia had found a substantial reason to be cordial with me.

I would not deny that being here was entirely . . . relaxing; it made me feel good to pull off being amongst these people. My thoughts were tranquil; they suddenly didn't matter.

Zahra, though, hadn't left her room since I arrived.

Milk had offered to alert her to my presence, but I refused, deciding to speak to her in my own time while I got to know the people my brother spent his time with.

"I was almost twelve and scared of what I was," Upper explained. "The royal family did not exactly love me before, so, I left."

I frowned. "Royal family?"

There was silence around as they looked at me with confused stares.

"You didn't know?" Elia asked first.

I shook my head.

"I thought y'all ran a storm of background checks on us?" Dog asked.

"We did," I answered. "Casmiro did," I clarified. "But I did not bother to check it myself."

"Why?" Milk asked.

"I did not care enough to waste time checking."

"Oh . . ."

"Why were you sent out of the royal family?"

Upper shifted uncomfortably. "I don't like to talk about it," he said, gaining Elia's attention. "It's, uh . . . very rough, panic-inducing rough."

I watched Upper's gaze lock with Elia's, which lingered for approximately three seconds before Elia looked away.

Sometimes, I despised my invasive, unnatural, and observant nature. I despised it because half the time I did not want to learn certain things, but I ended up learning them anyway.

"But," Upper said while breathing in, "one thing I want to do, after we get that gold, is start up my education again. Go to college, learn more, and get a job that pays."

"What about you, Dog?" Milk blurted out the question.

Dog's brows snapped down in a frown. "Why the fuck did you attack me like that?"

She blinked. "What?"

"You just asked like you have been dying to know what I would have done with my life and what I want to do."

She pressed her lips together, cheeks going pink. "I mean . . ." She was flustered now. "Isn't that what—what we're all doing?"

"Yeah, you just came on too—"

"Dog, just answer the bloody question," Upper spoke over him, glancing at Milk and deciphering her sudden distress.

What a mess.

Dog sighed, raking his fingers through his hair, scattering the already scattered arrangement. "Well . . . if there was one thing I could redo, I would ask my parents the question that had been burning in my mind when they brought me to Italy. The simple question of 'why?'"

"Care to explain?" Elia asked.

"My parents . . . they were murdered a week after they brought me here and took my—" He cleared his throat. "Well . . . my dad was an agent for the CIA, and my mom was a cop. When I get the gold, I will join the FBI and find out what happened to them. They were pretty big with people who were people, so with a little digging, I can get my answers."

He shrugged. "You don't know what people would be willing to reveal with a briefcase filled with gold on their desk."

"So," I started, "a thief wants to join the Federal Bureau of Investigation. How do you suppose that would work without a clean background check?"

"I have money. Nobody knows I'm a thief; my background is a clean slate. I'm smart, I'll train, I'll do whatever it takes," he said, determination in his eyes.

I nodded. "Impressive." I offered, "If you ever need to talk about this, whatever it takes, my doors are always open."

Dog blinked at me. "For . . . real?"

"Hm. I have a few favors owed to me by people who might be able to answer your questions; I can grant you a favor too."

"What's the catch?" Dog asked.

"You owe me a favor, one I probably won't have enough time to collect, but it could help you."

He observed me. "All right, we'll see."

I responded with a firm nod.

"What about you?" Upper gestured to Elia. "What would you change, and what would you do with the gold?"

Elia's gaze lifted to look around the group, settling on me for a bit, allowing me to see that he was caught off guard, despite knowing the question was going around. "I . . ." He trailed off, eyes unsure. "I . . ." He looked down at the drink he held and shrugged. "Don't really know. There's nothing I would change . . . there's nothing *to* change. As for the gold, I don't really care about it. I might travel, uh . . ." He looked *lost*, like he didn't know what he had planned or hadn't thought about it.

His eyes held this heavy cloud like his whole life had been a blank page. He didn't know what to write on it or where to start writing . . . the middle, the top, the bottom—or maybe I wasn't reading him right, perhaps this thing I saw didn't stem from how I had erased him. He cleared his throat. "Um . . . I don't know. I guess I haven't really thought about it," he said, drinking from his beer bottle like he didn't want to speak any further.

"And you, Marino?" Dog asked. "You're not taking the gold, so the question there is, what would you change?"

I thought about the question and allowed the silence to stretch as my gaze focused on the littered center table, a vivid representation of my life since I was born. A clear picture was painted before me, a mockery of the irony in my life.

I swallowed. "Nothing," I answered with the truth. "I would change nothing."

"Really?" Elia asked, shock evident in his voice.

"Hm. I believe the only people with the right to change something are the ones who deserve the do-over," I answered him, removing my gaze from the table. "I would change nothing, but it doesn't mean I will not correct everything."

Then it was silent.

"You see," I continued, "changing doesn't have the same effect as correcting. Changing means losing yourself and the person you've grown to become; correcting, rather, is most effective because you get to grow into something better, you get to look back at the past *you*, and you get to own the pride for how far you've come. Our past makes up most of who we are; the future is much sweeter, but the present is where the work is, what you're willing to do, to correct and to grow."

I watched them let my words sink in. Almost two minutes flew by; everyone was lost in their own heads.

"Thank you," Milk said, swallowing tightly. "You just answered a question I didn't realize I had been asking all my life."

"Me too," Upper echoed.

Dog raised his beer bottle to me with a tight smile.

While Elia just stared at me with a frown, one that didn't come from anger but concern.

"You're welcome. Glad I could . . . help"—I paused a little before adding—"unintentionally." I cleared my throat. "I should go check on the missing member before I leave; I have Casmiro arriving today."

"Oh yes, he told me he was flying in," Upper said.

I nodded, getting to my feet as Milk commented to Upper about talking to Casmiro; it brought up a debate I tuned out, walking toward Zahra's room, where Milk had gestured to early on when I arrived.

Standing in front of the door, I knocked three times.

There was no response.

I waited a few seconds before raising my hand and knocking again thrice.

When I got no response, I placed my hand on the knob, debating leaving it be or walking in without a response from her. Walking in would be rude; I would hate it if someone did that to me without waiting for a response . . . *but she did the same to me a long time ago.*

What if she needed help and couldn't talk because she . . . she . . . had choked herself with the wire of a . . . hair dryer?

Accidents happen.

The option of leaving it be lost the debate, and I found myself twisting the knob and walking into the room.

She was on the bed, on her side, eyes closed, sleeping.

I closed the door behind me softly. My eyes took in the room. It wasn't too big, but it felt and looked comfortable; the window was covered by a thin white curtain, giving the room a dark but light vibe that seemed comfortable for sleeping.

My gaze moved to Zahra again.

She didn't cover herself, so I had a full view of her naked stomach. The tiny shirt she wore stopped just below her breasts, and her shorts were folded at the waist like they were oversized. Her legs were on display, lips parted slightly, breathing steady, lost in sleep.

Comfortable but careless.

I silently kicked off my shoes, walking toward the bed.

I stood right before her sleeping figure.

Dipping one knee into the bed, her body followed my weight, but she didn't move.

I frowned, knowing how easy it was to overpower her this way. What if I had *actually* wanted to harm her? We would need to discuss this. It was one thing to sleep when necessary, but it was another to leave yourself completely vulnerable.

I placed a fist on the mattress beside her head, hovering above her, casting a shadow.

Apparently, that action was not enough to alert her—

Her eyes snapped open, unfocused, as her hand, with blinding speed, slipped under her pillow while her knees lifted, slamming hard against my stomach; I lost my balance. I was on my back, and she was straddling me, the cold barrel of a gun—*my* gun—pressing tightly against my throat. She unlocked it from the safety, but before she could pull the trigger, my hand forcefully swung hers away. The gun went off, the bullet shattering a vase by the side of the bed. She immediately brought the weapon back to me, about to hit me with the hilt, when I grabbed onto her wrist in midair.

Her chest was heaving with adrenaline, eyes burning in a dazed anger. "Zahra," I called firmly.

She still fought me, her hand pressing my right shoulder down while she tried to twist her wrist out of my hold.

"Zahra, hey! Calm down, it's just me."

"Oh, I know it's you, you motherfucker," she gritted out.

I blinked, frowning in confusion, locking my grip. "Then why are you still fighting me?"

"Why did you sneak up on me?"

"I did not sneak up on you."

"So, you just hover over random people when they sleep? That's fucking—*grade-twenty* creepy shit, Elio. Nobody does that unless they want to fucking kill you."

I relaxed. "Did it ever occur to you that I just wanted to kiss your forehead?"

She backed up like I had said the most ridiculous thing.

"Why the *fuck* would you come all the way *here* to kiss my forehead?"

I took in her face, momentarily getting lost before my gaze locked with hers once more. "Because it's a pretty forehead?"

There was a knock on the door before a muffled voice yelled, "Anybody dead?"

Her head turned toward the door and then back to me. She relaxed.

The voice came again. "It's gonna be a shit ton of work to carry a body out of this suite without drawing attention to a bloodied bedsheet, so I hope for you both it's a case of injured but still breathing."

The woman above me stopped fighting as she sighed. "It's your lucky day, Dog; I missed," she yelled back as I let her wrist go, and she dropped her hand and *my* gun.

"I can never get a fucking break," Dog muttered, his footsteps retreating.

Looking back at me, she sighed.

"You almost killed me," I pointed out, "with my gun, no less. Talk about finishing the job for me."

"Shut up. I would have killed you. Always call my name before you make me feel like you're about to suffocate me with a pillow. I kill first, ask questions later . . . most times."

"That is not wise."

"Your opinion was not needed."

"Hurtful."

She scoffed, like me and that word had no relationship.

"You still have my gun," I said, eyeing the weapon. "Why?"

She had taken the gun from me the night I almost killed my father. I didn't expect her to still have it. Keep it so close. Under her pillow.

Something tightened in my chest.

"I kept it for people who try to murder me in my sleep," she said.

I held back a smile. "Why did you respond that way when we texted earlier today?" I asked.

She raised a brow at me. "Are you seriously asking me that?"

"Yes."

She shook her head. "You have—You're so annoying sometimes, but I'll let it slide because you can be weird, but maybe next time, don't respond to me like you are trying to send an email to the mayor of Milan."

"I have never emailed the mayor of Milan; I have people who do that for me."

She glared. "Elio."

"I do not—" I breathed. "I do not know how to text like you want me to. If you want to teach me, then I will gladly learn as long as it pleases you."

"Oh, how kind."

"I am kind to you, even though you just tried to kill me, which is a clear message that you have no trust in me, which is wise. I must commend you, but you should appreciate me more. There are lots of terrible ways I could have reacted to subdue you."

"Well, you shouldn't have hovered."

I shifted a bit but stilled a wince. The muscles in my stomach ached from the impact of her knees slamming into my torso.

She noticed my discomfort because now there was a frown on her face. "You idiot," she said, her fingers going to unfasten the buttons on my shirt.

Oh?

My gaze left her fingers, moving to her face. My eyes took in all there was to see, but it was not enough; her hair, wild and curly, a mess . . . a beautiful mess.

She caught my stare, looked away, and then back in a double take.

"What?" she snapped at me, brows furrowing in annoyance.

"I like looking at you," I told her.

Her fingers paused their movement on my shirt, her eyes searching mine as I rose onto my elbows.

I watched her swallow, watched the way she flushed and her pupils dilate an inch, her blinking abnormal, alongside her breathing.

She looked away from me, fingers working unsteadily on my last button. "I think by now you should know those little flirty compliments do nothing for me," she said while she pulled my shirt apart, her fingers pressing softly on the bruise that was already forming.

"They don't?" I asked, supporting my weight with one elbow while I raised my other hand to her hair, smoothing loose strands behind her ear.

She raised her head, eyes locking with mine. "No—they don't."

"Are you all right?" I asked with a mock concerned frown, raising myself until I was at eye level with her, my hand caressing the side of her neck, below her ear, and inside her hair.

Her gaze dropped to my lips. "Yeah, why?"

"You're flustered."

"I'm not."

"It is cute."

"Stop it; those compliments make me cringe. I told you it does nothing for me."

I felt her breath as I drew closer. "You look quite taken by it."

"You are wrong," she said with a lowered voice, her pupils widening in size, our body heat mixing.

"I can even hear your heartbeat."

"No, you can't."

"Then maybe it is mine." My voice was hoarse and raspy but soft as I tilted my head to the side, drawing my face closer, the side of my nose brushing against hers. Our breathing mingled, our lips were so close, one push, just one push. "It gets hard to tell sometimes," I whispered.

She closed the distance, her lips catching mine in a kiss that tickled my reasoning. My hold on the side of her head held firm as our lips moved tentatively, testing the waters, basking in the soft, warm feel, dragging it along like we had all the time in the world to feel the heat that came with each other's taste, parting to allow the intrusion of our tongues. My heart, which had been hammering like that was its new function, had me feeling dizzy.

My teeth bit her bottom lip, pulling softly, letting us catch our breaths before we joined our lips together, completely in sync—*God, I love kissing her. I love it so much*. I loved how it made me feel like we were lost in a place where time had no effect, a standstill that had me thinking that we could do this forever, survive on the feverish high, a loop of us getting lost in each other.

Her tongue was soft against mine, and her lips perfectly fit mine.

Hell, the soft sounds that left her—unguarded, unshielded. A trance I couldn't escape—the perfect hypnotism.

This woman has cursed me.

I was aroused; her grinding on my erection served as a predator to the prey that was my control.

I held her firm as I switched our position, my arousal between her legs as I retook her lips, my hand holding onto her hip, squeezing before riding up the dip in her waist, her fingers burying themselves to the back of my head, tangled around my hair.

We broke away to catch our breaths.

My eyes searched hers. "I'm addicted, Sport." I bit her chin, my fingers working between her legs, touching her through her shorts. "I'm addicted to you."

Her lips parted as she let out a breathy moan, so quiet—for my ears only. I almost shivered; I almost asked her to grant me mercy. This was killing me; she was killing me. I was so hard, and it was so painful.

I never intended for this. I only wanted to talk. But just like every other occurrence with us, I could never predict it.

I kissed down her neck—no, I sucked down her neck, bruising her. She liked it because she arched, giving me more room as my hand left between her legs, moving up her stomach as I lifted the small shirt, caressing her breast in my hand, loving the feel as my thumb brushed her pierced nipple, the coldness of the steel having the same effect on my cock as the first time.

Perfect in every word. In every sense.

And now this is mine . . . she is mine to touch, my possession. My little witch.

Inside her . . . I needed to be inside her.

I lifted myself a little as my hand came to the folded hem of her shorts.

She got the message, her shaky hands coming to do the job while I got rid of my own clothes.

"The shorts are Dog's," she said, her voice heavy.

My eyes snapped to hers. "Do you lack clothes?"

"No?"

The nonchalance in her voice had me clenching my jaw; something ugly and unwelcoming burned in the pit of my stomach. "I don't like it."

She pulled the small shirt over her head. "That's something you'll have to sort out with yourself."

I was above her in an instant, her naked body beneath me as I held her chin, my gaze holding hers as I settled into my place. Between her thighs. "We'll discuss this later; for now, shut up."

Her brows snapped down in a frown. "Don't tell me to shut up—"

I kissed her words back down her throat, and she forcefully broke away with my lip in her teeth. A sharp pain pinned my bottom lip; I ran my tongue over the area, tasting blood.

My gaze locked with hers, a challenge in those eyes, mocking me, asking what I would do to beat that.

"You love testing me," I said.

"You forget your boundaries—"

My hand closed around her throat, and I slammed her head back down to the pillow, a choking laugh leaving her. "Feisty," she taunted.

My cock brushed her core, and she hissed. Her eyes filled with lust and thrill; she loved this, loved my control even when she wanted papers that proved she was in control at all times.

"What," she continued, taunting, "are you all—"

I slapped the pad of my fingers softly against her left cheek, very close to her mouth; her head turned to the side at the impact, clearly not expecting that reaction.

With my hold on her neck, I turned her head back until she looked into my eyes, those browns now filled with a new kind of interest.

My thumb grazed her cheek to below her chin, tightening my hold a bit before bringing my face and lips closer to hers as I asked, "Can't breathe?"

A smirk. "We both know I can have you on your back in a second, so don't—"

I thrust into her.

"Fu—"

I closed my lips around hers, stopping her loud moan before it could come out; as much as my being hungered to hear it, I knew we had to be quiet.

But . . . *God.*

Her slick, wet, tight heat hugged my length in a vise grip that had my fucking head spinning with desperation. Need—a craving about to be satisfied but with an intense longing to prolong it.

This feeling. This addiction. This obsession.

It would be my doom. My unraveling. I wanted it. I wanted all of it. I wanted her total consumption.

I broke away from her lips.

A breathy moan left her; it was ragged, loud.

"You need to be quiet, querida."

If ecstasy were a face, it would be hers; she defined the word perfectly, as I knew she would. My woman was capable of anything, and I was proud.

I drew back from her and thrust back in.

"Elio—"

"Shh, quiet," I whispered against her lips, my eyes locking with hers as I drew out and pushed back in, brutal, unforgiving.

Her moan died in her throat, a strained sound as she dug her fingers into my biceps, not taking her eyes off me as her teeth pressed down on her bottom lip.

"That's good," I told her, pulling out and slamming back in, her throbbing heat holding my length captive, a maddening tease, one that made my cock twitch. I pulled out and thrust back in, keeping my pace hard, a friction that had my pelvis brushing with her clit. "Spread your legs wide."

She did, and my hand went to her clit, rubbing as I thrust into her, fucking and rubbing those silent breathy moans past her lips, fucking and rubbing my name off of her tongue, fucking and rubbing her into a zone, lost in me, lost in this, into this feeling that seemed to be blooming in my chest.

Her hips lifted to meet my thrusts, rolling, grinding, turning me crazed. I dropped my head on her collarbone. "Fuck. That's good, so good; you're doing so fucking good, Zahra. *Fuck.*"

I don't curse often, but my whole damn vocabulary had suddenly gone extinct. I could only express myself in ways she had subjected me to; every word in my head started with an *f* and ended with a *k*—her body, her voice, her moans. They were all fucking with my mind.

I knew sex was good, I knew it was fucking addictive, I knew it had a sweetness to it that could make anyone melt—but I didn't know it could be this *all-consuming*, I didn't know it could make my chest ache, I didn't know I could lose myself, my mind, I didn't know it could be so engulfing, so . . . so—*fuck*.

She tightened around me, her legs came around my waist, and her release warmed my cock. Her back arched upward as I fucked her faster, sloppier, and—

Fuck, fuck, *fuck*.

My stomach was in knots, my chest was caving in on itself, and I came feverishly inside her, and her arms came around my shoulders, holding me like she knew I was about to break, mentally and physically.

Her lips sought mine, a kiss deeper than any we'd shared already passed between us.

Hot. Intimate. Intense.

My speeding heart was supposed to have calmed; my vocabulary was supposed to have returned, but—fuck, my heart was still a raging organ in my chest. Even as I pulled away from the kiss, sliding out of her and falling wordlessly to her side, I could still hear the pounding in my chest; my eyes latched onto the ceiling above the bed.

Zahra let out a contented breath. "Well, wow. It just gets better."

I didn't respond. My eyes were still on the ceiling, my chest rising and falling. My mind was numb, my body alive.

"You okay?" Her voice tried to invade my thoughts.

But something was happening to me; some part of my brain was foggy, some part of my chest had been left heavy, something changed and clicked into place, something gathered and stayed, and something grew. Something grew so fucking large, untamable.

Her weight shifted on the bed, and I felt her hand on my chest, her eyes on me. "Elio?"

I blinked, turning my head and swallowing when I caught her gaze.

"You look like you've seen a ghost. You just went pale,"

she said with a cautious laugh. "Are you getting a fever?" She pressed her knuckles against my neck.

I shook my head.

"What happened? Did you remember something?"

I shook my head.

"What's going on—"

"Do you have a chessboard?"

She frowned, my question seeming to have caught her off guard.

"Wh-what?"

"Do you have a chessboard? I have the sudden urge to play." *Make my brain work normally again.*

"Oh, uh . . . you were thinking about chess when you were fucking me?"

"I wasn't thinking when I was—" I stopped, refusing to use the *f*-word again. "With you, when I was with you—just now."

Something like wariness flashed through her eyes. "You're acting weird."

I blinked. "I think we should wash up." And then I was standing, leaving the bed, leaving her side, going into the en suite bathroom. I closed the door and let out a breath.

I locked my eyelids tightly together before pulling them back open, blocking my thoughts, blocking my mind, blocking whatever this was.

Dealing with it now was impossible, so I kept it, held it, and suppressed it for later.

I was back in my clothes, and Zahra was coming out of the bathroom when I moved to put my shoes on; she frowned at me. "You're leaving?"

"Yes, I have—"

"You just got here . . . I mean, if you want to leave, I'm not stopping you, but did you just come here for sex?"

I looked up at her just in time to see her sitting on the edge of the bed, wearing a faded green T-shirt and new blue jean shorts, watching me with a confused frown.

"I've been here for almost four hours now. I was with your friends before I came in here. My intentions weren't to have sex with you. It just happened because . . . well . . . it was—"

"Do you want to stay?" she asked.

I paused. "Pardon?"

She cleared her throat. "You hung out with everyone for hours . . . what about me?"

"What do you want to do?" I asked, schooling my surprise and suppressing the warmth in my chest.

She grinned suddenly. "Remember when you wanted us to watch that show about Lucifer?"

I had no interest in the show or sitting down staring at people reading lines from a script. "Yes, I remember."

"We can watch it now."

I had to see Casmiro. He would be arriving today, and I needed to fill him in on the progress with Kareem and attend a brief signing meeting with—

"If you don't want to, that's fine—"

"Let's watch it," I said, arranging my shoes back by the side of the bed.

She got to her feet, tilting her head as she approached me with a sly smile. "Canceling plans for me?"

"Are you going to put it on?"

She reached for me, wrapping her arms around my body, startling me with a genuine smile while she looked up at me. "That's really nice of you. No one has ever canceled plans for me."

I looked down at her with a frown. "When was it mentioned by me in the past few minutes that I canceled plans for you?"

"You didn't have to mention it."

"I won't comment because I believe everyone is allowed to be delusional."

She held my wrists, pulling me back toward the bed. "I hope you don't mind spoilers."

"What are spoilers?"

I found out an hour later when she told me all that would happen in the first episode before I had the chance to actually watch it.

At first, it wasn't annoying. I loved listening to her talk, but three episodes in, I wanted to be surprised by what was happening next. I learned from how the main character examined his thoughts, and was interested in seeing his story through. It was like reading a book but watching it happen.

Hours fell into hours, hours where I reprimanded her, kicked her off the bed, and decided to leave but stopped when she promised to quit telling me what happened, who the killer was, and why they killed the victim.

At some point, I sent a message to Casmiro, telling him I would be running late.

And yes, I ran late; the day turned into night. I was on the last episode of the first season. Zahra had left for almost an hour, brought dinner later, and I was still watching.

I watched until the second season started, and the person who'd roped me into it was fast asleep by my side.

I couldn't sleep, so I kept on watching . . .

I liked the show, I liked hearing her breathe beside me, and I liked being in the same space where Elia dwelled.

I felt wholly comfortable for the first time in a long while; all troubling thoughts were set aside.

All that mattered now was this. This show, this woman beside me, and this feeling slowly coming to life in my chest.

CHAPTER THIRTEEN

Elio

The man sitting opposite me was agitated. Flustered. Guilty of crimes I did not care to unearth; I only cared about the discernible fact that he was wasting my time. I had other pressing matters to attend to. But Casmiro had informed me that if it were something he could have overseen himself, he would have done it.

I sat at the head of the table, with the document the man had brought forward lying right in front of me, untouched.

Angelo sat on my left side with a laptop. Casmiro was on my right, with work folders requiring my attention in front of him. They were waiting for me to speak first, the room silent as a show of respect, but I remained quiet. Soldiers manned every corner in and outside the space, those who belonged to the stranger, Angelo, Casmiro, and me.

The minute the man walked into the boardroom in my suite, his eyes latched onto me like he was staring at a myth, like he had only just confirmed my existence. He still had a confident form, but his eyes laid bare all his weakness and strength.

I lifted my gaze to both men standing behind him, faces stoic, eyes forward. I looked back down at the lean man before removing the cigar from my mouth and blowing out the smoke.

The silence was loud, palpable, filled with tension.

Lifting both fingers that held the thick stick of my cigar, I motioned to his bodyguards. "Are they here to kill me?"

The man's eyes widened as he gestured for the men to find

another place to stand. They did so promptly, and the man threw an apologetic smile my way. "The Marino bodyguards of the Caporegime society take their jobs *very* seriously, Mr. Marino," he informed me. "They are well trained, skillful, and attentive. If you are ever in need of their services, we will have a team sent right to the headquarters, sir."

"Do my soldiers look incapable of protecting me?"

The man blinked rapidly, shaking his head. "That was not what I implied by my offer—"

"Offer?"

"I meant . . ." he blurted, sweat gathering between his brows. "My *suggestion*, Mr. Marino. A mere suggestion."

I kept my gaze steady on him, relaxing back on the soft leather chair. "Do your words fail you, Armato?" I asked, bringing the cigar to my lips again, taking a drag, and letting out the smoke, my focus still on the dark-haired man with the receding hairline. "Do you perhaps need water or a drink, or would you prefer a cigar to help you function properly?"

The man gulped, shifting in his seat. "I am all right, Mr. Marino."

"Hm." I nodded. "You came on behalf of the MCSS?"

"Yes."

"As their . . ."

"Spokesperson, sir."

I frowned. "Are you usually this transparent and uncoordinated when you conduct business on behalf of the Society?"

He cleared his throat. "Permission to speak freely, sir?"

I watched him for a few seconds before nodding once.

"Thank you, sir." He sat up, straightening his suit. "Forgive my lack of self-control; it's difficult to determine how to approach you. Your name is all we know, and what we have heard from different mouths is all we see of you. Some people in the Society can never put a face to the name, and our messages and requests stop directly at the door of Mr. Valerio. I act out of character because I am overwhelmed with the privilege of sitting before you, sir."

I suppose I have my father to thank for that.

"I see," I said. "You feel privileged and overwhelmed, yet you choose to disturb my vacation."

"For which I apologize, Mr. Marino. The matter was rather pressing, and my boss had tried and failed to reach you directly via email."

"He will continue to try and fail," I responded.

The man's mouth fell open and then closed again.

I sat up, pressing my cigar to the ashtray before picking up my glasses, putting them on, and opening the file. In my peripheral vision, I caught Armato's surprise, clearly not expecting me to take much interest in the file's contents.

Casmiro inched forward toward me, his seat creaking under his movement as he did. "It contains information for the shipment—"

"I can read," I cut him off without letting my eyes leave the pages.

He inched backward in his seat.

The room grew quiet as my eyes perused the pages, reading line after line. A clock was ticking in the background. The light vibration beneath my feet as the cruise ship hummed was extremely loud, and the breathing of every man in the room was careful, waiting—ceasing, when I frowned.

"If I am correct"—I turned my head toward Casmiro—"this shipment was the one that had been shifted due to two added containers?"

"Yes."

"That should have arrived, shouldn't it?"

"Yes, but it was shifted to a later date because three more containers were added at the last minute, as the information from the MCSS explains."

I nodded, looking back at the date written there. "August of next year. That is eleven months from now."

"Yes, as stated," Casmiro responded.

My frown deepened, and I turned my head toward Casmiro again. "Didn't you tell me you already signed off on it? Why do they require my signature?"

"It is a huge shipment. Due to the added containers, they would need your signature as the overall overseer."

"I see," I said, uncomfortable as I read through the last lines of the document to the space that required my signature.

I looked up at the spokesperson, Armato. Eyes wide in anticipation, like his life was riding on the signature I was supposed to give.

Something was wrong.

I looked at Casmiro. "Did you confirm what contents are in these containers?"

"I tried, but they told me they were not allowed to say."

"And who made that law?"

Casmiro cleared his throat, now looking uncomfortable and confused as he said, "You did."

I turned my head toward Angelo for confirmation, and he nodded.

"I see," I said, my gaze lifting to Armato. "The person who sent you to me, what position do they hold?"

Armato straightened up. "Federico Gennaro, the chairman of the MCSS, and his right hand, a Russian associate, Leonid Novikov, and their whole council."

The Russian name was unfamiliar, but I recognized Gennaro.

"And this council consists of how many countries holding a seat?"

"Ten, sir."

"It used to be five," I said.

"Yes, sir." Armato cleared his throat. "An invitation for the election and induction ceremony had been sent to you to welcome the new club members two years ago."

It was my fault for not being well-versed in the business of the MCSS. I never wanted to participate in the Society. They were just another part of my father's business I had pushed to the side when I took the seat—another one I would have brought to the ground eventually.

"So, from what I remember, there's Italy, Russia, France, Spain, the United Kingdom, and . . . ?"

Armato looked about ready to melt on his seat. "The United States, South Africa, India, South Korea, and Thailand."

My frown deepened, alarm bells ringing in my head. "They breached Europe?"

"Yes, sir, it was a huge event, a lot of—"

I snapped my head toward Casmiro. "Why did this information not reach me?"

Casmiro's jaw clenched. "You had placed strict orders about delivering information for the MCSS, though I did present the issue despite that, but you did not acknowledge it at that time, Marino."

"If I may," Angelo spoke up, "the MCSS is a sovereign society; though you oversee their affairs, they are allowed to make decisions of this magnitude without consulting you, as per the rules you set in place years ago."

When my father took over from his father, he had lived and ruled by their standing laws, but when I was old enough to have my own signature, he changed everything, using my name, *Elio Marino*, the mastermind behind their new affairs, the man who told his father it would be wise to call in capos from other families, the man whom no one sees, the man who reformed the grand society amongst our capos, including other caporegimes from influential families in neighboring European countries, as per my father's hand.

This new information was taking up a larger space in my

head, and I did not like it. It left a bad taste on my tongue, and I most certainly did not have the time or the space to give it more attention than absolutely necessary.

"So." I straightened my glasses. "The council needs my signature to allow the shipment a safe passage."

"Exactly, sir," Armato spoke.

The papers stated that the contents in the containers weren't in danger of tainting the family name, and it was tagged as "normal cargo," the same tag they've been using for decades.

I sighed, looking over at Angelo.

"We have more pressing matters. This is MCSS business; there's not much we can do unless you decide to conduct a full-scale investigation, which might take months. I checked the documents beforehand, and they are more or less the same format as their previous shipments," he stated.

I looked back at Armato, picking up my pen, uncapping it. "Extend my message to your chairman; tell him that the next time he decides to interrupt my time without proper preparations, I will be changing a lot of rules. It would be kind to include the important notion that it is a threat I intend to follow through on."

Receding Hairline swallowed, straightening like a rod. "Yes, sir, I will do exactly that."

The second I placed the pen to paper, a small chaos at the entrance stopped my hand. I frowned, raising my head at the familiar voice before I saw her approaching, hair straightened and styled with a bang, half pulled up in a short ponytail, and half left down. It confirmed my realization that her hair had grown a few inches longer than its normal length.

She wore an oversized sweater tucked upward to showcase half of her stomach and waist. Her legs were covered with white oversized pants, and she wore white boots. Like she was preparing to go out, with a stylish pair of glasses resting perfectly atop her hair.

Soldiers rushed after her like they were trying to stop her, but it was too late; she was already here.

"Oh." She grinned, looking around us as everyone at the table turned to look at her; soldiers around the lounge stepped forward in a move to contain her. "The boy band together again. No wonder these gentlemen didn't want me in here."

One of the soldiers moved to grab her hand, but she was quick to swing it from his reach, turning her gaze to his. "Touch me and lose a hand. I am skilled when it comes to mutilating; remember that."

I sighed, raising my hand to put them at ease.

"What is the meaning of this?" Casmiro spoke loudly, his voice laced with anger and irritation.

Zahra turned toward us again, approaching with a carefree grin, hips swaying, her confidence at its peak. "Hi, Cassie, I see you're back and feeling better; I did not miss seeing you healthy, just so you know," she said, slapping his shoulder before raising her gaze to Angelo. "Hi, Angie." She acknowledged him with a smile before her bright eyes settled on Armato, who looked confused at the change in the situation. "Hi, man I don't know."

And then she moved behind me, her arms coming around my shoulders in a hug from behind, lips smacking against my cheek. "Hola, my pretty-eyed boyfriend who never checks his phone for text messages, thereby forcing me to go through the extra hassle of coming all the way here, interrupting his meeting, for which he cannot get angry at me because I texted almost ten times. I think my thumb broke."

"Boy—what?" Casmiro asked with a wide-eyed, horrified look on his face.

"What's the matter, Cassie? Gunshots messed with your ears?" she asked, her voice closer to my ear, her perfume softening my senses.

"E, what the fuck is this?" Casmiro asked, spine straight, ready to tackle the trouble behind me.

I let out a breath, dropping the pen as I removed her arms from around me, pulling her to my side and meeting her stubborn gaze. "Can you come back another time? I am in the middle of—"

"Nope, there's a getaway boat waiting to take us to the city; I booked it this morning after texting you about coming with me to get a tattoo done."

"What the fuck is happening right now?" Casmiro asked.

"Zahra," Angelo spoke up, "if you could, please read the room and return when Marino is—"

"I am not canceling my plans," she stated in a firm voice.

I held her wrist. "Zahra—"

"I am still not canceling my plans."

I turned to the table. "If you would . . . give me a moment. I apologize for the interruption," I said, getting to my feet and pulling her with me toward the small door that led to the main suite.

"I am not apologizing."

"Okay, but stop being a nuisance, and put yourself away; when I am done here, I will come to you."

Her brows twitched, offended. "Right, I am being a nuisance for taking the whole morning, planning this fucking little trip so that we could go to the city together as a thank-you for being kind to my friends and getting to know them."

"That was—"

"It doesn't matter; I'll go alone," she said, already turning, but I pulled her sharply back, seeing as my hand was still around her wrist. She glared at me. "Punching you in front of the people who answer to you will not be a good picture for your boy band yearbook. Let me go."

"I do not disregard your efforts. You only arrived at the wrong time. It was a bit disrespectful on your part that you ignored—"

"Do I look like I give a shit?"

I heard Casmiro curse from behind me.

"Por favor, Zahra, wait for me; I'll be done here in a few minutes—"

"Twenty minutes, or I'm gone."

"Thirty."

"Twenty-five."

"Thirty-five."

She groaned, her gaze flicking behind me to the table, a frown on her neatly trimmed brows before she looked back at me. "Who's the sweaty guy with the receding hairline?"

"Someone."

"Oh no, secret stuff I can't know about," she said, her voice flat as I let go of her wrist. "Are the cats in the living room?"

"No."

"Fine, thirty minutes. Any more, and I'm out of here, with or without you."

"Thank you," I told her as my eyes took her in again. "You look amazing. Brighter than usual."

She pressed her lips into a thin line before widening it into a smile. "I know, but I mostly look brighter because I have a"—she tilted her head to the side, increasing her pitch level so everyone would hear—"boyfriend who is fucking me right!"

Casmiro groaned.

Zahra's grin faded into a glare. "Thirty minutes." And then she walked back the way she'd come in, and closed the door behind her.

A little mortified, irritated, and regretful, I returned to the table and took my seat.

"I apologize again," I said.

"Oh no." Armato laughed. "I understand; my wife gets into moods like that; you can never tell with our women these days."

I did not return his amusement; my stare remained blank, and his smile faded.

"Where were we?" I asked, picking up the pen, not looking at Casmiro because I knew he was frowning and would love nothing more than to bombard me with questions and unwanted opinions.

I signed on both spaces indicated, closed the file, and passed it to Angelo.

"Do not forget to pass on my message to your chairman, Armato."

"I won't forget," he replied with a firm nod.

A few minutes later, Angelo was escorting him out. The moment they were gone and the soldiers around us had reduced in number, Casmiro attacked me with questions.

"What the hell was that? You're in a relationship with her?"

"Yes."

His eyes widened. "Have you gone insane?"

"No." I frowned.

"She's trouble."

"I am aware."

He groaned in frustration. "I am only looking out for you, E. You saw the ruckus she almost caused today."

Sighing, I rubbed my eyes behind the reading glasses. "I tamed it."

"Still, you have to draw a line; what she did was unacceptable."

I nodded. "I will talk to her."

"Why are you responding like you don't care about anything I'm saying?"

I leveled him with a tired stare. "It's because you are repeating things I already know, *hermano*. I appreciate your care, but you must also show her respect—"

He looked offended, appalled. "Like hell I will."

I softened my voice. "She is my partner now."

"And I am still convinced she tried to fucking kill me."

"Casmiro," I started, and he grumbled, shaking his head, not supporting my decision. "I won't ask you to understand. The two of you certainly do not like each other for reasons best kept between you. I do not want to get involved because I care about both of you. But understand that she's a part of my life now, and you're also a part of my life, and you will have to tolerate it."

He looked like he wanted to peel my words out of the air before they reached him. "What about your brother?"

"He is learning to tolerate it."

"God." He shook his head, remaining quiet for a few minutes before shaking his head again. "This is . . ." He trailed off, allowing another stretch of silence. "It's none of my business, who you date, but I swear to God, one concrete piece of evidence against her, and I'm pulling this whole issue of my distrust back up, alongside a permanent solution to it."

"I understand."

"Good," he said, hands going to the other files on the table. "Now about the other matters—"

"We . . . will have to postpone that for another time . . . because she's in there . . . waiting."

"This is work, political work, that you roped me into, and now I am swimming in endless fucking minutes of meetings that I have to oversee and find solutions to. I am talking about areas that require *urgent* attention; I need your expertise."

My gaze shifted toward the door before falling back to Casmiro. "I want nothing more than to sit down and discuss politics with you, but that woman in there will not understand, and I—"

He shot to his feet.

"Casmiro."

"Let me know when you're free," he said, gathering all the papers without meeting my eyes, turning to leave before stopping, pinning a glare on the door, and then looking back at me. "Be careful."

"I will."

With a shake of his head and much hesitation, he made his way out of the lounge area.

I allowed a breath to fall through my lips as I looked back at the door. I knew why he acted this way. I knew he was feeling betrayed, wondering why I wasn't doing more to get into the matter of his attack.

"I am still convinced she tried to fucking kill me."

Casmiro's voice replayed in my head, but I suppressed it. Suppressed his worry, buried the tight feeling in my gut.

I am wrong. My gut is wrong this time. My mind has compromised my gut, and my mind is unstable, so there is a 7.5 percent chance that I am wrong.

I held onto that percentage. I held onto it tight.

"Sorry about the cheap car rental," Zahra said from the driver's seat of the 2010 Toyota Camry, one hand on the steering wheel and the other on a cup of coffee we had stopped to get while we waited for the car. She didn't accept my offer to pay for anything, so I let her handle it to avoid another argument. "Street and I spent a lot of money on the suite and the other cruise expenses."

I didn't respond; my focus was on my phone as I responded to Gemma's text with a frown.

Me:
This is what I keep talking about. Your carelessness and naivety. I care about you, which is why I will not tolerate situations that will inevitably hurt you in the near future.

Gemma (blonde car highway):
Omg, relax, my love, it's harmless, just one date.

I knew of her interest in Angelo, but I didn't know Angelo would entertain or reciprocate it. I have never cared about his romantic life; I only knew he never brought it into the business. I trusted him not to be careless with her, but his schedule was hectic and it would not end well for either of them.

Not to mention Casmiro, his focus would be off because, unlike me, he cared about Angelo's dating life and would become even more grumpy than he already was.

And that I could not deal with.

Me:
One date can create many inconveniences I want to avoid dealing with.

"It's funny how money can look so large one minute, and the next, you're wondering how the hell it's gone; it's not like we spend much." The car maneuvered onto another busy street. "But now I'm guessing being rich for a moment isn't even the goal anymore; being rich enough to remain comfortable is what we should aim for. The gold can get us there, and then we could invest . . ."

She was still talking when Gemma's response came in.

Gemma (blonde car highway):
You really have nothing to worry about; we'll be fine.

". . . I don't know which tattoo I'm going to get, but probably when I get there . . ."

Me:
Illogical, Gemma.

". . . this food place that serves amazing dishes; you'll be obsessed after tasting their daily special . . ."

Gemma (blonde car highway):
But I really, really really really feel a connection, and I don't want to lose that; you must also know how that feels.

"Who are you texting?"

I raised my head to catch her glancing at my phone and then me, before she focused on the road again.

"Someone," I responded, looking back at the screen and shooting off a final message.

Me:
We will continue this conversation when I return.

I pressed the side button and focused on Zahra.

"You were saying?"

She shrugged. "Never mind." She pulled in next to a tattoo and piercing store, which looked like a place I would never go. "We're here!"

"Why, if I may ask, do you need a tattoo?"

She turned off the engine, turning to look at me. "I already told you, but you didn't hear . . . texting and all, come on." She smiled. "I'll explain while we're in there."

The store wasn't too small or too large, but the music was odd and disturbed my ears. Sounds of tattoo needles on skin came from behind a door to the left. It was a little dark inside, black leather seats pressed against the artful black walls littered with several colors in drawings and eye-catching designs. It was a little warm, and the smell of ink couldn't be covered by whatever air freshener was busy spitting out fragrance every minute. There was a faint smell of sweat that also irritated me.

I hated the environment, but I kept quiet.

Zahra walked to the little reception desk, occupied by a woman with a buzzcut and piercings on her lips, nose, and brows; tattoos littered her skin. "'Sup, Tatty," Zahra greeted with a grin. "Been a while!"

Tatty responded with a surprisingly calm smile. "Zahra, I'm shocked; what has it been—a year?"

"Business these days—got myself in a bit of a situation that had me off the grid for months now. It's been crazy."

Tatty's eyes shifted to me. "Oh, I see; who's the beauty glaring at us?"

I was not glaring.

"He's with me, and trust me, that is not a glare," Zahra said, glancing briefly at me. "Where's Julio?"

A door opened on one side, and a big, tatted man emerged with a huge grin on his face. "Zahra, mi amor," he said.

She turned, and beamed . . . *beamed.*

"Julio, mon cœur, I've missed you!"

And then they were hugging.

Right there, a few feet away from me.

I had suddenly become invisible.

The man looked to be in his late twenties; he had a young face, and it was apparent that he visited the gym frequently.

They pulled apart, and the man's eyes took her in before settling on her chest, raising his hands in an attempt to touch her. "How are these beauties—"

My feet moved, and my hand grabbed the man's wrist before it could meet her chest; I squeezed it, aiming to shatter his bones beyond repair.

"Nng—Ow, ow, ow, amigo!" the man screeched, his body bending with my hold, trying to stop me from breaking his wrist.

Zahra's gasp reached my ears as she grabbed my arm, trying to release my hold. "Elio, what the fuck? Let go of him."

My stare burned into his. "Do you just touch women without their permission?"

"What the—No, I was trying to check—"

"Check what?"

"To see—Ah!"

"Jesus, Elio, let him go! He's Julio; remember the guy I told you about, the one who did my piercings?"

My grip tightened, and the man folded, dancing on his feet in pain, pain that was reflected in his face.

"You do not touch her," I told him.

"I won't. I won't!"

"That sounds like a promise made out of fear. Swear to me that you will not touch her again, and if you do, I am allowed to break your wrist and subject you to a life where you will run at the sight of a tattoo pen or any pen in general because not only will I break your wrist, I will *break you*. Swear it."

"I swear, no touch, no touching your angel, at all."

I let him go.

Zahra let out a breath, shooting a frown my way as she said, "You . . . God—" She stopped, her voice tight as she turned to Julio with an apologetic look. "Julio, I am so sorry."

"No, no apologies." The man couldn't meet my gaze. "I . . . I didn't know you now have a . . . spouse."

Zahra sighed. "Yeah, uh . . . can you bring out the design catalog?"

"Of course." The man rushed away, looking back at me. "I am sorry again, mister."

And then he disappeared through the door he had come out of.

Zahra turned sharply to me. "That was—"

"We are leaving."

"No, we are not." She fought me. "This place was a second home for me; I worked here for a few weeks, and—"

"I do not care, Zahra. We *are* leaving and going somewhere else."

"No." A glare, accompanied by irritation, flared in her eyes as she crossed her arms against her chest, her guard rising. "There's nothing wrong with this place, and you have no *fucking* right to tell me what I can and cannot *fucking* do."

"You were just going to let him touch you? Right in front of me?"

"It's norm—"

"Even if you weren't in front of me, you would have let him touch you?"

She sighed. "It's how we are, we—we're friends; I mean, he's seen all there is to see about my fucking titties, and I was here frequently during that time—"

"Did you hear what I just asked?"

"I did. And I'm telling you, it wouldn't have offended me if he had touched me."

I blinked at her, utterly dumbfounded, my anger eating away at my resolve. The fact that she even saw the need to argue with me on this.

"I am standing right here, and you are also standing right here, telling me you would have not been offended if another man had touched you that way, right in front of me, right in front of the person you are supposedly dating, the person you are supposedly in a committed relationship with."

Her mouth opened, closed, opened again. "I mean . . . when you put it like that—"

"I know you don't like me on a large scale, and we have our many disagreements, but a little regard and a little respect would be highly appreciated."

"Says the guy who was texting—" She clenched her jaw, stopped, breathed. "Fine. You are right. It's just, I'm used to that kind of familiarity with Julio, and I didn't think it would offend you because it never used to . . . offend me, and sometimes I don't think about the, you know . . . committed relationship thing. It will take some getting used to, but I realize how this could have looked." She cleared her throat. "Sorry, it won't happen again. No more letting men grope my boobies because now I have a big bad psycho boyfriend who owns my boobies . . . Does the commitment include that? You owning my boobies?"

"Stop saying . . . *boo—that,*" I ground out, knowing she was trying to make light of the situation, but I was still angry, still disturbed by what I'd just witnessed and what she had tried to defend.

"Right." She shot me a sly smile. "Sticking to titties . . . or my big roundish chest balls? Fleshy oranges? Chest growths? Uh . . . fluffy bosom, filled-up circles? Tropical chest coconuts? Heavenly—"

"Stop, just—stop." I rubbed my eyes. "Where are the car keys?"

Her smile faltered. "What for?"

"I will wait there until you're finished here."

Her face fell. "Why?"

"The car keys, Zahra."

"It's not that deep. I already apologized—"

"I would *hate* to argue in front of an audience." I looked over at the Tatty woman, who did not bother to hide that she was looking and listening.

Looking back at Zahra, I put out my hand. She sighed, fishing in her small bag for the keys. When she found them, she dropped them into my palm.

"Elio—"

I was already walking away from her and out of the shop, itching with a need to project my anger, the jealousy twisting my gut from her blatant ignorance regarding what that man had wanted to do.

They might have been friends who groped each other—*if there was a friendship of that sort*—but she had *me* now; it should have gone without saying that there was a fucking line neither of us should cross with other people.

Or maybe she saw no need for that line because whatever this was, it wasn't serious for her.

Overbearing and controlling were the last things I wanted to be. Those traits set off her alarm bells; I saw it in how she had locked her shoulders when I told her we were leaving; I knew she would bite off my finger instead of allowing me the space to demand we leave.

I wasn't blind to the privileges she had given me, the little trust she had let in, and I did not intend to misuse it. So I had to leave that space to contain myself because acting on my primal thoughts would have resulted in something more serious.

I did not want my anger to take away the little trust we seemed to have built. Or to supply her with the notion that I was exhibiting traits like the other men who had fed off the control they had on her.

It was apparent that, like her, I was clueless when it came to relationships.

I sighed, breathing in fresh air, before I got into the car, grabbed my phone, and placed a call to Angelo.

It rang three times before he picked up.

"Marino?"

"Do you recall that time I told you that if I needed relationship advice, I would come to you?"

"Uh . . . yeah?"

"Good, now is that time," I told him. "I need relationship advice."

CHAPTER FOURTEEN

Zahra

"Men, am I right?" I raised my hands, dropping them with a tight smile as I approached the counter. Tatty shot me a knowing stare that made me slump my shoulders and groan in exasperation.

"When I realized you two were together-*together*, I regretted not having popcorn to see Julio get beat up," she admitted.

Despite my worry, a smile tainted my lips. "Me too . . . kind of. But that's me and Julio, Tatty. That's how we play."

"Letting him touch your tits in front of a man who gives *I can squash you till you're dust* energy? Yeah, no, you were playing with Julio's life at that point. Besides, you've got yourself a man now; you can't be letting Julio touch you like that anymore, or talk to you like that in front of your man. That's not cool."

"Yeah, probably, but you don't know Elio, okay? He's—I mean, he can be a little extra sometimes, and it's not like I knew he would get offended. Besides, he ignored me throughout the ride here, and you don't see me being a bitch about it, in fact, I didn't care. Why? Because I am mature and I will not be that person. I'm bigger than that."

Tatty laughed, shaking her head. "I did not miss that attitude."

I grinned. "I know you love me, everyone loves me, they just like to pretend they don't love me, but I know they do. I am very lovable."

Her stare gave *Really?* as she snorted and said, "Okay, Zahra." She shook her head. "How did it go with that Devil kid, though?

You guys still roll?" she asked, assembling different needles to racks.

"Yeah, Elio's his brother."

She stopped. "You're dating the brother of your fuck buddy?"

"Yup—well, Devil's not my fuck buddy anymore. We ended it."

"So, you moved on with his brother."

I shrugged. "I mean, you've seen his brother."

"I *have* seen his brother, and I see why, but girl, you move fast."

I laughed. "Is Daiyu in?" I asked.

"Yup, with all you need."

My smile slipped off my face as I nodded.

"The operation is a go then?" she asked, and I shifted on my feet.

"Yup."

"Are you okay? To carry it through?"

I shook my head. "No. But if Daiyu's lead is right, and Handlers are really on the cruise, I don't care about anything else. Those kids need saving."

"Oh, God—he's gone." Julio's words came out cautiously from behind me, cutting our conversation short.

I turned with a sly smirk. "And you scream like a girl. What have I taught you, Julio?"

"Shush." He'd placed ice on his wrist, cautiously stepping out from behind the door, looking around like Elio might pop up with a gun to finish him off. "A little heads-up would have been nice. Where the fuck did you find him anyway?"

"Brother of the fuck buddy," Tatty supplied with a smirk.

Julio turned his head to look at me, staring blankly, the catalog tucked under his arm. "Why am I even surprised? Only you would pull something like that; family dinner must be eventful."

"Ha," I chortled, and grabbed the catalog when he turned

his shoulder, gesturing for me to take it, seeing as he was busy icing his bruised wrist. "No family dinners yet, but hopefully soon. I'll get popcorn, record the whole thing, and send it to you," I said, opening the catalog.

"What does he do?" Julio asked, leaning on the counter.

"Eh . . . politics, inside politics, business shit."

When I noticed their quietness, I looked up and between both of them before adding, "You know, that serious-people shit that helps the nation?"

Julio nodded.

"Yeah, that's what he does."

"Must be loaded," Tatty said, leaning against the counter while I looked back at the catalog in my hands, flipping page after page of the designs.

"He is," I agreed. "Hit the jackpot with that one."

Julio's laugh was mocking. "Not like it's any use for you. You have a whole ci—"

"We don't—" I looked around, my heart lurching as if Elio would pop out of nowhere. "We don't talk about that."

"I forget. Apologies, ma'am." Julio smiled.

"That gloved-hand friend of yours was here," Tatty cut in.

"Vitale?" I asked, my eyes not leaving the catalog.

"Yup, the hot creepy fucker," Tatty said. "Said he knew you would drop by here because you were around the area, and to give you a message."

I looked up, my attention grabbed. "What message?"

"*Bells are ringing,*" Julio answered. "He said to tell you that, word for word."

"What is that about?" Tatty asked.

I sighed, my annoyance spiking by the second, as I offered my clueless friends a tight smile. "He writes nursery rhymes, and, well—loves to drop hints of the new shit he's working on here and there. I'm pretty sure he dropped one for Layla because he knows I eat at her family's restaurant whenever I'm down here."

"Creep," Tatty muttered.

"You can't blame him; he was dropped too many times as a kid and has so many issues because of it. In fact, give me a sec; I'll call him to let him know that I got his message." I smiled, pulling out my phone from my purse as I moved to another spot in the reception area, placing a call to the fucking bone in my throat.

He answered on the third ring. *"I see your friends delivered my message."*

"Vitale, what is your problem? Ambushing my friends, ambushing me? *Threatening me?*"

"It got you to call me, didn't it?"

I rubbed my eyes. "Where the fuck are you?"

"Sicily."

"Great, stay there, and don't call or come here until I ask you to."

"Are you telling me what to do?"

"That's *exactly* what I'm doing."

"You wouldn't even ask me why I went back to Sicily quicker than intended?"

"No, because I don't care, and because I really wanted you gone."

"Ask me."

I closed my eyes, letting out a controlled breath. "Vitale, I don't have time for this."

"Ask me."

"Fine! What happened to you, sweetheart? Why did you leave so early? I really wanted to spend time with you, it's so unfortunate, but please tell me why you left. I really wanna know so bad because this aching in my chest, I can't—I can't control it. I just need to know why you left because I don't think I'll survive if you don't fucking tell me."

Without seeing him, I knew he was smiling. I rolled my eyes so hard it hurt.

I heard him clear his throat. *"Well, your, uh—recent bed-buddy asked me to leave. He didn't come to me, but he had people come to me. They threw around threats here and there, gave me hours . . . a head start."*

I raised my brows. "Oh, that's expected. I'm surprised he didn't kill you."

"Yeah, me too. But I am intrigued. You know me, I love a good drama," his voice drawled. *"I love playing in it. Especially when I know my role is one I would win at. I know what's coming so . . . this will be interesting."*

Anger sliced against my chest as I took the phone from my ear, closed my eyes, gritted my teeth, and let out a steady breath.

Opening my eyes again, I pressed the phone back to my ear. "Marino has nothing to do with this."

"Yeah, keep telling yourself that, Faizan."

"Stay *away* from him."

I heard him give a wistful sigh.

"I fucking mean it, Vitale. You fuck with him, then you fuck with me; there's no going around it."

He scoffed, then said, *"I'll be seeing you soon, Faizan."*

The call disconnected.

I squeezed my phone as I pulled it from my ear. "Fuck," I muttered, pressing the bridge of my nose. I wanted to hit something so badly, something that looked and smelled and talked and walked like Vitale fucking Conti. Schooling my features, I turned back to Tatty and Julio. "What did I say?" I walked toward them with a grin. "He was so eager to talk about his new addition to his upcoming album."

"That I understand, but what's up with the gloves?"

I blew out a breath. "Every man in their family wears gloves, don't even get me started on it. It's like some occultic tradition they can't talk about. Crazy." And that was the truth. Vitale always wore gloves like Manuel, their fathers, brothers, cousins, uncles, and nephews.

The Contis were a weird society I didn't want to get

involved with more than I already was. I had no reason to bother them as long as they didn't bother me.

"Let's see . . . I need a shoulder tattoo, something small but symbolic."

"Shoulder?" Julio asked, surprised. "That's too innocent for you."

"Trust me, I know. But I gotta cover a gunshot wound."

Tatty gasped, eyes wide, with surprise lacing her voice. "Gunshot?"

"Yup."

"You're usually more careful," Julio pointed out.

"That I am. It took me by surprise. Luckily, it wasn't fatal," I said, my eyes centering on a heart-shaped design. I dropped the catalog on the table, turning my head to an angle to see the shape of the design forming an E. I smirked to myself, pointing at the heart-shaped design. "This one, I want this one, but with some changes." I looked up at Julio. "We won't finish closing up the heart; we'll stop the curve at this point." I indicated with my finger. "And then from this other bit, it's going to have, like, a thunder shape design, but . . . one that looks like the letter *M*."

"Hmm, I can picture what you're saying, but maybe draw it out so we'll get the full picture?"

Tatty provided paper and a pen, and I carefully drew it out how I wanted it to look. "There, but with more expertise."

"Got it, I'll call up Daiyu."

At the mention of her name, my mind became burdened by the side mission I kept safely hidden from Street and Elio.

The things I would have to do to get them off that cruise ship.

I hadn't exactly lied to Elio about needing to get a tattoo done, I'd merely omitted the other reason this tattoo parlor was the very one I'd walked into.

CHAPTER FIFTEEN

Twelve years ago

Zahra

Mr. Handler was good.

Mr. Handler would never hurt me.

Mr. Handler cared for me, and loved me.

Mr. Handler was my friend . . .

But.

He made me cry. He lured me to his room. He pushed his tongue into my mouth. He carried me to his bed when I begged him to stop. He tried to touch me like our visitors did.

He hurt me.

It was the day after my twelfth birthday, and I stood by the yellow door, waiting for Miss Handler to bring my bags. She had told me earlier that I would be going to another house, and I would have new Handlers because of what Mr. Handler had done to me. It was then I realized there were other houses like ours where other brothers and sisters stayed, where we would be made to do . . . *things* for our visitors.

I realized a lot of things that morning.

Mr. Handler was confusing. His name was Manuel, and he loved me more than he did before. That was what he told me when he forcefully touched me with the same hands he used to give me ice cream and candy only hours ago when I'd smiled so big and laughed with the other children as we ate the ice cream and littered the ground with candy wrappers.

I realized something else.

Kids like me were business. A business that wasn't good,

and that was why they never let us go outside, or open the windows or see what the sky truly looked like in real time.

When Miss Handler returned with my bag, she carried a blindfold, and any hopes I had of seeing the outside died along with everything else in my chest. She left to get something else and Mr. Handler showed up. I wanted to move away from him, but he looked so familiar, like my friend, the one who gave me extra food, though he didn't give it to the others who asked. He couldn't look me in the eye but still went down on both knees in front of me, his head down. "I'm sorry, amore mio. I shouldn't have done that to you," he said.

"Will I see you again?" was all I could say, and he raised his head in surprise, like he hadn't been expecting me to talk to him.

"No. But I will find you," he said, holding my small hand in his warm one. "I will take you out of this; for now, I can't do much; I have to wait until you're older. Listen. When you are fourteen, your new Handler will take you away. And you will be given to someone else, your—your job will be more intense than this—I wish I could have prepared you for it, but I fucked it up . . . I'm sorry."

"When will you find me?"

He stroked my cheek, pressing his lips to my forehead. "My Zahra," he whispered. "When you're sixteen, I will come to you. Promise."

I nodded.

"Wait for me, amore mio."

Miss Handler pulled me away from Mr. Handler—Manuel. And I was taken to another house with different brothers and sisters.

When I turned fourteen, I was taken somewhere else, with some other kids who were also fourteen.

This place was terrible, and we were prepared for penetration. There weren't many older men; some of them were young, and they smoked a lot.

The first time I was penetrated hurt so much that I cried and bled. Our madam only gave me two days to recover, and then, the next time, it still hurt but wasn't as painful as the first.

In this place, I found out I had no mother or father.

I learned that I was a product of an underground operation for sperm and womb donors, where kids were being produced.

In this place, I lost all hope because I knew this was why I was born.

In this place, we were called *Plants*.

Plants were submissive and sellable. We were never to speak unless spoken to; we were tools. We were never to ask questions. We were business assets, not people. We were body parts and skin, not humans. We were dolls of pleasure with hearts and veins. We were to give, never to receive. We were nothing and no one.

I stayed with the madam and I served until I was fifteen, and then I was sent somewhere else. Our madam said I had been bought for a massive amount of money and had a new private owner.

The first time I saw my private owner, he put a bullet through another man's head.

I was kept in a small room in the big house, and almost every night, my new owner would come in and use me. He was always rough and sometimes slapped me when I wouldn't comply. Sometimes he would force me to swallow a pill so that I would want him, too; I hated it. I hated how my body felt after he gave me the drug, and I hated that I would need him to make my body feel much better. I hated him so much. But I endured.

A year passed, and I turned sixteen.

The day after my birthday, I heard gunshots, men shouting, and things blowing up. I was so scared that I backed myself into the corner of the room.

My door burst open, and I jumped at how loud it was, burying my head into myself as I pulled my knees up to my chest.

The footsteps rushed toward me, and my body shivered in fear. But the footsteps slowed, and I could tell the person was kneeling before me.

"Amore mio?"

I froze.

Slowly, ever so slowly, I looked up, my tear-filled eyes settling on that familiar face.

"My Zahra," he said breathlessly before gathering me into his arms, hugging me so tight. I cried into the crook of his neck, holding on to him for dear life. "I'm so sorry, amore mio. I'm so sorry it took me this long to find you; you're safe now."

He held me to him, and led us out. I couldn't even look at the dead bodies around me. His men were all around, too, and the shootings were still happening. He had done this; he had killed so many people for me.

He really does love me.

His home was very far away, tucked inside a vast compound he seemed to control. People parted ways for us as we walked in.

Before I could even get cleaned up, he called for a meeting, holding me by his side as he said in Italian, "This one is mine; the same respect you show me, you are to show it to her. Protect her with your life just as you would protect me. Any harm comes to her, and I will burn anything and everything any of you care about, and I will make sure you only die when the last bit of your flesh has been burnt. Am I clear?"

They all responded with small bows of respect, and he nodded, dismissing them.

"Where are we?" I asked him.

"Our home, in Sicily," he said.

"Our . . . home?"

"Yes. I have spent years building it for us to rule together. My father tried to stop it, but now even he cowers before me, and now, you share the same power, my Zahra."

I didn't respond but leaned more into him as he led me to

his bedroom. I let him strip off my clothes and carry me to the bath as he wordlessly washed my body, and I helped him wash his.

When we were done, he gave me one of his shirts, and I put it on before sitting in front of his dressing mirror and staring at the reflection of my thin face. My wet, waist-length hair made me look like a character out of a horror movie. So unnatural.

Manuel brought a hair dryer and started drying it, but I grabbed his hand. "No."

"What do you want, amore mio?"

My face remained expressionless as he held my long hair in his hands. "Can you cut it?"

He frowned. "Why? It's gorgeous," he said.

"I don't want it anymore, please."

"Are you sure?" he asked.

I nodded.

"Okay," he said, fishing for a pair of scissors. Then he placed it against my hair, still at a long length.

"No . . . higher."

He lifted the scissors until they reached my jaw; I raised my hand, stopping him. "There's fine."

He started to cut, and I closed my eyes. As he cut, I willed myself to forget every horror I'd faced until now. I shoved and shoved and shoved until I began to feel numb to the pain.

He whispered in my ear when he'd finished cutting and drying my hair. "Open your eyes."

Slowly, my eyes fluttered open, and my reflection stared back at me. I stared for a few seconds before my hand rose to touch the tips.

And for the first time since my last ice cream and candy night, a smile curved on my lips.

"I like it," I said with a scratchy voice. "I like it a lot."

CHAPTER SIXTEEN

Zahra

My mind stayed fixated on my argument with Elio as Daiyu applied the finishing touches to her work. I wanted him here, with me. Our disagreement had been unexpected, and I didn't think he would just walk away, as if he couldn't stand to be near me. I understood why he was upset, and maybe I didn't do enough to ease his worries. Maybe I didn't see why he should be worried because this wasn't something I'd done before.

Relationship. Commitment. Those were foreign words to me. Words I was only just starting to understand.

"Everything is prepared for the coming days," Daiyu said in Mandarin. *"Once you supply the coordinates, my people and I will take a getaway boat to the cruise ship."*

I nodded absentmindedly. *"I already have plans to get my friends out so I can assist,"* I responded in the language too.

She paused. *"You don't have to, Zahra. We don't know the ranks of these people. They might recognize you and send word to Sicily. I would hate to get you in trouble with Manuel."*

My chest tightened at the mention of that name. *"Don't worry about Manuel, he's taken care of,"* I said. *"And even if he wasn't and word gets back, he wouldn't care since he's no longer in the business. He left after . . . that incident."*

Daiyu nodded in understanding. *"Well, if that's the case, it wouldn't hurt to have the extra hand,"* she said.

I nodded, wondering what Elio was doing now.

"Are you sure your friends can't be involved? From what you've told me about Street, they seem like great guys."

"*They are,*" I answered. "*But the less they know about me, the easier it will be to protect them from . . . everything.*"

"*You don't think they can handle it?*"

I frowned. "*They might have been through hard times but they're innocent to this part of the world and the ugliness of it. I don't want to ruin that, I don't want to taint them like that. They deserve more.*" I sighed. "*We both know that being aware of this organization is literally the end of anyone's normal. They'd never be able to leave the box once they're in. I don't want them to be caged. I know how it feels, and I'd rather they hate me than ever have to feel what I feel every day.*"

"*You care about them.*"

I nodded. "*Yes. They showed me the meaning of family. The least I can do is make sure they leave unscathed.*"

Daiyu went quiet, but I could already hear the question before she asked it. "*You don't plan to be with them long, do you?*"

I dragged in a breath and let it out. "*I have many plans, and one of them is making sure they don't live the rest of their lives as . . . criminals. Whatever that might mean in the future, it's a burden I'm willing to bear.*"

Daiyu smiled, applying a cooling ointment to my new tattoo. "You never change, do you? Sacrificing your happiness for the sake of the people you care about," she said in English.

"That's the thing, Daiyu. I was never created to be happy. I was created to give happiness. At least now I get to choose how I do that."

She chuckled lightly. "Well, I can't argue with that."

I smiled.

"Anyway, while I might be okay with you helping, I still don't think you should risk yourself like that."

"It'll be fine."

The pain from the tattoo was dull, and my mind was moving between here and where Elio currently was. The thought of him distracted me from Daiyu's concerns. She was right to worry, but honestly, I couldn't be bothered, not when I was too busy trying to understand how the fuck everything with Elio had gotten so serious so fast, how I'd almost reached the finish line of this whole thing after starting the race without a heart or an attachment to anyone or anything.

But the past few years had impacted my life in a way I never thought they would. Street, Elio, our relationship—I was swimming with a boatload of denial, guilt, regret, and anger, heart-stopping, nerve-racking anger at the fact that I had to do any of this at all, that I had to fight in secret, a fight that was meant to be fought in broad daylight.

Hearing footsteps approaching, I turned my head toward the door. The room was occupied by Daiyu, me, and some guy who was getting his whole back inked. He had headphones in his ears. The door opened, and my eyes widened. All my previous thoughts took a back seat in my mind.

Elio walked in, his eyes finding me instantly while he closed the door behind him.

Some warm and fluffy feeling swirled around my chest at the sight of him. *He came back*. I didn't know why, but all that mattered was that he did. Maybe that was his way of showing me he wasn't mad to the point that he didn't want to be near me.

But he was here. He was around my past, around a story I'd never told. I brought him with me to create a picture, one that featured my present with my past. I wanted to see him in that lighting, to pretend even for a moment that he knew every single thing about me, and he accepted me, flaws and all.

I was careful not to move even though I had the urge to. "Hey." I smiled, but he didn't come over; he just settled onto the visitor's couch next to a kid of about eleven, who I supposed belonged to the guy getting his back tattoo.

"Hm," he responded.

"Why did you leave the car?" I swallowed. "Did something happen?"

He was looking around the room, displeasure in those

sharp eyes. "No. It was too quiet," he said before his gaze shifted to me, then Daiyu, then me. "When will you be finished?"

"Just a couple of minutes," I answered, my gaze lingering on him cautiously, trying to see if he still carried the anger he had left with, but his eyes gave nothing away, and his vibe was completely neutral.

And me, I was utterly overwhelmed, but comfortable, and weirdly happy that he was sitting there waiting for me, so dedicated.

The kid beside him had stopped playing on his phone; his head was raised toward Elio, jaw dropped, eyes wide in awe, like he was looking at something extraordinary.

Elio noticed, too, because he looked away from me to the kid by his side. He raised a brow as if to ask why the kid was looking at him.

"You are so . . . huge. Are you a wrestler?" the little boy asked.

Elio's frown grew very slowly, morphing into a glare.

I pressed my lips together, trying to suppress a laugh.

"Do you just make comments like that—"

"Elio!" I yelled, grabbing his attention and making him look at me. "He's just a kid, Jesus."

"A kid who needs to learn how to control his tongue."

"I know how to control my tongue," the kid fired back, sticking his tongue out to Elio, who inched back, looking seconds away from flicking the kid on the forehead.

"When will you be finished here?" Elio asked again, irritation lacing his voice.

"Just chill, okay?"

"I am *chill*. I would not be here if I were not *chill*."

"Okay, got it; I won't ask you to *chill* again."

Now the irritation in his eyes was directed at me.

He whipped out his phone and looked at the screen, which marked the end of the conversation; his eyes didn't leave the device until I was done and checking out the work in a mirror.

It was red, a little swollen, shiny but very neat, and simple, nothing extra. I covered it with my palm and gave a subtle nod to Daiyu before approaching Elio with a silly grin on my face. He was already on his feet, looking relieved.

"Now," I started, "I want you to tilt your head to this angle." I showed him, using myself as an example. "While you look at it."

He blinked at me, unamused. "Okay. I have no idea why you would . . ."

I removed my hand, and he trailed off.

A frown dragged his brows down, but then he tilted his head to the angle I'd asked him to, his gaze taking in the tattoo, and the frown slowly—ever so slowly—eased out of his brows, his lips parting, eyes softening sadly before they rose slowly to mine, locking, staying and searching, making my grin falter.

He looked . . . sad, appalled, terrified.

"Why would you do this?" His voice was soft, almost breathless like it took everything in him to ask that one question.

I blinked. "Why wouldn't I?"

"Those are—why would you tattoo my—my—my initials on yourself? *On your body?* Why would you do such a thing? You know this won't—you know this is permanent, right?"

I watched him warily, my excitement dying. "Yeah? I mean, I could just draw a skull over it if I get tired of it?" My gaze searched his as concern and confusion fucked with my head. "What's—what's happening right now? Why are you freaking out over this? It's not like it's a confession of my undying love or something; I have a reason for getting this one."

"What could compel—" He stopped, looked around us, and then back at me. "Can we go to the car? I don't feel comfortable discussing this here."

I nodded, and we left the room. I bid a quick farewell to all the familiar faces while rushing out with Elio right ahead of me; he opened the passenger door for me, meaning he was going to be the one to drive this time. I didn't comment on it as I got in, and he rounded the car, getting in too.

The second he locked the door beside him, his eyes latched onto mine. "Why?"

I sighed. "Remember your gun? The one that's always underneath my pillow? It has your initials, and well, you were the one who shot me with your bullet, so I tattooed your initials to the spot that you shot me, but as you can see"—I shifted my sweater to the side—"at first glance, it just looks like a heart shape and a letter *M*, but with, like, a thunder kinda font? So no one except you and me would get the concept unless, well—they turn their head that way . . ."

He shook his head. "You know the concept. That's my problem. You shouldn't have done this—you should have picked something else."

"Should I have tattooed a huge eggplant? Would you have loved that?" I snapped.

"No, it's—"

"Forget the fact that it's your initials; this was my choice, the only thing that it has to do with you is the fucking initials and the fact that you were the one who shot me there."

"Zahra—"

The groan that left my throat cut him off. "What is the big deal, for fuck's sake? I was so excited about this. It's the beginning of my tattoo era; I should be downing it with shots or something."

"It *is* a big deal." His voice was hard, same as his stare. "It will be a big deal when you look at it in the mirror every fucking day, and it reminds you of me."

I angled myself properly so my body was facing his. "*How* is that such a bad thing?"

He shook his head, hand going to mess up his hair. "Zahra,

tattoos are meant to be monumental; they're meant to mean something to you because they *stay*, okay? They don't leave your skin or fade away; they're supposed to be something you look at and—*feel* something, good or bad, depending on what they're there for. They're supposed to be *meaningful*."

"Okay?" I said softly, seeing where he was coming from. "You think you don't mean anything to me?" I asked, and his gaze fell from mine to the console. "You think I spend time or money on someone that means *nothing* to me? Do you think I'd even tattoo your fucking initials on my skin if I didn't like you so much it annoys the fucking hell out of me?"

He made some strained, uncomfortable noise that had me backing my statement.

"Elio, half of these things that I do with you, I've never done them with anybody else. I have never felt like this for anyone in my entire fucking miserable life, and sometimes I just look at myself and wonder if I'm still the same Zahra who left Sicily years ago. That's how much you affect me, you idiot, so yes, I tattooed your initials on my skin, and I love it; it's pretty, they're really fucking strong initials, and I'm wearing them proud—"

"And they're going to stay there." His gaze locked with mine. "They're going to be there, and I—what if I'm not here, Zahra?" His eyes worked, looking between mine, finding my response.

"I don't understand. Do you plan on going somewhere?"

He looked frustrated now, brows twitching between a frown and defeat before his unsure gaze fell back to the console, his lips a little downturned, eyes worried, his free hand clenching and unclenching on his thigh, which housed a leg that was now bouncing rapidly on his seat.

"Elio," I called.

He shook his head. "I apologize, but this is—"

"Just a tattoo."

He looked at me again, almost helpless, as he took my hand. "My head . . ." He looked into my eyes like he was trying to plaster his words to my brain. "My head is all kinds of messed up right now, Zahra. That—that little tattoo on your shoulder is ruining the reason why I drew this tattoo all over my body. You're undoing the only thing that I was living for."

"And that is what? Huh? To hurt yourself?"

"No. To fix this. To bring balance."

I leveled him with a glare. "A balance that involves you dying."

"You won't understand."

The scoff that left me was bitter. "I really don't want to be *that* person, and I know this is a shitty thing to say to you right now, but do you think you're the only one who's had it *tough*? People suffer worse shit, people are out there, *suffering* worse shit, living a life so despicable and vile and they don't want to fucking off themselves, and you're here blaming yourself for what happened to your family? That's not fair, Elio, because it's not even your fault! Do you think this is what they would have wanted? You think that's what your mom would have wanted?"

"Yes! This is what she wants. She told me—" He stopped. Color drained from his face. Shock filled his eyes at what he had just said.

"Elio—"

"No, forget I said anything." His voice was precise, clipped. He looked away from me; his leg stopped bouncing, his hands stopped shaking. His eyes stopped looking confused; his openness was gone. Now, all I saw was the blank wall he used to be. It was like his brain had turned, and he had just flicked on a reset button. "The tattoo caught me off guard. I did not think you would choose that kind of design. It is beautiful, nonetheless."

I blinked, unsure of what just happened. "I can't just forget what happened; you were saying something about—"

"I did not know what I was saying." He started the engine of the car. "It has been a stressful day; I think we should get food from that place you mentioned earlier; I cannot remember the name, but if you would—"

My hand covered his on the steering wheel. "Elio," I called, bringing his hand to me while I placed my hand on the other side of his face, turning his head so he could look at me. "You can tell me anything," I said, our gazes unwavering. "All jokes aside, all threats aside, I am here to listen to whatever—"

"I do not have anything to say. And stop looking at me like that. I am fine. I am not crazy."

I shook my head quickly. "I didn't say that. At all."

"Then stop looking at me like that; I don't like it."

"Okay, I just—" I blew out a breath. "Listen, if I had known the tattoo would affect you this way, I would have gotten something else."

He shook his head. "It is okay. I understand. As I said, it is a beautiful tattoo. I panicked for nothing. I am not used to this, so it is most likely normal that you do this, and it is okay. It is your body, and you can choose to do whatever you want to it. I will only support you and offer my opinions if asked."

I didn't like how he spoke, calculating his words before he said them.

"I—"

"And please, forget about me wanting to hurt myself. I do not, and I will not. I have too much to lose if I die now. So you do not have to worry; that was not what I implied."

I sighed, reluctantly letting it slide. "Okay," I said.

"Hm," he responded, detaching his hand from mine. "Now, where is that restaurant of yours?"

We ordered paella. No, *I* ordered paella, Elio just ordered what I ordered, and I wasn't sure he liked it. It was a special recipe, so it wasn't the typical paella; this one was fully garnished with prawns, beef, and calamari, and the rice was incredibly delicious.

When I took the first spoonful, I almost forgot why there

was a bit of tension between me and the man sitting opposite me in our booth. I was enjoying the meal, but then I looked up and realized he was picking at his food.

"You don't like it?"

He looked up at me immediately. "I do."

"Then why aren't you eating?"

He looked at the plate in front of him before settling his gaze on me again. "I like it, but I don't eat that much."

I scoffed. "Now that's a lie."

He raised a brow at me. "What makes you think it's a lie?"

I pinned him with a blank stare. "Seriously? All this coming from the guy who ate almost all the food in the fucking bowl I provided right after he fucked me in a tub?" I asked. "Or do we have to have sex before you eat like you did that day?"

He tilted his head like he was thinking about it. "Are you suggesting that we do? Because if you are, I would love to try that method."

A laugh bubbled from my chest and out of my mouth. "Oh my God, Elio, I can never figure you out."

The sides of his lips lifted a bit. "I was only considering what you said; besides, I think I ate that much because we were eating together."

"We *are* eating together now."

"I meant from the same plate or bowl, rather. Also, I do not really like . . . prawns."

I nodded. "So why did you order paella with prawns?"

"Because you ordered it," he stated.

"You could have just ordered something else."

"I couldn't see anything that was written on the menu. The font didn't agree with my poor vision, so I could not place the words. It made it difficult to read, and I did not bring my glasses."

Something softened in my chest.

"So why didn't you ask for help?"

He looked down at the food, using the spoon to push away the prawn closest to it. "We were not talking."

Jesus, this man.

I was convinced he was doing this shit on purpose. There was no fucking way. No fucking way he was making me feel like this by just being so fucking . . . ugh, adorable. Like a big baby. *My big baby* . . . I really did hit the jackpot with this one, didn't I?

One minute he's like the manliest man ever to exist, and the next, he's—*such a kid.*

A spoiled kid.

I shook my head, dropping my spoon and getting to my feet.

"What are you doing?" he asked with a clueless frown as I rounded the table and came to his side of the booth.

"Scoot over," I said.

His frown remained while he shifted, and I took the space beside him. I picked up my plate from the other side of the table and brought it over before pouring my food onto his plate, dropping the empty plate beside the overfilled one, and moving the prawns onto the empty one.

"We'll eat from the same plate, no prawns, no excuses," I said, knowing his eyes were on me, a piercing stare that made my stomach jump, one that made my heart thump, and compelled my eyes to meet his.

His stare held an emotion I couldn't even begin to understand if I tried.

I smiled. "Wha—"

He leaned in, pressed his lips to mine, and gave my existence a two-second glitch.

Soft and familiar lips lingered on mine, made me melt a little, made me weak, and drove me to a place where all the little issues we'd had since we left the cruise meant nothing.

He lingered a bit and then pulled away. I opened my eyes as he pulled his open.

"You want to know something?" he asked.

I nodded.

Elio worried his bottom lip with his teeth, his eyes flickering between my eyes and my lips. "I think . . . I think I *really* like you, Zahra."

This wasn't the first time he'd said it, but—this time, it felt like he meant it more than the last time he said it.

I smiled. "I think I really like you, too, Elio."

He returned my smile, his voice low. "Repeating my words?"

"You kissed mine out of me; your fault."

He placed his hand underneath my chin and raised my head. "I am sorry if I offended you today by leaving the tattoo shop. And also with our conversation in the car about the tattoo. I really do think it's a beautiful tattoo, and I'm flattered."

I didn't know it was possible for someone's heart to swell. But it felt like mine was swelling; I loved his compliments. Though I liked to pretend I didn't, I actually sought them out. It was why I'd taken extra care with my outfit today, applied a little bit of eyeliner and lip gloss, found my favorite sweater, and fussed about what to do with my hair.

It was why I was doing things that I would typically not do.

"It's okay. I'm not mad. I should be the one apologizing for Julio and—"

"You already apologized. I am not angry either. What I have with you beats that, right? It beats everything. These feelings, they're new for you too? Like you said in the car?"

I nodded. "Yeah."

"Then I have nothing to worry about. You are an exception for me, as you've implied that I am, also, for you."

I nodded. "Yeah."

He kissed me again, and I sank into it. His body called to mine, and I answered with my heart and my body . . . but my mind . . .

My mind was speaking a different language.

I was digging an even bigger hole for myself. I had fallen

into this hole, but for some reason, I was still digging, falling deeper into my own pit, but it didn't matter . . . the space around me felt good; it felt different, and I felt free.

But for how long?

How long can I keep digging?

How long can I keep lying?

CHAPTER SEVENTEEN

Zahra

I could feel eyes on me. Watching and waiting. Trying to listen, decipher, and decode me.

The annoyance that swirled inside me and the urge to turn and meet the person's gaze was strong. Still, I held firm, twirling the wineglass in my grip softly, as the transparent white scarf I'd tied over the bikini thong I wore blew this way and that with the evening breeze, the same as the unbuttoned, almost translucent white shirt over my bikini bra.

I'd tied my hair into two scattered buns on my head so that nothing would touch my skin; maybe that was why I felt the stalker's stern gaze on me.

"Yeah, I'll let you know," I said to Daiyu at the other end of the line before taking the phone from my ear and ending the call. I slipped the device into the breast pocket of my shirt and brought the wineglass to my lips as I turned.

The cold wind hit me first, accompanied by the smell of sea salt. The ocean was glistening with the setting sun, and the beautiful view had me feeling at peace until my gaze settled on the person staring at me.

I allowed an easy smile to stretch against my lips as I watched him casually standing there, one hand inside his pants pocket, not even hiding the fact that he was suspiciously looking.

With a sigh, I made my way toward him near the railing, a dangerous place to stand with the one person who had taken a dislike to me upon first glance. People were here and there, though, soaking up the evening sun and enjoying the last hours of the day.

When I reached him, I gave a toothy grin, and he frowned. "Casmiro!" I hailed. "It's a little pathetic that you choose to spend the remaining time on the cruise stalking me."

"Who were you on the phone with?"

I huffed out a laugh. "My lawyer, we were discussing putting a restraining order on your ass. You've been following me like a hawk from the fucking medieval times; don't you ever take a break?"

"I will take a break when I prove to everyone that you tried to kill me."

My smile remained as I tilted my head to the side. "Oh wow, that's a new one. Are you done trying to prove to everyone that I have other motives and I'm not who I say I am?"

His jaw clenched as he shook his head slowly, eyes filled with distrust and irritation. "I don't know why no one else sees it."

"Maybe because there's nothing to see?" I told him. "Cassie, you need to relax, smile more, be open and free, and while you're at it, pull out the fucking stick from your ass; not everyone who comes around your boss has ulterior motives."

He straightened, hard eyes pinning me with a stare that would have made me cower if I hadn't been in total control of the situation. "You have ulterior motives."

"And do you have proof to back your claim?"

His jaw locked.

"Good, you don't. Sometimes it pays to stay out of other people's business," I said, my eyes searching the piercing golden-hour blue of his as I took a step closer to him, curling my lips farther up when I spoke my next words quietly. "Maybe when you do, you might be able to avoid . . . unforeseen circumstances."

His nostrils flared, his form tight. "I knew you ordered the hit."

After a second too long of a heated staring contest, I broke the silence. "What was I supposed to do?"

The realization had his brows dropping, his eyes widening a bit like he had just been making his accusation without concrete evidence that was now indeed confirmed.

"You threatened me, Cassie, and I have come too far to let someone take away every fucking thing I have worked so hard for. I don't care who you are; you don't just speak out of turn and expect me to sit down and wait for you to shoot the next arrow, backing your words. I knew you were gonna do that, and I prefer to eliminate a possible threat before it becomes a problem."

"You bi—"

"Ah, ah." I wiggled my index finger between us. "The hit was meant to be a kill, but you survived; therefore, take it as a warning, Mr. Valerio. I am not someone you want to fuck with."

I could feel his body tighten with anger, and I smiled.

"I am also a very simple person to understand," I told him. "If you don't meddle in what doesn't concern you, then I won't meddle in your affairs. I have nothing to do with you or the Marino empire, so back off and live to fight another day *in* a fight that is *actually* yours."

"And what if I tell Marino all about this conversation?"

The laugh I let escape me was small. "Like the other times you've tried to tell him? I'm curious, Cassie, how did all the other conversations go?" I asked softly until my voice was almost a whisper. I took a step closer. "Did he listen to you?" Another step, and he sucked in a breath at my closeness, yet his eyes didn't stray away from mine. "Or did you both manage to enter another topic of conversation that took my name out of . . ." My gaze fell to his lips. "Your mouth?" I lifted my eyes back to his again.

"You think this is a game?" he asked me.

"I don't play games, Casmiro," I said, puckering my lips to the side as I let my hand trail up his arm, tingling and trailing atop every rugged ridge of his muscles, which tensed up under my touch.

"What the fuck are you doing?" he bit out.

I took the final step, my chest an inch from brushing his, but the man didn't back away from the warmth my skin supplied. Watching him, my tongue ran softly along my bottom lip, catching his eyes. "I'm trying to understand your obsession with me. What is it exactly, Cas?" I let my hand work up his shoulder. "Do you want me? Is that it?"

Disgust filled his eyes as he stepped away sharply like he had been burned. "You're fucking unbelievable."

I laughed freely now, stopping the vibration in my chest when I threw the drink down my throat in one gulp, letting the alcohol burn me as I swallowed, dashing him a grin. "What, I can't joke around anymore?"

"You don't deserve him."

My laughter ceased, and every facial muscle of mine settled into a glare. "He doesn't deserve *me*," I corrected. The hardness in my tone was one I had almost forgotten existed after setting myself up for this fucking journey. "You don't fucking know me, Casmiro; you don't know how hard I've had to fight for my place in this world. You don't know what it's like being born for a *despicable* reason, having your life snatched away from you before it's even yours."

Realizing that I'd said more than I should, I tried to calm myself, inching back from him and steadying my breathing. *I don't need this right now.* "Listen, I really like Elio. I care about him in ways I've never cared about anyone; I might not know how to show it, and it might seem like getting close to him is for a fucked-up reason, but it's not. I don't want it, but I'm dealing with it. Because I care."

I swallowed. "I commend your loyalty to him. It's hard to find these days, and I am so happy that he has someone like you to look out for him, but take your eyes off me, Casmiro, because I am not his problem, nor do I intend to be."

He said nothing after that, and I took that as my cue to leave.

I took the longer route to the side deck where most people were hanging out, celebrating their time at sea, although Kareem had organized a dinner party. I had gotten myself and the rest of Street invited, too, as Kareem had insisted on meeting my friends the last time we spoke.

I'd spent a little time charming Kareem into making me his favorite person, but most of my time aboard ship had been spent in Elio's suite. We finished watching the whole *Lucifer* series together. Started another one he said Angelo had recommended. We ate together and slept together most of the time.

Keeping our hands off each other was a struggle. I had suddenly forgotten how to control myself, but I knew it was him; it was all him, his body, the way he handled me, his shitty attitude that had stopped bothering me and instead turned me on half the time. It had been peaceful and blissful.

Quiet and normal.

But it was time to get to work, to get serious. I couldn't let the likes of Casmiro get to me or ahead of me; I couldn't let his words mess with my head because I was still in control of the situation. I still held the gun, the reins, and the lever. It was still my move, and I didn't intend to show my hand.

When I was calmer, I found Milk sitting in a corner, staring ahead at the people by the railing, five girls dressed beautifully in light clothing like us, smiling, laughing, and talking animatedly. I settled beside her, having refilled my drink on the way there.

My gaze shifted to the side, and I spotted Angelo, shirtless with white knee-length shorts, talking to Elio, whose hair was moving with the breeze. The loose black short-sleeved shirt he wore danced around his body, the top three buttons undone. His pants were a little on the oversized side, and the wind carried them as well.

His tattooed hand held a whiskey glass, half filled. There was a cigar between his lips, burning away as he listened to whatever Angelo was saying, a frown on his face.

I smiled to myself, wondering if I could grab a random person's attention and point toward Elio just to tell them he's mine.

By chance, he lifted his gaze my way, and I was filled with glee, my stomach doing a flip that had me smiling at him. He looked away without returning the gesture, and my smile died.

Never mind.

"Fucking rude prick," I muttered.

Milk blinked, looking over at me. "What?"

"Not you," I answered, taking a sip of my drink. "It's nothing, just another episode of 'my boyfriend's a prick to me, and I am trying so hard not to gut him.'"

She chuckled, looking back at the girls. "You and Elio share a very weird relationship."

"I know, that's why I like him," I said, following her line of vision again. "What's up with you? You wanna hang out with them?"

She snapped her head to me, eyes wide. "What? No . . . I mean, yeah? But they are, like, way out of my league in the social aspect of things."

I scrunched my nose. "They're normal girls who would probably kill to have your looks. And like you once told me, don't sell yourself short."

She sighed, turning her head to watch them again. "I'm not; it's just—beauty isn't everything, you know, and I love Street and you, but sometimes I wonder what it would be like to have a group of girlfriends, you know? Where you can talk about all the things and laugh freely like they're doing now. I'm not saying we can't or don't do that, but if I were normal and had a job, I could walk up to them and say hi, and if they asked me what I did for a living, I wouldn't say I cheat or steal from people. I would say I own a jewelry store or a shop at the mall, or a salon." She released a wistful laugh.

I pressed my lips together. "I get what you mean, but you gotta remember you didn't ask for this life, and we still have the future, and you're still young. You could still make lots of girlfriends who would kill to just say hi to you. I mean, you're one of the coolest people I know."

She looked back at me, her pale skin bathing in the setting sun. "Really?"

"Yup." I offered her a smile.

"Thank you, Zahra."

I nodded, looking back at the girls, my eyes zeroing in on one in particular. She was familiar.

Blond hair, pretty smile, and apparently, a beautiful laugh, and that aura—the aura of *perfection*.

I tilted my head to the side. "I know that one."

"Which one?"

"The blondie, the one in the short red net dress that screams attention?"

Milk's brows shot up. "Oh my God, she's the prettiest; I mean, they're all pretty, but she just outshines them all; she drew my attention to the circle. Where do you know her from?"

I squinted my eyes. "Hmph, the first night I spent at Elio's, she knocked on his door and apologized when she saw me; apparently, she had taken the wrong route, said something about having directional issues or some shit along those lines."

"Oh, that's odd."

My eyes shifted toward Elio; his gaze was on his whiskey glass, and he was nodding at whatever Angelo had said.

And then I looked back at the circle of girls to see the blondie's gaze shifting in his direction.

I frowned, watching her watch Elio and Angelo. Her concentration was not exactly on the animated conversation around her; she had a little frown on her brows.

"Why is she . . ." Milk trailed off, looking toward Elio's direction and then at the blondie. ". . . looking at them?"

I sat up straighter. "No idea."

Milk chuckled. "They're quite something to look at; why are we surprised?"

"That's not the 'Wow, they're hot' look, that's a 'What the hell are they talking about' look," I told Milk.

She shook her head, studying the situation as she said, "I don't even wanna know how you broke thaaaat . . ."

Elio's gaze shifted purposefully to the blondie, and it held for seconds too long before he looked away, shaking his head while removing the cigar from his lips and taking a drink before responding to Angelo.

". . . down," Milk completed. "I didn't just imagine that, did I?"

"Nope," I said, drinking the rest of the contents of my glass before dropping it beside me and getting to my feet. "Gotta go," I said, without taking my eyes off Elio. "I'll see you at the event."

"Hey, take it easy; it might just be a normal eye-lock thing; it happens with strangers all the time."

I nodded. "Yeah, I know." It happens with strangers, but I hated the tightness in my stomach. She was pretty, perfect, every guy's ideal girlfriend. I knew I was pretty, too, and the whole package, but I also knew when there was someone better than me in all aspects.

Beauty, style, charm, a perfect rich-girl childhood, awesome parents, and a remarkable upbringing.

I didn't want someone like that looking at what was mine, and I didn't like what was mine looking at someone like that and realizing they could do so much better.

I hated this feeling. It was pathetic. Rarely did I feel insecure, but after that conversation with Casmiro and my growing feelings for this man, there was no controlling the pathetic nervousness that made my palms sweaty.

With a last farewell to Milk, who had also gotten up to seek Upper and the guys, I made my way toward Elio, who spotted me before I reached him.

Angelo stopped talking as he, in turn, spotted me.

"Hey, Angie," I greeted, hooking my arm into Elio's, clinging to him.

"Zahra." He cleared his throat. "Wonderful evening."

"It is, indeed." I grinned, knowing I had interrupted some intense conversation between them. "Will you be attending the event?"

He shook his head. "Not immediately."

"Work?" I asked, and he nodded, prompting me to look up at Elio, who made no attempt to shrug off my hold. "Cut him some slack, all work and no play . . . how's he gonna get some?"

"He does not work for me," Elio responded, looking down at me, tone firm.

"I work for him. He loves to deny it," Angelo said, snatching the cigar from Elio's hand. "That's a third one too many." Then he turned to me. "Please try to monitor his cigars; it's getting worse."

"One more word—"

"I will do that, Angie, *fiercely*."

"I have no doubt," Angelo said, with a curt nod my way and then one last glance at a glaring Elio before he walked away.

I went to stand in front of the frowning man. "He's right; you should go easy on the cigars."

"You should go easy on your inability to abstain from situations that do not concern you," he stated, sounding irritated.

"That was rude."

He made no move to apologize; his stare was almost blank, save for the irritation lingering in those eyes.

I sighed. "It's just advice from people who care about your well-being." I closed the space between us, rising a little to kiss the side of his neck. "And your health."

"Hm."

I rolled my eyes, fully standing on the heels of my feet. "Give me a kiss; let's call a mini truce."

"It is unnecessary to call a truce when there was no war prior to—"

"Ugh," I groaned, cupping the side of his face and pressing my lips to his, hoping to God that the blondie saw it and knew he was fucking taken.

Breaking away from the kiss, my thumb grazed his bottom lip. "I have taken the liberty of getting you an outfit for the event."

He raised a brow, his throat working. "Why?"

"Because you don't recognize colors, and today, we will fix that by making you wear something different. We'll call it liberty day, where you do what you don't usually do. How does that sound?"

He gave me a warning stare. "I do not appreciate you implying I have trouble identifying colors, nor do I trust the mischief in your eyes."

"Trust me, you'll love what I selected." I held onto his wrist. "Come on."

CHAPTER EIGHTEEN

Zahra

I picked out a light brown round-necked, short-sleeved shirt, coupled with soft cream-colored beige pants to go with it, for Elio. He was going to shock many people tonight, and while I would love to see that, I really wanted him to get out of his self-made comfort zone for a while.

I had spent three days and two blow jobs trying to convince this man to attend this event, not because I really, *really* wanted him there, but because almost everyone who was anyone was going to be there, and he was going to be stuck here alone when everyone was having fun, living their lives and enjoying it.

I wanted to show him that his concept of life being better only when predetermined wasn't exactly ideal; I wanted to show him that it was okay to live for now and in the moment, and maybe I just needed him to loosen up so I could approach a topic I'd been finding difficult to discuss with him, given his very concerning ability to read me—I needed to get him off the ship without him suspecting anything.

Standing in front of the mirror in Elio's dressing room, I examined my sleeveless thigh-length, emerald-green dress. I'd selected it mainly because it provided easy leg movement and was very simple. Nothing too flashy, just something attractive and appropriate.

The only problem now was my hair; I'd tried teasing it, curling it, and leaving it straight, but nothing seemed to work. I wished I hadn't ignored the growing length and had done something about it.

I tried doing a short, low ponytail, but it would look awkward because it was long but not long enough to look pretty.

"Zahra, this is uncomfortable; it feels as though I am being strangled—"

I turned sharply after catching a glimpse of him in the mirror, and my jaw practically fell off.

"You look . . . lovely," he told me, his gaze moving down the length of my body.

"And you look . . ." God, when I selected his outfit from the cruise boutique when Milk and I had gone to get clothes for this event, I'd had a visual of how he would look in it, but nothing could have prepared me for this.

The shirt and the pants hugged him, not too much, but just enough, his chest, his biceps, his arms, broad shoulders, torso, his perfect narrowed waist. The way his pants showed off his muscled thighs and perfect legs and the way the whole brown and cream seemed to mesh with his skin color, and the color of his eyes; it was fucking new . . . Even though I had seen him in a white sweater before this, this was different. Elio in regular clothing was a new kind of sexy I was not prepared for.

I returned my gaze to his face, which now held a frown. "I hope that look is you telling me I should go change—"

"Hell no!" I yelled, and I felt the force of my voice from my chest. "Change never."

"What?"

I blinked, swallowing. "I mean, you look sexy. Very sexy, off-the-charts sex appeal, sex on legs, on strong, strong legs, very sexy material—" *What am I saying?*

"This is not decent, right?" He looked confused.

"It is very decent in a sexy kind of way. Definitely not professional," I told him as I walked closer, his cologne melting my resolve. He smelled so good. "But it's liberty day, so, yes, you are wearing this to the event." Sucking in a breath, I ran my hands up and down his biceps, feeling him up as I muttered what was supposed to have stayed in my head. "Lord, do I want to use this body . . . fuck me."

"Now?"

I snapped my head up to look at him. "Oh no . . . I meant, uh . . . I was cursing myself because I am really appreciating you and your awesome, awesome body. Carved for me." I smiled at him.

He watched me. "It was not technically carved for—"

"Shut up, just go with it," I told him. "And please, you look good, like really good, like no-one-is-going-to-stop-staring-at-you good. You look like some mundane banker who frequents the gym and has a lovely girlfriend who he is loyal to."

"Is there a hidden message there, somewhere?"

"Of course not."

He nodded. "Thank you for saying I look good; I quite like the color, but I would have preferred something less—slinky. You are very flushed right now, querida."

"All for good reasons." I smiled. "But trust me, it is perfect and decent, but different, and it's liberty night for you, so we're going with it."

"Liberty night is not a real thing."

"I know, but it's our thing now." I smiled.

"Okay," he responded, a light tone in his voice to show that he liked it. He liked "our" thing.

"Great, now I just gotta figure out what to do with my hair."

His gaze moved to it, and then he raised his hands, his wristwatch glinting in the light as he brushed the wavy mess back. "Would you like my help?"

I raised a brow in inquiry. "Can you help?"

"Irrelevant question; I would not have asked if I couldn't."

"A simple yes, Elio, just a yes was all I needed." Walking back toward the mirror, I groaned, and he followed behind me.

"Stop asking irrelevant questions, and I will stop giving irrelevant answers."

"You're too much."

"I am not."

"You always have to get the last word in, don't you?"

"Yes, I do," he said, pinning me down on the stool in front of the mirror.

I met his gaze in the reflection and smiled, and he returned it with a small one as his hands fell to my hair. "It's longer than it used to be."

"Yeah, I haven't had the time to cut it." My hair grew fast, and I always made sure to stick to my preferred length, but these past few months had been, well, too much.

"I like it like this. I like long hair," he said.

"Well, good for you?"

"Will you let it grow more?"

"I most certainly do not plan to."

I caught him nodding. "That's a shame." He met my gaze in the mirror, his hands falling from my hair. "Before I start, I have something for you."

"What?"

He dipped a hand into his pocket, and I frowned, wondering what he was pulling . . .

My thoughts stopped as a silver necklace surfaced; it was shiny, with a butterfly pendant. My lips parted, but I didn't utter a word. I couldn't.

He got me a present?

He cleared his throat. "I got this the day you went to get your tattoo. It came in a small necklace case, and it was not very expensive because I could not go far after I left the car." He cleared his throat again. "Long story unnecessary, I could not find the right time to give this to you, but I reckon it would look good with your dress."

I smiled, meeting his gaze again as I moved my hair out of the way. "Put it on me?"

He nodded, placing the necklace around my neck, and *God*, it was beautiful, and I knew then and there that I was never taking it off.

I touched the pendant once he had hooked it together.

"It's beautiful, Elio."

He placed his hands on my shoulders. "It is."

"Thank you. I really love presents; I don't get them often."

"I see."

I played with the pendant, the sparkly butterfly representing how fast my stomach was dancing and how wide my chest was swelling, as I secretly swooned, loving this gesture more than I should.

He got me a freaking present . . .

Wow . . .

I kept staring at him while he made do with his promise to style my hair; I couldn't think straight at this point because something just clicked into place inside me.

He got me a present . . .

I smiled, but it slowly faded, my chest tightening with guilt.

Fuck.

The event was, well, massive. Golden light spilled from crystal chandeliers, catching on the rims of champagne flutes. The air smelled of sugar and money, a mix of expensive champagne and rich chocolate cake that clung to the back of my throat and my tongue. Laughter rolled through the room like static under music, the kind that made everyone sound a little wealthier than they were.

We'd been there for over three hours now. As predicted, Elio had caught the eyes of many, especially Kareem, who was surprised and was talking at the top of his lungs, going into a monologue about how much Elio needed to start embracing other habits and life being too short to be so routine oriented.

Street and I had gotten our chance to speak with Kareem, and he had—as expected—taken a liking to Milk.

I spent half the time with Street while Elio had been with Casmiro, Angelo, and some other men I did not care to acquaint myself with.

Milk had gushed about the necklace, and I'd tried to act like it wasn't a big deal, but it was—it meant a lot to me that he'd given me something so pretty—I felt special, and the gesture went to my head, toying with my emotions.

Another hour passed, and I observed my surroundings; people were everywhere, and familiar faces were scarce.

Another hour passed, and I asked Milk what the time said; it was almost midnight, and I stretched the stiff muscles in my neck—excusing myself from Street before seeking Elio.

I found him alone in a secluded area. It was quiet, the night sky directly showing in the open space behind him. He was sitting there, observing, bored, probably irritated. I almost felt guilty for leaving him to himself, but Street and I had engaged in our usual rating-people game, and it got rowdy when some group of guys and girls joined our table, and I lost myself in the sheer youthfulness of it all—*mostly bracing myself for tonight.*

He raised his gaze in my direction.

"Hey there, stranger." I grinned, settling beside him on the soft white couch, pressing my body against his and breathing him in. His arm came around my shoulder.

"You left me alone," he said.

"Sorry." I kissed his jawline. "We had a full table, and I couldn't leave because we had this game with some real cool-ass people, and Milk had been feeling sad about us not making enough girlfriends, and it was just fun . . . liberty night fun." I grinned.

"What do I have to do to become a priority? One that comes before your friends."

I laughed softly, wrapping my arm around *his* shoulders.

"We have a long way to go till then, buddy. Where's Cassie and Angie?"

"Gone. Around. I have no idea. But Casmiro told me he would be retiring early."

"And your security detail?" I looked around.

"Liberty night. I do not like them following me around. Besides, not many people recognize me like this. I like it."

I grinned at his admission. "I told you, and you're in good hands; Kareem's security detail is pretty strong."

"Hm," he said, his hand caressing my naked shoulder as he pressed a light kiss there. "When do we leave?" he asked quietly.

"Soon," I told him. "I was hoping to talk to you about something now that we're partially alone."

His gaze rose to meet mine. "What is it?"

I pulled back a little from him. "Well, nothing serious. It's just about the painting."

He watched me. "What about it?"

"I want Street back in your search."

He drew back farther, his brows drawing down in a frown as he said, "There is no need for that."

I sighed. "But we were in the game before you shoved us out, and we're still on the quest. I just think it would be better if we work together."

"I have it under control; if it is the gold you are concerned about, I have plans to get it to you and your friends without you having to work for it."

"There's the thing." I didn't take my eyes off his. "No one takes care of our business for us; we like the hustle."

"And I have an easy way out." His voice was straight. He didn't like talking about this with me. "I am buying the manor."

I paused. Blinking at him. "What?"

"Hm. Once I buy it, I buy everything in it. Security will be doubled, and no one will go there unless I authorize it. I will take a tour with Kareem himself and have him show me everything."

"And how long will this whole buying process take?"

"A couple of weeks—"

"We don't have that much time, Elio."

His frown deepened. "Why are you in a hurry?"

"*Because* everyone else is in a hurry. Word is out that all the paintings found in that warehouse are counterfeits, and it's only a matter of time until someone figures out where exactly the original is. We're not the only ones searching for this thing."

"I am aware."

"Then why are you willing to wait weeks to actually have it with you?"

"Because my gut says so, and there is no way you are getting to tour that manor before I do; that being the case, there is no way for you and Street to get the painting before me."

I watched him carefully, breathing out. "What if I can get a tour early, like, let's say, the day after tomorrow?"

"Impossible; Kareem gave me his word," he shot back, confident.

"But what if?"

"I would not bet on it."

"Well, I would." Sighing a little, I allowed a smile to stretch across my lips. "In fact, I bet I could go talk to him now and get myself that tour."

Elio watched me with a calculated stare, trying to understand where this was leading.

"You would fail," he said.

"I love a challenge," I told him, straightening. "Let's bet on it."

"Zahra, this is un—"

"Come on," I urged, "let's bet on it."

He sighed like he was only trying to indulge me. "Fine. What would you like to bet?"

"If I fail to get myself a tour," I swallowed, "then I will sit back, swallow my pride, and let you do all the work for me."

"I like that."

"Yeah, I know you do."

"And if you manage to get the tour?"

My lips curled at the side as I shifted closer to him again, letting my hand rest against his chest. "I get . . ." I drawled, "a onetime pass to take over in the bedroom."

His eyebrows shot up. "Interesting . . ." Suspicion was in his eyes, but curiosity soon clouded it.

"What do you say?" I asked.

His hand came to rest on my waist. "I say we have a deal."

I smiled, pressing a closed-mouthed kiss to his lips. "I knew there was a reason why I liked you. Why don't we drink to it? Seal the deal."

"I've had enough drinks for tonight."

"Liberty night, Elio. We are dropping self-made laws, remember?"

He hesitated but then nodded. "Okay."

I grinned, inching away from him before my gaze moved to the semi-distant crowd ahead of us. I found the waiter by the side and gestured him over.

When he reached us, I picked two drinks from the tray, which held four; I passed one to Elio and thanked the waiter as he went off.

"Ah, cheers to me winning again." I clinked my glass to his.

"This ego of yours is a problem you need to address," he said, bringing his glass to his lips. I drank mine in one go while he drank half of his.

"Ugh, it's not even strong alcohol." I grimaced. "Should I get another one?"

"It is fine; this is all right," he said, setting his half-empty glass on the table and checking his watch. "It is almost midnight."

"The party always starts at midnight. Look around; people are just arriving," I told him. "Also, I still have a bet to win."

He shook his head. "Maybe I should retire before you. I have a little work to get done and some papers Casmiro needs me to look over. And I should probably go speak to Kareem about a certain tour."

I watched him as he straightened.

I laughed lightly. "Right . . . I'll let you go."

Something in my voice must have made him look back at me with a slight frown. He probably didn't think much of it . . . until he moved to stand and stumbled back on the couch.

Then he blinked.

Once, twice.

I watched him swallow as he turned to meet my gaze, eyes unfocused but hard. "Did you . . ."

"Yes?" I asked, shifting closer and holding him to stop his swaying body.

"Did you . . . I don't feel . . ." He blinked a few more times. "You fucking spiked my drink?" His tone was low and slow, dark and angry.

I held him close to my body. I could tell he was trying to get out of my hold, but he had no control anymore. Even though he was tense, he was mine to control.

My heart hammered as my fingers danced in his hair while my other hand rubbed his back.

"We made a bet. You didn't say we couldn't cheat," I whispered in his ear. "Lesson for tomorrow, Marino, whenever you make a bet with me, discuss all the terms included."

His forehead dropped against my shoulder, his breathing unsteady. "Zahra—"

"Shh," I cooed, rubbing his back.

It took only a few seconds for his body to slump entirely against mine.

I closed my eyes, breathing and grinding my teeth hard before opening my eyes again. Fear painted my insides red at the fact that I had managed to knock out *Elio Marino*, make him completely and totally vulnerable, at my mercy. But relief eclipsed the feeling of fear when it dawned on me that I had managed to pull this off.

Before I orchestrated this, I knew it was nearly impossible to get him like this, especially when he saw through me, since he was never careless.

He trusted me. And the guilt raged because I knew I had just misused it.

I raised my hand a little and didn't have to look before I heard footsteps rushing toward us.

I still held him to me, my hand still caressed his hair, and my heart was still pounding.

"Transport him safely to the penthouse. No one sees you. No one comes into the house. Full security. Await further instructions."

"Yes, ma'am."

When he was taken from my arms, I refrained from watching him get carried away as I gulped down the guilt I felt for removing him from the ship.

Letting out a breath, I flexed my shoulders.

One down, four more to go.

Time to get to work.

CHAPTER NINETEEN

Zahra

My heart felt like I'd placed a bag of cement on top of it as I loaded my gun. I knew I'd messed up, with Street and with Elio. I'd broken their trust, crushed it with deceit and lies and actions I would never be able to take back.

Although there were many lies I could tell to salvage it—in fact I had a few lies ready and waiting, with facial expressions practiced to make sure they bought them, and I knew I had a good chance with salvaging it with Street . . . but Elio?

I'd have to give him a truth he'd believe. I couldn't tell him about this, but I could tell him about how close he'd been to losing his life tonight, and how I saved him.

It was a long shot, after taking away his free will like that, but it was all I had to fall back on.

This mission, those kids, this area of my life was all I was living for. Daiyu might not know it but she wasn't the only one who had gotten out of that organization and decided to dedicate her life to ending them. She was going about this on a small scale, but I couldn't do that; not only was it mentally challenging but it was dangerous.

To handle something as big as the organization that made me required specific strategies, ones I'd been laying out for years.

And yes, yes, I'd built strong relationships along the way . . . with Street and with Elio, but my goal remained the same.

Get in and get out.

Stop these guys before they realize someone out there is trying to stop them.

Nothing was going to change that. Not my connection to Street and not my feelings for Elio.

My stomach sank.

I swallowed, shoving the Glock into the holster on my left side and loading another one.

My chest was burning, drawing together in a tightness that made me feel breathless.

Guilt was such a horrible feeling.

I couldn't even entertain the thought of shoving the people I cared for aside without feeling like I was making a huge mistake.

How the fuck did I get so compromised? How did I slowly forget the reason I left Sicily? When did I start thinking I could actually have it all?

I should know better. I *used* to know better.

If today, and all I'd had to do to get them out, had taught me anything, it was the fact that Street and Elio lived very far away from the life I'd been born into.

Too far . . .

"Hey, we're good to go."

I snapped my head up at Daiyu, who was dressed in the same black-on-black gear as me, a gun in her hand. "Oh, okay."

"Are you good?" she asked, her voice and eyes filling with concern.

I looked away from her, cocking the gun in place as I nodded. "Yeah, sure."

Her eyes softened. "Zahra, you know there's still time to—"

I met her gaze. "I'm not backing out."

She watched me for a moment before nodding. "All right then, did you get your guys out okay?"

I nodded.

"And Marino?"

I flinched, startled.

She shrugged. "I did a little digging after I saw him at Julio's. Is he the guy you were texting the other time?"

I looked away again, shoving the second gun in the waistband of my pants and grabbing my hair tie from the bed. "Yeah."

It was quiet as I tied up my hair.

"Does he know?" she suddenly asked.

I let out a sharp breath. "Considering the fact that I just risked my neck by drugging the boss of the Marino fucking empire who also happens to be a guy who—for some odd reason—I really, really like, just to get him off of the ship so we can do this, no, he doesn't know."

"Zahra—"

"No, it's—" My hands left my hair, digging into my eyes instead. "I was stupid for thinking I could be a Plant and still have a normal life." I dropped my hands. "I'm not fucking normal. None of this is . . ." I sighed, swallowing the bitterness in my throat. "What kind of a person drugs the people she considers family just to make sure they never catch wind of the shitty life she once lived?"

Daiyu's shoulders dropped.

"What kind of person clings to lies like it's her only lifeline? What kind of person am I, Daiyu? I don't know anymore—I mean, I can't be a good person if my first response to literally anything is deceit, and lies, and violence, can I?"

Daiyu sighed, taking a step closer to me. "Listen, Zahra, I wish I could tell you something different, but I can't. I've made my peace with the hand I was dealt a long time ago. I could never have normal friends, or a serious relationship or . . . or a family. It's like you said, we weren't born to be happy. No matter how much your people promise to be there for you, it doesn't change the fact that when they know, it'll change everything about the way they look at you, and to live like that . . . to have the people you love see you the same way you see yourself when you look in the mirror, it's—"

"Scary," I finished for her.

"Yeah." She smiled sadly. "It's why I avoid connections like that. It makes my existence easier to deal wi—" She frowned, angling her head a little to the left, her hand lifting to her ear as she said, "Copy." Her eyes met mine. "My people located them on board. The chaos from the event you were at hasn't reached them yet, but it might soon. We need to leave before it does."

I nodded, our earlier conversation forgotten as I removed the gun from my holster and followed her lead, rushing out of the room. "Do we have rescue on standby?" I asked, my strides just as long as hers.

"Yeah."

"Any idea the number of attackers we're looking at?"

She shook her head. "None, but I hope to God we have enough ammo to get out of here alive without needing backup," she said, and we turned down an empty hallway where a few of her men were already assembling.

Daiyu collected a strap-on communication radio from one of her guys, tossing it to me. "Put that on."

I caught it, hooking it onto my vest. "Where are we going?"

"Engine room," she said. "We have the element of surprise so Team A will cover Team B while they go find the level twos and get them out."

"I'm guessing we're Team A?" I said.

"You guessed right," she said with a grin before turning to her people. "Spread out, everyone in position."

We scattered, some of the guys running down the opposite hallway—after studying the layout of the *Celestial*, I knew they were going to charge from behind while we attacked from the front, covering them while they got ahold of the kids.

Daiyu, a few others, and I ran down an empty narrow hallway, guns outstretched before us as we took the stairs that led down to the engine room. The air was thick with smells of old oil and sea salt, but my breathing remained calm.

Voices and laughter reached us from inside the engine

room, and I watched Daiyu silently signal to the guys with us, and they each spread out to different aisles in the engine room.

The smell of metal, and the sound of pipes clanging and hissing covered the sound of our footsteps, the thrum of the ship causing a trembling that masked any vibration our presence would have revealed if we were on land.

I slipped behind a large compartment, the heat from whatever was inside burning through my clothes as I peeked behind, catching at least eight men standing around with drinks and cigarettes in hand, laughing and talking about God knows what. There were other voices coming from different areas that told me there were more than eight people here.

My gaze met Daiyu's at the other side where she was leaning against another metal compartment. She gave me a subtle nod, and I returned it as we both sharply left our hiding spots, and chaos erupted.

The blast and echo of our gunshots had my ears ringing and my heart racing. We managed to take down four of the guys from that circle before they brought out their weapons, shooting back at us. Their bullets blasted through steel pipes, white-hot steam bursting out and fogging the air as I quickly rushed to take cover.

Shouts and gunshots filled the space around us.

I was hot, and my heart was pounding. A bullet slammed against the compartment that was my cover, rattling the metal. I moved to fire shots at the guys shooting at me. A sharp grunt told me I'd hit someone. But it was hard to see, everywhere was clouded with steam.

I got at least two other guys before my gun gave a click and I threw it aside, slipping my hand into the small of my back to take out my second gun, now smeared with sweat.

More gunshots filled the air, drawing nearer, and I knew they'd called in their caval—

"Argh!" Daiyu yelled from my side, and I snapped my head to see her crouching over.

No . . .

Without thinking, I ran toward her, shooting blindly to cover myself as I dropped to my knees, skidding the remaining way over to her, and dragging her body away from the line of fire, behind the compartment she'd used as cover.

"Are you hit?" I asked hurriedly, my voice shaking as she fussed with something behind her.

"Just below my vest." Her chest heaved. "I'm fine." Her breathing sounded strained. "Head to Team B. They need help."

"Like hell I'm gonna lea—"

She pulled out a flash grenade. "I've got this, Zahra. Go, I'll cover you."

I shook my head. "Daiyu, there's many—"

"You need to go." She breathed. "I already knew what I was signing up for."

My stomach turned. "Daiyu . . ."

"The kids, they're the ones that matter now," she said. "We gotta get them out, Zahra." Her eyes were bright with a determination that hit me square in the chest.

I swallowed, clenching my jaw hard, looking away.

"Fuck," I gritted out.

"Listen," she said, and I met her gaze again. "I was—I was wrong, earlier."

"What?"

"If you think they can handle it, and you think being honest might give you a chance at a normal life and a better ending than this one promises . . ." She swallowed, breathing. "Take it. Don't let it go. You deserve to be happy."

My chest tightened, eyes stinging.

"We all do," she said. "Now go! Let's finish this."

I hesitated, the grip I had on my gun tightening. "I'll come back for you."

She smiled. "I'll see you on the outside, Zahra."

I nodded.

She returned it, gaze hardening as she engaged the flash grenade, throwing it right at our attackers.

The moment the bang blasted, I made a run for it, dashing down three aisles and straight for the area where Team B went through.

"Team B, stat!" I yelled.

"Route to the workers' station, men down!" someone shouted from the radio where the gunshots were just as loud as they were here.

"On my way!" I yelled back.

The route to the workers' station was tight. Hot steel pipes lined the walls on both sides of me, a loud whirring sound making it difficult to really use my ears to scope my surroundings; it was why when I turned a corner with my weapon before me, a man sharply turned with his gun pointed right at me.

"Drop it, lady," he said, voice hard.

"What if I say no?"

His jaw ticked, then a smile curved at the side of his lips as he raised his gun, like he was surrendering. "Why don't we fight fairly? Give me chance to beat that *no* out of y—"

I pulled the trigger, watching him drop to the ground with a thud, my bullet sitting right between his eyes.

"Sorry, but I don't have time for that," I muttered, stepping over his corpse just as the sound of hurried footsteps reached my ears. I sighed when another man with a gun came into view. He charged at me, and I fired at the pipe right beside him, steam blasting out to the side of his face.

He screamed, staggering back, distracted and shooting blindly.

I dove out of the way, shooting back until—click.

"Shit," I cursed.

Charging him, I connected my gun with his torso and my knee with his groin, making his knees pinch together, his gun clattering to the ground. I snatched it up sharply, shooting him twice in the chest.

I encountered three more armed men on my way to the workers' station. I finished the bullets on them. Received one and then two really fucking hard blows to my sides. Met up with Team B and separated when they gave me cover to go before them to the workers' station.

Quietly, I climbed up the tiny stairs from the engine area and through the small door to the workers' station, my gun leading the way as I came into a long empty hallway, doors on each side.

The dull hum around me was the only sound I—

Wait a minute.

I paused, frowning as I stopped to really listen.

A familiar sound was coming from one of the rooms, dull, but I heard it.

A song . . .

Chills ran down my spine, fear trickling up my stomach to my chest.

The gun shook in my grip as a very weird, twisted version of Connie Francis's "Pretty Little Baby" echoed softly down the hallway.

Red-hot dread had my insides tightening as I moved, the sound growing louder, just as my breathing did. I could feel panic setting in.

Why . . . was it playing? Why *that* song?

I forced down a swallow, stopping in front of the door the music seemed to be coming from.

Every muscle in my face was twitching, vibrations stretching from my fingertips to my head.

I felt faint, lightheaded, my stomach churning with anger and fear and confusion.

Panic locked inside me and I kicked the door open, my breathing cutting out as my gaze met that of scared fourteen-year-old boys and girls, all huddled around each other.

My throat tightened as my gaze flicked to a table where a vinyl record player was turning, the music spewing out.

With my teeth clenched, my heart raging, I pointed my barrel at the record player, and fired bullet after bullet after bullet until all I heard was click, click, click.

The music stopped.

My chest was heaving, my panic clawing, eyes wide as I looked at the kids. "Who was here?" I asked.

They didn't answer. All I saw was fear, raw, unfiltered fear staring back at me.

"Who put that fucking music on!" I yelled, and some of the kids flinched and yelped, drawing farther away from me.

I dropped my gun, my shoulders falling as I walked backward until I hit a wall, slumping down and covering my face with my shaking hands, unable to breathe. "I'm sorry," I whispered, hot tears gathering and falling from my eyes. "I didn't—mean to yell. I'm sorry."

When I looked up again to meet those eyes, those reflections . . .

Reflections of me.

Of where I used to be, *what* I used to be. What . . . deep down, I still am.

Scared. Uncertain. Voiceless.

My lips trembled, my vision blurred as I managed a small smile. "It's okay, I'm the good guy," I said. "You're all going to be okay now."

I wiped my eyes, knowing I wasn't going to receive any response from them as I clicked on the radio attached to my vest. "Does anyone copy? I have them."

Static, then, "We're on our way to you now. Our backup has arrived."

Relief flooded me.

"Daiyu?" I asked.

Silence followed, and my throat grew heavy.

"She didn't make it," the voice replied.

I closed my eyes, fresh tears sliding down my cheeks as I nodded. "Got it." My voice was thick with tears. "Have the boats on standby, we need to get out of here before authorities are alerted. And prepare for cleanup."

"Copy."

CHAPTER TWENTY

Elio

I have been too lenient, too trusting, and too kind.

It was nearly laughable, this situation I found myself in: cuffed like a helpless starfish to a bed that wasn't my own, to sheets that weren't familiar, inside a room decorated with candles and dimmed lights.

Mostly naked, save for my briefs.

My wristwatch was on the bedside table, and my clothes had been folded carefully and placed on a dressing table on the far left. The room was big, and the bed was king-sized; the large window by the side of the balcony door showcased city lights—I wasn't on the cruise; I was high up—a penthouse.

Unfamiliar.

I laughed.

It was low, it was carefree, and it was humorless, a sound lost to my ears because somehow, anger had eluded me. I was left stupefied, and my skin was crawling.

I had lost time.

There was what I could presume—a blank space in my existence, hours I could never get back, minutes of forced vulnerability, seconds where I had no control.

Stripped, cuffed, *violated* in a way that made my hands curl into tight fists at a memory I did not like to remember.

If my father could see me now, he would be laughing. He would say, *"I told you so. You only know yourself. You only trust yourself. No one else. Foolish boy."*

I was, indeed, foolish.

I laughed again, shaking my head and keeping my eyes trained on the ceiling.

There was nothing else that could surprise me at this point.

Don't let your guard down, and you are blank, a plain piece of paper no one understands; ruthless, wicked, heartless to the point of damnation, setting yourself up for a life spent alone with your unsteady mind, drowning in self-pity and trauma, growing without a conscience and prepping for an eternity spent in the pits of hell.

Let your guard down, and then you're careless, weak, and incapable. Opening doors for people to walk all over you, you lose respect; you lose yourself; you become vulnerable and trusting; you allow your heart to lead your being to its preferred destination.

You let your mind take the back seat in the moving car that is your life, and you let your heart sit next to you on the passenger's side. You smile at her; you embrace the feeling that came with her; you welcome it with open arms, lost in the beauty of her eyes, the effect of her care, the spell in her words, and the warmth of her body—so lost in her that you forget you're driving, until you run headfirst into a tree.

I always alternated between "raising my guard" and "letting it down," but I'd never considered the gray area in between.

Why . . .

Why was I holding on to a humanity no one recognized . . . a humanity that had been challenged multiple times, one that had been pushed and tested?

What would he do if I did this? Would he shoot me? Would he skin me alive? What exactly made him wicked? If he was wicked and only killed with a gun, then everyone else who kills with a gun is wicked. What is he truly capable of? Let's test him, let's defy him, let's poke him to get a reaction, let's—

Then I show them. I shut them up. I cease their chanting and their poking; I have every right to because I warned them.

I hated myself the most when I couldn't understand myself because then I knew I was capable of anything and everything. All wrongs would be the perfect rights in my head.

This is me now. I don't know what I'm going to do. I can't tell what I want to do. I am terrified of what I would do.

I was outside my body, watching the unrecognizable stranger on this bed. Wary and longing to take back control.

I knew it would be irrational to jump right to conclusions. I knew I should give Zahra the benefit of the doubt and wait to hear what she had to say.

But for the first time in months, my mind was working faster than my heart—and I let it.

I let it because I had missed this. I let it because the urge to hurt was intense—it was so strong that it made my skin thrum. It made my head heavy; violent lucid images plagued my mind, and I needed to release this numbness.

If my woman didn't plan to kill me, her first mistake would be letting me out of these cuffs, seeing as every sliver of the sane person she could goof around with was gone.

She crossed a line she shouldn't have; she tapped into a space she shouldn't have.

She took me back to the first time I'd lost myself and my sense of place.

Seventeen. Happy. At peace with the fact that I'd managed to impress my father. Until he gave me a drink, and I woke up naked next to two women I didn't remember meeting.

It was much like the situation I found myself in now. I was at peace, comfortable with someone I never thought I would grow fond of, someone that made me weak in all aspects, a careless addiction that I was beyond grateful for, my partner, the one I didn't even realize I trusted until she broke it with a drink.

Until I woke up in a panic, sick to my stomach, unable to move.

She had resurrected demons I buried a long time ago.

It was so odd because this feeling was not directed at her. It was directed at me. I wouldn't change anything. I would only correct, adjust, and rewrite.

I would test the gray area. Manipulate it in my favor. I would make sure there was no room for this to happen again. No room to hear my father laughing at me, so clear and loud, even if he wasn't there. No room to be this vulnerable and defenseless without my permission.

My lack of control over my own mind vexed me.

It fucking hurt me that I had been shoved back into this space by *her*. The first person I'd dropped my guard for, the first person I had wholly trusted without even acknowledging it to myself, seeing how naturally it came.

This woman had seen me in ways nobody else has, no matter how important the reasons for her actions might have been; I thought we'd grown to the point that we shared a certain understanding.

I did not care if she had no idea how much her actions would affect me. She should have cleared it with me first.

I closed my eyes and swallowed hard before pulling them back open.

Almost simultaneously, the door pushed open, and in came Zahra.

The woman behind my turmoil walked in with a champagne bottle in her grip.

She wore a transparent robe that gave me a clear view of the sinful lingerie underneath; it was a red one-piece that did wonders for her curves. My cock twitched in response. Despite my animosity toward her, I couldn't deny her body's pull with mine; I couldn't look away from her beauty. I couldn't help myself.

My chest squeezed.

How had I given her the reins to my sense of self? When did my body become dependent, always waiting to answer the call of hers?

Her head moved in my direction, and her eyes widened.

"Oh my God, you're awake." She almost doubled over, dropping the bottle on the dresser and quickly coming toward me, climbing up the bed, her warmth enveloping me, the familiar smell of her, sweet and mind-consuming, filled my senses, made me feel light, made my chest burn.

She was over me, on top of me, her hands were on my face, and her eyes were searching mine. "Are you okay? Do you have a headache? Fuck—I didn't check if there were any side effects from the drug because I was in a hurry and had to get you off of that ship. I—" She stopped, guilt swirling in her eyes as she took in my expression. I didn't know what it was, but if it was based on what I was feeling, then her abrupt stopping was understandable.

"I'm sorry," she finished, swallowing. Her thumb grazed my cheek as she leaned farther down, and my eyes remained open as she kissed me on the lips and said again, "I'm sorry." Then she started kissing my whole face and saying sorry repeatedly, and I failed to understand what exactly she was apologizing for.

I was so detached from this moment that it took me a while to register the sincerity in her eyes.

It saddened me that I couldn't understand the sincerity.

"You're angry, I understand. You have every right to be. But I need you to understand that I did it all for a reason. I have receipts to prove that this was for a good cause, aside from the fact that, well—I love seeing you bound up—but I just need to make sure you don't want to kill me for drugging you." She swallowed. "Because you look like you want to kill me."

I didn't respond.

She sighed, her teeth chewing the inside of her cheek, obviously worried.

"You know I would never hurt you, right? Unless you did something to hurt me, and you haven't done anything to hurt me, so . . . you know this was not done out of animosity, right?"

I didn't take my eyes off her and didn't release the pressure on my brows or the frown on my face; my facial muscles did not agree with me.

I don't know what I'm doing.

"I knew you would be angry." She sounded disappointed. "Why wouldn't you be?" She sighed, raking her hair back from her face. "I don't know how to be open, I don't know how to share. Maybe if I knew how, you wouldn't be looking at me like I squeezed all the blood from your heart."

My brows eased after that statement, and I broke eye contact with her, allowing my gaze to roam down her body, her neck, to the tattoo on her shoulder, her chest, her breasts under the beautiful lingerie, her stomach, her center over my torso, both knees on either side of me.

A body.

A woman.

Sex.

"Listen, it was important enough that I had to get you away from the ship, okay? And it wasn't just you . . . All of Street, too, because there was something important and time-sensitive that I had to oversee, and I needed you guys away because—I needed Street away because they don't know that part of me, and I needed you away because something else was going on, and there were people—"

"Did you get the tour pass from Kareem?"

She blinked at me, caught off guard. "Yes . . . I did, and it didn't really take much convincing. Why are—"

"I am cuffed to your bed," I said, my eyes lingering on her chest. "Completely yours to control. We made a bet. I lost. You won." My gaze trailed up. "And now you have control." I locked eyes with her. "Take your prize."

A body.

A woman.

Sex.

Her mouth fell open and closed before she managed to

gather her words. "Oh . . . wow, you don't—you don't want to know why I—"

"You said you have receipts, correct?"

She frowned a little. "Yeah, but—"

"Then I will see them later," I said. "But I want you now. Your choice of clothing is very distracting, so even if you chose to tell me anything now, I would not listen."

She breathed in deeply, then exhaled. "You're not angry? You don't want to talk first?"

"We will later."

She nodded, letting an appreciative smile fall to her lips as she sighed in relief, leaning down to kiss me.

I accepted it, kissing her back, her soft lips a familiar brush against mine.

When she pulled away, she looked at me with a softness in her eyes. "I appreciate your understanding. You don't know how much I've been overthinking ways to tell you what happened and still have this time with you."

"Hm."

"Would you like me to uncuff—"

"No," I cut in immediately, and she frowned as I quickly added, "please leave the cuffs on; I will tell you when I want them off."

She shot me a sly smile. "So, you *are* into kinky things, you big whore."

"I am into whatever you are into . . . little slut," I told her. "Just don't go overboard."

"No worries." She grinned, bringing her lips to my ear. "You can trust me," she whispered, kissing my cheek before getting off me and taking off her robe.

My eyes followed her movements, locked to her ass, her hips, her legs.

A body.

A woman.

Sex.

I chanted again in my head, blocking any emotions from this.

"Sooooo . . ." she dragged out, bringing a small purple box to light before turning and beaming nervously at me.

I short-circuited.

The emotional drive forced its way through.

My chest expanded, but my mind shrank that expansion almost immediately. The wall over my chest pushed out any of the lightness that bloomed whenever I caught her smile.

"I *most definitely* have not been planning this for a while, and I *most definitely* did not lure you into that conversation because I knew I would win the bet," she said, her tone a little smug.

I didn't speak.

"I got a toy." She bit her bottom lip, placing the box at the edge of the bed. "Nothing serious . . . but I've been waiting for it to go on the market for a while."

"A toy . . ." I let the words trail off before adding, "A sex toy?"

She nodded.

"For who?" I asked, and she must have heard the thick question in my voice.

Her eyes widened. "Oh no! Nothing like that . . . You are enough for me. Although . . . it's for you . . ."

"I do not do—"

"No penetration, don't worry."

I visibly relaxed.

"But, um . . ." She smiled. "This is . . . a little more intense," she said, opening the box. "Have you ever heard of a cock ring?"

I tilted my head as she brought the object out of the box. It was purple and long, with two circular hoops and a thin silicone plane over it.

I did not know what I was looking at.

"That is supposed to be around me?" I asked her, meeting

her bright, deranged gaze as she reached for a remote-like device in the box.

"Yeah, and it's an e-stim."

"Elaborate."

She inspected it. "It's an electrostimulation device, has different intensity levels, and touches *every* sensory organ and stops you from coming; it also gets you hard . . . really hard," she informed me.

"And you control it."

Brown eyes, dark and lustful, rose to meet mine. "I control it." Something in her voice darkened as she reached inside the box again, pulling out what I could decipher was an eye mask.

"I assume that is for me, also?"

"Yes."

"Why do I need to cover my eyes?"

She didn't answer, but she picked up the box from the bed and discarded it somewhere before she crawled up to me; my eyes took her in, her soft movements above my body, tentative . . . sensual. It made my head spin.

She looked so beautiful. Bewitching. So *mine*.

My cock stirred in my briefs, and the bulge became evident. I was livid, I was hard, and I somehow . . . wanted this, curious to see what she would do to me, how much she could make me fold into her—even in this state.

I responded to her, and I shouldn't. At least not this much, not this completely.

She smiled softly at me. "You'll see," she told me. "Do you trust me?"

I watched her, my eyes searching hers, unable to hide my visible swallow. I would have been able to answer that question without hesitation before, but now I hesitated, supplying a tiny nod.

A lie. A false truth. I didn't trust her . . . just like I didn't trust myself. But I needed a release of this anger, something to take away the tightness in my chest, the hotness in my head.

I needed this. Her.

My chanting was forgotten.

It wasn't just a body. It was Zahra's body.

It wasn't just a woman. It was Zahra. My woman.

It wasn't just sex. It was her.

And I still can't understand myself.

"Let me take care of you," she said, kissing my lips. "You don't have to see what I'm doing; you just have to feel it. Is that okay?"

Feel . . . Was she reading my mind? Did she somehow see in my eyes that the last thing I wanted to do was feel? Could she sense my turmoil?

"Elio?"

"Yes, it's okay."

She smiled before placing the mask over my eyes—and I was plunged into darkness. My heart picked up its pace, and I felt her hand on my chest, her lips on my neck, and my anticipation . . . grew.

I couldn't see what she was doing; I could only feel it.

A warm tongue licked down my collarbone as her body moved, along with her lips, kissing down my chest, torso, and the hard plane of my stomach, down to the lines that led to where my straining cock dwelled.

"I want to taste every inch of your skin," I heard her say, her breath on my skin causing a different sensation.

She rubbed me softly through my briefs, her warm palm edging my arousal.

I parted my lips, letting my breaths come out. I felt her fingers on the hem of my briefs, pulling them off my body, and then I felt her hand on me, wrapping around my cock, which was rock hard, a subject to my woman's hand, allowing whatever torture she had for it without a fight. I felt myself growing harder as she stroked softly.

Her hand took the precum, dragging it down my length, and then I felt her warm tongue licking from my tip to the base.

I hissed.

"You have the most attractive and beautiful cock I've ever seen; you know that?"

"Should I thank you?" I ground out.

"I didn't say you could respond."

I didn't speak after that.

She sucked me into her mouth, and my world rocked; feeling her hand on my naked thigh as she worked me to total hardness, the sensations heightened—I was surprised, wondering if this was because I couldn't see what was happening.

Her hand felt so good wrapped around me, and my heart was hammering. I felt a rush of excitement, a budding expectancy I couldn't explain.

I swallowed as she kissed the throbbing length like it deserved a little peck for being so responsive to her touch.

I felt her shift and then a soft click. Nothing happened for about six seconds, but then her hand was suddenly on me, and I bucked up a little, not expecting her grip, and then something came around my length. It was the toy she'd shown me; I felt a tight hold against the head of my cock and the base—locked in place, and the feel of it alone, wrapping me like a vise, had my lips parting to suck in a sharp breath.

It felt different . . . *good.*

"Are you okay?"

"Yes," I said, sounding almost breathless as I felt her body move again, and I felt her familiar weight above me. Her hand grazed my chin.

"Good. I like you like this. You're so fucking hot like this."

"Hm," I ground out; it was hoarse and rasping.

"Things might get a bit intense, so I'll give you a safe word in case you feel over—"

"¿Me estás insultando?"

I heard her chuckle, and I could imagine how her eyes narrowed and shone without seeing her. That was how much I had mastered her expressions, how I knew the kind of face she made after speaking, how I had recognized the smugness in her voice seconds before she had drugged me.

Even then, I decided to ignore the slight tightness in my stomach until I couldn't stand and lost all control of my body.

"I'm not insulting you. We need to be safe, so I think we need one."

"I won't need it," I told her firmly.

"Still," she said, and I felt her thumb trace my bottom lip. "I'll give you one." Her teeth clamped down on my unsuspecting lip, her tongue replacing her thumb as she softly said, "One of my favorite colors . . ." She trailed off, her teeth biting gently and releasing as she whispered, "Red."

I gulped down. "I will not use it."

"Let's hope you don't," she said, tapping my cheek softly. "Give me a moment; I'll be back."

Movements—and then she was off me, the soft patter of her footsteps and a door opening and closing, then . . .

Silence.

A silence so heavy even my thoughts couldn't find a space to infiltrate and torment me.

After a short while, she was back, the door closed, and I heard soft movements and her footsteps here and there, on my left, and then my right . . .

"What are you doing?"

"Fixing the temperature of the room," she said, and then light shuffling sounds followed.

"What are you doing now?"

"Getting naked." I could hear the smile in her voice.

A moment later, I felt her on the bed again above me.

"I have a few rules," she said, the mischief in her aura making my stomach jump, her skin grazing against my waist area. "Don't flinch or move while I explore you . . . if you do, I'll dial up the intensity of the ring around your cock. For every flinch, there is a repercussion. Am I clear?"

"Hm."

"A yes or no, Elio."

"Yes, you are clear, Zahra." I didn't understand why I would flinch. What was she planning?

"No. Call me ma'am."

"Te estás divirtiendo con esto. ¿Verdad?"

"Sí," she responded. "Mucha diversión."

"Fine, you are clear, *ma'am*."

I knew she was smiling; somehow, she made me see it without seeing it. And it was beautiful, soft, stretched the sides of her lips, her eyes alight in admiration and respect.

The sound of something uncapping met my ears, and the smell of chocolate filled my nostrils.

I frowned, wondering why there was choco—

Hot burning liquid met the skin of my chest, and I flinched at the impact.

A light vibration in my cock had my hips jerking off the bed a little, and my mouth fell open as my body tingled. Blood rushed to my cock like it had been summoned, and I felt a shudder skid through me.

What is . . .

Fuck . . . the zing-zap sensations crawling through me felt so good.

"You flinched," Zahra said. "I told you not to flinch."

The smell of chocolate was still around us, and I could still feel the burn of whatever she had placed on my skin.

With my cock throbbing and my head in a daze, I felt her lips over the spot she had burned with the . . . chocolate. Her tongue—very cold like she had been sucking on ice—licked whatever liquid she had placed on my chest, soothing the burn, but the pain from it and the sound from the fucking toy around my length made me strain my wrists against the cuffs, unable to move, to see and touch—I could only *feel*.

"Thick, hot chocolate with your skin tastes divine. Best fucking dessert I ever had." She kissed me there. "I can still see your skin turn red even with your tattoos."

My chest was heaving slightly, but I still had control; the sensation from the stimulation was beara—

I flinched when hotness spread over the other side of my chest, the burn running slowly to the middle, and the intensity of the ring doubled. I had the instinct to touch myself and soothe some of the aches, but I was restrained; my muscles tightened and tensed up at the new sensations traveling all around my body at once.

It was mind-curling, my feet tugging at the restraints. A sensation in my spine traveled up front to my stomach and my girth, hard and strangled against the rings.

My breathing grew louder every minute my cock twitched from the sweet, sweet sensations taking their time to trickle and settle inside my body.

Once again, her cold tongue licked up from where the hot liquid had been dripping to where she had initially poured the chocolate.

I heard a devilish chuckle leave her like she was having the time of her life.

While I was fucking breaking a sweat, loving the pain too much—and the pleasure. It was ticklish, a little overwhelming, but controlled—

The sudden feel of a burn spreading in a circle around my left nipple had me flinching—again, and almost immediately, the vibration from the cock ring grew louder, and I heaved out a loud breath, my chest warming, my stomach tightening.

"Fuck." I breathed out a curse as her mouth enclosed my nipple, cold and tantalizing as she sucked the chocolate off me, her wet tongue intensifying a sensation that didn't need to be inflamed.

The ring was gripping the head of my cock, squeezing me like it wanted to provoke a release, but it didn't; it just kept me there, on edge, vibrating, pulsing—

Another burn on my other nipple, and my body jerked at the effect; the intensity increased—

"Fuck, Zahra." My head was pressed back firmly into the pillow, my eyes squeezing shut at the new feeling erupting from my cock; I was drawn up tight, my stomach muscles tensing as this wicked woman licked me clean while I pulsed, ached, and fucking *felt*.

It felt like the same sensation hitting my cock was hitting every part of my skin.

My heart was pounding, the vein in my neck pulsing, sweat building and erupting from my—

I flinched as hotness suddenly dropped down my chest, and the intensity doubled. A deep groan was dragged out of my throat as I gripped the sheet hard beneath my cuffed hands.

My cock was dripping precum, and I was so fucking hard to the point that I thought I would erupt on the fucking spot without being touched; I was pulsing and erect.

Almost sore.

The pain was driving me mad, but it paved the way to this rush I couldn't stop, this shiver that had acquainted itself with my body.

"My God, you're so flushed. You should see how hot your skin is," she said in a breathy moan, sounding like she was overly affected by the way she completely undid me—

More unexpected heat on my torso. It burned my skin—the pain causing yet another flinch that sent a jolt to my cock even before Zahra increased the intensity again.

"Ah!" I hissed sharply, the sound, a moan, a groan, and a choke mixed to form rubbish in my ear. My heart was racing, vigorously trying to find a finish line, but I could find none.

I wanted release so badly, but the edging was fucking bittersweet; I was charged with sensory stimulation that had even my toes fucking curling, and all nerve endings in my body had rushed to my angry erection.

Zahra's breathing was getting loud.

"Are you—are you touching yourself?" I asked.

"Mmm, yes."

"I want to see."

"No," she breathed and then brought her fingers to my mouth. "Open, taste me."

And I did, taking her finger into my mouth and sucking in the familiar taste of her. My tongue swirled around her fingers, and I was aching to fuck her, lick her, touch her, hold her. She removed her hand all too quickly, and I wanted to taste more.

I felt her shift a little; I was still going mad with the sensations around my cock, how hard I could feel myself twitching and spilling out precum like it was the new fucking normal—I wasn't coming; I wanted that orgasm so intensely, I had never wanted to orgasm so badly. I—A burn at the side of my stomach, and I flinched.

Intensity increased.

"F—" I ground my teeth together so hard as my hips jerked upward like I wanted to spurt out cum, but nothing came out; it was painfully but pleasingly brutal, and my body shuddered, the same as my breathing. I was sweating, my hair was matted to my forehead, and I was stubborn. The vibration of the rings was very audible now.

I had never been so hard in my entire fucking life; it seemed like I was swollen and thick to the highest capacity of my length.

I was sensitive all over.

Zahra traced where she had burned me with her tongue, but then ice—ice touched my skin, and I couldn't help the fucking flinch that came again, and the intensity went up higher, the vibration strengthened to stronger pulls, the rings felt like they were around my throat even when they were not.

No release, no relief, no—

Another burn. Another flinch. The moment I felt another increase, a fast, sharp, intense sensation gripped my whole body, and I was tapping the bed.

"Oh! Fuck, Zahra, red, red, red, red."

The vibration stopped immediately.

My breathing was all I could hear; I could feel hurried shifting, and then the eye mask was being removed. It was blurry when I opened my eyes, but I managed to catch Zahra's horrified expression. "Are you fucking kidding me?!"

I would have laughed if my breathing wasn't coming in short gasps.

I blinked the blurriness away, and a teardrop slid from my eyes.

I hissed, a shiver rocking through me, my body twitching. It was so intense, so fucking intense, painful, and good . . . I felt too good. Too charged.

I breathed in and out a few times before acknowledging Zahra's glare.

"Take it off," I said with a sharp breath.

With a frown, she shifted slightly to do as I asked. When she touched me, I flinched in a hiss, and her head snapped to my face again.

"Gently, I'm too sensitive."

She shook her head and carefully unclipped the toy, slipping it off my length, and I was still hard, swollen red—but it felt good, even though it was painful.

I loved the mix. It was the perfect release I needed.

"Uncuff me," I told her, and without meeting my gaze, she proceeded to do as I'd demanded. Her naked body wasn't doing my situation any favors, and I needed to be buried inside her.

When free, I inspected the little bruises on my wrists and body.

She climbed back to the bed, watching me. "Why the fuck didn't you use the safe word sooner?"

"I did not need to use it. Come—"

"You *clearly* needed to," she cut in indignantly.

I let out a small laugh, cracking my neck from left to right, feeling more alive than I had in weeks—except it was not in the way that gave me peace of mind.

"You think this is funny? I could have hurt you!"

"It would not be the first time, Zahra."

She blinked at me, clearly lost. "What the fuck do you mean by that?"

"It does not matter, come to me; let's finish this."

She watched me for a few seconds before sighing and moving onto her knees toward me, her eyes falling to my cock, which still looked too sensitive to touch.

My hand curled around the side of her face to the back of her neck as I pulled her to me, her lips falling against mine, and the urge to tighten my grip pulled strong, but I didn't give into it.

Her tongue brushed mine, and I tasted chocolate, which she had been using to burn me. I sucked on it, drawing out a whimper from her, the kiss making her body soften toward me.

I broke it off, and her eyes fell on my cock again. "Shit, that looks painful."

"Hm. It does, doesn't it."

Her gaze rose back to mine, which hadn't broken from her as I said, "Suck it."

A frown dropped down her brows. "Are you demanding, or are you asking?"

"Does it sound like I'm demanding?"

"Yes. Don't use that tone on me; I don't like it."

"What tone would you prefer I use?" I asked, my grip tightening on the back of her neck. "Hm?" I voiced. "You want me to be polite?"

She swallowed. "It's the bare minimum, Elio."

"Hm." I gripped her thigh and pulled her leg over me as she settled into a straddling position. "Fine, don't put your mouth on me."

I managed to catch her frown as I fisted my rigid length. I lined myself up with her entrance, and she hissed at the soft brush. The urge to glide my cock over her wetness like I loved to do hit me fiercely, but I held back and pushed the swollen crown of myself into her tight heat.

She gripped my shoulders, a gasp leaving her lips. "Please go slow. You feel so fucking thick."

And she felt so tight. Perfect.

I held onto her waist before both my hands palmed her ass, squeezing and lifting her as I sank her onto my length, also raising my hips slowly until I was completely sheathed inside her. I let out an almost feral groan. She gripped me, wrapped me around her walls—hot and pulsing.

Soft gasps escaped our mouths at the same time, in sync as always—my chest burned.

My heart was slamming, aching to let myself feel this, to let myself go with this, knowing it would feel so much fucking better with the emotions I held for her, with how much I cared.

I fought for control.

"Grip the headboard. Hard," I told her, and her hands left my shoulders as she steadied herself, her breasts in my face, begging for a suck that I couldn't help but succumb to, my tongue curling and sucking against the firm nub of her pierced nipple.

She rotated her hips around me, seeking friction. I gave her the friction, lifting her with my hands still gripping her ass as I pulled far out and shoved back inside her again.

A moan tore from her lips as she rocked her hips, sucking the breath out of my lungs as I thrust inside her slowly, rolling my hips as she followed my pace. I took my time, going deeper and slower like I wanted her to fill all of me, every inch, every vein, every twitch and pulse that rocked through my length, as it begged for release, begging to take her harder, shatter her beyond her mind's comprehension.

My mind was winning. The emotions were piercing, my thoughts were turning, gears shifting, and I was driven by pure lust and anger.

My grip tightened on her as I pulled out and thrust back in with one hard push, the force working her body, making her breasts bounce, making her moan loudly as I filled her tight cunt, and fucked her.

I fucked Zahra, hard and fast, relentless and merciless, rough and raw, my hips slapping against her skin, sounding like fucking poetry to the soul.

The necklace I bought for her glinted as she moved, pressed against her skin, sticking to the sweat that had taken hold of her body, just like mine.

Her breaths shot out in gasps and whimpers; her eyes screwed shut in pain and pleasure. I took her in, sucked in every expression she gave, and planted them tightly in my memory.

Pain split my chest in half, and I closed my eyes and dropped my head on her shoulder as I pounded into her, my fingers going to rub her swollen clit, sensitive to the touch, addicted to the feeling against the pads of my fingers.

"Elio," she moaned my name, a prayer on her lips. I loved it, and I hated it. My pretense was fighting with my feelings.

My mind was a maze, lost to the pleasure she gave me and the pain she dished out.

I was taking it all, accepting it, embracing it . . . fuck—

I wasn't cherishing this body, I was using it. I wasn't keeping this body, I was manhandling it. I wasn't adoring this body, I was disrespecting it. I wasn't worshiping this body, I was fucking it.

I flipped our positions until she was on all fours, and I was slamming into her again, piercing her with my thrusts, harder and faster with each push. I ravaged her, squeezed her ass cheeks, slapped them, and I loved the gasp that left her. I bruised her perfect skin, loving the imprint of my hand on her.

My woman was moaning loudly, screaming, begging, sweating, completely undone, just like she had done to me, but she was meeting each of my thrusts, speed for speed, challenge for challenge; she liked it rough, liked me rough.

"Elio, please," she begged.

"You want more?"

Her hips buckled, her ass bouncing and shaking with each slap of my hips. "Oh *fuck*, yes."

"You like this? Do you like it rough? Hm? Is this what really gets you off? Have you been faking it with me all this time, little slut?"

She cried when my palm connected hard with her cheeks. I loved watching the spot go red; I loved it so much that my chest strung tight.

I had never been this rough with anyone. This was carnal. An act I didn't know I could pull off.

Zahra Faizan made me feel everything differently: hate, anger, addiction, and care, a deep-rooted care that had woven thorns around my heart, strings connecting directly to her.

I felt my release edging close; at the same time, her heat pulsed around my rock-hard length.

I pulled out. Flipped her over again, her back to the mattress as I lifted her leg, raising it to rest on my shoulder, spreading her glistening pussy, the deep-pink shade pulsing with need.

Our gazes locked, and so did my chest. Her eyes were hooded, red-rimmed like she was biting back tears. Were they of pleasure? Or could she feel the anger buzzing in me?

I shifted my gaze, refused to indulge her stare as I eased into her again, and a strangled noise left her throat as one of my hands encircled it, squeezing, not enough to make her pass out, but enough to bruise her.

I rocked my hips, in and out of her, appreciating how she clenched so fucking tight around me.

The other hand that held her leg to my shoulder went down to her clit as I rubbed the same pace I fucked.

Harder and faster, and faster and faster, until my mind was blank. I could feel the dig of her fingernails on my forearm, and I caught her eyes rolling back, and her cunt held tight against my cock.

"Oh fuuucck," she cried. She convulsed, she shattered, she was a mess of body shakes and tremors as she erupted, coming all over my cock, her moans tight—she was so wet and lubricated, so fucking good that I drew tight, and could feel my orgasm at the edge.

I pulled out and fisted my length, and with three strokes, I spurted against her stomach, my hips jerking at the force of my release, a groan falling from my lips as I spaced out for seconds on end, my body shuddering.

I released my hold around her neck, placing my palm flat beside her head as she calmed down from her high.

"You didn't come in me," she noted, her eyes looking wary, a distant heaviness I couldn't understand.

"Too intimate," I told her.

Her throat worked as her lips formed a slight downturn, and she shifted in discomfort.

"You're angry at me," she noted yet again, and my eyes held hers.

I don't know how long we stayed there, staring at each other, unspoken emotions swinging this way and that between us, until I found the courage to speak.

"We need to talk."

CHAPTER TWENTY-ONE

Zahra

Elio didn't notice the bruise on my side.

He was too busy leaving the one currently on my neck, the one currently slicing my heart in two, the one that made me want to throw up.

I know I fucked up. I know.

But . . .

From my reflection, my shaking fingers rose to graze the print of his hand on me.

Irritation and anger at myself, burned in my chest.

I'd given him full control and he . . . the only person I trusted with my body, he . . .

My lips trembled and I took my hand back down, a shudder racking me from head to toe as I locked eyes with myself in the mirror.

I stared.

And stared . . . watching tears fall, and fall, my face scrunching up in a silent cry. I couldn't let it out because why . . . why, if he was so angry, did he . . .

Never, he'd never, not once since we got together, made me feel . . . like *that*. Like the thing staring back at me.

Why . . . why would he take from me . . . why . . .

I sniffed, flicking on the faucet, filling my palms with water and splashing my face.

I dried off and returned my gaze to my reflection, letting out a breath to calm myself, because this was Elio. I knew him. He wasn't himself. He was angry. I crossed a boundary, and he did too.

We both did.

Whatever the result of the talk would bring, I would respect it. I wanted him. I wanted to see where this could go . . . but I wouldn't be surprised if it ended today.

Being with him was like cheating the system of the world I was still trying to escape, and if there was one thing I knew, it was the fact that I couldn't cheat the system.

Daiyu never even tried and she still died by the hands of it.

What hope was there for me?

CHAPTER TWENTY-TWO

Elio

Zahra had been in the bathroom for almost fifteen minutes.

To say it was extremely awkward between us would be an understatement. She hadn't spoken a word to me or met my eyes. It was obvious that she did not want to look at me, and to be fair with myself, I'd rather not look at her either—with the thoughts swirling in my head, it took more than willpower to remain here.

I busied myself trying to decipher what else was missing from my body. I somehow did not feel complete, and my gaze swept around the room twice, but I couldn't find any of my belongings still lying around.

Sighing, I dropped my head, waiting—a distinct feeling of anxiousness clawing at my insides—but I could still feel a tiny bit of numbness—self-misunderstanding, and maybe slight anger if I dug deep enough.

My phone had been left behind on the *Celestial*, and I needed a way to contact Angelo or Casmiro. If they had somehow figured out I wasn't on board, this whole thing might get nastier than necessary.

Just then, the door to the bathroom opened, and I raised my head.

She came out wearing a familiar black oversized hoodie sweater that covered most of her. Still, I knew she had on checkered boxer shorts underneath, as it was her preferred choice of indoor clothing.

I recognized the sweater as one of mine and wondered

how she had managed to get her hands on it without my knowledge—then I stopped wondering when it registered in my head that she was a thief, so it would have been easy for her.

She closed the door behind her and raised her gaze to meet mine before dropping it and heading to the dressing table, pulling out a drawer and a thick file from inside it.

Closing the drawer, she visibly let out a breath, then walked toward me, extending the file as it shook slightly in her grip, showing me that her hands weren't steady. They were shaking.

Ignoring that, I accepted the file.

"Those are the receipts," she said, her voice surprisingly firm. Too controlled. "I collected everything because I knew you would have questions." I watched her sit on the edge of the bed, right in front of me, slightly curled into herself—uncomfortable—as she fumbled with the neckline of the hoodie, dragging my gaze to the imprint of my hand around her neck.

I'd bruised her. I took from her instead of giving. I sated my anger with her body.

It was wrong but now was not the time.

I removed my eyes from her, letting the silence stretch on while I looked back at the file in my hand . . . not reading, not waiting for a papered truth that might as well be lies—I shouldn't even stand here for this. I should leave. Give no room for explanations, no room for this.

I shook my head, dropped the file on the table behind me, and crossed my arms.

She tentatively looked up from the file and then to me, a question in her eyes, a heaviness I could read perfectly, one stemming from the way I'd treated her, like those other men from her past, but I ignored it.

I should apologize.

I should.

"You're not checking it?" For the first time since I'd known her, worry tainted those eyes, uncertainty ruled, courage was nowhere in sight, and the usual stubbornness that kept me on my toes had vacated.

"I do not see the need to look through heaps of papers supplying me what could very well be lies. If you do not deem it fit to justify your actions by actually *talking* to me, then we can call it a day."

She swallowed, slowly and laboriously. But she remained silent.

I ground my teeth, clenching my jaw. "We can start by *you* telling me where the hell I am; that is, if your silence is drawn from your inability to find a proper beginning."

Her hands fisted around my sweater, hugging herself slightly. "It's . . . Vitale's penthouse . . . He rented it for a month, but he was never here because he returned to Sicily after your warning," she supplied.

A warning he foolishly adhered to. An idiot I couldn't wait to teach a life lesson. I loved biding my time, but this information from Zahra had my skin burning and my head hot with anger. This wasn't necessarily his fault, but since I could not hurt Zahra, he would take the blow in conjunction with the one I had been waiting weeks to give him.

"You brought me," I started, "to another man's house—"

"Don't put it like that, he didn't even stay here, and he wanted to let them rent it out to someone else, and if I had let him do that, the money would've gone to waste. And I had all this planned, and I didn't have enough money to get someplace better, so I just asked him to let me use it."

I watched her for a while, not detecting any lie, even as she shrank beneath my stare.

Something had changed in her. An odd aura she gave off in my presence. A vulnerability that wasn't there before, one I could tell—with her body language—grew from insecurity.

Just as she had crossed me with her actions, I had crossed

her with mine. I should say sorry—sit beside her, take her hands, pull her to me, and say I did not mean to be rough or brash or to have spoken to her that way.

But I would be lying. The only truth there would be my apology. But the rest had been purposeful. I had not been myself. And I wanted to make a point because I was still that man who did not worry about consequences.

"What exactly did you want to use the penthouse for? The elaborate sexcapade? Or is there something else? Because I fail to understand why you would take away my free will, like you did, what could be so big and terrifying that you would feel the need to drug me, Zahra."

"Your life being in danger," she answered.

"Elaborate."

Silence followed before she sighed and started talking. "I got a tip from Sicily, from the people working the painting case for Manuel—the ones who informed me about Chika? They told me a dangerous Elite group knew where the painting was. And they were on the cruise. To assassinate Kareem. Word must have leaked out that you wanted to buy the manor, and I put two and two together and realized that the Elite group wasn't there to assassinate only Kareem; they were there to assassinate the person who wanted to buy it too."

My mind flashed to an odd formation I had noticed at the party, one that had me going back to the secluded area to observe before she interrupted me, and I had wanted us to leave before whatever chaos I sensed ensued. But a part of me wanted to see it happen, except without Zahra's presence.

"I see," I said.

"The Elite group arrived a week before the event. Milk and I mingled a bit, and we scored an invite to a party they hosted to throw Kareem's security detail off their scent. While I was there, I snooped," she said, inhaling and exhaling. "I saw Kareem's victim profile, two other men who talked to him just before you did, and then . . . you. They had everything about you."

She breathed. "I didn't know what to do, and I wanted to inform Angelo. I took some pictures, and after I confirmed he was going to be at the party that evening, I sent them to him with a follow-up of my plans. This was why I created liberty day; this was why I chose a different color of clothing for you, because it would be harder for them to recognize you, as you never change the color you wear."

I looked away from her, shaking my head. "It was all a ruse. Everything."

"To protect you, Elio."

"And telling me beforehand would have broken one of your limbs."

"Elio—"

"And Angelo—he didn't tell me anything. Nobody told me anything because suddenly, the boss doesn't need to know that there was a target on his head. And Casmiro—"

"Angelo informed me that he told him. They worked behind the scenes to ensure the Elite group was caught. You telling your guards to leave due to liberty day helped move you easily. We couldn't trust anybody, not when word got out that you wanted to buy the manor. The news wasn't public. So, it was either a flaw from Kareem's side or yours. My bet is Kareem's side."

I have, indeed, been too lenient.

"The information you provided still doesn't answer the question of why I was not informed."

"Have you met yourself?" She frowned. "Would you have done anything to protect yourself? You chase death—you do, I know you do—and this was the perfect opportunity for you to embrace it without having to move a fucking muscle. Liberty day or shit, you're the first guy in this fucking business who I know would be willing to spend the rest of his life putting his safety last. And I know you; I know you knew something was up, but you didn't move. You didn't leave."

She was right. But I would not admit it.

"So, drugging me was the great idea you had. You did not stop to think how that action would have affected me."

"And I'm sorry. I *meant* my apology. I am sorry I did that, but I will not apologize for saving your life, Elio. I will not."

"No, I appreciate you taking the initiative. I do. But you could have also trusted me. If you had told me everything you figured out and not kept it all to yourself, acting like a hero I never asked for, you would not have had to drug me and make me relive a memory I had drowned myself in tubs, cigars, cuts, and fucking burns trying to forget."

Guilt smeared her eyes slightly red. "I am sorry, Elio. I didn't think—"

"You never think; there is no surprise there."

She clamped her mouth shut, shaking her head like she was disappointed in herself.

"How about Street? What was the need to remove them? Were you scared of stray bullets meeting them? Did you drug them too?"

"Yes."

My jaw clenched. "You drugged my brother?"

Her teeth skidded across her bottom lip. "Yes."

"To protect him too? I recall you saying there was another reason you took them out."

She blinked rapidly like she wanted to clear her vision. "A lot happened tonight."

I was losing my patience. "What does *a lot* entail? Care to elaborate?"

She shifted uncomfortably, looking down. "It's not something I can . . . speak about; I don't feel comfortable speaking about it right now."

I nodded. "This is good," I said, making her look back at me. "This is good that we are airing out the things we are uncomfortable with. For example, I am currently *very* uncomfortable with this relationship."

"Elio—"

". . . and I know you wanted me to tell you beforehand when I got tired and wanted to end it, but unfortunately, I do not have enough patience to wait for you to review my decisions and see if I am worthy enough for you to deliver an answer to."

Her shoulders dropped, eyes on me with a plea in them. "I *want* to tell you, but I—I don't know how to."

"And I am not pushing you to tell me," I informed her. "It is your choice. I am only putting an end to what I started," I said, and in response, something clogged and tightened in my chest at the way her face fell.

She carefully rose to her feet, about to step toward me, but hesitated. "Let's talk about this."

"You keep saying that, but you never say anything."

"I am *trying*, Elio. I am." Her voice shook. "Don't—please don't make a decision right now. I know you're angry, and you deserve an explanation, and you feel like this isn't—like I'm not open enough, and I know you probably think this was a mistake—"

"I would not call what we had a mistake. It was not one. I only thought the two of us could be good together, but apparently I was wrong. This is toxic. I cannot read you; I do not know you as well as you know me. I try my best to be open *for* you. I leave everything bare, but you give me only what you think I need to know. I do not know what is real or false, I keep building trust, and you keep breaking it."

She swallowed. "I never mean to."

"How am I sure?" I pressed. "How will I know that you won't decide to take matters into your own hands and do something that would make me want to fucking strangle you? How do I know that I can trust you? You are not giving me anything emotion-wise, and I am giving you everything. Do you know how one-sided that feels?"

She shook her head. "It's not one-sided," she said, voice quiet.

"How do I know that when you won't talk to me?"

She didn't respond, and I waited and waited; my head yelling at her to say something, anything. But she did not speak.

Not one word.

"You won't say anything?" I asked.

Nothing.

I released a breath and shook my head, looking away from her, biting my tongue till it was sore before I decided to break the silence.

"Thank you, for saving my life, for preparing all of this. This has been—" My words cut off in my throat, and I didn't know how to finish that sentence. I didn't want to say something I would regret, so I settled with, "I hope you find someone you can willingly give your trust to, even if that person isn't me."

She took her eyes off me completely, and the silence that followed was deafening to the point that I decided I was done standing there.

No effort. Her easy acceptance had me confirming that I was the only one dedicated enough to keeping this relationship afloat.

I hurt her, *maybe*. Her expression, though a little flat, gave nothing away.

But she hurt me . . . and it was not a *maybe* feeling, the curling and twisting in my chest at the realization that she had chosen whatever burden she refused to share over this . . . over us.

It felt like I had been dating myself for the duration of this relationship—like it was always bound to end, and she knew that, so there was no point trying to save a sinking ship.

How I didn't see this before was unbelievable.

I shook my head, sighed, and walked away from her and out of the room.

CHAPTER TWENTY-THREE

Elio

The penthouse was easy to navigate, and from the number of rooms and the interior decor, I knew a lot of money had been used to reserve this place for a month. I understood why she brought me here.

She was trying to save me and do what she thought was right, even if she did it wrong. I understood that we all made mistakes, but I failed to understand why she would not open up to me as I had done for her.

I needed to know—*truly* know the woman I had fallen for.

My heart felt so heavy, and I needed to leave.

There were no guards in the house, and as I moved to the elevator, I brought my wrist to my view, aiming to check the time, but my watch wasn't around my wrist.

Then it clicked in my head, what exactly I had forgotten to put on.

"Fuck."

My wristwatch. It was still on the bedside table.

I turned and walked back in the direction of the room. Reaching it, I hesitated for a few seconds before pushing the door open, letting out a sigh of relief when I didn't find her in the position I'd left her, which only meant she'd gone to the bathroom again.

I locked the door behind me, spotting my wristwatch where I had last seen it, and then proceeded to fetch it—putting it around my wrist and noting that it was 5 AM, almost dawn. It gave me enough time to figure out what to do about Casmiro and Angelo.

I could not let this slide.

Their subordinates would handle their duties. I did not want them in the compound. They were too close to me to consider a permanent solution to their defiance, and honestly, I did not care enough to exact dire punishments. They did, indirectly, try to save my life, but that didn't excuse the fact that they'd carried out something significant because they thought I would not care to know. Of course, I wouldn't have cared to know, most likely I would've ignored it, but still. I would insist they leave the compound until I thought it necessary for them to come back.

It was an order that would not sit well with them; they would hate it, and so it was the perfect punishment, giving them limited access to me—and giving myself the space to get to work without them watching me.

Clipping the wristwatch in place, I made my way back to the door, but the moment I placed my hand on the knob, a soft sound came from behind the bathroom door.

It made me halt, frown, and listen; I didn't hear myself breathe for a second. It seemed as though I'd stopped my heart from beating to make sure what I heard wasn't my mind playing tricks.

It came again, a small sniff, a soft sob, uneven breathing—*crying*.

The frown fell from my face, and my hand slowly and softly dropped from the knob, detesting what I was hearing.

Fuck—it cut me. The sounds of her crying—it cut me deep, and to know I was responsible for that . . . I did not like it. Not one bit. I walked quietly to stand in front of the bathroom door, her crying much more audible.

I placed my hand on the door handle, wanting to push it open and stop those sounds. Stop her crying because it was odd. Zahra never cried—this was the last thing I expected.

I ground my teeth together so hard the clenching hurt my jaw.

Resigned, I swiftly kicked off my shoes and softly knocked on the door. "Zahra. ¿Qué estás haciendo?" I said softly. "Hm?"

"Zahra. What are you doing?"

The soul-torturing sounds didn't stop.

I sighed, dropping my forehead against the hard surface of the door, closing my eyes, and swallowing as emotions moved through me, decisions falling and shattering, my mind discarding affirmations, and taking a back seat again, allowing this stupid heart to lead *again*.

I was so gone.

"Zahra," I called again, pulling my eyes back open, but only her crying met my ears.

It was melting my resolve—it had *already* melted my resolve; I could barely remember why I had left this room, ending us.

"I'm coming in, okay?" I said, waiting a few seconds before I pushed open the door and stepped inside.

She was leaning against the sink in front of the mirror, hands covering her face, shoulders heaving as each sob left her.

She was crying like she had been spending months holding a lot of things in and had only just decided to let them out through tears.

Closing the door behind me, my throat worked again, and I walked over to her, seeing the wet streaks flow down the visible parts of her cheeks, falling onto my sweater.

I didn't know what to say, didn't know how to comfort her. I'd never been put in a position like this, and it didn't help that it tore me up to witness this—I was seeing a part of this woman I never knew I would hate to see. It seemed as though she just became even more human than she once was.

I took another step closer until we were toe to toe, and one of my arms curled around her waist, pulling her flush against my body, while the other went to the side of her head, caressing her neck beneath her ear before my fingers disappeared into the depths of her hair, settling on the back of her head as I lured her to rest her head gently against my chest, while I caressed her scalp.

"Deja de llorar, por favor," I told her softly before adding, "Seeing you like this is breaking my heart, querida."

Stop crying, please.

Her hands broke free between us as she put them around me, letting me hold her while she held me, trying to tame the tears. Her body shook in my arms, and I knew then and there that I might just be a small part of the reasons why she was crying. Something else was making my woman unravel like this before me.

No filter. No barrier.

I tightened my hold around her. "Is this about what I said?"

No response, just more tears while she held me.

I sighed. "I am sorry about tonight." I let the words flow out. "I am sorry I hurt you that way; I should not have touched you while I was angry."

Her grip tightened around me. "I am sorry too." Her voice was heavy with tears. "For drugging you. That was stupid. I should have told you—everything."

"I know. I know you're sorry."

She sniffed, trying to calm down. "It's just—everything—everything I had to do and see today just took, took so much from me. And knowing I would be with you at the end of the day—it made me feel relief. But I—I fucked that up too."

I shook my head. "You didn't know, and I didn't mean most of the things I said. I am very comfortable with you," I assured her, caressing her scalp. "I just needed you to see that it was *okay* to trust me, even if you feel like I would ignore you. I know I have my days, but when have I ever ignored anything you truly wanted from me?"

She shook her head, calming down.

"See, next time, just talk to me. Do not take matters into your own hands. And this is not just for me alone, but for anyone at all. For your team, what you did was wrong, and I am positive that if you had told them you needed them off the ship immediately, they would have listened without question because they trust you. But you drugging them might have taken that away."

She shivered in the aftereffects from her tears. "I know now, I was just—I'm not used to—I stopped asking for things years ago. I get what I want because asking always—for me—comes with consequences, but I'm trying to be better. I am."

"I know," I responded. "I also know I am not without fault. I should not have pushed you to tell me what you were clearly uncomfortable with."

She pulled away softly, shaking her head, letting me see her flushed cheeks and swollen eyes as she wiped her tears. "No, no, you're right. It's . . . I . . . Today I—I lost someone."

I frowned. "What?"

"Her name was Daiyu. We knew each other when we were kids, and today I watched—" She swallowed. "Today she died." Her fingers fidgeted with the sleeves of my sweater.

"Zahra, we don't have to—"

"No, I have to. If we want to take this any further, then you should know—you should know me." She met my gaze firmly. "I trust you. I do. And I want this to work. I want us to work because I really, *really* care about you." She pursed her lips. "And I might lose my eyes, so I gotta lock it in before you can run."

I frowned again, confused. "What?"

"I cried . . . over you, and I once said I would stab myself in both eyes the day I cried over a guy, so . . ."

"Oh."

"Yeah." She sniffed, smiling sadly as her hand covered mine. "Come on," she said, pulling me with her as we made our way out of the bathroom and back to the bedroom's warmth. "I'm glad you realized your wristwatch was still here."

My frown deepened. Of course she had noticed.

Zahra settled on the bed, and I settled beside her.

"Why didn't you tell me I left my watch while I was leaving?"

"It was expensive," she stated. "I thought I would have a good cry and, tomorrow, find a buyer. Get some cash. No regrets."

I scoffed. "Greedy thief."

"Psycho killer," she said with a small smile.

Silence befell us, but it was not awkward. I waited patiently for her to tell me what she wanted to reveal.

She cleared her throat, unable to meet my gaze as her voice filled the space between us.

"You pretty much know the basics. I was born in Saudi Arabia, but almost immediately, I was carted off here to the headquarters for Italy."

"Headquarters?"

She nodded. "There's this organization; it's secret. I don't know how they operate or who runs the show, but they make children—based on customer orders, as I learned early on," she said, and a sick feeling twisted my stomach. "They call those children *Plants*. It's a trafficking ring—children are being made to—to pleasure adults, and then later, when they turn fourteen, they graduate into more . . . sex trafficking, and all the crazed shit that comes with it." She sneaked a glance at me. "That, um—that's how I'm here. I am one of the Plants. Not many of us get lucky enough to leave without either dying or running away and then being found and dying later."

I took her hand in mine. "And you have no idea who they are? The people behind this?"

She shook her head. "All I know is that it's huge. They have branches and headquarters everywhere, and children—all different ethnicities. I know I'm of African and Saudi Arabian descent; the sperm must have been trafficked and taken to Saudi Arabia to get a womb donor, so I would—well, look at it like this. It's happening every day. With different people. Different children."

This was the most despicable thing I'd ever heard. It made me see red that she had gone through this and that there was nothing I could do to erase those memories.

"I don't have a family, background, or place I come from. I don't have ties to anywhere in the world. I wasn't made to have ties or roots. I have my name though—even if it was given to me to . . . to suit someone else's desires."

My heart swelled for this woman, as I raised my hand to tilt her chin up and switched to Spanish. *"You have a strong name, querida. You own it. And it is very beautiful, just like you are . . . bright, shining, and very—ultimately—brilliant."*

A smile curved her lips. "Thank you for saying that."

"Not often do I offer to speak the truth, but this is one reality you need to be assured of," I said, brushing her chin to her jawline with my knuckles. "Tell me more."

She nodded. "As I told you before, Manuel saved me, took me out of the business. But it didn't erase the fact that I went through that shit. I grew up having different—*people* in my mouth, in my body—"

I squeezed her hand, and she squeezed mine, too, appreciating the comfort.

"The houses were built like foster homes, with children. We have two Handlers, one woman and one man. They take care of the children, oversee the adults who visit, take the money, and make sure to keep the children happy. My Handler at that time was Manuel, and also Miss Lola. She passed away a couple of years ago."

"Manuel was in the business?"

I nodded. "His father was in charge of the house where we lived, and he asked Manuel to oversee it. There was"—she let out a shaky breath—"there was a time when he tried to hurt me; I'd just turned twelve. It was traumatizing, and I should have hated him for it; I should have seen him for the monster that he was, but . . . I thought, I thought he was my saving grace.

"Even when I was taken to another house, and he promised to find me again when I turned sixteen, I waited every damn day for him to save me. It was a long wait, but he did come; he showed up for me. No one had ever done that for me, no one had ever loved me the way he did, and that easily fooled me.

"But staying with him, being by his side, being in his bed, being *used* by him was just—it was terrible. He was my worst nightmare and my saving grace. I battled with my feelings for years, trying to figure out why his love hurt so much. Until I realized it was not love. Until he woke up one morning and decided I wasn't what he wanted anymore." She swallowed. "He threw me away."

The darkness I caught in her eyes was a budding rage I could tell she had spent years managing to tame.

"He let me go," she said. "What he had for me wasn't love, it was an obsession with my body and my face, and he was just done—like he couldn't look at me, but even all those times that I still stayed, trying to make my decision, I would catch him standing there, just watching me. I was confused because he made me feel insecure, and confident at the same time, and I had had enough. So I left."

And then she was quiet, something distant in her eyes telling me there was more after that, but I didn't push.

"Did you love him?"

She shook her head. "No. I wouldn't call what I felt love. It was toxic. It was not a happy feeling. It was a feeling of longing for something less overbearing. Back then, I thought it was love, and it was okay for love to hurt, but after leaving him, I realized that I was just in my head, wishing for something that wasn't there."

Looking up at me, her eyes searched mine. "What I feel with you, Elio, it's different. It's new, and it's scary because it brings out this side of me that I didn't know I had. Sometimes I don't recognize myself, but I love it because I feel normal. I feel like this is the best side of me. And I'm always eager to see what else I can be, do, and feel with you."

That brought a smile to my face.

She returned it. "You still wanna know why I needed Street off the ship?"

"Only if you feel comfortable enough to tell me."

She nodded. "I do," she clarified. "I needed them off because after we stopped the Elites and the whole massacre happened, I had to help Daiyu, the girl I mentioned earlier. We stayed in the same house, but I left earlier than her. She reached out to me a couple of months ago, and I learned she had somehow managed to get out.

"She had this group of people hunting down houses here in Mexico and nearby cities. It's a small, secret organization dedicated to saving as many children as they can. She needed my help to get her people on board. We were supposed to be intercepting a shipment for level-two kids. That's what they call the fourteen-year-olds moving up to . . . sex trafficking. It was rough, she got shot, and well . . . we managed to get them out, and I came back here."

"It must have been hard . . . seeing them, the kids."

She nodded. "Oh yeah, it was . . . inside the room there was this song Manuel used to hum to me when I was little." She went silent, then swallowed. "It was like stepping into my personal hell, like a reminder that nothing about me is normal. But the kids, God . . . they were so young, and scared and familiar, it just—it hurt to see them, to be there."

"But you took part in saving them, and that's a good thing."

She nodded. "Daiyu's organization is outstanding. But they lack resources that would make their jobs better. I wanted to tell her that if they needed any help, I'd be happy to help them. I know Street would be, too, but if I approach them with this, and they put two and two together, they might find out about how I grew up. They might see me differently."

"I doubt that," I countered immediately. "I don't see you differently. You are still the same Zahra. And I know Street won't see you differently, either. Take those thoughts from your head."

A sigh left her. "They're here," she said. "Street . . . dead to the world, but they occupy the other rooms in the penthouse, and I have much explaining to do, but I don't think I'm ready to tell them yet."

"And that is okay. I know you will figure something out; you are a better liar than I am, after all."

She frowned. "I don't know if that is an insult or a compliment."

"It was a compliment."

A small laugh left her.

I brushed her hair back from her face, seeing the tiredness in her eyes. I was happy she'd told me this and confided in me. I knew how much it took from her, but somehow, it made me feel closer to her. It made us feel more intimate than before.

I leaned forward and pressed a soft kiss to her forehead.

"Thank you for telling me all of this, Zahra. I will conduct a little personal research myself, and find out what I can about this organization."

She smiled, taking in a shuddered breath. "You will?"

"Yes, they need to be stopped," I said, watching her smile widen as she stifled a yawn. "You are tired. You should sleep. It is almost daylight; I have to find Casmiro and Angelo—"

"I can send them the address here . . . if you want," she blurted.

"No, that is all right; I will go."

She sighed, brows dropping at the idea of me leaving, the tiredness vanishing. "Can we still—still talk about this? I know you might need space after everything, but I don't want us to end, Elio."

I frowned. "I thought we covered that already?"

Her shoulders dropped. "Yeah, I know, but I assumed after we talked you might—I don't know—want to reconsider your decision to . . . break up?"

"I reconsidered my decision when I walked into the bathroom." I grazed her cheek softly. "I am still in this with you, Zahra; you don't have to worry."

She let out a heavy breath. "Next time, just fucking say it out loud. I'm not smart enough to read minds."

"I will make note of that."

She leaned in, joining our lips in a tentative kiss, one I fell into without second thoughts or second-guessing.

When she pulled away, she whispered, "Stay. Please. I will send your location to Angelo, and he'll forward it to Casmiro, and we can discuss it in the morning about the painting and everything that went down."

I didn't have much reason to object to that, so I stayed, and we lay down together like we had been doing for the past few months.

She spent the next few minutes in my arms, telling me how she would placate her team by explaining that she'd wanted to surprise them with another one-month vacation to explore all of Mexico while staying in this penthouse she had supposedly rented from personal savings—at some point, she completely relaxed, and then, she stopped talking, and her breathing deepened.

I checked and saw she was already asleep.

Lying there for a while, just watching her, unable to find sleep as usual, I pressed a kiss to her hair, detached myself from her, left the bed, and put on my shoes.

I quietly left before she woke up.

CHAPTER TWENTY-FOUR

Zahra

In the vague dream I was having, something was buzzing. Continuously, urgently, and distant. It maintained a sequence that just stretched on—nonstop.

The sound slowly dragged me out of my sleep daze and back to reality, my eyes opening up, heavy and tired. I groaned into the pillow and angrily fussed above the sheet, as the buzzing continued.

With a frown that I was almost positive would burn the device, I raised myself a little, searching for my phone, and finding it on the nightstand at the other side of the bed that was quite cold, very neat—*I'd woken up alone*—my annoyance sank immediately. I dragged my body to the other side of the bed and picked up my phone.

Vitale.

"What the hell does this fucker want?" I groaned, dropping back on the bed as I closed my eyes, answered the call, and pressed the phone to my ear. "What is it?" I snapped.

"Where did you keep your phone? I've been calling all morning; do you think this is fucking funny?" The anger in his voice held a seething tone that had my eyes snapping open and my senses on alert. I brought my phone to my view and caught that the time was one in the afternoon.

Placing the phone back to my ear, I rubbed my eyes. "I was asleep; I had a rough night. What's going on?"

"Oh no, sorry to disturb your beauty sleep; nothing really is going on, just my fucking life being ruined, that's all!"

Something shattered on his end, telling me he had flung a fragile object to the wall or ground.

Frowning, I sat up. "What happened?"

A strangled sound left him. "Everything is ruined, Faizan, every fucking thing—everything I've worked my whole life for is gone."

"Slow down—slow down, what do you mean?"

"The seat, Faizan—" He sounded broken, his breathing ragged. "Eight years, I've worked tirelessly for eight fucking years, and now it's gone, slipped out of my hands . . . everything."

Oh God.

I got off the bed, unable to stay still, sudden sweat beading on my skin inside the hoodie I wore. "I thought you said they didn't take a vote until the middle of next year? You had all the Society members in your corner; we made sure of that."

"We did," he practically growled. "But guess what?"

The menace in his tone ignited goose bumps on my skin. "What?"

"Somebody suddenly decided to be generous . . . fifteen fucking million pounds went in support of my drunkard brother. They got him in . . . they're yet to make a final decision, which they informed me they would make next week, but we both know who is getting it." He laughed humorlessly. "You wanna take a wild guess at who donated that money?"

"Marino? That's crazy, he can't influence the decisions of the Society unless he previously had ties with them."

"Well, apparently years ago, his father did."

I closed my eyes, gritting hard. "Fuck."

"Fuck indeed! What the hell did I even do to your fucking boy toy—"

"Vit—"

"He ruined my whole life, and for what!" Something shattered again. "Because I spoke to you? Does he know how hard I've had to work to take my father's place in the Society? Does he know what is on the line and what happens if my fucking brother takes that seat? My mother—everyone, everyone who has put their trust in me, Faizan . . . I'm finished."

"No, no, you're not. There's still time, we can still—"

"We? There's no 'we.' You left me! If you had been here, if you had been by my side like we fucking planned, I would have gotten that seat—"

"It's not over, V. The final decision is made next week, yes? I will talk to Elio and make him undo whatever he did."

"No need for that, there's nothing to undo." I could tell he was pacing furiously, his breathing was uneven. "I want to kill him. I will kill him. I will fucking murder that bastard and then murder his soul and fucking spirit until there's no entity tied to his fucking being."

"Vitale, just breathe. We will figure this out—"

"I want him dead, Faizan. He fucking played a bad hand. A terrible hand, and I am itching to show him what I'm capable of."

"Continue along that path, and you will be dead before you can even raise your gun to shoot him, Vitale," I said, rubbing my head at the headache that had begun to surface.

He went quiet, letting out a shuddering breath.

"Listen to me. Now is not the time to lose your cool, okay? We can't have people see you like this; we've come too far for you to go batshit over a little stone in your path; you need to get your shit together. Where are you?"

His breathing was all I heard as he forced out the word. "Home."

"Is anyone there with you?" I asked him.

There was a strained sound from him again, and I knew he was holding himself back from completely losing it. "People are around, yes."

"Go to your room. Now. Align your steps with each breath you take."

After a short while, I heard his heavy footsteps and incoherent counting, and then a door opened and closed.

"Have you been drinking?"

"What the fuck does that have to do with anything?" he snapped again.

I blew out a breath. "Vitale. I am asking because I can hear your breathing pattern, and I need to know if you need to take your meds now or—"

"I am fucking fine!" he yelled. "My life just got fucking ruined, and you're miles away asking about some stupid meds, pretending you care if I live or die! You don't get to do that, Faizan! You don't get to fuck with me like this when you're fucking around with someone else." Another shatter and a sharp shuffle as if he had left the phone elsewhere.

What followed next was chaos, and I pressed my eyelids closed as different clashes followed, some shatters, some thuds, angry groans, and grunts—more shatters, more and more and more; I didn't even know how long it lasted. I just stayed on the line, listening to this man who had managed to stay calm for almost six years—after almost hurting someone he cared about—lose control in just a few minutes.

He cared so much about himself that he didn't let something as manageable as anger issues mess with him. He got himself help, and he was better, better than he used to be, but hearing this, I knew how hard the blow of Elio's actions had hit him.

Hell, even *I* felt the blow. We had worked our asses off to get him to a position above his brother with just wits and cunning.

Elio . . . *God.*

That man had targeted Vitale where he knew it would hurt the most, where he knew the damage would create more damage. He didn't kill him—no—he was torturing him from the inside out—like he had done proper research on what exactly would tip off Vitale and drive him to the very brink.

He had given him time and space and made him believe he was let off the hook with just a primal warning—then he had struck, and he had won.

I felt terrible because I knew how hard Vitale had worked and how far he'd come to be in this place mentally, only to mercilessly break like all his growth had meant nothing.

Elio had played his hand well, and he was *apparently* still playing it.

I could see it clearly, the way the mind of my boyfriend worked.

First, he instilled shock in Vitale's mind, and then devastation, before it slowly progressed into anger, Vitale's only flaw—the one he had been burying so deep all these years and was successfully healing from.

Then, slowly—ever so slowly—he would lose his mind and play right into Elio's trap; he would want to attack. He would give Elio the perfect opportunity and excuse to do whatever he pleased without retaliation from the Society because then, everyone would know that Elio's empire never struck first; Vitale was the one to throw the first punch. Therefore, it was within the rights of the Marino empire to take him out.

The clashes and shattering stopped, and only loud, distant breathing was heard. He was trying to calm himself, but I could hear a tiny wheezing sound that got higher and higher as seconds passed. I heard footsteps and hurried movements, drawers opening and slamming closed until they stopped, and then a strong puff of air down his throat—an inhaler—I knew because he rarely got asthma attacks, but whenever he did, it was around the house, within reach. His mother would never take that chance.

I waited a few beats, listening to him calm down, as my nerves did.

His calm breathing drew closer, and a slight shuffling followed, indicating that he had probably picked up the phone.

"Are you calmer now?"

"Yes."

"Good. I know how this looks and how hard you have

worked to get this far, but you cannot break now. That's not what we do, remember?"

"Yes."

"Now, more than ever, I need you to trust me. There might be nothing we can do about it since the money has already been paid, and your brother has already been sponsored. But I will talk to Elio and try to get him off your back. If you attack, I guarantee you're the only one who will get hurt."

"I can't just let this slide. If he wants to play a game, he must know I am happy to play too."

I sighed. "He knows that, and that is exactly why you will lose. Let it go, Vitale. Let the position go."

He shot out a laugh that was born from withheld anger. "Have you lost your mind?"

"No. I am saying you can get something even better." I allowed my words to sink in. "Do you want to be the one that's voted in? Or the person who approves and makes the final verdict on who gets voted in?"

Silence, and I knew I had caught his interest.

"What do you mean?"

"If we get that flash drive, we hold the power over your family name; we hold every secret the current Serpent head has tried to keep from the public eye. With your power, my power, and your impending inheritance, we can take him out and put you higher than your enemies, and then you could even choose to do whatever you want with your brother."

"That sounds too good to be possible."

"It's not impossible. Not impossible for me, or you. I need you to trust me, Vitale."

"For how long?"

"As long as it takes. If you want something this good—this far-fetched—you have to be patient and observe. I know you hate to hear this, but you could learn a thing or two from Elio. Study your enemies, know exactly where to hit them, and make them bend to your will. It is not time to let your emotions take over. It is time to watch and bid."

He sighed. "Okay . . . I hear you." I could almost see him running a gloved hand down his face.

"Listen, I know I'm not there, and I know I'm in a relationship with the one guy I should probably not be in a relationship with. I know how this looks, but you know me, Vitale, you know where my priorities lie. Stopping the trafficking ring, bringing down that organization, making sure no other Plants are created, and getting you to a high-standing position in the Society. I haven't forgotten. I am still with you in this, regardless of whoever I'm with, or whoever I have feelings for. I will never forget where I come from, why I'm here, and what I left behind, okay?"

"Okay," he responded with a breath, one that sounded like it was from a place of relief. "Okay, Faizan."

"Good."

He groaned. "Fuck, my room is a mess."

"Your seven minutes of madness is to blame. Deal with it."

"I was going to," he gritted out. "I didn't say that so you could comment."

"Whatever, I'll call you if I have any news. Call me if something happens."

"Yeah."

I ended the call and immediately found Elio's number and placed a call to him. It rang and rang and rang, with no answer, until the line disconnected. I tried again—the same thing, and then I tried a third time—it rang twice before he declined it.

"Motherfucker."

I made my way out of the room to check on Street—upon reaching the rooms where I had been sure they'd been last night, each one was empty.

"What the fuck?"

The penthouse was too quiet. After searching for a few

minutes, it registered in my head that no one was there and I was alone.

Where the hell did they go?

Fear flashed inside me, and I quickly reached for my phone and dialed Milk's number. It rang about five times before, thankfully, she picked up, and I spoke first.

"Hey, what's up? Where are you guys?"

"Hi!" she said cheerfully, heaving a breath; distant sounds of people chattering met my ears. "We're at some adoption home under refurbishment, and I'm currently scrubbing toilets. There is so much black mold on the ground, and I don't want to think about what it was before it turned into mold."

"Hold on, wait, what are you talking about? What adoption home?"

"Oh," she said. "He didn't tell you?"

"Who didn't—wait, you guys are supposed to be resting—What adoption—Who—"

"Is that Zahra?" Elio's voice sounded from the background.

"Yup," Milk answered.

"Give me the phone; I will talk to her."

A little shuffling and his voice became more pronounced. "Zahra."

"There better be a good fucking explanation for why you declined my call."

"Yes, there is indeed one," he started. "I did not hear it ring the first two times you called, and when I tried to answer the third time, the screen of my phone got a little too dark, and I could not see it because the sun was affecting the brightness—and by accident, I declined instead of answering."

Knowing how possible that was, I ignored it.

"What's going on? What are you doing with my friends? What adoption house was Milk talking about?"

"Are you well rested?"

I blinked. "Did you hear what I just asked?"

"Yes, and I apparently ignored you, if that wasn't clear," he said. "Are you well rested, Zahra?"

I let out a sharp sigh, my patience running thin. "Yes, I am well rested, *Elio*," I gritted out.

"Wonderful. I will have your friend share the location with you so you can join us. We need more hands on this if we want this organization to open next week."

"What organization? What are you talking abo—"

"When you arrive, I will explain in detail what I mean. Please arrive wearing something that permits you to do hard labor . . ." He trailed off, his voice going low. "I would not want to inconvenience the apple of my eye."

"What the f—"

"See you soon."

The call disconnected, leaving me standing there, my heart swelling and my cheeks growing warm at the phrase he'd used.

Always manages to leave me speechless—this man.

The location was sent shortly after, and I got to work getting ready to see what was happening.

It was chaos—okay, maybe not exactly chaos—but people were everywhere, some on ladders, some moving in furniture, some working on rooms I could only peek into to see what was happening. I almost bumped into someone carrying a bowl of black—oil?

I looked around, confused beyond belief.

A new set of furniture came in, gray couches carried by some stranger and Upper, who looked like he had been dragged from hell to do hard labor.

In a swift glance my way, a crazed look touched his lips. "Oh, hey, Zahra, you will *bloody* pay for this," he said with a pained smile that didn't leave his face as he and the stranger disappeared around another corner.

"What the—" I blinked, my gaze drawn somewhere far off, at a ladder; Dog stood at the top of it, with a paintbrush in his grip, shirtless, with only jeans on, his body covered with gray paint, a rolled-up joint tucked in place behind his ear, with a permanent frown on his face.

I didn't see Milk or Devil, but I knew from the phone call that Milk would be in the restroom areas, and Devil should be around here somewhere—

"Sport," Elio's voice had me spinning around.

He was in a typical black button-up, untucked from his pants and rolled to his elbows. His hair was a bit rough, but it still somehow looked great.

His eyes took me in swiftly, lingering on my shorts as his gaze grew darker. "Welcome; I appreciate you adhering to the dress code."

I wore a faded black T-shirt and sweat shorts that stopped midthigh, and my hair—let's not even go there.

"Right, what is happening?"

"Come with me; I will explain," he said, brushing past me and around a corner. I spotted Devil conversing with three people and jotting things down on a notepad in his hand. He looked equally tired and stressed, and when our gazes locked, he frowned, shook his head, and looked away.

Okay, obviously, they're all angry. I already knew I had some explaining to do, but first, I needed to figure out what exactly I would be explaining for and what in the fuck was happening.

Elio entered a small office, holding the door open. I shot him a wary look and walked past him into the almost empty space—save for a small table, covered with papers and a framed picture of a group of children, and two chairs.

When I heard the door close, I turned—and was immediately attacked by lips on mine, hands on my body, and my back being pressed against the table. One hand held my waist firm, and one knee separated my legs as his mouth ravaged mine in a kiss that had my heart racing.

The shock at the sudden change of situation lasted a few seconds before my mind forgot my apprehension as to what was happening around me, and I gave in to the pull of him, fisting the collar of his shirt and pulling him closer to me, parting my lips for his tongue to swiftly swirl in to taste mine.

His muscular thigh rubbed against my center purposefully, building up pressure as a small pulse began to build and build, aching for his touch.

The coldness of his rings pressed against the side of my neck as we slanted, deepening the kiss, a groan from him and a breathy moan from me.

My nipples hardened, and I pressed my body flush against his chest and felt his hardness against my belly while I tangled my fingers into his hair.

We were joined together like we hadn't spent almost all of last night being together.

We pulled apart to catch our breaths, and his beautiful hooded eyes locked with mine as he breathed out in a ragged rasp filled with arousal. "Hi."

I smiled, astonished. "Hi."

His lips went to my neck, and he kissed softly down to my throat and over to the other side of my neck like he was apologizing to it for the light bruising that still showed there due to his roughness last night.

I did not hate him for it; I just hated how it made me feel. What it reminded me of.

But I'd forgiven him—his hug restored every doubt I had, and I trusted him. I trusted him, and one day, when all was said and done, I'd give him the last piece of myself.

Pressing one last kiss to my neck, he returned his face to my view. "I really want you, but here's not the place."

"Here's a perfect place for me."

"Hm," he drawled in a deep groan, the sound vibrating from his chest as he shook his head. "The walls are thin, and I want to make you scream."

I smiled. "You really are horny, aren't you?"

He took my hand that was fisting his shirt and brought it down to the hard bulge in his pants, leaning in to whisper against my lips, "Very." He took my lips in his again, kissing me softly and slowly, sucking and working my lips as I undid his fly, and his hand disappeared into the elastic band of my sweat shorts, and inside my underwear, touching me where I was wet and aching.

His lips still moved tentatively over mine, in accordance with his fingers spreading the wetness from my opening up and down my clit.

I watched him when he broke the kiss, bringing his fingers out of my shorts and removing the two rings around them before bringing the fingers to his lips, sucking swiftly, and making them wetter before he slid his hands back into my shorts and underwear, circling my swollen clit in a motion that made my hips buck and my lips part—a sweet feeling that rose as he rubbed my clit in a pattern that made my heart squeeze in pleasure, loving how he knew the right way to satisfy me. A soft sound left my throat, and he slipped both fingers into me.

He collected my gasp by taking my lips again, his fingers pumping slowly in and out of me—it felt so good.

With slight difficulty, I slid his hard length out of his briefs, his warm skin perfect and rigid against my grip as I stroked him, my hand giving attention to the head of his cock as he leaked out precum that added lubrication up and down his shaft.

We were quiet, kissing softly but lazily, without focus, our hands working on each other—slight hitch of breaths from either him or me.

When his fingers increased tempo, pumping in and out of me, I followed the same sequence with my stroking, and we broke the kiss apart, his forehead resting on mine as we breathed through our mouths, feverish and intimate with our movements completely concealed between us.

The sounds he made were low and lust-filled, his lashes

beautifully down, watching my hand stroke him and the movements of his hand inside my shorts.

He was so hard and, like me, so close to the edge.

We made it last longer to enjoy the pleasure we gave each other. Still, the force with which he began pumping his fingers into me had my knees buckling, my hips meeting his thrusts. My stomach was woven so tight, alongside my clit, and I was shuddering before him at how good it felt—it didn't take long before my walls gripped his fingers tight, and I was coming all over them, a moan escaping my lips, my legs growing so weak, standing became a chore as I gripped his shirt, my cries breaking as I rode his fingers down my high.

When I was a little calmer but still in a daze from my release, he took his fingers out of me and brought them to his lips, licking them clean, before bringing his lips to mine in a kiss that had me tasting myself on him.

His tongue tasted like me, and he tasted like mine, and I got drunk on it, on him, before he pulled his lips from mine, and I watched him, my hands still moving against his hardness. "This was not what I planned, coming here today."

"I loved your shorts a lot," he admitted.

"Really?"

"Hm. I love whatever you wear," he admitted again, his stare deep and piercing. "I love whatever you do, and however you look. Drives me crazy every time, and I love it."

I smiled, going down on my knees before him, and raised my gaze as hooded eyes looked back down at me while I took him in my mouth, earning a groan as his hands went to my hair.

Sucking and twirling my tongue around the head of his cock, I took him as deep as he could go, letting my tongue lay flat inside my mouth to aid his thick length moving farther down as I hollowed the inside of my mouth, sucking him to fervent curses.

He was so undone, fighting to be quiet as I worked on

him, cared for him, and teased him with my tongue the way he liked.

His fingers caressed my scalp in silent appreciation as I moved up and down his length, his thickness filling my mouth, his taste driving my senses wild—I wanted him inside me; I wanted to get tangled up in a sheet with him until I didn't know where my body ended and where his began.

I wanted to make love to him, fuck him, ride him, suck him, touch him, kiss him, take him till I was sore and broken. I wanted to own him, and I wanted so very much for him to own me.

I knew he was already so close, but I tried to edge him a bit before letting him hit the back of my throat—in a few thrusts, his orgasm struck, spurts of cum shot down my throat, and I dutifully swallowed. I loved it; I loved getting on my knees for him and having him in my mouth.

I loved that *I* got to do this and not someone else. Sometimes, I wished I could read the minds of all the women who ogled him whenever we were in a public place; I needed to know who exactly I would be plucking eyeballs from.

When I got to my feet again, we kissed as he tucked himself back in, putting his arm around me—so mundane, so natural.

My heart was racing just being close to this man like this.

He broke the kiss but didn't let go of me. "I missed you all morning, but I did not want to disturb you . . . I knew you were tired."

My hand on his biceps picked off invisible lint from his shirt. "Did you even get to sleep?"

"Hm, no. But I plan to sleep tonight."

"You shouldn't plan to sleep, you should sleep every night; it's what normal people do."

"I am not normal people."

I raised a brow. "What? You got some superpower I don't know about?"

"Yes . . ." he drawled.

"What is it?"

"I know how to make you squeal."

"Wh—"

He lifted me suddenly, and a loud squeal left my mouth as he dropped me on the table, placing himself between my legs.

"That was so fucking cheesy."

A smile gently curved his lips, lighting up his eyes as he said softly, "It made you squeal, did it not?"

I rolled my eyes. "It did." I played with the collar of his shirt, his gaze lingering on me like he couldn't look away. "What?" I asked; his stare wasn't unnerving, just—heavy, so heavy it made me feel heavy too.

"You are adorable," he answered, and the compliment went straight to my chest, making it feel all fluffy and weird, like I was levitating or something. I didn't even know why my toes wanted to curl.

For some reason, I wanted to shy away from his gaze. "What's up with you today?" I asked with a smile of my own, one I couldn't even stop from forming on my lips if I tried.

He shook his head and wrapped his arms around my body until we were pressed together. He buried his head in the crook of my neck, breathing me in deeply. "Zahra," he called my name softly, in a small, breathy way that told me he wasn't calling for me to answer him; he was just saying my name like he was sinking into the very essence of me.

Against my chest, I could feel the fast pacing of his heart, wild and raging, a copy of mine, but his was so fierce that it had me falling even deeper into him—*for him*.

This felt good; a comfortable silence of him holding me, so warmly, so intimately, like it would break him to pull away—right now, a lot was unsaid, but plenty was shown. Plenty was felt, and I allowing my body to grow soft against his, wrapping my arms around him and letting the feelings take charge of the moment.

I was falling for this man, without sequence, without grip,

a free fall that came with fear, passion, and something mind-twinkling—but for the first time since I felt this soft connection with him, I didn't pull away, I pulled in. Because I needed this feeling, I craved it like food for my soul—a secret potion to keep me sane and functioning.

For a fever of a moment, all was forgotten—the reason I had set a course for this journey; my life before I met him—before I *knew* him—was forgotten. All I wanted right now was to be in his arms, to stay here, and let him kiss my flaws back to perfection.

So, I let myself free-fall into him until my mind knew nothing—absolutely nothing, but him.

CHAPTER TWENTY-FIVE

Zahra

It baffled me how he'd successfully diverted my attention from why I was here and what was happening.

While I didn't want to leave his warm embrace, we needed to talk about his active plan to destroy Vitale and why he had my friends working on this building.

I pulled away softly from him, catching his gaze.

"You have just realized that we need to talk," Elio stated like he knew whatever charm he'd placed me under had now worn off.

"Yes, what's going on?" I asked as he pulled farther back, hands still on my waist.

He watched me carefully, trying to work out my mood before speaking. "Right before you drugged me, you'd been trying to get Street back into the quest with my own team. You thought it would be better to work together."

I nodded, eyeing him warily and wondering where he was leading.

"Good. I recall myself telling you that I already had it under control, though it might take weeks to collect, and you told me we did not have that much time—"

"Yes, yes, Elio, you don't have to repeat our whole conversation; I have a really sharp memory."

He frowned, amusement in his eyes. "I apologize; I was under the impression that you sometimes lose vital information from your memory bank. I will make sure not to make any assumption of that sort in the near future."

My smile was not genuine, and I wanted to connect my

forehead to his nose but held back. "It's the way you insult me and still sound polite while you do."

He nodded. "Yes, I have that skill." He raised a hand to graze my cheek. "I love it when you are observant about little things pertaining to me."

"Yes, I love it, too; I'm also very observant of the fact that in about two minutes, you might sustain a nose injury if you don't cut the shit and start talking."

His lips tugged at the side, but he didn't comment further as he continued, "Right before I was about to be assassinated along with Kareem, I told you I would have the painting and the gold delivered to you once I collected it. To which you responded, and I quote, 'No one takes care of our business for us; we like the hustle.' In my mind, unbeknownst to you, I formulated a plan that could satisfy the both of us without quarrel."

I watched him with a calculating frown. "What plan?"

"I already have the painting in my possession."

My eyes widened. "What?"

"Kareem was very kind as to grant me ownership of the manor earlier than expected; a threat was made on his life, and the poor man did not anticipate how important that manor is to me and—now to many people." He drew away ultimately, walking around the table to sit in the chair behind it.

I spun around, unable to ignore the clouds of suspicion covering the fluffiness I'd gotten earlier. "What are you talking about?"

I watched his eyes shine with pride—a pride that I was sure grew from whatever scheme he had concocted.

"The victim file you found when you infiltrated the condo of the assassins sent to kill me; how accurate was my file?"

I blinked, my mind pausing. "Too accurate."

"Correct," he said. "The Marino empire does not have a mole—it would not *dare* to have a mole because I provide them anything they want and more, and because they know I will know if they dared to cross me. The only person who could have delivered the information I wanted to buy the manor would have been Casmiro, Angelo—or me."

"I don't understand."

"I will break it down, Sport. Have a seat." He motioned to the chair by the far end; I pulled it closer till it was opposite him and then settled onto it.

"If you did not know this about me, I do not like making noise. I *despise* it. I love sticking to my business so no one would feel the need to *know* my business," he said. "My father was loud. I am quiet. Being too loud is often known to be careless. But when you are silent and use your head instead of a gun, you tend to breeze in and out of chaos unaffected."

Something clicked in my mind. "The school bus incident?"

"You are very sharp indeed," he commended. "The news about the painting and the quest was splashed across all media channels. It got people to start digging, and even though it had later been proved to the public that it was nothing but an elaborate miscommunication and a scheme to make money—not everyone bought it. It was a big mess.

"Arturo's adopted son, Chika, had paid several media houses to cover the story, throwing off the original people searching for the painting so that he could get to it before anyone else did. He had figured out where it was when he landed here in Mexico. But I'd had people take care of him before he could do even more damage."

"You didn't kill Chika?"

"Only a few people are worth my bullet. He was not worth my bullet. I had my people do it. I had them question him, too, because I was too busy stopping the mayor from having a heart attack while chaos ensued in his city, thanks to you and your team."

I became uncomfortable. "So you mean—it isn't just you who knows that I—about how I brought him in?"

"No," he answered. "But you need not worry. That is

neither their concern nor their verdict to judge. They only passed information I asked them to retrieve."

"Right . . . right . . . How does this relate to Kareem and the assassins?"

"A lot of noise had been made, so it was only a matter of time before someone randomly put two and two together and discovered the real location of the original painting. What better way than to be the person who caused the first chaos?

"I decided to buy the manor, knowing it would take weeks to secure. Kareem, while kind, was too slow. He would have loved to peel me open, to make me a friend before his association with me was severed. I did not need friendship; I only needed his signature. I did not desire to cause him any harm, but I also needed to speed up the process and take it on without noise.

"I was unsure what you and your team had planned, but I had a gut feeling it would have backfired, and one of you would have gotten hurt. So—I found myself some assassins—or better yet, one anonymous buyer had found them and promised them a lot of money to assassinate Kareem and the person who wanted to buy the painting."

I blanked out slowly, my head working, piecing things together, how his whole demeanor had changed when I informed him I needed Street back on the mission. He was quick to dismiss the idea; also, last night, when I informed him of the assassins, he was more concerned that I'd drugged him and hadn't trusted him enough to tell him. He didn't even ask about their origin or why—if they'd been after the manor's owner—they would want him dead or the other two men they had gotten victim files on.

Elio clearly stated that I wouldn't have needed to drug him if I had told him, but I'd taken it all in stride as his usual ignorance—and his chasing death. I didn't think it was because he was already aware, but still—some pieces did not fit.

"Why would you hire assassins to kill Kareem if you didn't want to cause him any harm?"

"They were not to touch Kareem, just the other men with him. Those ones were already planning to take him out, and while I would normally not care, Kareem had shown me nothing but kindness and trust and even offered to pray for me for no reason. It was my way of helping him without his knowledge and getting my hands on the manor and that painting as soon as possible."

"But you told me it would take weeks before you secure ownership. Why would you wait for weeks if you wanted to get the manor as soon as you could?"

"I answered based on the way you phrased your question. You asked me how long the buying process would take, not how long it would take for me to get the painting—and I lied by omission and told you it was a gut feeling telling me it was all right to wait weeks because I did not want noise, and because I was not aware you knew about the assassins," he clarified. "If you had told me—or if Casmiro and Angelo had *deigned* to inform me, the events that followed could have been avoided."

I frowned. "That goes both ways. If you had told me about the assassins, I wouldn't have had to drug you and be scared for your fucking life." My voice increased in pitch. "And you were so angry at me and almost broke things off with me, for what—"

"Do not misinterpret this, Zahra." His tone was sharp as he sat up. "I was not angry because you tried to save my life—no—I was angry because you drugged me, and at that time, I was clueless as to why you did it. You hadn't exactly been forthcoming when divulging information; what the hell was I supposed to feel?"

I scoffed, clenched my jaw, and looked away while trying to suppress my anger.

After a long silence, he sighed, leaning across and reaching for my hand. I looked over at him.

"Zahra, I don't want to fight with you, we have already discussed this issue. While I was angry that you drugged me, I was not lying when I told you I appreciated your taking the initiative to save my life. According to how it all turned out, the assassins had ventured off course because the plan was to attack when we were touring the manor. I needed to taint that place for Kareem so he would let it go quicker than he would if he loved it.

"When I noticed the formation at that party, I knew something was wrong, and I wanted to observe, so I left the crowd. If you hadn't intervened and I had fleshed out their new strategy, I would have gotten you and Street out of there before they brought out their guns. The lesson here is that a lot could have been prevented with trust from my end and yours.

"Aside from that, I planned this because I knew it could only get worse, and I knew my brother was involved—I knew *you* were involved alongside the people you both cared about. That was why I wanted it to happen on my terms. I did not want any more chaos that would endanger your lives. I do not want to live through that any more than I have to, Zahra."

I softened my features. "I understand. But why would you include yourself to be assassinated?"

"We both know a threat to Kareem's life would not go unnoticed by anyone. I did not want any loose ends. So I took the liberty of taking myself off the suspect list," he said. "In a way, I am glad you had intervened because I would most likely be dead if you hadn't. Loyalty changed with the people my disguised-self had hired . . . or maybe it was greed after they discovered what they could gain if they worked alone. They would have killed anyone who got in their way, and I wouldn't have seen it coming because I underestimated them."

"And Kareem? The men who are after him?"

"I was kind enough to tell him about it. His people will deal with them. But that chapter is closed with me, and the manor is now in Marino hands. No one would infiltrate the building even if the painting had been there."

I breathed. "You really went to great lengths to stop Street from doing any work."

"For your protection, Zahra. It would have been a bloodbath if I hadn't intervened. Dangerous people were after that painting, and now, we have to be more guarded because finding the painting is just a small part of this quest. Finding the gold from the map would be much worse. Eyes are on us, and they are following. People with a lust for money, and dangerous people who hunger for the power those flash drives would give them."

I nodded. "I know . . . but why do you have Street working here?"

He relaxed his shoulders. "Like I reminded you earlier. You told me you all liked to hustle for what you want. Since I have the painting and decided to bring your team back on the hunt for the gold, this minor work they are doing should be able to cover up the ego talk about working hard to gain something. In other words, it covers the stress you would have endured to retrieve the painting."

"My God."

"I was merely working on the information you provided me. You should thank me because I told them I was in on the plan to get them to the penthouse as a surprise, and if they wanted to get the final piece of that surprise, they would have to work for it."

"So now they are probably angry because they think I am making them work for the surprise."

"Hm. Not if you grab a mop and a bucket to assist Milk in the toilet. A show of good friendship."

I rolled my eyes. "You are impossible."

He nodded as if I had given him a title he would never forget.

"Why this building, though?"

"I came across it in listings of several houses needing volunteers. This one was far worse and in dire need of refurbishment. And thanks to a Good Samaritan, I learned recently that there might be some children in need of a home and proper medical care."

My heart stuttered. "What?"

The children Daiyu and I rescued with her team.

"I did not speak to her people," he informed me. "I am hoping you will relay the information that you found a perfect home for them while they heal from the mental stress of what that organization put them through."

I calmed instantly, not knowing exactly what to say to show how grateful his thoughtfulness made me feel, so I got up, went around the table, sat on his lap, and hugged him. "You don't know how much this means to me."

His arms came around me. "I am glad I can help in some way."

"Thank you." I pulled away, smiling at him, eyes searching his pretty, relaxed ones. "You're giving them a home—it's so generous."

"It is not enough. I am still asking around, seeking information. Once I find out who the people doing this are, they will pay."

"I have no doubt, as long as you include me in whatever you're planning."

He cupped my face in his hand. "I wouldn't have anyone else fighting by my side, Zahra, trust me."

I joined my lips with his to further show my appreciation. It wasn't a kiss filled with hunger or lust, but it made me feel light. Safe.

When I broke away, I looked around. "Whose office is this?"

"The manager's."

"So not yours."

"Not mine."

I grinned. "We managed to christen a place that isn't ours."

He tilted his head. "Hm, not the way I would have liked, but yes, there is a point there."

"Who knew you could be this naughty?"

"It's all you. Your effect on me. You make me insatiable."

"That is an honor."

He nodded. "It is, I must admit. Wear it proudly."

I laughed. "Where's Cassie and Angie, anyway? I didn't see them around."

A frown dragged his brows down. "They have been dismissed from their duties."

I blinked at him. "You cannot dismiss your underboss or your consigliere."

"Says who?"

"That's like the normal etiquette code thingy of the Mafia?"

"Mafia?" He frowned. "While some people use that term, I prefer to call my family an empire. Holds more weight."

I dismissed that. "You know it's not their fault. You should have told them your plans—they were worried about you."

"I would have told them before it happened. I had plans to tell them—"

"And you wouldn't have gotten the chance to either way."

"That is correct."

"So why punish them for a scheme that fell apart?"

His eyes narrowed, something cunning lingering in them. "I suppose you're right. But they still have to learn lessons from it. If I were some other boss who found out their most trusted—even though he doesn't show it—had kept something as grievous as that from him, they would be dead," he said. "But I know Angelo's mother, and Casmiro's family, and I swore to them that I would protect my own. I will not go back on my word. Therefore, they have to accept a little punishment."

"Until when?"

"Until I am ready."

"Ready for what?" I frowned. "To forgive them?"

He watched me but did not answer. A long minute passed until I understood what he was doing.

"Ignoring my question?" I asked.

"Yes."

"I hate you sometimes."

"Hm." He shot me a knowing look, his hand rubbing up and down my back. "You don't."

"You did say it was okay to be delusional," I said. "Now that I'm here, I might as well broach the topic. There's something I wanted to discuss with you."

His lips pressed against my chin as he pulled me closer to his body. "What is it?"

"I got a call from my friend . . . Vitale."

He paused his movements; even his breathing stopped momentarily as he raised his head to look at me—frowning. A deep, hard, menacing scowl blanketed his face and made me swallow down the nerves that had suddenly clawed up my throat.

"I don't like it," he said.

"You don't like what?"

"His name on your lips; I do not like it. If you want to broach a topic about him, refer to him as something else. Not his name."

I frowned. "Why shouldn't I use his name?"

His eyes hardened, clearly hating that I chose to fight him on his request—no—*demand*.

"It gives him more meaning, and I am very uncomfortable with that."

"Okay . . ." I blinked, needing him calm to even bring this up. "Okay . . . I'll—uh—I don't know what exactly to refer to him as—"

"That man. Just say 'that man,' don't say his name."

"Okay—"

"Make the conversation snappy because I do not want to be angry."

I gave a sharp nod. "Right." Then I frowned. "Did something else happen? Why—why do you hate him so much?"

"I don't hate him. I would not spare a lesser man that kind of emotion. He irritates me. And he held you—roughly, unapologetically, and I promised myself I would kill him. And I will."

"I mean—"

"He also left a scar on you a long time ago, and he's still breathing. I recall you saying no one leaves a scar on you and lives. I understand in our case, it's different due to recent developments, but you still talk to him. I do not want to portray myself as possessive because you are your own woman, but I will not deny that your constant communication with him bothers me."

I sighed. "There is absolutely nothing for you to worry about with Vit—"

"Zahra," he warned.

"*That man*—sorry—you have nothing to worry about; he's just a part of my past—"

"That you still talk to."

I smoothed my hand over his shoulder. "He . . . was not a bad part of my past, Elio; in fact, we were good friends, and he showed me what being a normal teenager felt like. He hated Manuel as much as I did."

"Why?"

"Manuel and Vi—*that man's* brother, Ignazio—made his life a living, breathing hell. Aside from being bullied to near death, they deprived him of everything good—just for fun. Ignazio is a terrible person and doesn't deserve that seat you sponsored for him."

Elio raised a brow. "So he asked you to talk to me? Get me to change my mind?"

"No. There's nothing we can do now. But I know that move you pulled wasn't your last—"

"Oh, it was not my last. That bruise lasted three days on

your arm. I have barely started dealing with that man; when I am done, he will be too dead to be dead."

I don't even want to know what that means.

"He didn't offend me, Elio. He doesn't deserve that. Trust me, he just—The bruise didn't even hurt me."

"I am glad it didn't. But that does not excuse the painful fact that seeing it on your arm for those three days hurt me. Do you know how much willpower it takes to ignore killing someone who is supposed to be dead? The mental stress it caused me, who will pay for that? Hm?"

"Come on, it's not that deep."

"His disgusting gloved hand gripped your arm *deeply*. Yes, it is that deep."

I bit back a laugh, and he caught it.

"This is not funny," he clarified. "I do not like that you are trying to vouch for that man."

"I'm not vouching for him; I'm just letting you know he's not worth the trouble. Trust me. Leave him be; you'll have more peace of mind when you do."

"Were you involved with him?"

The question caught me off guard. "What?"

"Before . . . were you and he . . . intimate?"

He watched me intently, and upon my silence, something dark crossed his eyes. "You were."

"Only once," I blurted, "and it didn't mean anything to me."

"What about him?"

I sucked in a breath from my parted lips, letting it out with a response. "Not anymore."

"You do not sound sure."

"Elio, it happened years ago—"

"But you still speak with him, knowing he might harbor feelings for you. You care about him—"

"Baby, the only person I care about romantically is you."

That shut him up—in fact, his whole body froze beneath me. Was it from me using that term of endearment or from my declaration? I wasn't sure, but it had the tips of his ears growing a shade redder as he cleared his throat and shifted on the seat as if he didn't know what to do with himself.

"Well," he started, looking everywhere but at me. "I already made my decision. I will make him suffer, and then I will kill him."

"Jesus, Elio—what if it upsets me?"

His gaze snapped to mine. "Do not threaten me like that."

"It's not a threat. It will upset me because the only good thing in my present is killing the mildly good thing in my past."

"What if the good thing in your present wants to be the only good thing in your life and in your future, and in order for him to be sane, he has to kill the mildly good thing in your past so that you can see and know him as the only solid good thing that ever happened to you?"

"Yeah, you lost me."

"I will not change my mind. If I let him go, he will not learn his lesson."

"He already learned his lesson, okay? He's pretty fucked up right now and very angry."

"Precisely what I wanted."

"Let him go . . . please, for me—for little old me who you *really* care about and would hate to anger because she would not let it go and would most likely bug you till your ears bled and you had no other choice but to do her bidding when you could have just accepted when she asked nicely?"

He sighed, shaking his head as the frown slowly slipped off his face. "Promise me he won't interfere with us because then I will not wait to make him suffer. I will just kill him. In cold blood; I would make sure I don't use a gun so that I can feel his life slipping away with my bare hands."

I swallowed. "I promise. Your pretty little heart is safe with me."

"It is?" he asked, the hint of a different meaning passing between us.

"It is. Completely safe."

He nodded. "Good. I will call off the hit on his mother."

"Jesus—"

His lips covered the loudness of my voice as he hugged me to his body possessively. When he broke away, his eyes searched mine. "No more talk of that man. It upsets me."

"Duly noted."

He supplied me with a firm nod. "Would you like to see who the children you rescued will be staying with?"

CHAPTER TWENTY-SIX

Zahra

The children were playing outside in the expansive backyard; many booths had been set out for them to participate in different games, get healthy snacks, or get their faces painted with all colorful things. The tiny voices, innocent laughter escaping through mouths with braces and several ones with a few gaps here and there, filled me with a peace I had never once experienced.

By the side of the booths, clowns made children laugh, and a small kids' band was also close to that area.

A huge fort was set up close to the building in case the kids were tired from all the fun and games and wanted to rest while they were there and work was being done inside.

The innocence of the surroundings made me smile.

"I have secured a building not far from here; that is where they can rest for the night until the work inside is done. They will come here every day if they wish to have fun. The manager here arranged everything, and I just paid whatever expenses she might have needed," Elio said.

"It's like a little camp for them. They don't look tired at all." My smile widened but didn't reach my eyes.

"Hm." Elio shifted closer, putting his arm around my shoulder and pulling my body to his.

"I honestly didn't think you were this generous," I told him, accepting the warmth his body provided.

He shrugged. "Children should not have to spend their childhoods being sad. They have their adulthood to cover that."

I looked up at him, scrunched my nose as I raised my hand, and poked a finger into his hair, pushing his head slightly.

"Ouch," he said, not a muscle shifting on his face to indicate that my action had hurt him.

"You say the most fucked-up things sometimes."

"Stating facts is not 'fucked up,'" he answered. "Everybody gets sad sometimes; it's harder on some of us adults because when we were kids, we did not have a childhood. We did not play outside. Did not laugh freely. Did not . . ." He trailed off, his eyes distant as he watched the kids. "Did not know what true happiness felt like." His voice was quiet.

A solemn kind of calm washed through me. "Yeah, you're right."

"Now that we are adults, the least we can do for the children around us is to make sure they do not grow up knowing what being an adult feels like before they actually become adults."

The care in his voice almost caught me off guard. I had seen how he was with that kid back at the tattoo place, and I didn't think for one second that though he might have frowned at the kid like he wanted the poor boy to melt, he still cared.

"What do you think of them?" he asked.

"What?"

"What do you think of kids, of children in general? Would you like to have some of your own one day?" he asked, head dropping as he looked down at me.

My hand went to my throat, playing with the butterfly pendant around my neck as I swallowed. "They're precious little beings; what woman wouldn't want to have them?"

"I meant you."

I met his stare. "Are you fishing for something? Thinking of having kids with me? Because if that's the case, you need to slow down. I don't think we are there yet."

He frowned. "Are you uncomfortable with the question?"

"Why would I be?"

"Because you are not answering."

"Why are you asking?"

"I am curious."

"Why are you curious?"

"Why are you getting defensive?"

I poked the inside of my cheek with my tongue, looking away from him as I looked back at the kids, letting the silence stretch before I spoke. "Yes, if I could, I would have loved to."

When there was silence from his end, I looked up at him, expecting the question I saw in his eyes.

"I can't have children," I informed him, a tremor in my fingers as they stroked the butterfly.

"What?"

Not wanting to see what he thought in his eyes, I looked away, back to the innocence of our surroundings, before I answered. "How do you think they made sure none of us got pregnant?" I asked. "No female Plant can have children. We can't reproduce because we were not made to reproduce."

He stiffened beside me, and my heart almost sank.

"Does that change anything for you?" I let the question slip out before I could stop it.

With a snap, he was turning my body to face his, and with great effort, I met his gaze, which was angry and harsh. "Do not speak nonsense."

I bit my tongue.

"Do you remember what they did to you?"

I dragged in a breath and let it out. "When they took us to the—When we were fourteen they took us somewhere before we were prepped for penetration. It was a doctor's place. I don't think it was registered, but it was an equally big organization, too . . . I didn't know then; they just made us sleep, and when we woke up, we were taken back. But as I grew, I learned it was tubal ligation."

"So, it can be reversed."

"In some cases, yeah. I went to reverse it . . . but the doctor told me there was a lot of damage and the possibility of me ever getting pregnant was, well—zero to none. And we've had sex unprotected a lot of times and nothing—so . . . yeah."

A familiar look flashed in his eyes.

I pursed my lips before speaking. "I've had years to get over that fact, Elio; you don't have to pity me."

"I do not pity you. I pity the people who did this to you."

I laughed, but he did not join me.

Pulling me into a hug, he whispered in my ear, "I promise you, Zahra, when I find the people who did this, the world will know."

The tone of his voice told me he meant every single word he said. It sent a chill down my spine—but my mind loved the idea because it was what I also wanted, and with him by my side, I was more assured that we would find them, and we would rain hell-fucking-fire until there was nothing but ashes beneath our feet.

"What kind of sick motherfucker makes someone work for a fucking surprise?" Dog bit out, pinning a glare my way as he slid into the space beside Milk, hitting her shoulder not so gently.

We were at the newly refurbished cafeteria in the building. Some of the tables were filled by other workers who'd decided to have a late dinner too.

"Personal space, Dog? You still smell like paint," Milk pointed out, biting on a fry, her hair pulled up in a rough ponytail.

Dog directed his glare at her. "And you smell like toilet, but you don't see me pointing it out."

"You just did," she said, offering him a blank look.

"I just did," he repeated, his gaze lingering before looking away and shaking his head. He reached for one of the burgers on the table, and took such a big bite out of it that his mouth was too full to chew properly.

Upper didn't speak; when he got to the table, he just started feasting on his burger like it was the last food on earth, grumbling occasionally. Devil was the last to join us after escorting Elio out of the building.

Elio was flying back to Milan early due to work, and I had convinced him to call back Angelo and Casmiro. He had promised to think about it, but I highly doubted he would, as he informed me that Casmiro was back in his hometown with his family and it would be good for him to visit since he almost died recently, and they had been worried. He also said Angelo had recently gotten into a relationship, and he wanted him to cater to it adequately.

I didn't push further after that. I let him be, and he promised to call when he landed, leaving me to deal with Street.

"Did he get off okay?" I asked as Devil took the space beside me, reaching for one of the chilled Cokes in the middle of the table.

"Yeah, a whole parade and shit—they just came out of nowhere like they were waiting for him to exit the building or something—said he'll call when he lands." He flexed his shoulder, taking a swig of the Coke, but kept drinking and drinking and drinking like he couldn't get enough.

Milk rubbed her neck, tired.

Upper looked like death.

Dog was angry-eating, and Devil kept drinking until the bottle was almost empty.

"What kind of drug did you give us?" Upper asked. "I have urges to throw up, but I cannot throw up, and I'm so bloody hungry, but I'm so full."

Guilt gripped me. "I'm so sorry, guys. I don't know what I was thinking."

Dog—not being able to talk—just gave me the middle finger.

I deserved that.

"I mean"—I cleared my throat—"at least we got the painting? Right? And now we have a map—"

"And security twenty-four seven while we're here," Devil supplied. "I am not happy you drugged us. But I'm happy we're back in the game."

"Right after I try not to die from the effects of the drug and scrubbing toilets all freaking day," Milk said, the side of her head dropping to the table, cheeks pressing flush against the flat surface.

"I helped out?"

Her gaze shifted to me, eyeballs huge like she was possessed, thanks to the stern glare she shot my way.

I shifted closer to Devil, shrinking from her stare—the guy in question threw his hand around my shoulder, pulling me tighter into him.

"What's the plan now?" he asked.

"We study the map and watch our six because I don't think it will take people long to figure out we have what they want."

Dog swallowed, drinking his Sprite and burping loudly.

Milk's face scrunched up in disgust. "You are so disgusting it hurts my eyes."

"You love me still, pinky brain." He smirked her way, and she delivered him the middle finger this time as she raised her head. "The map is all colors of messed up; it will take ages to figure it out."

"You only think like this because you're all drugged up. Wait for the fog to clear," I told her.

"At least we have the penthouse," Dog injected. "Though Zahra claimed she rented it with invisible savings we all know shit about."

"Yes." Upper tilted his head, studying me. "Why did you serve your boyfriend that story, and why did he buy it?"

"He didn't buy it," Devil said. "He was the one who rented it, and Zahra—with her pride, she didn't want Elio to let us know that he did it—made him lie."

"Still sounds like bullshit to me," Dog said, his eyes trying to parse out the truth as he watched me.

"Whatever. We'll have our fun and break for a month, and then head back to Milan. Elio told me he would arrange a place for us outside the compound, but within the district, so that's awesome. But for now—all animosity aside, we need to fill our pockets because a lot was spent on that cruise, and, well, a little thievery here and there wouldn't hurt, would it?"

"Sounds like fun if we survive this drug, as Milk pointed out," Upper said.

"You'll survive it, and I'll make up for it—"

"Oh, you will," Dog said. "All fucking errands will be run by you. You're our little puppet until we leave Mexico."

"I accept without complaint," I answered, knowing it would all be forgotten when we woke up more refreshed tomorrow.

For now, I ate my food.

Easy and jabbing conversations passed around the table swiftly while glares turned into smiles and smiles turned into laughter, and we didn't even notice when evening turned into night.

I was relaxed, content, in my element, and with my favorite people.

I looked forward to our break because when the time came to work, relaxation would be the furthest thing from our minds, and fortunately, we were more than prepared.

CHAPTER TWENTY-SEVEN

A month later

Elio

The room smelled like blood and spilled guts.

The odor was repellent, circulating in the area that had once been cold but was now warm due to the mutilated bodies around me and the body heat from four of my soldiers who would, unfortunately, have to clean the mess that had resulted from my anger and empty mind.

I flexed the muscles around my neck, blowing out a breath of relief as one of the soldiers passed me a cigar and a lighter. The moment my gaze settled on my hand as it collected the items, I struggled to see my skin. All that met my vision was blood; coated around my hand, splashed on my forearms, and digging under my nails.

It irritated me, and the urge to soak myself in clean water pulled strong.

I placed the cigar between my lips, lit up the end, and inhaled the smoke until it stroked every nerve ending in my body. I turned back to the massacre.

Five bodies . . . there were supposed to be six. The Elite people I'd hired were supposed to be fucking six. One of them had escaped. One dead man was still breathing, and a sense of unfinished business touched a nerve that made me picture a gruesome punishment for every man involved in finding these people—for their carelessness and inability to get the job done—Angelo and Casmiro included.

I knew my actions were a little . . . erratic. The Elite had no idea who had paid them for the job. Still, it was *me*—they diverted, made noise, made things inconvenient for me, and I despised flaws in schemes I had taken the time and energy to build. They brought in flaws—*greedy thieves with no regard for courtesy.*

I had waited two weeks to do this and wanted to wait a few more weeks—make them sweat a little—but today, my mind had been a void of its own making, webs of anger and a need for blood, and relief had woven itself around my insides, and the urge to visit this little team had plagued me till I succumbed.

Waking up, I wondered why the neutral mood I had carried from the day before never followed me to the new day. In fact, I had been on a phone call with Zahra and, at some point, fell asleep naturally—without taking any pills to aid it.

We had been talking about anything and nothing for hours on end. It started from the time they reached a club, and she'd retired to a private corner to speak with me, distracting me from reading, as she talked about the most random things. She refused to disconnect the phone—for some reason—thinking I was bored to death and her company was the only thing she thought would keep me sane.

I didn't mind because I enjoyed hearing her voice and the voices of her friends in the background.

Even when she returned to their penthouse, and they had dinner, I was still connected to the call until she went to her bedroom, and I finally settled into bed and drifted off with her still talking and on the brink of sleep herself.

One would think that after all that and a night of perfect sleep, I would wake up feeling light and regular—but no—I felt heavy, and when I picked up my phone to check the time and then caught the date, I knew why I felt like I had the weight of the world on my shoulders.

It was December 1st, my birthday, and I hadn't mentally been prepared for it.

After my nineteenth birthday, I always took care by schooling my mind a day before my birthday, but things had been going smoothly for the past few weeks. I was happy, I was content, and everything was normal; but somehow, today became so gray. I tried to think of reasons to be happy and grateful, but thinking about them made them gray, too, and the feeling ignited anger. Uncontrollable anger that seemed to sink into my skin and body.

I had taken the longest shower, went back to the bedroom to arrange my bed, and did not like the little crease by the side, so I redid the whole thing; there was a little crease in the middle, and I redid it again—up to five times before I was satisfied—but the work made me angrier.

Going to find clothes to wear, I despised how everything in my wardrobe seemed dirty; even if I knew they were clean, they somehow managed to look dirty.

I succumbed, selected a standard button-up, and ironed it even though it was already well-ironed. I performed that action—over and over and over and over again, burning myself on occasion and swinging the machine into a nearby wall out of anger. I went back to pick it up, inspected it for damage, and returned to ironing.

I had woken up at around eight in the morning and was leaving for the torture rooms at noon.

I could not eat anything. I did not crave food. I craved alcohol, anything that would make me feel numb.

I decided to finish with the Elite group on time, but after I saw them, it took two hours to kill five people completely. Torture and maiming—blood, opened flesh, screams, cries, terror, and gore—somehow, I wasn't satisfied.

Blowing out the smoke, I tilted my head, studying the one with strawberry-blond hair, now soaked in blood, his fingers still twitching.

"Gun."

It was in my grip in an instant, and I angled the barrel to the dying man's head and rapidly pulled the trigger until his brain particles started to slip out of his scattered head.

Angling the gun back up, I studied my work for almost a minute before nodding. "Hm." I stretched out my hand that held the gun to the soldier who had given it to me. But for some reason, the weapon remained in my hand.

Slowly, I turned to look at the soldier; his face was pale, eyes on the man I had just shot.

"Was he a friend?"

The soldier snapped upright, blinking back as he looked at my forehead, unable to meet my eyes, body shaken up. From his young face, I could tell he was in his early twenties.

He shook his head fiercely, fear in his eyes. "No, sir. No, sir, I—I am sorry, sir."

I frowned, irritation biting at my skin. "What in God's name am I looking at?"

Dread tainted his eyes at the disdain and irritation in my voice.

"Sir, I'm—"

"Go, get out. Make sure I never see you again. Ever."

"Yes, sir," he said before hurriedly rushing out of the room.

I looked at the other soldiers, their faces stoic, eyes ahead, awaiting orders.

I stretched my gun toward one, and he quickly collected it. Body firm, trained.

That was what I liked to see.

"Inform the recruitment manager that I would like to meet with him. I will not tolerate little mistakes like this."

"Yes, Marino."

"Pass a message across to the data team. Tell them that if they do not locate the whereabouts of the last member in the Elite group before the day ends, I will seek out anyone and everyone they care about, and then I will pay them a farewell visit."

"Yes, sir."

I stepped out without another word, two soldiers following automatically behind me as I walked from the torture room to my house. Everyone who passed by avoided my eyes and stayed out of my way; some had fear in their eyes, and some were stoic.

I itched to pick out the ones who cowered—in fact, I would add it to my agenda to do a personal inspection of every man in the empire. It would take more than a day and even more than a week—but the urge to pluck out blunt thorns was very strong—or maybe the anger simmering underneath my skin compelled these thoughts because usually, I would not care.

When I entered my house, the soldiers didn't follow.

I headed straight to my bedroom, discarded the cigar, and started taking off the dirty clothes on my body—entering the room half naked, I walked into the bathroom and straight to the sink, turned on the water, and placed my hands underneath it. The water that came out clean and clear from the faucet was tainted with blood when it met my hands. I cleaned and cleaned, wiping off dried blood with soap as the bloodied water went down the drain.

When I was satisfied after what seemed like the longest time, I turned off the faucet and went to the bathtub, turning on the cold water as it filled up.

I took off the remainder of my clothes. As I got into the tub and the water rose around my body, my muscles were still wound tight even at the coldness on my skin.

I let my head fall back to the tub's edge, closed my eyes, and swallowed with effort as I tried to calm my breathing.

It wasn't working.

When the tub was full, I let my body sink into it. My chest, shoulders, neck, and then my head until I was completely under. A soft kind of calmness claimed me, and I stayed that way for a while, holding my breath with my eyes closed—when I was at my limit, I opened my eyes underwater, and the silhouette of my mother leaning by the tub was what I saw next.

She was still in that black dress.

I was about to come up, but her hands came into the water, holding my shoulders down.

"It's okay," her muffled voice said with a smile as she held me down, grip strong, while I fought to come up for air. "It's all right, Elio; you will be with me soon."

Even though I struggled, my whole body felt like it was paralyzed. I couldn't move, and she held me tightly, firmly. But somehow, I was still struggling—in my mind, I was still fighting to move, get up, and intake oxygen, but my body wouldn't respond, and my mother wouldn't let go of me.

I couldn't hold my breath any longer and was forced to part my lips underneath the water, both my nostrils and my mouth filling my lungs with liquid—and I was drowning.

Suddenly, she let me go, and the paralysis slipped from my body as I emerged with a force that had water pouring out of the tub to the floor; my hands—shaking—gripped the edge of the tub firmly as I coughed out the water, taking air into my lungs, wheezing.

My chest and eyes burned, my body shook—and no one was there . . . I was alone . . . I had been alone.

My mother was not here.

My mother is dead.

When I'd managed to cough air back into my lungs, I lifted myself from the tub and grabbed a towel by the side, wrapping it around myself firmly as I carelessly stepped out of the tub, forgetting water had soaked the tiles.

One second, my leg was on the floor, and the next, it was slipping, and my body was plummeting right underneath my feet, and I met the ground with a forceful, sharp thud that sounded like a slap.

Something shattered, and a sharp pain sliced into my elbow. There was also a tingling burn inside my mouth.

For a few minutes, I remained in that position on the ground. My body hurt. My head, light—and my mind, still a void.

December 1st.

I hated every single fucking bit of this day. Bad luck always followed. Everything always went wrong. Even if I prepared myself the day before, something would ruin it. Something that would hurt me, either mentally or physically.

Even today, I still could not pinpoint what or who exactly had jinxed me the day I turned nineteen.

Was it because I had woken up on the wrong side of the bed that day? Would things have turned out differently if I had woken up on my right side? Was it because I did not eat with Elia on that day? Or was it my sister's words, which still echoed in my ear if I stopped and listened for her voice amongst the chaos in my head? The last three words she ever said to me.

"I hate you!"

A sigh left my lips as I started to move, trying to inspect the damage on my arm.

I had broken some glass objects during my fall, which injured me.

Looking in the direction where the pain came from, the bite intensified when I saw the gash.

The skin above my elbow had been slashed—deep enough to need stitches. The ground was messy, stained with blood and water.

"Fuck."

I managed to stand, tremors still in my hands, as I headed to the mirror to check the damage inside my mouth.

I bared my teeth; they were all bloody. I'd injured my upper gum, but it didn't hurt as much as my elbow.

I spat the blood into the sink and rinsed my mouth and teeth until the water ran clear.

Then I started inspecting my elbow wound, also managing to find a first-aid kit. I washed off the blood that had slipped down my hand before cleaning the damage and treating it.

Fishing out a bandage and trying to work that open with one hand and my teeth, I managed to free it, but it rolled right onto the ground, the cloth getting wet with the water and blood on the floor—another mess.

I closed my eyes for about ten seconds, trying to tamp down the sudden urge to break something out of annoyance.

At that same moment, I heard the door to my bedroom open and close.

"Elio?" Zahra's voice met my ears, and I froze. "You in the bathroom?"

Her footsteps drew closer until the bathroom door opened, and her eyes found me—the smile on her face dying instantly when she caught sight of the blood and the mess.

"What the fuck happened?" She rushed toward me, inspecting my hand as concern filled her eyes. "Are you okay?" She reached to touch me. "Let me see—"

"Don't," I said, tugging my hand from her reach. "I will take care of it."

She looked up at me and then back at the wound. "It's okay, I can help cover it—"

"I will do it myself, thank you."

She reached for me again, but I tugged away.

Her brows curved in a frown, brown eyes showing equal parts care and annoyance. "Let me help you."

"I am very capable of tending to myself."

"But it looks terrible; how did it happen?" Her gaze moved around the bathroom. I took that time to scan her from head to toe; her hair was left loose and styled to perfection, and she wore a red dress that stopped high on her thighs and showcased too much cleavage. She smelled good, too, fresh out of a probably less traumatic bath than the one I had just experienced.

What is she doing here? Yesterday, if I recall correctly, she was in Mexico.

Her gaze fell back to me, searching as she reached forward again. "What's wrong? Why won't you let me help?"

"Because there is no need for that."

"You don't have to be stubborn about it. You clearly can't do it yourself; your hands are shaking—"

"I can do it myself."

"E—"

"Can you give me space?" I snapped, irritated. "I will tend to myself and then join you in a moment; can you do that?"

She blinked, probably sensing I wasn't in the mood for an argument. She hesitated a moment, sighing, and thankfully backed off. "Okay, I'll wait for you outside the—"

"The bedroom, outside the bedroom."

She was taken aback, her lips thinning downward, and then she nodded. "Okay."

With that, she left the bathroom, closing the door behind her. I waited until the bedroom door opened and closed, and then I let out a breath of relief, not realizing how much I hated her seeing me like this.

Shame was the most prominent emotion.

It took a while, but I managed to finish up with the wound and clean the mess in the bathroom. When I reached my wardrobe, all the black button-ups seemed . . . *bloodied*, like the one I had taken off earlier.

Unable to stand it, I went to another section in the wardrobe and found a white one. I felt satisfied as I put that on quickly and made myself look presentable before leaving the room.

I found her in the kitchen, leaning on the table with her fingers tapping furiously on her phone screen.

Her legs were on full display, tanned, brown, and so beautiful. The dress seemed to be made especially for her, and the urge to hug her from behind was there, but I knew she would probably smell the oddness of my mood and not my cologne.

She didn't notice me until I was in line with her vision, and she did a double take while my eyes zeroed in on the cake right by her side on the kitchen counter.

My stomach—something was wrong with my stomach.

"I love the shirt," she said with a genuine, surprised smile, putting her phone away.

"Thank you," I said, ignoring the cake and the feeling it evoked, before moving to the whiskey collection on the shelf, turning away from her as I got a glass and a bottle.

When I turned, she was rounding the counter and putting her arms around me in a hug that warmed me and relaxed the muscles the water in the tub and my connection with the ground had made tight.

"I've missed you. Happy birthday," she said. The smile and brightness in her voice made me feel even heavier than before.

"Hm."

She pulled away to look up at me as I dropped the items in my hand on the counter.

"You didn't hear me say that on the phone when it was midnight? I wanted to be the first to wish you a happy birthday."

"Very thoughtful," I responded, pouring myself a drink as silence reigned. Finally, she sighed.

"What's going on, Elio?" she asked, and I glanced at her, noting a bit of confusion, anticipation, and a little excitement as she spoke. "Are you mad because I didn't text you? If you are, there's a reason for that. Aside from being on the flight and having it delayed by an hour, we arrived back at the condo you rented for us, and Milk and I had to get things from the store while we tried to help Dog bake a cake. I told Street it was your birthday, and Dog saw it as a good opportunity to bake. It was chaos in the kitchen, and then we had to let the cake cool for hours after it was done baking, and then we decorated it—I helped with the whole thing and it took great efforts and you need to try it, I—"

"It looks wonderful," I cut in, holding the whiskey glass and taking a sip as I eyed the cake and then her.

She was looking right at me, eyebrows brushed; eyes brighter due to the light color she had applied; her lips were glossed, and she looked terrific—she'd taken her time to look amazing for this—but my mouth spoke before my head. "I see the efforts you made with the cake, and I appreciate it, but I am not very keen to eat it. Not because I do not think it will be good, but because I am not in the mood."

The anticipation and excitement in her eyes vanished like I had squashed it.

She sighed. "This is the first time we're seeing each other in a month. Why are you acting like this?" Apprehension laced her tone. "Did something happen?"

"No." The sip I had taken of whiskey was enough to make me realize that I didn't need a drink, so I put it down.

"*Clearly*, something is wrong."

"What gave you that notion?"

She waved her hand as if trying to gather my aura. "This, all of this. You're too . . . straight."

I tilted my head, confused. "I am straight."

"That's not what I mean. You're too bland and off—You're acting like you don't want me here."

"Maybe I don't."

Fuck. That was supposed to stay in my head—those three words were supposed to remain in my head, not fall from my mouth because I do want her here, I do, but I just don't want her to see me like . . . this, and the way her eyes widened, looking like I had slapped her with my words, had me completely frozen on the spot.

I'd hurt her feelings.

She shook her head, looking away from me as she walked back around the counter and grabbed her purse from a kitchen stool. "You can throw away the cake if you don't want it or whatever you do to things you don't want." With that, she made her way out of the kitchen, her footsteps getting fainter and fainter.

My common sense was working very slowly today, and it took me seconds too long to make my body move and chase after her.

She was almost at the door and out of the house when I caught onto her wrist, and she spun around, her bag swinging and getting me right in the nose.

It stung, and I held it immediately, the pain sending warmth to my eyes.

A sharp gasp left her, and she dropped the bag to the floor instantly, eyes wide. "What the fuck! Oh my God, I didn't hear your footsteps—Are you bleeding?"

"One—one moment."

She tried to see it, hands on my face. "Fuck, I'm sorry. It was instinct, and I didn't hear you behind me and—"

"What do you have in that bag? Christ." I wasn't bleeding, but it hurt more than the elbow wound.

"It was made with a bit of metal—God, I'm sorry."

"No, no, it's good," I managed out, knowing the skin around the area was already growing red. "It happens. I would have gotten hurt one way or another; it's fairly normal."

"What the hell does that even mean?"

"Nothing you need to worry about." I removed my hand from my nose, blinking my vision clear. "Lo siento," I apologized. "For earlier, I did not mean for you to leave . . . I am just—I am having a very bad day, and I did not want you to see me like that."

Her gaze softened. "You were okay yesterday . . ."

"Yes, I was. But I don't know. It happens like this . . . sometimes."

She nodded. "You want to go somewhere to talk about it?"

I eyed her. "Where?"

"I may or may not have reserved a spot for us at a restaurant. For your birthday, in case you wanted to leave the house?"

The pain in my nose had subsided a little; thankfully it wasn't serious. "You had a day planned for us?"

She nodded.

"Why?"

"It's your birthday," she answered. "Birthdays are special, and from the looks of it, you don't really celebrate."

"I never have," I confessed. "That cake on the counter is the first I have ever received. In my entire life. So, if I acted weird about it, you know why."

Her lips pressed into a thin line. "Well," she said quietly. "Now you have me to show you why having a birthday cake is normal. Most especially one made with so much . . ." Something swirled in her eyes, and she raised herself, pressing her lips to mine in a light kiss, before pulling away, her pretty eyes looking between mine as she completed her sentence. "So much . . . care."

Somehow, I could materialize a smile from the chaos in my head.

"I rented a car. A better one this time, and you're driving us to the restaurant; we'll eat and talk and fill your stomach and get you back in a good mood; what do you say?"

"All right, okay, yes."

CHAPTER TWENTY-EIGHT

Elio

About an hour later, the woman I considered my partner was taking too much pleasure in my awful day. I'd already concluded that she had terrible table manners, and it didn't bother me anymore. The glare I sent her didn't have any weight as she tried to stifle her laughter, her eyes going red with the efforts she was making to hold it in.

"I really don't know why I like you," I stated, shaking my head as she raised a hand as if she were stopping the laughter, but when she tried to speak, laughter was all that came out.

"I'm sorry," she wheezed, her face red. "I'm sorry, I'm just—I'm just trying to picture it. You"—laugh—"falling from"—more laughter—"the bathtub"—a wheeze. "It's so—it's so not—I can't picture it."

"People fall, Zahra. People fall all the time. And mine was almost fatal; you should not be laughing. I could have died."

She sucked in a shaky breath. "I'm glad you didn't, but—do you happen to have a—a camera in the bathroom? I just—I gotta see that shit for myself."

"You are a very terrible person," I pointed out.

She busted out laughing again, drawing attention from people around us.

She blew out a breath in an attempt to calm herself. "What? People falling is—there's just something about it that—I don't know—especially you? Mr. Never-careless-always-careful-and-proper."

I leveled her with a stare. "I must admit that I can never be too careful. I am only human, after all."

"Oh, now you're trying to seem more human to placate yourself."

"And you are becoming less human by bullying me with your laughter. On what is supposed to be my birthday."

She rolled her eyes. "Swear that if it was me who had that bathroom accident, you wouldn't be laughing at my expense."

"I wouldn't. Because, unlike you, I would hate to see you hurt."

She raised a brow. "You wouldn't try to picture it, not even one fucking bit? Lie and tell me that you wouldn't."

"I wouldn't."

"See? That's a lie."

I shook my head. "Why do I even try to indulge you?"

"Because I'm the most sensible person you know?" She batted her eyelashes.

"You would really hate to hear my thoughts right now," I told her, evoking a small laugh.

"You know . . . this is, like, our first real date, like, we came out for the actual purpose of going on a date."

"I thought it was for my birthday?" I asked.

"Yeah, it is, but this place is a little fancy, and I reserved it two days ago. So it's a birthday first date. I've never had one of those."

I smiled. "I think that statement should be rephrased. You've never had one of me."

"Look who's getting cocky now." She chuckled.

I shrugged.

"So what do you do on your birthdays? I know you don't celebrate, but what do you do?" she asked.

"Get hurt, unintentionally. Almost every birthday of mine. It's like one of those curses in paranormal books."

"Paranormal books? What's paranormal?" she asked with curiosity in her eyes. She truly did not know what paranormal meant.

"Someone or something supernatural."

Her brows shot up. "Oh . . . like, horror things, scary things?"

"Along those lines, yes."

"Well, I think you're just jinxing yourself. Sometimes our minds unknowingly manifest these thoughts, and our lives take hold of them, and we jinx ourselves without knowing."

I nodded, seeing sense in what she was saying, although the feeling did not touch the surface of what I actually felt. I did not comment on that because the last thing I wanted was to trouble her with how I truly felt.

Our conversation veered into another direction. I tried to keep my mind on track with her—often getting lost in my body and coming right back whenever she laughed or covered the side of her mouth from others' views when she wanted to eat messily because she couldn't help herself.

Soon after, she excused herself to the restroom when our starter was cleared and the main courses came out. I checked my phone, seeing a *happy birthday* text from Angelo and a picture of a package his mother had organized for me. There was a birthday wish from Gemma, with tons of red hearts and a promise to shower me with presents when we saw each other again; there was also a small video clip from Gran Louisa.

It was a short *happy birthday* message and a reminder to bring Zahra over.

Still getting lost in the messages, I stopped when I felt Zahra's presence. I turned my phone screen off, looking up to see she was just two feet away from me when a woman trying to leave a table bumped into her.

"I'm so sorry. I didn't see you there." Zahra apologized politely, but the woman, who looked like she had been angry before bumping into her, shot her a glare, muttering something in a language I didn't understand. From the way Zahra's politeness quickly shifted to a frown, I knew it was something foul.

Zahra responded in the same language, a slight frown on her face.

The woman didn't back down; she quickly sized her up and probably thought she could take her if worse came to worst. I picked up my fork, cut through the meat, watched the scene unfold, and eyed the man sitting at the table the woman had been bolting from; he was also watching the scene.

The woman responded to Zahra, firming her stance, the language falling out of her mouth obviously nothing pleasant. Her pitch was increasing by the second, causing a scene. Everyone was paying attention to what was happening, though I was sure nobody understood the back-and-forth unless they understood the language.

I saw the exact moment Zahra's calm snapped; it was almost the same time the man stood up behind the woman, whispering something in her ear and cautiously looking around as if embarrassed.

When Zahra spoke, the venom in her voice could not be mistaken as anything other than anger, and with the way the woman's eyes widened, I knew my little witch had struck a nerve.

Staff began to gather at the corners, needing clarification about what was happening.

The woman stepped forward. "What the fuck did you say?"

"You heard—"

Zahra was cut off when the woman pushed her, and almost like she had gotten the opening she had been waiting for, she moved to retaliate, but the worm by the woman's back encircled his *dirty* hand around Zahra's arm as if to hold her back from attacking his companion.

I looked away, the grip I had on my fork tightened, and I picked up the knife, forcefully slicing through the food on my plate as I spoke. "If you want to keep your hand, you will take it off my woman."

My voice was surprisingly calm, audible enough to shift all attention to me.

The restaurant became silent, and my soldiers, who had been discreetly standing in the corners, all took a step forward, increasing the silence as I dug the fork into the slice of meat I had cut and then carefully carried it into my mouth. I raised my gaze, chewing slowly, my eyes solely on the man.

"Would you like to keep your hand?"

The man swallowed, letting his hand drop as he tugged at the woman who now seemed afraid, same as everyone around who—telling from their features—were a bit uncomfortable with whatever aura I appeared to possess at the moment.

One last glance at Zahra, and the woman was about to oblige, taking a step back, but I shook my head, and her movement halted as my gaze settled on the man.

"You do not leave until you apologize," I said.

Apprehension stained the woman's eyes as she looked at the man.

A sigh came from Zahra. "It's all right, E—"

"You do not leave until you apologize or you lose your hand. My patience is running very thin." My voice covered Zahra's, and I heard some gasps from tables nearby, but I was unbothered as I watched. I dug another cut into the meat, and ate it without looking away from the man.

He gulped down and turned to Zahra. "I'm sorry for—holding your arm. It was wrong of me."

I nodded, looking away. "Some people do not understand basic manners," I muttered, raising a dismissive hand, and I could feel my soldiers retreating to their positions.

The music in the restaurant that had lowered in volume increased suddenly, and the couple walked out hastily, heads down in embarrassment. Zahra resumed her position opposite me, the usual murmurs resuming.

"That was quite unnecessary; I was handling it fine," she said.

I cut another piece of meat, not looking at her. "I know you were. My problem was not with the odd woman. It was with the worm behind her."

"Still, it—"

"What language was that?"

"Polish," she answered. "You didn't have to—"

"You should drop the subject." I put the piece I had cut in my mouth and, without looking at her, proceeded to cut another while I swallowed. "Or I will be very compelled to cut off more than his hand."

"It's not—"

"Do not remind me of the people I let live."

Silence passed between us, and she sighed, dropping the topic.

We had recovered from the weird air around us, and I was driving us back to the compound after she had pushed us to go to the cinema to see a movie about people who were robots. I had wondered briefly why she didn't want us to go back just yet. I was not really tired, but I was burnt out from being around people and things I did not want to see.

I honestly would have preferred a little quiet evening with her. Still, I indulged her because she seemed to love going places with me, mainly because I was a novice to most normal things people do, and according to her, she gets a certain kind of high from being the one to introduce me to new things.

Right now, she was on her phone, looking quite relaxed, though her eyes were focused as she texted whoever she was texting.

I took one of my hands from the wheel, placing it on her thigh. "Everything all right?"

Her head snapped up to mine, wide eyes telling me everything was not all right. "Yeah!" she said almost too cheerfully. "I mean, no . . . not really . . . could you, um—drive a little faster? I really need to pee."

I eyed her. "Indeed?"

"Yup . . . we finished a whole bottle of wine, so . . . yeah."

I nodded, keeping my hand on her thigh as I stepped on the gas, eyes back on the road as the car sped under a small bridge, and I didn't take care passing other cars, pressing my foot deeper on the gas as the car accelerated.

"Uh, Elio . . ." Zahra's voice was shaky as she inched back in her seat. "When I said fast, I didn't mean—"

The car went a bit off course, and a sharp squeal left her mouth as I took my hand from her thigh and tried to steady the vehicle again; we emerged from under the bridge, passing cars that were veering away from us like we were about to cause a fatal accident.

"I think I'm gonna puke," she squeaked out.

"Remember, the car is a rental."

"You're a terrible driver, and your license should be revoked."

"Hm. I suppose I would be worried about it being revoked if I had one."

She paused, then, "Oh God."

In under twenty minutes, we arrived back at the compound. I flexed my shoulders, mentally preparing myself to ask her if she would be willing to give me a shoulder massage. I still felt body pains due to the fall earlier today.

Stepping into the house with her, I didn't consider the darkness around the space too concerning. It was all the different smells of perfumes, drinks, and food—the lights suddenly came on, and different voices yelled "SURPRISE!" before music blasted from speakers, and my eyes took in the people in my home.

All of Street, Casmiro, a few of my associates that lived not too far from the compound, strangers that I was supposed to know—and the lights—God, the lights were too bright, and I didn't even register half of what was going on—people were walking up to me wishing me a happy birthday, voices were everywhere, strange, disturbing music—I think I was sweating, and my pulse was—

"Happy birthday, boss," Casmiro said with a shoulder pat. "I feel bad that I always thought it was December third, and I always wished you well on that day, and you never once corrected me—but I don't blame you; I should have known."

His voice was light and a little slow, and something told me the drink in his grip wasn't the first one he was having of the night. He raised a glass to Zahra, then walked away, allowing more people to approach me.

Everything happened in a blur, and I was forced to talk to different people all night long . . . drinks were passed around, people were invading spaces they should not invade.

I received so many gifts from everyone, including soldiers who dropped by for only a second.

Words from here and there told me Street had planned the whole thing.

Zahra had been away from me most of the time, and Elia was the one who kept me company even if I supplied one-word answers because my entire being was too tense to deliver more than that.

Elia had told me he just realized why I'd stayed extra hours with him on this particular day, and he told me I should have told him . . . To be honest, I could not comprehend the answer I gave him then.

I was having an out-of-body experience—emotions flickering between angry, sad, happy, bad, and angry and sad and happy and bad.

I was forced to eat the cake, even if it tasted good, and I think I told them so; I still wasn't feeling my mind working properly.

It took almost three hours into the night before I decided I wanted to head to bed. People were already leaving, and just a few close people remained.

Zahra followed me. We showered together; I kissed her, lifted her, and pressed her back against the shower wall. I was inside her, lost in her; my mind was my own again; she was real, and this was real, and everything that had happened today was real.

Real, Elio, real.

Real shouldn't feel like a time-lapse.

I was on the bed again, and she was in my shirt as she held a small box in her hand, a shy smile on her lips as she joined me under the covers, tucking her hair behind her ear.

"Your present," she said, and I lifted myself to my uninjured elbow, collecting the box from her and hoping the smile I gave reached my eyes.

"The whole party wasn't your present?"

She chuckled. "That was mostly Street's idea, and getting Casmiro and Angelo to authorize it was a pain. But they did because I kinda bribed them that it might put them in your good graces again."

"Hm," I said, opening the box to see a silver necklace. Almost the same pattern as hers, but the silver was darker, and the chain wasn't as thin as the one I gave her; it was a little thicker. The pendant, though, was what made me stop.

"Do you like it? It took about two weeks, but it was worth it."

It was the same shape as the tattoo on her shoulder, the heart and *E* shape, with the little *M* by the side.

I looked up at her. "This must have—this must have cost a lot."

"No, not really . . . I had some friends make it, and it was discounted."

I nodded. "It's beautiful, Zahra, thank you."

She smiled, taking the jewelry and pulling it out. The chain around it was long enough for the pendant to reach the midpoint of my chest. She hooked it around my neck and snuggled closer, quietly asking, "Are you happy?"

I pulled her close to me. "Hm. Yes, I am. Thank you for everything."

"Shut up, don't thank me, it's kind of my girlfriendly duties."

After that, we whispered between each other, her going off about how future birthdays would go, and then we slowly went off course, having an out-of-context discussion about how time flies and how far we will be in a matter of years. I honestly didn't know how the conversation morphed to discussing a possible future together or how we looked at possible reasons for why we would separate if we were ever to separate.

It was primarily meaningless bickering that took us hours into the night until she fell asleep, and my eyes remained wide open.

I hated it. I was so tired and worn out that I just needed to sleep it all off—that void, the out-of-body feeling that still plagued me, and even as I detached myself from Zahra, walked into the bathroom, and fished for my sleeping pills, it felt like someone else was controlling my body.

I popped two pills in my mouth, even though it was prescribed to take only one. But one was never enough to knock me out in a few minutes; it would have taken time before it started working—two did the trick. I swallowed them dry, closed the pill case, and locked the mirrored cabinet.

I returned to the bathroom door and stopped right before I opened it.

There was a silence.

There was a deafening silence inside my head, telling me my thoughts had indeed vacated. In fact, I stopped and tried to listen to myself, but nothing was forthcoming.

I was functioning solely on action and not thought.

Even as I stepped back from the door, once, twice, like my being was in reverse, going back to where I once stood over the mirror cabinet, watching my reflection and seeing a stranger staring right back at me . . . I tried—I really tried to remember who that person was, or what I was, or what my name was, or how I came to be here, what I had done seconds before I came back here to stare at a reflection that didn't reflect anything back to me.

Robotically, I raised my hand, opened the cabinet, picked up the pill case, and opened the lid before tipping my head back and throwing every pill into my mouth.

CHAPTER TWENTY-NINE

Zahra

Not often did I let anger rule my mind or my actions, but that was precisely what thundered through me when I stormed into the room and caught the man who had practically been dead to the world—just yesterday—inserting cuff links into the wrists of his black shirt, not once looking up when I entered the room.

This was when I felt the second tug of tears, ones I had held back for almost a week since I found him.

His hair was brushed back, cut, and tamed. His shirt was tucked into his perfectly fitted black slacks, and his black shoes were spotless. He looked clean—like he was heading out, getting ready to start his day like nothing had happened. Like he still didn't look pale. Like this was just a typical day when he woke up and dressed to go to some important meeting . . . like he wasn't—like this wasn't—

My fingers shook as I quickly locked the door behind me, took out the key, and slipped it into my jacket.

He raised his head briefly, gaze trained on the door, before focusing back on the cuff links, not once looking at me. "Whatever you are trying to start, I suggest you abort now. I am in no mood to indulge it."

I scoffed loudly, disbelief making the anger beneath my skin bubble, and I stomped my way over to him, stopping when I was right before his tall and broad frame. "Fuck you, and f-fuck your mood."

My voice shook. My body shook. The breath I dragged into my lungs shook. My vision blurred as I watched him, angry at his nonchalance and stupidity for abruptly leaving the hospital area of the compound.

The anger I felt gave way to sadness. I was sad that he couldn't look at me—that he wouldn't look at me, but at the same time, I was glad . . . glad that he was okay, relieved that he was standing and that he was here . . . still here . . . still alive . . . more alive than he had been a week ago.

My throat tightened, gathering a lump as I blinked a tear down my cheek.

One week . . . it had been one week since I found him in that bathroom. Motionless. His chest wasn't heaving, his nose wasn't producing any breath, his fingers were still warm but were growing cold, he looked pale, he looked *dead*—it had been a week, but my throat was still sore from how fucking loud I had screamed, how I had stumbled to my knees beside him, seeing the empty pill case right next to his body.

Seeing him now, the whole thing replayed in my head, bit by bit.

With shaking hands, I felt for his pulse, and there was nothing; his neck was slowly slipping from warm to cold, telling me he hadn't been unconscious for long. I held both sides of his face, shifting closer to his body. "Hey," I called softly, tapping his cheek like that would bring him back to consciousness. "Elio—" It was in that moment that my gaze had landed on the pill case beside him, and gears began to turn and reconstruct in my head.

Fear was the next thing to hold my reasoning captive, and an urgent need to get him to breathe rumbled inside me as I placed my hands on his chest, pumping hard.

"Come on, Elio . . . come on." I pumped and pumped, leaning over to pinch his nose, covering my mouth with his and blowing steadily.

Nothing happened.

"Fuck, fuck, fuck." I panicked, starting compressions again, pumping and pumping, and sweating and fighting off the fear clouding my senses.

I pinched his nose, covering my mouth over his again as I tried to blow air back into his lungs before rising to see nothing happening again.

I started pumping again, harder this time, my own heart hammering so fast against my chest.

"Please, God, no. Please, God, no, please, please, please."

I was crazed, breathing sharply as I applied enough strength to his chest.

"Come back to me"—pump—"come back to me"—pump—"come on, Elio."

Thirty compressions, my arms were going weak. I pinched his nose, tilted his head a little as I blew breath into him, and rose to check.

Nothing happened.

A sharp sob left me as I started compressions again immediately, the situation suddenly becoming more real. Frantic, I screamed for help but knew no one could hear me, not from here. His room was literally the last one downstairs. I knew Casmiro was in the building, Devil was, too, probably most of Street, but I wasn't sure—I wasn't sure of anything at the moment; all I knew was that I needed this man to breathe—tears clouded my vision—I just needed him to breathe.

I continued the compressions. I wouldn't give up until I feel something. I wouldn't give up.

"Elio, please, please, come on, come on, breathe for me."

Leaning over to pinch his nose and blow into his mouth, I checked to see if his chest moved.

Nothing.

My lips trembled as my stomach tightened, and I let my tears fall, starting compressions again, but it was weak because my bones suddenly felt like jelly, and I wanted to curl up beside his body and keep him from growing cold like he was doing beneath my palms.

"Please . . . please . . . God, please, this cannot happen to me. Elio . . . wake up, come on . . . come on, come on, baby, breathe, breathe, come back. I'm still here; come back." I pumped harder. "Wake up, please . . . I can't lose you. If you can hear me, please—fuck." I raised my forearm and wiped my tears and sweat as I repeatedly pumped his chest with more strength until I wasn't sure if I was breaking his chest or giving him compressions. I just needed his heart to wake up.

I was shaking everywhere as I hit him. I hit his chest repeatedly; the sound of my fists slapping hard against his skin, where his heart was, almost made me sick.

I pinched his nose, tilted his head back, and pressed my mouth down to his as I blew air again, rising to see his chest moving slightly.

I almost doubled over, a strange kind of strength coming over me the next instant as I took my compressions back to the normal rate, continuing the CPR for a few seconds before I got on my feet and rushed back to the room with blinding speed, finding my phone while running back to Elio, feeling his neck for a pulse to see that it was weak, the weakest I'd ever felt.

But it was something. I dropped the phone beside me, turned Elio's body to the side, brought his chin up after I dialed Devil's number, and he picked up, voice groggy.

"Z?"

"Medic!" I yelled. "Hurry up, it's Elio!"

He cursed before the line cut.

All that happened next was a blur. Casmiro had rushed in shortly after with a medic, and soldiers were everywhere. I was still in shock, still couldn't process what had happened, and even when Angelo arrived the next day and asked who had found Elio, I still couldn't remember half of what he said. Still, I knew he had taken me away from all the chaos and from a confused Devil who was having a conversation with Casmiro about Elio's health issues.

The empathy in Angelo's eyes was something I would never forget. He thanked me, tried to talk me out of my head, told me about the first time he had found Elio, told me about his sister, and eventually asked if he could trust me with sensitive information about Elio. I told him yes, and he told me of Elio's special training in the army. I had been sad then, but the sadness that touched my insides didn't compare to my fury. It was a violation—all on the orders from his sick father.

A sick father who Elio seemed to believe was alive, in that motel, where he had tried to hurt himself, and his supposed father who had a gravestone right here in the compound, right beside his mother and siblings.

I didn't question it then because I had been more focused on getting him to give me the gun.

He had made me promise not to tell anyone about his father being alive, but I had meant it when I told him there was nothing to tell because his father was dead, and he had been dead for years.

Right off the bat, after he confirmed he had faked the man's death, I had told him he needed help—and I had also meant that.

But now wasn't the time for thinking all that. Now was the time to talk.

"You should be on bed rest, Elio. You should be in bed, in that fucking hospital, resting; you should be on your way to get a fucking shrink to help you—in fact, I hope that's where you are getting ready to go."

"No."

"No?"

"I do not have time for this, Zahra," he stated plainly, reaching behind me to grab his suit jacket from where it hung. He put it on. "Give me the room keys; I have a week's worth of work to see—"

"Are you fucking serious?"

He picked up his watch, fixing it around his wrist without looking up.

"Are you trying to act like you haven't been unconscious for a week after OD'ing?"

He fixed his collar, gaze still not meeting mine. "I am fine now, no? Do I seem unwell to you?"

"Elio," I called, trying to bring him back to his senses.

"Room keys. Stop being a nuisance."

"Can you even try to fucking look at me!" I yelled.

His body stopped looking for things to distract itself with as he sighed, finally looking down at me, his gaze locking with mine. No remorse. No regret. No guilt. Nothing.

"Keys," he stated.

I shook my head, sniffing and wiping the tears from my eyes. "That's all you can say to me? Keys? Like it matters?"

"It does matter. You locked the door when you came in; I need the keys to unlock the door in order for me to go out."

I bit the inside of my lip. "Elio . . . you almost died. Hours after your birthday, do you remember?"

"I am aware. While it is quite unfortunate, I am now back, alive *again*, and everyone is happy, yes? I do not want to speak on it, nor do I want to dwell on a past that I cannot vividly remember, nor can I change, so if you would give me the *fucking* keys and let me go my way, that would be most appreciated."

"No. I want to talk about this now."

"For the love of God, Zahra, I am barely managing to stay composed before you right now."

"I don't want your composure!" I yelled sharply, stepping closer to him. "I don't *need* your composure, Elio. I need to know how you feel; unearth. Tell me. Explain. Give me something. Anything to make this guilt stop eating me from the inside out because I have spent all this week thinking this is all my fault! Thinking you tried to hurt yourself because of me, so please, just *talk* to me."

Whatever mask he had been wearing slipped off him instantly as he closed the remaining distance between us, cupping both sides of my face in his hands, thumbs going to my cheeks to wipe the tears before they could fall even farther down. "No . . . never . . . this was not your fault. Please do not blame yourself. You have no reason to blame yourself."

"It wasn't the party?"

"No. No, Zahra, of course not. The party was astounding. I loved it. I was happy. I don't know what happened. I wanted to sleep. I was tired, and I went to take my pills to help me. I took two of them, and then I woke up today and learned I had been unconscious for days."

"You took more than two, Elio. You took everything."

Silence followed; he stood watching me for a few beats before he dropped his hands from my face, his fingers raking through his hair, ruining the arrangement. "I have no idea what you want me to say. I cannot remember what I did; my mind has blocked it out because I wasn't there at that moment."

"Okay . . . then get help, get help so that this doesn't happen again."

He shook his head, stepping back from me and turning to the bed. "I do not wish to."

"Why?"

"*Because* I do not wish to."

I rushed around him until we were face-to-face again. Unable to continue this conversation in English, I switched to Spanish. *"Why the fuck are you so stubborn about this!"*

"I do not have to answer to you."

"Don't give me that bullshit!" I yelled, shaking my head. "You clearly need help, and you will get it. Whether you like it or not."

The softness that had been in his eyes vanished. "Who do you think you are?"

"One of the many people who care if you live or you fucking die. You will treat yourself."

His laugh was humorless. "Honestly, it would do you good to forget it happened."

"Forget?"

"Yes. Forget it; erase it from your memories because I will never heed your wishes. It is not what I want."

I nodded. "Right." My eyes searched his. "That's all right. But know this: if you don't get help, I don't think I can be in this relationship."

"Of course you would end the relationship just because I don't agree with you. You're toxic."

That had my eyes widening, fury scratching painfully on my skin. "Toxic? *I* am toxic?"

"As if you weren't already aware."

Is this motherfucker—

"You wanna know what's toxic?" I gave him a pointed glare, sharpening my arrows. Stepping closer to him, I didn't break eye contact. "You really wanna know what's toxic, Elio?"

His jaw clenched, but he didn't speak.

"It's waking up"—I poked his chest—"in the middle of the fucking night, going to the bathroom, and seeing you lying there . . . pale, cold, and not breathing." He didn't move back as I moved forward, my chest brushing his. "You wanna know what else is toxic? It's me using these hands"—I brought my palms before me, placing them on his chest—"to try"—I sucked in a breath—"to try to bring you back to life . . . over"—I pushed him, and he stumbled back—"and over"—I hit his chest in a push that had him stumbling back again—"and over again!"

"Zahra—"

"Toxic? Toxic is the fucking fear I felt for you! It's the fucking tears I cried for you! It's my heart breaking seeing the look on your brother's face when you were carried out, looking like you wouldn't make it through the night, Elio."

I sniffed, wiping my cheeks. "I'll be damned a thousand times over if I choose to accept your death wish and hold that kind of fear in my heart for the rest of my life, waiting for the last shoe to drop. If you won't get help, then this is done. I'm sorry, but I won't go through that again."

Again, silence reigned.

His gaze was unsteady as he looked at me, something like defeat lingering in his stare; it was heavy, it was dark, it was breaking, and it was sad. He took a few steps away from me before taking off his jacket and dropping it on the bed, sitting beside it, and running his palms down his face.

It was silent between us. Him with his palms covering his face, fingers massaging the sides of his head like he was trying to keep down his headache, and me at the other side of the room, trying to calm the raging beating of my heart.

Then he nodded and spoke. "I understand." His eyes met mine as he brought his hands back down, his right thumb digging into the palm of his left hand. "I understand if you want to leave me. I would hate to put you in that position again—I am sorry that I put you in that position—If I could have predicted that it would happen, I would not have—" He stopped, his head dropping as he looked down at his hands and shook his head slightly.

It was silent once more, and my nerves were skyrocketing.

He glanced up at me, eyes sad, dark, red-rimmed—he was holding back tears, trying to control emotions begging to be let out.

He looked back down at his hands, stopping them from shaking by digging his thumb deeper into his palm. The rigid flex of his biceps and the clench in his jaw told me how hard he was trying to hold himself together.

"I understand if you want out. But to be sincere with you . . . I don't want you to leave me, Zahra."

He looked up again, and I caught the glistening in his eyes. "If you leave me, then I don't—I don't know what I am living for." He managed a slight shrug. "It's not Elia because I had already decided to end it all, even with him in my life. You are my constant, Zahra; if you go, I have no reason to hold back." A tear slid down his cheek. "I don't know how long I'll last here if you walk out that door."

I shook my head. "You can't tell me that."

"It's the truth," he said, keeping his eyes locked on mine. "Eres mi vida, Zahra." *You are my life, Zahra.*

I shook my head. "No."

"Eres mi vida."

"No. No, I'm not. You can't say that to me when you refuse to protect the life you claim is mine. Not when you want to take it away from me."

A frown dropped his brows, hurt swirling in his eyes. "You think I want that?" he asked. "You think I want to take my life? I gave up revenge because I chose to be here for you; I chose this, I did, I *want* to live. I had already made that decision when you became a constant, but my mind doesn't get that I want to live. It doesn't understand that I don't want to die. My mind wants to die because it's tired, Zahra. And I am tired of it; I am tired of my mind.

"I am tired of the person that I am; I am tired of hearing my name. Of this weakness and abnormality, I am just so tired of spending my life being this person who fights daily to be normal. I *long* to be normal. You have no idea how bad I wish you never got to see this side of me; you don't know how ashamed I am of even being in the same space with you, knowing what you had to go through to bring me back." He looked down again. "I don't want you to leave me, but I will accept it if that is what you want."

I walked toward him, crouching before his body and holding his hand in mine.

"Elio," I called softly, "look at me."

He raised his gaze, and I let my hand reach his cheek, wiping his tears.

"I don't want to leave you either. I want you to let me in. Let me see where exactly the problem is coming from. I want you to walk me through that darkness in your head. Let me in so we can figure this out together. Please, Elio."

He pursed his lips, and then softly, he nodded.

I sighed in relief as I pushed his suit jacket to the side and took the space beside him.

He intertwined our fingers but didn't look at me. He was quiet for a while before he finally spoke.

"Sometimes," he started, "sometimes I have this feeling . . ." He trailed off, seeming lost. "This feeling like I'm outside of my body, like a stranger, looking in . . . it doesn't happen often, but when it does, I become a complete stranger to myself. And anything I do in that moment becomes action . . . without feelings. Without self-consciousness. I must admit that was how I felt throughout the birthday party.

"When we were together in the shower, I wanted that moment to feel real. I chanted it so many times in my head due to how badly I wanted to make it real . . . and while it did feel like that for that moment, I lost it again. Everything else that happened . . . I can't really remember. It was like a time-lapse in my head. It all moved too fast."

It was silent between us again . . . he wanted to say more, and I waited patiently for him to speak.

He swallowed, tightening his hold on my hand. "I see things, too . . . sometimes. I see my mother, and I hear her voice. When she touches me, it feels real and familiar, but I know she's not there.

"I also hear voices from people I've met and talked to over the years. Sometimes, they're loud; sometimes, they're just murmurs; sometimes, they make me talk out loud and hallucinate. I can't sleep because it brings hallucinations, vivid ones that are . . . that are of things that I have done . . . One particular thing . . . Elia . . . what I did to Elia."

"What?" I asked, confused.

A shudder went through him as he spoke. "He was the first person I ever killed . . . they were able to save him, but . . . I can't stop—I see—I see that version of him all the time; he stands at random places all over the house . . . watching me, taunting me . . . Sometimes, I beg him to leave and tell him I never meant to do it; sometimes, I just pick up my gun and shoot at him until he disappears. Sometimes I don't even know if I shoot at him because it's all in my head, and I am so tired, Zahra."

"Do you think it's something medical? Like an illness?"

He nodded. "Yes. My mother was schizophrenic. Maybe I inherited it? I don't know, but I wasn't always like this . . . It didn't start until much later . . . after the army. After the fire, everything that happened. Maybe the stress just woke something that had been sleeping all along? Maybe it's not even genetic. Maybe it's trauma. Maybe it's all the things I've seen . . . all the things I've done . . ."

He looked up at me, the tiredness reflecting in his eyes. "I sometimes think when my mind can't cope, and when it all gets to be too much, I have that out-of-body experience, and I do things that I don't mean to do or say things that I don't mean to say. It's a never-ending cycle, and I really, really want it to end."

"You know it doesn't have to end with you dying, right? You could get help."

He looked away from me. "I can't."

"Why?" I asked, trying to catch his gaze. "Is this because you think you're undeserving of it?"

"I know I am. I am positive I am undeserving of it."

"Angelo told me about what you suspect was done to you in the private army facility?"

He sighed heavily.

"Elio, I think they made you believe you're undeserving of help."

His Adam's apple bobbed up and down. "Possibly. My father was hell-bent on never getting me medical help, so there is a possibility that was one part of the special training."

"So why are you still conforming to it?"

"Because I can't stop. Because my father is alive and—and

I don't think I will ever stop being affected by what they did to me at the camp—as long as he's there, as long as he's still breathing."

My stomach sank as I watched him, hoping to God that my suspicions weren't true. "You could put an end to it today."

His eyes searched mine. "By killing him?"

"Yes. He is one of your demons, the obstacle in your path, and if you don't kill that demon, I don't think you'll move forward, Elio."

He was listening to me; I saw the resignation in his eyes as he nodded. "Will you come with me? I don't think I can do it alone."

I swallowed, and it was almost painful. "Yeah, sure."

CHAPTER THIRTY

Zahra

He took no security detail. No one questioned us leaving the compound, but I sent a quick text to Angelo, and to Devil, telling them that all was well and that I might have gotten him to finally get help.

I might have.

But we had to take care of this situation.

The drive took about an hour and forty minutes, but we arrived at the motel.

I watched him greet the receptionist, who looked at me with surprise, probably in shock that he'd brought someone here after so many years.

With my heart in my throat, my body buzzing, and my chest tight, I followed Elio down the hallway, which was lit with yellow lights that gave the space a warm feel and somehow added to my nerves.

The jangle of keys as he stopped right in front of a door and proceeded to unlock it had my heart pounding.

When I heard two lock clicks, and he pushed the door open, I braced myself as he walked in, and I followed behind him.

I closed the door and looked up as he pointed to the middle of the room. "There he is."

My gaze settled on the chair facing the window.

My. God.

I couldn't speak because my heart was breaking.

I felt his eyes on me. "Why are you quiet?"

Swallowing, I looked up at him, at the question in his eyes. "There's no one there, Elio."

His frown drew down slowly before he looked back to the chair in a double take.

He froze, also growing quiet.

"Elio—"

"He was just there." He stepped forward, looking confused. "He was just here, now."

"There was—"

"No, he was just—I saw him seconds ago . . ." He trailed off, shaking his head like something wasn't adding up.

"Elio."

"No." He shook his head again, his breathing frantic as the seconds passed. "No, I know what I'm talking about. He was sitting here when we walked in, Zahra." He gripped the neck of the chair. "He was here; I know what I saw." His eyes fell to me. "You didn't see him?"

I shook my head slowly.

"That's impossible . . ." He blinked. "That's impossible . . . that's impossible," he repeated.

Cautiously, I took a single step forward. "Elio, it's okay—"

"No." The confusion in his voice was evident. "No, he is always here." He looked back at the chair, his chest heaving. "You don't understand, Zahra. I talk to him, I always—I always come here to talk to him." He looked back at me. "I bring food, and he eats, and—no—he's here, maybe he—when I looked at you—the bathroom . . ." he said as he rushed to the other side of the room, pulling open the door and stopping dead when he found no one.

"Elio, there's no one here," I said softly, unable to stop my voice from shaking.

He turned sharply to me, his eyes unfocused as he walked back to where I stood, putting his hands on my shoulders, his breathing uneven, shaking like his body was. "You have to believe me."

"I believe you."

"No, you do not; you're looking at me like you think I'm crazy."

I shook my head. "I don't think you're crazy, Elio."

He looked intently into my eyes. "Then you saw him?"

I shook my head. "No, but I believe that you thought you did—"

"No, I faked his death, Zahra. Everyone *thinks* he's dead, but I left him alive because I had this—I had a plan; you have to believe me, he was here, he is always here, and we talk, and he talks to me—the last time, the last time I was here, I hit him, I felt him—"

"Just like you feel your mother?"

He went quiet.

"Elio, you told me that you saw your mother. You felt her touch you. She seemed real, but you knew she wasn't there. Sometimes when people go through things like this . . . when the mind tries to protect itself . . . it creates things that feel real, even when they're not. This isn't the first time your mind has created things, Elio."

He let go of me, repeatedly shaking his head as he paced the room. "No, no, that's different. I can—I can differentiate it, I know when it's real or not—my father—my father was—that man was real, he was here, he was the reason I started this whole thing. I wanted—he was here because I wanted him to feel how my mother and brother and sister felt in that fire, we were supposed to—we were—it was—this was—" He was breaking right before me.

"Everyone knows he had an attack," I said softly. "A heart attack that killed him, and it was rumored that you were the only one in the room. Everyone thought you caused it . . ."

Tears fell from his eyes, his breathing coming out of his mouth now, loud as he shook his head and paced, recalling what I just laid out. "No, no, no, no, he was—I remember that day, we were—we were arguing, okay? And he—and he fell—he didn't die—he didn't die, Zahra, he didn't die because he doesn't get to die like that. So I faked it—right? I faked his death, and I brought him here, with me—and he's been here since then, and everyone thinks he's dead and buried, but he's not—I know—I know because I see him, I see him here, you have to believe me, please."

"Elio, it's okay—"

"It's not!" he yelled. "He can't be dead because I don't want him dead . . . not yet! He couldn't have had it so easy when they didn't get to have it easy. When I don't have it easy!"

He broke. Crumpling to his knees, both hands covered his eyes, and sobs left him . . . ragged and pained.

I was in front of him the next instant, gathering him into my arms, hugging him tight as I cried, breaking while he broke. "It's okay."

He wrapped his arms around me, buried his face in the crook of my neck, and cried, the wetness from his eyes touching my skin.

"I killed them, Zahra," he muffled out. "I wasn't there . . . I wasn't there to save them; I should have never left them. It's all my fault."

"It's not. It's not your fault."

"They were screaming for me—if you could have heard it—God, Zahra, they were screaming my name, and I wasn't there . . . I was too late . . . they were gone . . . they were dead, I couldn't even—I couldn't even recognize them, couldn't—they were—it was bad . . . it was—they didn't—there was no skin—there was nothing—I couldn't bury anything—I couldn't do anything, and I can't even tell them I'm sorry."

"They know." I rubbed his back. "They know you're sorry."

"They hate me—they would know that I didn't—I didn't kill him for letting it happen. I didn't take revenge for them—I didn't do anything."

I held him tighter. "I know you'll hate to hear this, Elio, but sometimes . . . revenge isn't the only solution . . . all you need is a good cry, a good talk, a good sleep, and acceptance. You haven't allowed yourself to move on after all these years, and I am positive they would have wanted you to be happy. I don't think they hate you; that's just what you think. You need to, for once, take care of yourself, your thoughts, your mind . . . you need these things to function, and only when you own them will you be happy."

I pulled away, and he looked at me; his eyes were so red, so broken, as I held his face. "My presence in your life can only do so much. You said it yourself. You tried to bring yourself back even when you were with me, and you did, but you lost the grip on your mind again, even with me in the picture. If you—if you use me as an anchor, it's only a matter of time before I lose the ability to keep your mind afloat; your problems will sink me, too, and you will drown even with me there . . . it's happening already, that's why you have to treat yourself, *please*."

His throat worked, and he nodded. "Okay."

"Okay?"

"Yes. I will get help."

"You're not making false promises?"

He shook his head, shoulders slumped. "No. I want to get help, and I will get help. Now. I will see a specialist now, if possible . . . if you'll come with me."

I couldn't fight the smile as it grew on my lips. I wrapped my arms around him, hugging him. "I will. I'll be there with you, and I'll hold your hand, and I'll do whatever I can to help you through this."

He relaxed into my arms, and the space that had opened up in my heart for him opened even wider, and I closed my eyes, hugging him back to calm him while accepting that I didn't just like this man, nor was I just fond of him—no—realization made goose bumps rise on my skin as I held onto him even tighter.

I was falling in love with Elio Marino.

Hell . . .

I think I already fell.

CHAPTER THIRTY-ONE

Zahra

The mission had been compromised.

The reason I left Sicily, the reason I woke up every morning with determination to continue the day, the reason Street was created.

Everything was compromised.

I couldn't afford to jeopardize my relationship with Elio . . . or Street. I had to tell them. They needed to know.

Years ago, leaving Sicily, my heart had been impenetrable. Gathering Street had been purely for my own selfish reasons. But then we became a family. They became my world. They became important, people I knew I couldn't carry on in my life without. Each lie I told them turned from small stones on my conscience to big rocks.

Then Elio came into the picture, and my heart, the heart I'd believed was too broken to ever develop feelings for anyone, was cracked open by him. Slowly, unsuspecting. He crept in.

And now . . .

Everything was complicated.

I blew out a breath, digging my hand into my pocket, pulling out my phone, and dialing Vitale's number. I pressed the phone to my ear, my eyes taking in the vast expanse of Elio's compound from the roof where we'd kissed for the first time, where this whole thing started.

Vitale picked up on the fourth ring. "Wow, pigs really *can* fly. Zahra Faizan initiating a call to me willingly?" he said in greeting.

"Hey, Vit."

"Hey." There was silence . . . then, "Are you okay?"

"Yeah. How are you?"

Another silence, longer than the first time. He soon broke it. "I'm . . . good. How are you?"

"Good too."

He scoffed. "Okay, what's going on? You can't be calling me for no reason."

"I'm tired of lying," I blurted, and he went silent again. I swallowed, closing my eyes and letting out a long breath before opening my eyes again. "I'm tired of lying to them, Vitale."

"Faizan—"

"I have to tell them why I'm here. I have to tell Elio about the flash drives. I know he'll understand and help because he wants to help, he told me he'd help me find them and—and imagine all the progress we can make if I tell Elio everything I know about that organization. We could—"

"Zahra." His voice was sharp. "Stop for a second, and think, please."

I closed my eyes. "I can't keep lying to them."

"You're almost at the finish line. Everything is going according to plan. You have the map, and soon you'll find the flash drives—"

"It's getting harder; the map took us to Brazil, and it was a bust. A dead end."

"Of course there would be dead ends. I'm positive Street will get it right. You specifically brought in the best of the best. We've tested them out from petty crimes to the big leagues."

"Vitale, I can't—"

"Remember *why* you're there, remember how long you've put everything on hold to find those fucking flash drives. Remember where you truly belong. I can only hold the fort for so long, Faizan."

"Fuck." I raked my fingers through my hair. "Fine, I won't tell Street . . . but Elio, he already knows about the organization; I just need to tell him about the flash drives."

"Faizan—"

"I won't betray him, Vit. We're changing the plan."

"Jesus Christ."

"When we find the flash drives, I'll hand them over to him and ask him to give us the one we need."

"And you think he'll just hand it over to you?"

I could almost see his frown. I sighed. "I trust him. I know he'll understand."

He was quiet for a while before he spoke. "You're making a mistake, Faizan."

"Call off the operation. Let me handle this on my own."

"I can't just—"

"I'm not asking, Vitale. That's an order."

He scoffed, didn't respond. The silence dragged on until he asked, "And what about our deal?"

"That's a discussion for later."

"Right."

"A lot has changed, Vitale," I pressed. "I have Elio now, and I can't—"

"I don't even wanna hear it. I hope you know what you're doing, Faizan."

The line disconnected, and I stood there with the phone pressed to my ear for a minute before tucking it back into my pocket, blowing out a breath, and hoping . . . hoping with all I had that I wasn't making a mistake.

CHAPTER THIRTY-TWO

Zahra

Me:
Hey baby.
So, since you're in London for the week, and our last operation in Brazil was a bust, Street and I would like to use your house to study the map more. We need good security and space, and your home is perfect for it because of its safety and freedom within the compound.
I promise we won't touch the wine or whiskey.
Please . . .

There, I sent it. I didn't abbreviate it for effect. Give it a few seconds, and we'll get our yes, some expensive wine, and a clear mind to get to work," I said to everyone gathered around the table.

Devil offered me a pointed stare. "I see no reason why we should go to the compound. There's enough security here and enough space."

"It's the wine," I answered.

"And the kitchen," Dog added.

"The game room, too; I got lost in there at the birthday party," Upper said. "Have you ever tried drinking good alcohol while having a wild 4D experience with cars you know you could never drive?"

"There are also many picture spots for the gram." Milk shrugged.

Devil sighed. "It all depends on his response. Besides, if Dog plans to cook, he will trash the kitchen; Elio doesn't like a mess."

I narrowed my eyes, keeping silent.

Dog's face scrunched up. "The fuck are you trying to imply? That I'm a messy cook?"

"Exactly," Devil said.

"Zahra and I will help him clean," Milk said. "Besides, isn't Elio going to be back in a week or something?"

"A week and a few days," I answered, not exactly knowing or caring to know what kind of work he had traveled to do. He'd told me, but I had zoned out when he started talking about politics—and I might have said the word "awesome" too many times—which he had innocently taken as my keen interest in the topic. However, I couldn't understand the meaning of half the words he had used while talking.

"See." Milk grinned. "That's enough time to clean up whatever mess we make."

"And I'd be a fool to believe you guys would leave that house today if he actually says yes," Devil said.

I shrugged. "I mean . . . it's not like he'd be back today or something . . . it's a long week. A big house, with amazing drinks, and a good game room, with a fully stocked kitchen, very spacious, absolutely luxurious. A mini cinema room. Why the hell wouldn't you want that?"

Upper tilted his head at Devil. "Weren't you given some privileges in the compound? We literally don't need permission when we have you."

"Ah, why don't we use the brother." The sarcasm from Devil's statement didn't seem to reach Upper.

"No, no, I mean, don't you plan on using some of those privileges?" Upper asked.

"We're still trying to build our relationship; I don't think being overbearing is the right thing at the moment."

Upper's brows shot up, eyes widening in surprise. "Wow."

Devil frowned at the tone, his gaze falling directly on the dark-haired boy who had returned to focusing on the complicated map.

"What's 'wow'?" Devil asked

"Nothing. I didn't say anything," Upper said.

"If you have something to say, say it, don't be a coward."

"Bloody hell, relax." Upper met his stare. "I have nothing to say to you."

I looked between them. They obviously hadn't talked about their relationship. I didn't know why, or if they ever planned to visit it, but there was some animosity between them, and I wondered how they could still share a room with all that negative energy in the air.

"Guys," Milk cut in, "no need to fight; let's just hear what Marino says, and then we can move forward."

"Yeah," I said, watching the little stare-down that Upper broke with a shake of his head and a frown. I cleared my throat. "I understand where D's coming from, but I think Elio might want us in the compound for whatever heist work we want to do. The only reason we're outside the compound is his little show of making it clear to us that we're not his prisoners and—"

A sound pinged from my phone, and I rushed to grab it from the table, knowing it was his response.

Big Baby:
No.

I blinked at the message. So abrupt. So decisive. So. Fucking . . .

I blew a calm breath and remembered that his intention wasn't to sound mean.

"He said no."

Dog's eyes widened. "Now, what kind of boyfriend denies his girlfriend entry to his house when he's not home? Sure you both are in love?"

I gave him the middle finger, my shoulders slumping. "I guess we're stuck here for the week."

"Hell no, I didn't spend all last night thinking of drinking that addictive wine and cooking in that kitchen to end up in this decent fucking dump." Dog removed his feet from the table, pinning Devil with a stare. "You're gonna text him and ask."

"Where's the logic?" Devil asked him with a bored look. "Why do you think he'd say no to her and yes to me? She *literally* just asked him *minutes* ago. He's totally not going to sense something weird going on. At all." Sarcasm, again, which meant he was growing annoyed.

"It's a gamble. If you do it and he rejects it, then fine, we'll stick to the decent fucking dump, but if you don't do it, we'll just break into his house and the compound, possibly die if we're caught—or get injured or some sad shit where we'd probably lose Upper in the process—"

"Why me—"

"What do you dig?" Dog asked over Upper's voice, watching Devil intently.

Devil's jaw locked; his gaze steady on Dog, who raised a challenging brow.

With a groan, Devil reached for his phone in his pocket and started typing furiously while reading aloud what he typed. "'Hello, brother, can Street and I stay in your condo to sort out some stuff we can *also* sort out in our own con—'"

"Tell him we won't touch the wine," Milk quickly added, earning a glare from Devil, but he continued typing.

"'We won't touch your wine collection unless we decide to touch your wine collection, which we probably will—'"

"Tell him we might cook too," Milk added again, earning another sharp glare.

But Devil continued typing.

"'We will use and trash your kitchen and will probably miss a stain on the counter, which you might come back to see. It will probably irritate you until you decide to move out, so please, it is very, *very* okay to say no to my request to stay in your condo when we can as easily stay in ours.' Send." He dropped his phone by his side. "There, done."

"How in hell's arse do you think he will ever say yes to *you*, basically telling *him* to say no?" Upper asked.

"I did what the Dog asked me to do."

"Point of fucking correction, it's just Dog."

"That's what I said," Devil answered.

"No, you said *the* Dog, which just made it seem like you were calling me a dog. And you've done that, like, a couple of times before, and I have corrected you a couple of times before, but a fucking douchebag will always be a fucking douchebag."

"And I won't stop until all of you stop trying to use my supposed last name as some ticket to getting away with shit you indirectly pull with my brother."

I sighed. "That's not what we're trying to do, and it's not like he's gonna say yes anyway."

Milk nodded. "Upper's right; you kinda did tell him that it was okay to say no, and—"

Devil's phone pinged, and we all went quiet as he picked it up, swiped up at the screen, and widened his eyes. "He . . . said yes."

"What!" I yelled, snatching the phone from his hand and bringing it to my view.

Elio:
Of course. Anything you want.

My jaw dropped. "What the fuck?"

Milk peeked over my shoulder and cooed. "Aw, he said

anything you want! Ugh, to have a big brother . . . Think he's looking to adopt?"

Devil grabbed his phone from my grip. "No, he is not." And then he looked at Dog, who relaxed back on his chair. "Happy?"

With a smirk, Dog responded, "I knew he would say yes. Who wouldn't do anything for a brother who has never asked him for anything like that before? Simple logic." His gaze landed on me. "He also probably said no to you because he knows you're always up to no good, or you guys probably got into a fight we don't know about, or . . . he doesn't really fancy you." His smile was proud. "Again. Simple logic. You're all welcome."

I rolled my eyes and fought the urge to call and give Elio a piece of my mind.

We hadn't gotten into any fight; in fact, I was mainly at the compound all through last week, and I had followed him to most of his therapy sessions. We talked, we ate, we had sex, we hung out, we were perfect, and I was positive that he most definitely—to Dog's fucking disappointment—fancied me. Plenty.

Or does he?

Or is this how he'd act with any other woman he *fancies*?

Does he fancy any other woman?

No. Nope. I'm not thinking this.

We spent the next hour packing up our things and heading out. When we got to the compound, we were escorted by a few soldiers who addressed Devil with the same respect they would have given Elio.

The frown on Devil's face didn't exactly tell me if he liked the new attention or the power—it reminded me a lot of the times when Elio would frown, and you wouldn't be able to tell exactly why he was frowning or what might have triggered his silent anger.

The urge to call the mean man tugged at me, and surprisingly, it was not to call him out for saying no to me and yes to

Devil. It was to hear his voice—even if we had been on the phone hours ago when he called to check up on me. For no reason at all.

I didn't know small gestures like that could make the heart flutter, but it made mine flutter. I had rolled my eyes, but I could still not stop the smile from curling on my lips.

We all settled into the huge kitchen, Upper setting his laptop on the mini dining table, which was for—I don't know—food tasting? A much grander dining table was a closed door away—an entirely different room.

I spread the map on the table, and Milk laid out notes to put down coordinates and make our own description of the map while Devil studied it.

Dog popped open a bottle of expensive wine while trying to find something good and fast to cook.

"Arturo Garza was either a phony motherfucker or a mad genius who knew how to make simple coordinates seem like the bane of everyone's existence. Everything we've got so far has been dead ends," I pointed out with a sigh.

"Brazil, Australia, Dubai, the Netherlands . . . all dead ends," Devil said. "All that matters is that the location of the gold and those flash drives are hidden in this madness somewhere."

"We just gotta open our eyes," Milk said.

We all went quiet, looking at the map.

"I feel like we're missing something," Upper finally said. "Maybe it's like the painting? He distributed it around the world, meanwhile the original was in his manor all along. It's just like the map taking us to Brazil, Australia, Dubai, the Netherlands, Croatia, Cabo Verde . . . and it's all dead ends, fake locations."

"Hiding the gold somewhere in Mexico would be too obvious," I said.

"Maybe it's not in Mexico," Milk pointed out. "Maybe it's here, in Milan, the place where he stocked all the fake paintings? Maybe it's like a reverse kind of thing?"

Upper nodded. "That does make sense. He chose Milan to hide all the fakes. Milan is where his great-grandfather went to school for a few weeks before moving away. So obviously Milan means something to him in a way?"

"Okay, I think we should focus on Milan this week, map out every coordinate with ties here," Devil said.

"Yes, also, we'll need a list of all the properties he once owned in Milan. They're all liquified assets now, but there might be something worth checking out there."

Milk and Upper got to work.

"Where is the wine?" I looked up toward the kitchen just in time to find Dog dropping the opened wine bottle and crouching down. "Dog? The wineglasses are literally behind you; what are you doing?"

"There's a locked cupboard here," he said, and the sound of him trying to pick the lock reached our ears.

"If it's locked, then leave it," Devil responded. "It literally means the person who locked it didn't want anyone to open it."

"Why would someone have more than five unlocked cupboards in a kitchen and lock the sixth one? Doesn't that make you guys curious?" Dog asked.

"Nope," Upper answered him.

"Just leave the damn cupboard, and come here, we have shit to do," I said, looking back down at the map with a frown.

"I'm curious," Milk spoke up.

"Thank you, pinky brain. Devil, Zahra, and Upper have become so"—the sound of the cupboard coming open reached us—"boring these days . . . What do we have here?"

I looked up with a frown as Dog rose to his feet, holding a big yellow gift box in his hands.

"A locked-away birthday present," Dog said, looking at both sides of the box as he walked out from behind the counter and straight toward us.

"We shouldn't be snooping," I said, eyeing the box.

Dog dropped the box on the table, looking at me like I had lost my mind. "Your boyfriend has an unwrapped birthday gift covered in yellow sparkly shit, locked in a cupboard in his kitchen, and you still think we shouldn't be snooping?"

"I didn't see this amongst the gifts he received, and I was in charge of the presents," Milk said with a frown.

"We need to learn to leave shit alone," Devil said, eyes on the box. "But . . . even if we open it, it's not like he's gonna know, right?"

We all looked at him. Surprised.

"Upper," I called, straightening. "Security cams."

"Way ahead of you," he said, his fingers jamming on the keyboard of his laptop before he connected a USB cord from his phone to the laptop, typed some more, and then nodded. "We're on loop, but not for long."

Dog opened the box, and I frowned. Yellow petals were everywhere, but amidst them was an average-sized yellow teddy bear with a huge heart-shaped design between its hands, the words *Happy Birthday, Elio!* sewn onto it.

"Wow, someone went to great lengths to make a customized teddy bear . . ." Milk said.

There were other things inside: several chocolate bars, all with yellow packaging, a wine bottle, beautifully painted sea shells—all colorful and handmade, a beautiful glass casing that housed a set of silver rings, a cute yellow mug with his name on it, a yellow tie, and a card, which Dog picked up.

My heart was hammering, and I was very fucking confused.

The person who sent this had packaged the box with extra care.

He had hidden it.

Why had Elio hidden it? And who had sent it?

"From some Gemma Parisi," Dog spoke up like he had heard my thoughts. As he read the card, a frown drew his brows down, deeper and deeper and deeper, heightening my anxiety.

"What does it say?" I asked.

He looked up at me, eyes guarded. "Uh . . ." he drawled out. "Nothing . . . nothing, uh . . . just some—"

"Let me see." I outstretched my hand toward him.

Dog looked to Devil like he was asking for help and then to Upper, who looked scared for me. It seemed like the three boys had shared a brief conversation in their heads with only that quick eye contact.

"What's happening?" Milk asked, looking around the table.

"Hand over the fucking card, Dog."

He sighed, passing it to me. I snatched it from his grip, and my stomach dropped as I read.

Hey, my love!
Happy birthday. I am so sad that I couldn't be at the party today! I heard from Angelo that you were going to have one! I was so excited to attend until I realized you hadn't told everyone about us! But that's okay, I understand. I can't wait to see you and hug you and shower you with plenty of kisses until you're sick of me! Gran Louisa wants to send you a video message; she's writing it all down so she won't make mistakes. Our baby, Sailor, misses you so much; she's been crying all day. It's like she senses your absence. Anyway, this is long! I hope you have a good, beautiful birthday with lots of good music and lots of cake! Love you! And call me!

Kisses,
Your best girl,
Gemma

I blinked, and the card shook in my hand.

Milk dropped back down to the chair. I hadn't realized she had been behind me before.

Devil collected the card, and I dropped my hands with a disappointed sigh.

"Let's not . . . jump to conclusions. That is totally out of context, right, Milk?" Dog said, and Milk shook her head.

Upper whistled, sitting back down, having read the card with Devil, who placed it back inside the box and covered it.

I still couldn't process what I had just read and what it could have meant.

My heart quickly ran to my throat, knowing Elio might have some other woman on the side who could possibly have a kid with him. A little girl named Sailor?

But then again, I knew that man—*or I thought I did.* He would never do that to me.

To anyone.

Elio would never hurt me like that. It was out of character . . .

You thought Manuel would never drop you because he was obsessed. But he did right after he found a new obsession while still obsessing over you . . .

I shook my head. "Did he ever mention her to you?" I asked Devil.

Devil met my gaze. "Of course not. I have no idea who she is. Never heard him mention her."

I nodded.

"You all right?" Upper asked.

"Look her up. I have to know who she is. This doesn't make any sense."

Upper nodded as he got to work on that. We all settled in behind him.

He typed her name into a private illegal database network.

A grainy picture of her ID card came up with her address, old and new. Height, weight, high school and college details, birth certificate, and other useless information like her bank statements and shit I didn't care to know about.

The face on the ID card was what drew me in. I couldn't

see much of it, but I recognized that blond hair, and I swear my heart skipped a fucking beat.

"Gemma Parisi, age twenty-six. French and Italian descent, parents died when she was five in a brutal car accident, and she's been living with her grandma ever since." Upper summarized from what he could pick up and the details I didn't see.

"She dog-sits and babysits?" Milk mused aloud.

"Yup. Income is nothing to write about, but it's enough for two," Upper said.

Devil frowned. "Is this legit?"

"Yup. She's clean," Upper said.

"Too clean," Dog muttered. "Too clean, it's unnatural. Can you dig more into the parents?"

Upper navigated the cursor, and another tab opened, revealing two other ID cards for her mother and father. "Mother was a social worker; Dad was in construction. His criminal record isn't spotless—vandalism, arson—but those date back to his teenage years, nothing suspicious in recent times prior to his death."

"The cause of the car accident?" Devil asked.

"Collision. A truck driver," Upper answered.

"The truck driver still breathing?" Dog asked.

Upper typed something, and another tab opened. "Uh . . . was in a coma for a couple of months, but he died soon after. He was a normal guy, too."

"Huh . . ." Dog said. "So, she's actually clean."

"Yes," Upper said.

"I'm not getting any bad vibes either," Devil said. "Which means Elio isn't acquainted with her for business purposes."

"Can the database provide more pictures of her? She looks familiar," Milk said.

"No. The only picture we can get from here is the one from her ID, but we can check Google or the gram. The gram is safer." Upper opened a tab that already had his account on display. He went to the search tab and typed out her name.

There were many Gemma Parisis, but one caught us after looking through the list. This one had a single underscore before her full name. When Upper clicked on it, my heart stopped.

"Oh my God," I said breathlessly.

"You know her?" Devil asked.

"She was—she's the one from the cruise," Milk spoke up. "The one who was looking at Elio!"

"And the one who came to his suite and said she had directional issues . . ." I raked my fingers through my hair, gripping it as my chest tightened with hurt. "Oh my God, how could I be so stupid?"

"Hey." Devil was quick to interject into my mini breakdown. "It might not be—"

"Shit," Upper said, drawing our attention. "They went together. There's a picture of the private jet—and . . . there's Elio."

"This motherfucker," Dog gritted out.

Seeing the picture, I looked away, feeling betrayed.

Cheated.

Used.

"Zahra—" Milk was rushing to me, but I quickly raised my hand.

"I'm fine. I just need a little—a little space; I'll be back."

I walked out of the kitchen area and down to Elio's bedroom. Only when I was inside, locking the door behind me, did I breathe. It was heavy, and my heart was breaking.

I didn't want to believe it. I knew how fucking hard my senses had tried to tell me about this, but I had ignored it because I trusted him in that respect—in that respect and more. I didn't think he would do this. He had preached about his respect for women and how he wouldn't want to repeat what his father had done to his mother.

But apparently, that was fucking bullshit. Elio was no different.

I wouldn't cry.

I swallowed the lump in my throat and blinked away the stupid sting and burn in my eyes.

No. I wouldn't cry.

This wouldn't be the first time somebody used me. No. But I would make sure to fucking hell it was the last. The last time I would open my heart to someone and let them hurt me.

If he hadn't wanted me—if he had wanted that perfect fucking Barbie—why did he lead me on like this? Why would he make it seem as though I was the only one that he wanted?

My vision blurred, and I shook my head with a frown, whipping out my phone as I paced the length of the room.

Anger came next. Mixing with the hurt as I opened his chat box and started typing.

I deleted the rubbish line of questions and typed out another again, but deleted it. My fingers were unsteady, and the anger inside me wanted me to say the meanest fucking thing my brain could come up with, but each time I typed it out, I ended up deleting it again.

I didn't want to hurt him.

But he had hurt me. *He* had hurt me, so why was I sparing his feelings?

Fuck this.

Me:

We found ur little yellow-wrapped gift from ur sweet Gemma Parisi.

I don't kw what to say because I never thought u would do this. After all the crap examples u gave of ur father, u turn out to be no different.

I sounded like a fucking fifteen-year-old, but my angry fingers kept typing. I wasn't thinking, wasn't stopping, just typing and sending, spamming.

Me:

I don't kw what gave u the impression that u could cheat on me and get away with it like I'm some easy fuck by the side that u could sway with stupid words that mean absolutely fucking nothing.

Even knowing how guarded I am about relationships, u still did this to me, made me look like a fool the day she came to ur suite on the cruise. U were fucking some other woman while trying to rope me into a relationship with u for some fucked-up reason.

I'm pretty sure u were laughing at me in ur fucked-up head when I told you I couldn't have kids. u already have someone who can give u kids.

Why are men like this? Why the fuck did u see the need to lead me on when u know u have someone even more perfect on the side?

I can't believe I didn't see it. You're good, I'll give u that. Always acting like some innocent fucking freak who

would never switch pussies when he gets bored. You'll pay for this; I swear to u I won't rest until I find u and fucking gut u until you're nothing but blood and body parts. Not before I cut off ur fucking dick and feed it to u. I'll also find that Gemma bitch and tell her that her baby daddy is out there, lying and hurting other women for fucking kicks. In case you didn't get the memo, we're fucking done. Piece of fucking shit.

I threw the phone on the bed after sending that last one, not even remembering what I typed out. I dropped to the edge of the bed, covering my face in my hands as I tried to tame my breathing, anger, and hurt.

"I'm so fucking stupid," I whispered to myself. To think I wanted to ruin a mission that had been in play for more than six fucking years. For him.

I shook my head, replaying the day Gemma had come to his suite . . . he didn't say anything, pretended he didn't know her, but they were there together. I believed her lie, I trusted him.

"God, I'm such an idiot." I dug my hand into my eyes, trying to hold back the sting.

I didn't know how long I sat there, but I knew I was too ashamed to face Street. Not after knowing they knew I wasn't good enough for Elio—and I was probably being played this whole time.

Even Angelo knew about Gemma.

"Fucking idiot," I whispered, letting my eyes grow wet, unable to stop the emotions swirling around my chest.

Now I knew why Upper, Devil, and Dog had shared that look. They knew how bad it looked, they knew, and they probably pitied me.

Pitied the foolish girl.

I was *indeed* foolish—I dared to step out of my comfort zone because my heart had led me down the wrong path again.

Except this time, my anger wasn't just anger. My heart thumped abnormally, each beat accompanied by hurt, loss, and disappointment. Feelings that made my limbs weak. How quickly I let myself fall for Elio—thinking he was possibly the sincerest man I'd ever meet when it came to relationships. I should have known better.

Trusting someone this much was something I strived hard *not* to do.

The one time I decide to give in, I get cheated on. I still can't believe it.

"I'm so stupid," I whispered again.

The vibration from my phone got me out of my thoughts. Sluggishly, I flipped over the device.

My heart cut.

He was calling.

I watched it ring, wanting nothing more than to answer and hear what he had to say. But I couldn't.

The call cut off, and the phone started vibrating almost immediately—his nickname flashing on the screen.

I declined the call and switched off my phone as I got to my feet, pocketed the device, and rushed out of the room.

Reaching the kitchen, the hushed conversations stopped when they spotted me.

That damned box was still on the table.

"We're going to find the bitch."

Devil sighed. "Maybe you shouldn't jump right to conclusions. I know Elio; he would never hurt you like that."

"Do you really know him? Is it written on the fucking forehead of every man to grace the earth, who would cheat and who wouldn't?"

"Z, just—"

"We're going to find her," I said, looking around the group. "Anyone who doesn't want to come with me, that's fine. I'll go on my own."

CHAPTER THIRTY-THREE

Zahra

So, are we just gonna sit in this minivan until one of these proper people calls the cops on us?" Upper asked. "I cannot get my name into the system."

"Shut up, rich boy," Dog said, eyes scanning the neighborhood from his seat near the window at the back. "She's processing."

I was biting my thumb, my leg bouncing as I pinned my gaze on the house through the closed window of the passenger's seat.

The house was literally—perfect, just like the woman who lived there.

"I still don't think Elio would do that," Milk said. "He doesn't seem like that kind of guy."

"And I still think you should have heard him out. He's called everyone, which means he has an actual excuse that might make sense," Devil said from beside me in the driver's seat.

"Or he doesn't."

"Z, just—"

"No one answers his call. Doing that would be an act of betrayal, and I will never forgive any of you."

The car was silent again as I looked away from the house. "I bet my whole life savings that he spends most of his time here, fucking hypocrite," I muttered.

"Are we going in?" Devil asked with a sigh. "What exactly is your plan? We've been sitting here for over an hour now."

"I'm thinking," I gritted out.

"While we think," Dog spoke up, "I'm starving and would

like to distract myself. Why don't we play another reveal game?"

"Like last time?" Milk asked.

"Exactly. Last time, we shared the meanings of our names; this time, we'll share our real names. Who's in?"

I let my head fall back on the headrest and took everyone's quietness as acceptance.

"I'll go first," Dog said. "You laugh, and I snap your necks." He cleared his throat, silence, then, "My real name's Wesley Reagan."

I pressed my lips together.

"Your real name's *Wesley*?" Devil shot out without missing a beat, looking back at Dog.

"Yeah. But most people call me Reagan because I always tell them never to call me Wesley. Or I'll snap their necks," he said pointedly.

"Right," Devil said.

"Wesley is an okay name—just doesn't suit your face," Upper said.

I sat up. "I really can't imagine—"

"No comments from you, Zahra; I really don't wanna hear what you have to say about my name."

"Then can I laugh?" I asked.

"Yeah, sure. We drove past a cemetery on the way here; laying you to rest will be easy. It's night, no one will see."

"I think the name Wesley is pretty . . . compared to mine," Milk said.

"What's yours?" I asked, angling my body to look at the back seat.

"Typical name . . . very common," she said.

"Still wanna hear it," Dog said, watching her.

She sucked in a breath. "It's Penelope. Last name's Canavan."

"You look like a Penelope, unlike Wes," Devil said.

"I swear to God, Devil. I swear to God."

"Penelope is a beautiful name," I said.

"I agree, it is not bad, dear Pen," Upper said, lightly tapping her head.

She grinned.

Dog didn't comment on her name.

"I'll go next," Upper said, clearing his throat and rubbing his hands together. "I'm Archibald Avington Otto Farraday, the fourth—or fifth, I can't be sure . . . I didn't stay in the palace long enough to study the family history books before I was booted out, so I don't know exactly how many Archibald Avington Otto Farradays there were before me."

"I can't remember anything you just said," Dog voiced.

"Me neither," I admitted.

Laughing, Upper relaxed on his seat. "My name's Archie."

"I knew," Devil said, looking out the window.

"How?" Upper asked.

Devil's response was a shrug, and that was that. He wasn't divulging how he knew. "Everyone knows my last name. My first name's Elia."

"That sounds like a girl's name. Like the female version of Elio," Dog said.

Devil groaned and gritted out, "It's unisex."

"Your father was cruel," Dog said.

"He disowned me when I was six. Right after killing my mother in front of me. Cruel doesn't do him justice," Devil said, bringing a bit of silence.

I broke the silence with a clearing of my throat. "Well . . ." I spoke, quickly calculating the consequences of what I was about to reveal. But Elio's people knew it and still didn't know *me*. I was also positive Devil and Dog hadn't caught on to Chika using my last name after he had us on the school bus.

"My name's Zahra. Zahra Faizan."

I caught the instant freeze in Devil's shoulders.

I stopped short when he looked at me, and I caught the recognition in his eyes; his brows were furrowed just a bit as he observed me like I had spoken a lie that would fuck up this version of me in his mind if it were true.

I didn't back down from the stare, but he looked away first.

Did not utter a word.

He knows something.

"You look like both your names," Dog said.

"Yeah," Milk agreed.

"It's pretty," Upper said.

I took my eyes off Devil and met Upper's gaze with a smile. "There's just something—"

Three audible knocks from the driver's side window had us shouting and jumping in fright.

My hand was already on my chest as I snapped my head to see the blond standing there, trying to look in.

"Motherfucker." Dog released a breath upon seeing her.

And so did everyone, collectively.

"Didn't mean to scare! Can you guys—wind down?" Her muffled voice reached us.

Devil looked at me, the previous suspicion in his eyes long gone. Concern was all that remained there now. "Should I?"

I looked back at the blond, knowing she couldn't see us.

Cracking my knuckles, I sucked in a breath, trying to calm the hard thumping in my chest as I nodded. "Yes," I said, putting on my mean face. "Wind down."

CHAPTER THIRTY-FOUR

Zahra

Devil pressed a button, and the window opened.

My stomach twisted with jealousy. She was even prettier up close.

"Hi!" she chirped, looking into the minivan. "Oh, it's a—it's a full house," she said, fighting to keep her grin from slipping as her gaze fell to Devil, and then her grin turned a little brighter like she was genuinely pleased to meet him. "You must be Elia. I see the resemblance, the whole hair color and ch-chin, like—yeah." Her grin turned into an awkward smile as she glanced at me.

I leveled her with a glare, and she quickly averted her eyes from me. Intimidated. Yes. Good. I liked that.

She cleared her throat. "You guys have been out here for an hour now. Would you like to come in?" she asked, swallowing. "My nonna just finished making dinner; I think there is enough for everyone—"

"Oh, thank God, I was starving—"

"Dog," I warned.

"What?" he whined. "We haven't eaten in hours, I'm dying here."

"The cemetery isn't far. Remember?" I gritted out.

Gemma's eyes widened in fear at my statement.

"And you." I pinned her with a stare. "Do you just randomly invite strangers into your home?"

She blinked. "Uh . . . well . . . you're—you're Elio's girlfriend, and he's Elio's brother . . . I mean—when I saw the minivan, I recognized it and knew it couldn't be Elio because he's not in Italy.

I tried to call him, but he wasn't picking up, and then I figured it might be someone from—you know? His work? I wanted to call the cops, but the minivan was familiar, and I just wanted to make sure."

"So, you came out of your house—not sure if it was a serial killer waiting to kidnap you or hurt you—just to make sure it was okay to call the cops?" Devil asked.

Gingerly, she raised her hand to reveal pepper spray. "I have . . . pepper spray?"

I looked toward the back seat to my friends, with a question in my eyes, only getting shrugs in return.

I turned my gaze to her. "You know us."

"Yeah." Her voice shook. "From the cruise, um, the *Celestial*? The first time we met at the suite, when I—when I knocked . . . and lied . . . because I panicked."

I frowned, wondering why she was revealing this much.

"I saw you guys around Elio often, and I've always wanted to introduce myself. The minute the window came down, and I saw that it was you, I realized that, well—well—I figured since you're here, you might have found out about me? And since you're here without Elio, then maybe you have—uh . . . questions."

"Can we take this inside? Where there's food?" Dog chipped in.

"That would be great!" Gemma nodded, smiling like she wanted to take my friends, too, and then she looked at me. "I promise, Elio and I have absolutely nothing romantic to do with each other—we're just very good friends. Like, very good friends, and I really don't know why he's not answering his calls, but I am trying—and I will try my best to explain anything you want."

"Good friends?" Upper popped his head out so he could get a good look at her. "A good friend he has a baby named Sailor with?"

"Huh?" Gemma's eyes widened in shock. "Oh no . . . oh

no, no, no, no. Oh God, the gift box . . . that must be it. Uh—Sailor's my cat. The ginger one? With Mimi? Elio told me she spent some time in your suite on the cruise. I wanted to thank you guys for your hospitality, but Elio hadn't introduced me yet. If I could get ahold of the man in question, he would explain perfectly because I'm pretty sure I'm making a mess of this whole conversation, and that is the last thing I want." She took a long breath, and her smile was now forced, uncomfortable, panicked, like she was scared of making matters worse.

I blinked at her. "So . . . you're not . . . you're not his . . . *baby mama*?"

"Jesus Christ, no! I'm dating his friend. Angelo? That's my boyfriend."

"Oh," Milk said from the back seat.

Devil looked at me with a blank stare. "We should have answered his call."

I swallowed, starting to see things in a different light. "But wait—you called him your love."

Gemma sighed. "I call everyone that. I didn't actually mean it like he's my actual love. I call literally everyone I see 'my love.' It's like a habit I got . . . I don't know when I started doing it. But I've been doing it for as long as I can remember; I even call my bosses 'my love,' and it's just something I do, and I'm sure you didn't need all those details."

My shoulders dropped as I rubbed my eyes. "Are you fucking shitting me?"

"I'm sorry," she squeaked. "I am a big people person, and—God, Angelo told me he hadn't given the box to Elio because he was still recovering and didn't want to trigger anything. I didn't know what Angelo did with it after I gave it to him . . . like, weeks ago. I'm sorry if I caused anything. I just—I just wanted to do something nice because—well, he doesn't celebrate birthdays, and gift boxes are always perfect, especially yellow ones because they're like sunshine, and sunshine is always great for moon minds—God, what am I saying."

I breathed out, slumping back on the car seat as my shoulders relaxed in relief.

"It was all a little misunderstanding, I promise," she added.

I nodded, the pain in my chest disappearing as I closed my eyes. "I still have questions, and I really hope your grandmother made enough food."

"Ah, yes! I like full house. Many people come to eat my food!" Gemma's nonna said with a grin as we entered the house.

It was normal, welcoming, colorful, and cozy. I couldn't picture myself living here long term, but I wouldn't deny it was a beautiful home. A regular home with ordinary people. A pattern of life I knew nothing about.

"Oh, I know that smell." Dog brushed past me and straight to where I supposed the kitchen was, but not before stopping to ask Gemma's nonna a question, to which she smiled at him and responded with a vigorous nod.

"I hope we aren't imposing," Devil said. "We can leave if that is the case."

"Oh no, that's okay. This is totally okay." Gemma smiled with a nod, sneaking a glance at me.

"Well, I'm Milk," Milk spoke up, stretching out her hand to Gemma with a broad smile. "Pleasure to officially meet you. I saw you several times on the cruise; you're gorgeous."

Color filled Gemma's cheeks. "Oh—thanks! Coming from you—that's, yeah—uh, thank you! You're pretty, too! The extraordinary kind, very—very pretty."

Milk's smile widened. "Why, thank you!"

"I'm Upper, and I'll go make sure Dog doesn't touch anything in your kitchen because he seems to believe all kitchens are his. All kitchens."

"That's totally okay, too!" Gemma said.

I studied Gemma's body language. She was pretty overwhelmed by everything happening right now; maybe a little uncomfortable, but a people person and a people pleaser would definitely never tell you if they're uncomfortable.

At least, not her kind.

Poor girl. This world we're in would crush her fragile mind, and I bet she had absolutely no idea what Elio really did.

"Where is the Zahra?" Gemma's nonna made her way toward us, her eyes as blue as Gemma's pinned right on me.

I shifted uncomfortably.

"Hmm, you are the fuck friend turn girlfriend."

"Nonna, come on," Gemma chided, sounding embarrassed.

"Shh, I must do inspection." She squinted her eyes at me, and then both hands came to my face, turning it from left to right.

From the corners of my vision, I caught Devil leaning against the wall, eyes filled with amusement.

"I see . . ." the woman drawled out, "I see same ears . . . same eyebrows . . . same eye shape but more in woman form. Hmm . . . what else . . . frown for me."

"Why the fuck would I—"

"Frown now!"

I frowned, not because she asked me to frown, but because this was really weird.

The woman smiled. "Perfect. Soulmate."

"I am so confused," I said.

She took her hand from my face. "My mother always tell me if a woman meet her soulmate, her true soulmate, they will have some similar thing in look, in manner, and sometime in thinking. That is how I know me and Maurice, my dead husband, are not soulmate. That is also how I know my Gemma and that Giacomo fool she date before are not soulmate. But you and Elio, soulmate."

I turned to see a big grin on Milk's face. "I read that

somewhere too!" she said, tilting her head. "And now that I think about it, you do look—"

"You have a beautiful home." I cut Milk off before she made the whole situation even weirder than it already was. "It's . . . it's homey."

"Yes. My Gemma work very hard for it. Hope everybody like spice! I will check on turkey now. You, pink hair, come set the table. Elia, come, let us talk as you help me carve the turkey."

When I was alone with Gemma, I turned to pin her with a look.

She stood straighter. "Listen, Zahra, I know how this must all seem, Elio and me, but I promise that it's nothing like that, and I really don't want to cause problems between you two. And honestly, Elio really, *truly* does care so much about you, and I feel like he's going to hate me for this situation, and—well, maybe the gift box was a bad idea; I just really wanted to do something nice. I'm sorry if it seemed otherwise."

"How did you meet him?"

"A ride. I gave him a ride in my car many months ago."

I scanned her from head to toe. "Huh . . . Why didn't he mention you?"

"He told me he was finding the perfect way to tell you. I really wanted to meet you, but not in this way. In a normal way."

"Right . . . and you have no ulterior motives." I studied her.

"I don't think I have enough in me to have ulterior motives," she answered.

"You're just friends with him."

"Just friends, I promise."

"You don't think he's hot."

She blinked. "I—I think he's all right and perfect for you."

"And not for you?"

She swallowed. "I like Angelo. Very much. I promise you, you have nothing to worry about regarding my friendship with Elio. I care about him as a friend, and that's it."

"Hm." I nodded. "He didn't call you to tell you we might be coming?"

"When I saw the van, I called him, but he didn't answer. I haven't heard from him in like two days, but I always see him around when I FaceTime Angelo."

"Do you usually let people push you over?"

She blinked. "Wh-what?"

"You let people step on you too often?"

She swallowed. "I, uh . . . I don't know what you mean. I really don't want to offend anyone and—"

"Yeah, I don't really care."

I liked that I was still in control of the situation.

Looking around to make sure no one was coming or listening in, I took a step toward her, and she inched back a bit. "I'll make one thing clear, *Gemma*. He's mine. And if this friendship thing rubs me the wrong way, in any way, shape, or form, we will be having a less cordial conversation. I'm going to set some boundaries. I don't care if you call everyone your 'love,' you don't call him that, and you don't give him kisses, you don't do any of that shit."

She nodded. "Got it."

I let my hand settle on her shoulder, and a smile curved on my lips. "Good talk." I patted her shoulder, looking around as I stepped away from her. "Your choice of wallpaper is perfect. Aesthetic."

Her throat worked. "Thank you."

"Also, you shouldn't just let people into your home like this . . . even if they're friends of your friend. It's not safe. Not everyone is who they say they are or who you think they are."

She nodded. "Yeah, of course."

I nodded once before turning and heading to the kitchen.

CHAPTER THIRTY-FIVE

Zahra

When we left Gemma's after being there for a couple of hours—hours of eating and listening to Gran Louisa bad-mouth her late husband nonstop, we went back to the compound, worked a little on the map, brought out some coordinates, and waited for confirmation before we decided to call it a day and leave the compound.

I leaned my head against the car window; eyes closed as I imagined the soft bed waiting for me back at our condo. I was tired, worn out from all the emotional and mental distress I'd gone through.

I opened my eyes when I felt Devil make a curve into the house's small gate.

Milk was already fast asleep, her head on Dog's shoulder. Upper's eyes were closed, but I knew he wasn't sleeping.

When the house appeared, I sat up straighter, stretching my limbs and suppressing a yawn.

"Elio," Devil said, and my heart cut as I froze, spotting the figure leaning against a car right in front of the house. He raised his head as we approached, his gaze following us.

I frowned in confusion. "What the hell is he doing here?"

"Do you want me to stop here? Or should I head to the garage first?"

I took off my seat belt. "Stop here."

Devil nodded, slowing down and stopping at the far end.

Elio didn't move; he was still leaning on his car, watching us.

"We'll be inside," Devil said.

I nodded before getting out of the car, and they drove off to the back of the small compound toward the garage.

When I looked up at Elio, he was already looking at me.

Face, as usual, expressionless. In his hand was a lighter he was flicking open and closed, over and over again.

I blew out a shaky breath as I walked over to him, watching his eyes follow me until I was directly in front of him. He looked stressed but composed.

"London was too cold for you?" I asked, wondering why the hell I had decided to lead with that.

He didn't say anything. He just watched me. As expected. The sound of the lighter filled the space between us.

"What are you doing here?"

"Nobody was answering my calls." Flick. "You turned off your phone after your . . . numerous text messages. I could not reach you, Elia, or anyone. So, I flew back."

Mentally, I punched myself. Somehow, I had forgotten the text messages or even my phone.

"Elio, why would you come all the way—" I sighed. "Those messages weren't—they're no longer valid."

The flicking continued, but still, he wore no expression. "What does 'no longer valid' mean." It wasn't a question.

"I know everything now about Gemma and your friendship with her. We went there—to her house, and talked to her and Gran Louisa, and I cleared it all up."

"You cleared it up," he stated.

"Yeah," I answered, trying to read his mood.

He stood upright, the flicking stopped, and he shoved the lighter back into his pocket. "I am glad you did. I'll be on my way."

I frowned as he started walking around the car.

Hugging myself against the cold, I tried to tame the anger bubbling inside me. "So you're mad," I called out, and he stopped, letting his shoulder fall, allowing a minute to go by, before turning to me. I took in his blank stare. "You think you have the liberty to be mad right now? You think you're the victim in this situation?"

"I never said anything, Zahra."

"Yeah. You flew all the way from London, only to leave after exchanging a few words with me and acting like I was the one who hid someone of the opposite gender from you."

"I never made a comment," he said, straight-faced.

I ground my teeth, taking a step closer but leaving enough distance. "I had every right to be angry."

"I did not say otherwise."

"Why are you acting like a fucking asshole right now?"

"I am?"

I counted to five in my head, ascending and descending. "If you have something to say, just say it."

"Now you want to communicate."

I took another step closer. "That's why you're angry? Because I didn't answer your call or listen to you? I was thinking the worst—"

"I concluded that from your messages. I reread them multiple times; I could even recite them word for word. You *indeed* thought the worst. I understand and am aware of my fault in this. I did not tell you about her, not because there was anything to hide.

"One reason was because I was preparing myself to join two parts of my world together. Another was because you had already met her on the cruise, and if I recall, we were not together then, and I did not tell you I knew her because right then, at that moment, I was not in the suitable headspace to have that conversation with you.

"There were other opportunities to tell you; I am aware of that too. I admit I treated the matter with ignorance because I knew it would be challenging to make you understand since you had already seen her, and I never said anything then. But I was going to take you to Gran Louisa because she wanted to meet you. You can ask Angelo; I already scheduled a day to do it after we got back from the trip. That is if you still think I would have never told you about her."

"I already know—"

"About the gift box. I had absolutely no idea it existed. Allow me to stress further that if I had wanted to hide it from you, you would have never found it."

I sighed. "I know that now."

"I know you know that. I knew you would have been angry, and I know you had every right to be. But to assume or to believe that I would do something as despicable as infidelity?" His expression was quick to switch from indifference to hurt. "You know my history with that, Zahra."

I sighed. "I know—"

"Yet you said those things. You *thought* those things about me."

"I didn't mean them—I was just angry. I knew you wouldn't do that to me, but I was sad, the note in the card was pretty convincing, and I believed it because it was better to believe it than to not believe it and be disappointed and hurt more later on if it turned out to be true."

He shook his head. "You still doubted me after everything. I know I am not good with actions; I know my words sometimes are the only things I can show you, but I promise you, Zahra, I have *never* lied to you about my feelings for you. I mean every word I say. I don't joke with us. I don't fucking joke with you, Zahra."

My heart was hammering, and I was regretting those text messages, recalling how I had told him his words meant nothing.

This time, he walked closer, taking up the remaining space between us as he raised his hand to smooth my hair away from the side of my face. "Do I have to spell it out?" he asked quietly as I raised my head, our eyes locking. "Hm?" he questioned, tilting his head as his knuckles brushed from my chin to my jawline until he was cupping the side of my face.

My mouth went dry.

"If the fact that I told you that you were my life and that you mean everything to me doesn't make any sense to you, if you want me to say how I feel in layman's words, in a way that doesn't touch the depths of what I feel for you, then all right. I love you." His fingers caressed my neck, his bright gray eyes searching the browns of mine. "I love you, and that is the simplest way I can put it."

I couldn't speak. I wasn't even sure I was breathing. But it was suddenly difficult to take in oxygen, and to stand, and to do remotely anything.

Elio pressed his body even closer to mine, placed his forehead on mine, closed his eyes, and breathed feverishly.

"Te amo, Zahra," he said. "Tú tienes mi corazón."

I love you, Zahra. You have my heart.

The warmth from his body flowed into mine as he moved, leaned farther in, tilted his head, and pressed his lips to mine. A kiss that had me holding on to his shirt, a connection that had my heart mirroring the exact rhythm of his. An intoxication that had my stomach going to war with itself.

Anger failed me, agility betrayed me, and the fight in me no longer existed. Everything in me was him and this, and I kissed him back with as much attention, as much detail, and as much fervor. My hand left its hold on his shirt and moved to the side of his face as I got on my toes, parting my lips, brushing my tongue with his, tasting him, feeling him, wanting him.

He loves me.

Me.

I buried my fingers in his hair, tugging and breaking the kiss as my eyes searched his. "You love me?"

"I do."

Something swelled in my chest, and I joined my lips with his again—I didn't understand why I felt the urge to cry. But I could feel what he felt. I knew the love he carried because I carried it too.

I could feel the pounding of his heart against mine.

I loved that he could tell me. I loved that at least one of us could voice it. I loved the way he had expressed it.

I appreciated that he did.

I wanted to voice it, too; I wanted to tell him—break this kiss and tell him how I felt, how light and free he made me feel.

But I couldn't. I couldn't do it. Not now, at least. Doing it meant giving away the last piece of myself.

I wasn't ready, and with the way he kissed me back, I knew he understood. He placed no pressure on me, and I appreciated that as well.

I never bargained for this when I took back my freedom, but one thing I knew was that I was never letting go of this feeling. I was never letting go of him.

For now, his confession would suffice. He loved me. I had someone I could hold, kiss, and talk to—and he loved me.

That was enough reason to drop every guard I had put between us.

Enough to prepare myself to reveal why exactly I had left Sicily. I trusted him, and we were already working toward the same goal.

It wouldn't hurt to have him be on my side and in my plans, even if it meant finding another way to help Vitale.

It might not be wise, it might be foolish, but for once in my life, I was taking the risk.

And I knew in my heart that it would be worth it.

CHAPTER THIRTY-SIX

Zahra

It took weeks, but we narrowed the coordinates on the map for Milan down to three locations.

We'd stormed the first one, but it had been an empty warehouse, a fluke to throw us off our game again. Two days later, we set out for the second location and were attacked by three other groups looking for the painting—there, we learned that our movements were being monitored. We'd expected it. Elio had clarified at a meeting that though we had the map, we shouldn't be naïve to think people didn't know we had it.

Then again, he'd also said it wasn't a matter of who had it, it was a matter of who had the most firepower. If we were being monitored, we needed to have enough arms to protect ourselves.

I knew all this before he raised the awareness.

I knew many things—things I was scared to speak about because the consequences meant losing more than I bargained for.

At the third location, we found absolutely nothing, like I'd suspected. And then a few days ago, Upper had cracked another coordinate that happened to border with land that was in Arturo's name. The records of the purchase were buried so deep it took Upper a while to pull out all the information we needed.

I had no doubt that the gold and flash drives were sitting pretty somewhere on that property.

Those damned flash drives.

While I'd come to Milan to investigate the flash drives' whereabouts, I'd also been spying on P. Deluxe Corp.

Leaving Sicily at nineteen, I'd had one thing in mind. Bring down P. Deluxe Corp—the organization behind the trafficking ring or at least, that's what I thought they were called. From the different transactions, placement documents, and payment receipts I had found in Manuel's records of the time he had been in the Conti Serpent Society, all executive orders came from this P. Deluxe Corp.

I had done my research about them.

Public records indicated that the corporation was a private research facility owned by a man called Pedro Lombardi, who was now deceased.

Vitale had told me that finding the corporation was too easy—and something was amiss. But I had looked at every directive and intel from spies I had in different places, and they all pointed at P. Deluxe Corp.

A week ago, Elio also mentioned their name when he told me of his findings. These were things I already knew.

We couldn't take up the matter with authorities or make a case against the corporation being a false research facility, but we could destroy it.

As for Elio, I was going to tell him everything today—I knew he would understand why I held back, and I knew he would be by my side because if I was frank with myself, I couldn't do it alone. Destroying this organization had been a massive part of my life since I had discovered myself. Who I was, what I wanted, and what I would die doing.

I wanted no child or adult to go through what I did. I knew stopping this particular ring wouldn't stop pedophilia around the world, but it would prevent children from being born into the business.

Vitale already had our people on standby, waiting for my word to bring down the operation. But I wanted to finish here first, get the flash drives to Elio, tell him everything, and hope to God that he let me have the flash drive I needed. It held the information Vitale's people required to get into the organization's system, finding every branch and house, before blowing up the building and bringing down those bastards.

My heart was in my throat, and I was nervous.

I had to get it right if I wanted a chance to salvage all the relationships that might be destroyed today.

Right now, Devil and I were on our way to the new location, and a long convoy of Marino SUVs was behind us. Ready with arms in case any other group decided to join the fun.

Dog was in one of the SUVs with Marino's people, and Milk and Upper were working behind the scenes, as this location required several invisible eyes rather than physical bodies.

My hand was on the gun strap around my waist, my focus dead set on the road ahead, and my mind was a chaos of its own.

"You good?" Devil's voice reached inside my head from the driver's side.

I looked toward him, noting the frown on his brows, but it was one of concentration.

"Yeah, I'm good."

His lips pressed into a thin line, but he didn't speak after that. I studied him for a bit, knowing that despite our little jokes here and there over the past weeks, we had been tiptoeing around each other. I didn't want to broach the topic because the last thing I wanted was to be at odds with any of them.

"Hey," I said, calling his attention as he glanced over. I tapped my comm, gesturing for him to turn his off.

When he did, his frown deepened. "What's wrong?"

"I feel like we need to talk."

His grip on the wheel tightened. "About what?"

"Don't play pretend. Ever since I told everyone my last name, your eyes have been on me, and we've been walking on eggshells around each other. I'd like to know why."

His body grew tense, and I knew he didn't want to talk about it; he wanted to play dumb, imagine he hadn't heard or realized anything so the little bubble he was in wouldn't burst. He was at war with himself, and it only piqued my curiosity to know what he knew.

"It's nothing," he said.

I sighed. "Look, we're about to enter a battleground together; I just want to ensure we're good before we face possible death?"

After a second of quietness, he let out a breath. "Do you recognize the term *E2*?"

I went quiet, watching him with a frown before I asked, "How the fuck do you know about E2?"

He glanced at me, his eyes reflecting the same void as always. He had the unique ability to never move any muscle on his face. He looked back to the road.

"I don't *know* of him. I *am* him."

The silence that befell us was very heavy. At first, I heard his voice repeat in my head as I tried to make sense of the revelation. "I don't understand."

"There is nothing to understand. I know who you really are. We communicated prior to me finding you or Street."

I looked away from him. "Fuck," I muttered. "I can't believe you're . . . Fuck. How come this never came to anyone's notice?"

"You're one to talk." He glanced at me with a stern glare.

"When I said my name, and you realized who I was, why didn't you react then?"

"I was also at risk of revealing who *I* was. I am not one to meddle in shit that doesn't concern me, and I stopped being E2 when Street was created."

I sighed, my chest growing heavy as I looked his way again. "So, you've let me hang around your brother for the past couple months, knowing who I was and what I'm capable of?"

His jaw clenched. "You promised not to hurt him, and I believed and trusted you. Even after knowing your last name."

My eyes turned from him and back to the road. "Well, you're right. I have no intention of hurting him. He means more to me than you know."

"I'm guessing he doesn't know." His voice was stern.

"I plan to tell him," I stated.

From my periphery, I knew he was shaking his head.

It was quiet for a short while until he broke it. "Was everything with Street staged?"

I swallowed. Hard.

I squared my shoulders, keeping my gaze trained ahead. "We're almost nearing the location; we should turn on our comms—"

"Was everything staged, Zahra?"

I turned to look at him. "I love Street, okay? I love each and every one of you. You guys are like the family I never got to have, and while it didn't start like that, it doesn't mean that everything we've been through together doesn't mean shit to me."

"Will you tell them?"

My heart and nervousness went a bit wild. "I will. When I get everything I want."

Another tense silence passed, and he broke it again. "You were my last job."

"What?"

"You. I was paid to kill Zahra Faizan. I only got your name, which I recognized from when you were my client. I didn't take the job or any other information about you. Shortly after, I found you, and you made Street. I left that life behind and became Devil."

"Who sent you to kill me?" I asked.

"Ignazio Conti."

I rolled my eyes. "Of course," I muttered. "What other way to get the seat than to kill me off so Vitale wouldn't have standing? He's going to be a problem."

"You're a problem," Devil muttered angrily under his breath.

I faced the road, clenching my jaw. "Only to those who are a problem to me," I responded, looking his way. "Are you going to be?"

He went quiet, jaw clenching. He didn't reply.

I nodded, looking away from him with a frown. "Turn on your comm; we have work to do."

We pulled over at a lone dirt road, and I looked left and right, seeing nothing for miles, just dried-up weeds, sand, and withering farmland outside.

We got out of the car, and Dog walked toward us from the car he had been in. He looked around, eyes taking in our surroundings. "You sure we're at the right place?"

"Yes," Upper said in our ears. *"You're standing where the coordinates led."*

"Maybe we need to be looking for something unusual," Milk offered. *"We might not see what we're supposed to see because the whole area is disguised to look like nothing but a dirt road."*

"Yeah . . ." My eyes zeroed in on a lone healthy apple tree a few meters from the woods.

Looking to either side of me, I saw Dog and Devil staring at the tree too.

"I have a very crude Adam and Eve joke that would be so inappropriate to say right now," Dog said.

"Keep it to yourself," Devil ordered, surveying the area.

"Admit you're dying to hear it. You're legit on the edge of your seat to hear it."

"I'm not sitting."

I stepped forward. "We should—"

The revving of multiple engines halted my statement as I spotted numerous cars driving toward us from afar with blinding speed; Marino's men were quick to get into position.

A biker group was arriving from our left side, the roar of engines filling the area.

"Shit," Dog said, pulling out his gun at the same time I pulled mine out.

"Mr. Marino." One of the soldiers rushed toward Devil with a phone outstretched. "The boss wants to speak to you."

Devil collected the phone as a set of soldiers came around us.

I rechecked my gun while surveying our area, watching our right as the cars neared.

"We have to move," I said, not listening to what Devil was saying to Elio on the phone as we started rushing toward the tree, at almost the same time the people on the motorcycles opened fire.

Loud bangs were coming from everywhere around me.

But we were well covered against the shooting happening around us. I could feel a strange kind of heat that rocked the severity of our situation straight to my head.

"Hey, he wants to talk to you," Devil said, handing the phone over to me as he got his gun out.

Collecting the phone, I pressed it against my ear, turning off the comm while letting my gaze settle on the woods and bushes behind the tree, spotting movements. "Now's not a great time, Elio."

"I am aware. I can practically hear it," he spoke. *"The gold and the flash drives are kept in different locations. I just arrived at the hotel where we'll meet."* He sounded so calm, like his brother and I weren't currently being shot at or surrounded by people who wanted what we were going for.

"How do you know they're in different locations?"

It was quiet for a second too long before he responded.

"Intel. It is in the same building, but the flash drives are kept in a safe."

"Building? All I see is a fucking tree, Elio."

"Yes, but there is an installed lock system by the side of the tree; Upper and Milk will give you the code to open the underground building. If I am correct, you are currently walking or running—based on your breathing—on top of the gold."

"Isn't that just awesome?"

"Do not panic. Casmiro has sent more arms your way; this mission is ours to win. All you have to do is keep calm and ignore the other people trying to get there before you. Remember, you're ahead."

"Really loving this pep talk, right now of all times," I said as we reached the tree, and I spotted the installed lock system while Devil and Dog hurriedly communicated with Upper and Milk to get it open. "How does it feel sitting peacefully in an expensive hotel room while your girlfriend is one bullet away from being killed?"

"You insisted you wanted to find the gold with your team, remember? You like to hustle for what you want. Besides, I have something important to oversee, and I trust you not to die. My trust aside, I paid you one hundred million dollars. The money was not free, querida."

"Fuck you, seriously, fuck you."

My heart was thumping so loud as I joined the men in covering Dog and Devil, one hand holding on to the gun as I fished for targets, getting too close to where we stood. My other hand was holding firmly on to the phone.

"Zahra," Elio called.

"I'm here," I said, my gaze shifting slightly to the woods again, lingering as I listened to Elio.

"Do you want me there?"

"No," I said. "I've got it."

"All right. I need you to get those flash drives yourself. Elia, Dog, and my men should be able to handle the gold perfectly."

I paused, dropping my brows down in a frown. "Why do you need me to get them?"

Another second too long of silence.

"Like I told you, the flash drives are kept in a safe. Only I know the password to open this safe. That was Arturo's favor to me, for petting his Chihuahua and not running from it. I will never understand his logic."

"Me neither."

"I can only trust you with this information."

I nodded, even knowing he couldn't see me. "Of course, I'll get the drives to you after we're done here. But hey—we need to talk; there's something important I have to tell you afterward."

"Stay alive, and we will talk."

I rolled my eyes. "I don't plan on dying today."

"Good," he said. *"The password is Rory."*

I frowned. "What?"

"That's the name of his Chihuahua. Nobody ever asked him, so he made it the password."

"Rich people."

The ground rumbled beneath my feet, and I stepped back simultaneously with Devil, Dog, and the other men around us.

A large round portion of the ground was rotating, going downward as it did, like a huge drill paving a safe passage for us. It revealed sets of metal stairs as it continued going down. The walls on the circular ground were also metal.

"Found the passage?"

"Yes."

He gave a *"Hm"* of approval. *"Be careful, Zahra. I expect you unharmed."*

"You will get me unharmed."

"Hm." It was quiet as some of the men went in first. *"Zahra?"*

"Yeah?"

"Te amo."

My heart missed a beat, and all the air rushed out of my lungs on cue. He didn't say it often, but when he did, the effect was long-lasting. I blew out an uneven breath and spoke quietly. "I'll see you soon."

The line disconnected, and I returned the phone to one of the men by my side, looking toward the woods again.

"What in the *Stranger Things*." Dog whistled as he followed behind some soldiers down to the open ground.

I was about to follow suit when Devil held my arm back as he turned off his comm. "Elio said you are getting the drives."

My eyes looked between his. "Yeah."

"He trusts you," he pointed out.

"I know. That's why I'm going to get the drives to him."

His eyes shone with suspicion.

I let out a sharp breath. "Come on, Devil, you've known me for almost six years. When I say you can trust me, I mean it. I will get the drives to him and tell him everything, and if I can convince him to let me look at one of the drives, we'll be saving many lives. Please trust me on this."

He stared at me for a bit longer. "Okay."

I let out a breath, about to leave, but he held me back.

"I'm choosing to trust you, Zahra. Don't make me regret it."

I turned on my comm. "I won't."

After a nod from him and confirmation from me, he let go of my arm as we climbed down the metal stairs and into the ground together.

CHAPTER THIRTY-SEVEN

Zahra

The lights above us were sensor lights; they only turned on when we were beneath them, and as we walked through the straight hallway, I created a brick wall over my mind, reminding myself why I was there. I hadn't bargained for a full-blown quest, but I admitted we had come a long way—*I* had come a long way—and finally, I was going to do all I had set out to do from the beginning.

I could still hear the shouts, echoes, gunshots, and thuds from aboveground. It was chaos out there, and if more arms and men didn't arrive to support the ones outside, we might as well prepare for the chaos that would be transferred here.

"I hate underground tunnels," Dog's voice echoed. "I've never been underground, but I hate it."

"We've lost connection to Upper and Milk," Devil said.

"Upper did say it might happen," I said, looking around.

Our footsteps echoed on the metal walkway. The smell of gas, fuel, and metal filled the area, and I allowed myself the liberty of letting out a breath. The device in one of the soldier's hands started beeping as we reached an intersection. There were two hallways—one on the left and another on the right.

"The device is picking up the location of the gold from the right," the soldier said.

"That means the flash drives are on the left side," I said.

Devil looked toward me with a nod. "Two soldiers will accompany you, just in case."

"Sure. I'll grab the drives and meet you guys back there," I said.

"Be careful," Dog said, and I nodded.

"You too."

"Call for the extraction team," Devil said to one of the soldiers as he and Dog headed down to the right, and I made my way toward the left side with two soldiers following me.

I turned another corner and didn't have to look too far to find the black box attached to the wall, alongside an alphabetical keypad and a small screen.

I looked back at both men who escorted me. "What time is it?"

One of them dropped his brow in confusion as he checked his watch.

"Twenty-nine minutes past three."

In about a minute, I would be certain my order had reached my people on time because I shouldn't have spotted them in the woods earlier.

They shouldn't be here. I fucking told Vitale to call this off.

The moment I turned back to the box, a loud explosion rocked and vibrated the walls, sending cracks along the metallic ceiling as sprinkles of sand fell from above.

Inside the building, gunshots rang so loud, echoing around the space, alongside yells from men and the thuds of bodies dropping.

I took off my comm, stared at it for a long, long minute before dropping it on the ground and crunching it with my boot. "Fuck," I cursed under my breath as I quickly pulled out my gun, removed the safety, and turned. "I'm sorry, guys." Their eyes widened with realization as I pulled the trigger before either of them could raise their weapons.

I shot one in the neck and the other straight to the chest, their bodies dropping as I turned to the box and typed out the password with shaking fingers—jumping slightly when another explosion rocked the building.

Footsteps rushed in my direction as I pressed enter after typing the password.

A soft clicking sounded from the box, and I rushed to pull it open.

There were six flash drive casings; only five were occupied, but the sixth was empty.

Someone's been here before me.

I closed my eyes. "Elio," I whispered, my stomach turning. "Goddamn it." I snapped out of it, opening my eyes and grabbing all five casings, checking the names carved onto them. Four of those names were familiar; one wasn't.

"Ma'am." I turned toward the voice as the footsteps halted, and a rumble shook the ground again.

My frown turned into a glare as I stared at the man who had spoken. "Nobody got my orders? I specifically asked everyone to stand back until they heard from me!" I seethed out.

"Mr. Conti overruled it," the man said, handing me a phone. "He's on the line."

I glanced at the phone before taking and pressing it to my ear. "You better have a good fucking explanation as to why you just ruined my whole plan, Vitale."

"Is the corporation shifting base a good explanation for you?"

My heart stopped for a second. "What the fuck are you talking about?"

"They know we're on to them. Now they're moving. We don't have time to wait for your lover boy's approval before we destroy these fuckers."

"We can't even destroy them! I didn't find a flash drive with their name on it."

"Impossible."

"There were six casings; one is missing, and it's definitely not theirs. Four of the flash drives are labeled with names of four of the most powerful families and political bodies, and get this—there's nothing on the Marino empire. Elio's name isn't on any of these."

"And the last one?"

"Something called MCSS."

"Hold on, I've heard that name before or seen it somewhere in Society dealings. I'm not sure, but we should check it out. It might just be what we're looking for."

"All right, I have to find Devil and—"

"Ma'am, we have to leave now," the guard said as the crack above us expanded. "This whole place is about to come down."

"I can't leave my friends."

"Faizan, get it together! Before your friends, there was your mission," Vitale's voice rang in my ear. *"Follow the guys, and get the fuck out of there so we can bring these bastards down once and for all."*

Fuck, fuck, fuck!

"I'll have them call you back when I get to safety." I ended the call. "Let's go," I said, brushing past the men as my mind tried to push away the fact that I was ignoring the missing drive, knowing exactly whose name was written on it.

There was smoke everywhere as we rushed back in the direction I had come. Men were all around me, protecting me from everyone running around with stacks of gold, even as the building was on the verge of collapsing. I couldn't spot Devil anywhere, but as I rounded a corner, I spotted Dog on the ground, fighting off another man who was trying to aim a gun right to his head—his head that had a gash that covered half his face in blood.

I wanted to rush toward him immediately, but the men around me stopped my movement. The small shift had Dog's head turning a little, his gaze locking with mine as I was being ushered out; his stare dropped to the flash drives in my hands and then back to me before his brows drew down in confusion and realization.

His opponent took that little opportunity to slam the gun right at the side of his head, knocking him out as another explosion rocked the building, and a loud rumbling reached my ears.

"We need to leave!"

I aimed my gun outside the circle of the men flanking me, shooting the person who'd hit Dog in the face. But there were more enemies coming, and he was lying there . . . vulnerable . . . I—

"Ma'am, we need to go now!"

My eyes stung as I looked back at Dog's unconscious body one last time, before turning and leaving the chaos behind.

A convoy was already awaiting us as we made it out of the hole, and I was ushered into a car. My heart was pounding; my eyes burned as the vehicle moved hastily. It was a disaster. I fucked up. I left them behind when I could have helped. I chose my mission and my goal over my family.

A decision I couldn't take back, a decision I would never be able to take back.

I prayed to God that Devil had survived and got to Dog in time before the whole place collapsed in on itself.

"Give me a phone," I said, and a device was passed to me. I typed in Elio's number and placed a call to him.

My chest grew tight when the first ring came through; I waited and waited and waited until the line cut. I called again, anxiety grazing the string of nerves in my body.

He didn't answer.

I tried three more times, and on the last try, my vision blurred, and I gave up. My hands shook, and I bit my bottom lip hard to stop the tears threatening to let themselves out.

I couldn't shake the feeling in my gut telling me how big a mistake I had made, but I hardened my mind, set my jaw, blinked away the tears, and held on.

All good things. You're doing a good thing. This is the right thing. You're saving lives. You're doing the right thing.

It took two hours, but we got to a safe house, and I was handed a laptop after placing a call to Vitale.

"You better be right about this MCSS. Because I swear

to God, Vitale, you'll pay dearly if anything happens to my friends."

I could almost see him rolling his eyes. *"We don't have time for your melodrama, Zahra; everything you have worked your ass off for is on the line, one bit of information away from being screwed to hell. The last things you should be worried about are your friends with weird names."*

I ground my teeth together. "Just letting you know," I said as I inserted the USB drive into the laptop. Nerves racked my body as I clicked on the small icon displayed on the screen and stopped short.

"Marino Caporegime Sovereign Society?" I read aloud, my heart beating so fast against my chest.

"He's there after all; what are they about?"

Names of different countries were labeled in different folders.

"Hold on," I said, clicking on one of the folders marked ITALY. Tons of documents were displayed on the screen, dating back years before I was born. "Hold on . . ." I trailed off, squinting as I opened one of the documents dated a few years ago.

My heart stopped, something shifted, my mind drew a blank, and I wasn't breathing.

"Faizan?"

Shipping details . . . bank transactions . . . names and numbers of children, dates of birth, birthplaces, trafficking receipts, details of newborns needed—the when and the where, details of women and men designated to houses in different cities and regions in Italy. Names of headquarters in disguise like . . . like P. Deluxe Corp.

Everything . . . everything . . .

I opened and closed so many documents, my eyes burning as I read words that breezed past my head, words that hurt to read . . . my vision was blurry, my cheeks were wet, my hands were shaking, and my breathing was loud.

"Faizan, talk to me, what's happening?"

Everything, every authorization, the largest funds collected from the disgusting details right in front of me, every fucking line and link of the whole damn operation went back to one person. One name.

Elio Marino.

Even to the year I was born, the year I was trafficked, down to the Handler houses and the sex slavery base; his signature gave the final authorization.

I felt faint in the head. I wanted to pass out and die and scream and vomit.

"Zahra, talk to me."

"It's impossible," I whispered.

"What?"

"It's impossible, Vit. It's not him."

"What are you talking about?"

"The MCSS. It's them. They run the trafficking ring and so much more. P. Deluxe is a tiny portion of how large they are. This whole thing is bigger than us, Vitale. And it says here that Elio authorizes everything, but I promise you he doesn't know about this. He can't know about this."

"What?" He sounded as shocked as I was.

"I don't believe—he would never . . . he doesn't know this."

"How does he not know about something this big?"

"I don't know, but he wouldn't do this."

"You think? Zahra, I'm pretty sure every proof of his fucked-up agenda is right before you. I should have seen this coming."

"But it's not—"

"Open your eyes, Zahra. Would he really tell you about something so secret? Something that pertains to you? You think you know everything about Elio Marino?"

I couldn't respond to that. My chest drew tight, and I felt so betrayed that I wanted to pull my walls down and shoot everyone trying to get in.

"I warned you. Fucking hell, Zahra, he's been distracting you from the bigger picture. We have to act fast and act now."

"There's no acting now." My voice was hard as I straightened, wiping forcefully at my cheeks. "This is big, Vitale. It's more than we prepared for."

"We can start by bringing down P. Deluxe."

I tried to level my breathing as I exited out of all the documents, finding the one regarding P. Deluxe and sending the details to Vitale. "I sent you all you need. Bring it down."

"And you?"

"I have to handle Street. I'll call you." I ended the call.

I had deviated, forgotten how ruthless these people could be, forgotten what had made Elio who he was. I had forgotten that he was a liar, just like me, and he was skilled at it, perfect—if not more perfect than I was.

Even after registering all this, I still needed to hear him say it. I needed the confirmation of his deceit, of his lies. I needed a reason to kill this feeling of betrayal and replace it with the hate I so badly wanted to feel.

But more than anything, I wanted to be wrong.

I needed to be wrong.

CHAPTER THIRTY-EIGHT

Zahra

It was nighttime before I reached the location I had traced Street to. I had spent hours getting information about what had happened after I left. Not all the gold had been removed, but about two containers had left with Marino's people before the place collapsed, leaving many dead.

I had no information about who was hurt and who was not, but I knew Street was in a hospital in the city.

Walking into the building, I spotted some of Marino's men around the area; they watched me but didn't stop me. Something in the air told me I wasn't welcome here.

I knew that, too, and that was why I wouldn't be here for long.

The receptionist directed me toward the room they were in.

I was nervous and a little scared. I carried a heavy heart as I stepped out of the elevator, walked toward the room, and stopped in front of the door.

This wasn't exactly what I had planned. But it was nobody else's fault but mine.

I breathed, hoping it would calm the tightness in my chest. When it didn't, I pushed the door open and walked in.

Their talking halted, and my gaze zeroed in on Dog, who was on the bed, sitting up—alive—he was all right, even with the bandage around his head and a broken arm. He was okay, he was alive.

This time, when I released a breath, it freed some of the tightness in my chest.

Milk stood beside Dog on the bed. Upper was on the seat at the other side of the bed, and Devil was by the window; all eyes were on me.

"You sure have some fucking nerve coming back here and showing your fucking face," Dog said, and the hate in his eyes was new, something I never thought would be directed at me, from him.

The look strangled and squeezed my heart in a brutal vise.

Upper looked away from me like he couldn't bear to look at me for a second longer.

And Milk? There was nothing there. There was nothing in her gaze; she just looked at me like she was looking at a stranger.

Devil—with the way he looked at me—was disappointed.

"Get the fuck out," Dog said.

"I will. I just wanted to—" I let out a small breath. "I'm sorry, I know I fucked up—"

"You more than fucked up. You crossed over the line of fucked up, and we don't wanna hear it," Dog said. "Get the fuck out."

"At least hear me out, I'm sorry—"

"We don't even know who you are," Milk said. "You had a whole freaking convoy to usher you out. Did you forget we had eyes outside that area?"

"And you left them there to die," Upper said. "You betrayed us, and you betrayed Marino. I don't think a simple *I'm sorry* will be able to fix anything."

I didn't leave because I wanted to save only myself. I left for a good cause. I could tell them that, but I was done being selfish—I had brought them together, and now I had to let them go. I was going to be in this for the rest of my life, I always knew that. I couldn't pull them down along with me. This was too dangerous, too personal, it was too fucked up for them. I couldn't ruin them with any of it. I already took too much. I had to become one of their bad memories because I didn't deserve to leave this unscathed.

I couldn't have my cake and eat it. They deserved better.

"I'm not here to fix anything," I said, and Devil frowned. "Honestly." I huffed out a laugh. "I don't fucking care about any of this shit you guys are trying to throw at me. I know I left, and I betrayed you guys. I know where I'm at fault, and I'm fucking owning it and apologizing for it, and if you guys can't take my apology, then so fucking be it."

"This motherfucker," Dog gritted out under his breath.

"Zahra, whatever you're trying to do, this is most definitely not the best way to do it," Devil said with a glare.

"I don't care," I replied, squaring my shoulders. "Street was fun, and this was nice. But I created it, and now I'm uncreating it. There's so much going on that you fuckers don't know about, and shit just got very fucking real for me, and everything I've worked so damn hard for is on the line right now because I chose this path." I let out a shaky breath.

"Let me guess," Milk started. "We were a means to an end for you, weren't we? A small piece of whatever grand scheme you're a part of."

"If that's what you wanna hear, then yes. I specifically picked each and every single one of you because there was a lot to benefit for my whole personal fucking selfish gain. All skilled people, alone, looking for a home, looking for friends, ambition, riches, fucking purpose. I gave you all that shit, and now in a way, I've also given you gold. I'm the bad guy, ta-fucking-da."

"Get out," Devil said; the anger in his eyes held firm. It was promising. But the promise wasn't anything good. "Seriously, fucking leave."

"I was leaving anyway," I said, my heart squeezing even more. "Upper was leaving, too . . . I thought I should mention."

Upper's head snapped up, his eyes finding mine, wide with apprehension. "What the bloody hell, Zahra!"

"What? You weren't going to tell them?" I laughed, but it

was humorless. "This was a fucking sinking ship, we all wanted different things."

"You're leaving?" Devil directed the question to Upper.

"No, it's not—I didn't make the—"

"Also, Devil knew who I was for weeks and didn't tell any of you. I'm not the only one who isn't loyal and is capable of betraying all of you."

"What the hell is wrong with you, Zahra?" Milk asked, looking at me with disbelief.

"Oh please, don't pretend to be all fucking innocent now. You haven't always had it easy here. I know you still have nightmares about your mom, and you wanted them to stop. Street was supposed to be your escape but ended up being a prison where we do the same things your mom always did to you . . . The pretty face, the beautiful body, your only assets, your only actual value in Street. What was it you said on the cruise? How you wanted to be normal, and have a normal life? News flash, Milk, you can't be around us and have a normal life, and you know that. And somewhere deep fucking down, you're looking for a way to leave. Am I wrong?"

She couldn't speak, and the tears in her eyes told me I had broken something between us that could never be repaired.

I looked around us and almost broke into tears then and there. I couldn't see any of them clearly due to the tears filling my eyes. "You've all got the gold; you've all got a second chance to be who you want, to take revenge on life and experience all the things you've missed out on because of your fucked-up parents. So you each take the gold and get the fuck out of Italy and these fucking streets.

"Forget about me. I'm nothing; I ruined us. I'm one bad dream, another black spot in your past because, truth be told, if I could turn back time to when we were underground, I would choose myself over each and every single one of you. Over and over again. That's who I am. That's Zahra Faizan."

"I bet you're proud of it," Dog seethed.

"Oh yes, I'm very fucking proud," I said. "I started this whole thing. Not because I wanted a family or friends. I had a job to do; I needed the perfect pretense, and Street was created. I succeeded. I got what I wanted, and now I don't really need any of you anymore."

"You are fucking disgusting," Milk said.

"You're not the first one to tell me that; get in line, Pen."

"You carry on like this," Dog said, "and your ego will be the very fucking thing to kill you, mark my words."

I swallowed, pausing a second before I spoke. "Yeah, already marked," I said. "Like Milk said, Street was a means to an end for me, and this is that end. Hope you all have good fucking lives," I said, maintaining a stoic look as I turned and stepped out of the room. The mask I had put on my face fell immediately. I covered my mouth with my hand as tears fell freely from my eyes while I rushed to the elevator, tapping it repeatedly until it opened. I stepped in, collapsing against the wall, sliding down when the doors closed.

Sobs left me. I didn't shield them because my heart was breaking, and I was letting it break because I didn't want this—I didn't want this at all.

But I was cursed, and I'd spent the past six years escaping that curse, but now it had caught up with me.

I could never be happy—nor could I have anything good. I wasn't born to escape a miserable life; I was born into it, and I would die being miserable. That was the curse attached to every Plant.

Cursed to be lonely, never to be loved, only to be used and controlled. I had found a way to eradicate being used and controlled, but the loneliness would forever remain, and I allowed myself to dream.

But not anymore—now was the time to ensure no child was born with that curse ever again.

Now was the time to destroy the MCSS; I couldn't be weak. Not now, when I was at the start of another race.

I just had one more stop before I took off on the run.

I pulled out my phone from my pocket, calling Vitale. He picked up on the first ring.

"Faizan."

"I took care of Street. I'm pretty sure they'll be out of Italy in the coming weeks."

It was quiet until he asked softly, *"Are you okay?"*

"No." I sniffed. "Spread the word, get everything in order, and tell everyone." I wiped my tears. "Tell every motherfucker that I'm coming back to my city."

CHAPTER THIRTY-NINE

Elio

Loyalty was a word I liked to think resonated with who I was as a person—at least, most times, in certain situations.

An outsider looking in might be the first to think otherwise; not everyone knew who I was, but everyone made assumptions based on what they saw and heard.

Yes, I might be a liar. I might say one thing and then do the opposite, but if I made a promise or an affirmation to someone I cared about, I was bound to follow through. I was constrained to honor it in a form best suited for the situation, no matter how adverse it might be for the person or how much they despised my methods of keeping a promise.

Of course, not everyone was built this way, and I completely understood that. I understood many things I should probably question, but my heart, mind, and being had pushed my head into withholding my suspicions and keeping my conclusions to myself until I heard from her.

Until I heard from Zahra—I raised the flash drive I had been holding on to for a day—until she told me why exactly her name was imprinted on this drive.

Why she had left the underground with the flash drives, accompanied by people she had never once mentioned.

Why she had left behind her friends. Not once looking back.

I knew she would be here; I counted the hours, the minutes, and the seconds. I was ignoring the doubts tearing through my insides, little by little, knowing she would come back to me, and even if she didn't return for me, she would return for this drive and whatever content it held.

After all, that might have been the reason she was here in the first place.

Though I knew she had another motive aside from finding the gold with Street like she had claimed, I never once asked because I saw past whatever she was concocting.

I saw her.

I fell in love with her.

I cared for her and had ignored whatever deceit came with her because I trusted she would eventually feel comfortable telling me whatever she had been keeping to herself.

But then again, I could have handled every scenario of possible things she would have wanted out of coming here and doing things under my protection, but the last thing I expected was this.

A flash drive dedicated to her.

I didn't check it.

The last thing I would do was learn something about the woman I loved through a hardware device made by someone who could speak the truth and still not be as in-depth as it would be coming from her directly.

I drank from the whiskey glass, dropping it on the table as my eyes returned to the drive.

ZAHRA FAIZAN

The first time I saw the drive in that box after reaching the underground a day ago, I had completely ignored the drives labeled MCSS and THE SERPENT SOCIETY. I picked up and left with the one I'd never expected or predicted would be there.

I couldn't determine the future, and I had no idea how their mission had gone today, but I couldn't risk her flash drive entering into the wrong hands, so I took it and left the rest.

Casmiro had tried to convince me to check it and to grab the one marked MCSS. But I didn't care for those. They could fall into the enemy's hands—it would most likely be doing me a favor. I didn't care about their affairs, seeing as they were sovereign—but I hadn't found a flash drive with my name on it, nor had I found one with my father's or my empire's names. I had found one with *her* name on it, and I needed answers.

Asking her to be the one to get the drives wasn't a test per se—she was supposed to piece two and two together when I gave her the password and told her the flash drives would be in a separate space from the gold.

Upon seeing her flash drive missing, I expected her to know who was responsible. I was the only one who knew the password, and if the safe had been hacked prior, she would not have needed a password to get to it.

I did not know what she was hiding, but I knew I had already forgiven her—that is if it had anything directly to do with me. I wanted answers because I'd failed to predict her actions; I was beyond positive Zahra would return to me with the flash drives.

But she hadn't.

I needed to know what had gone wrong, if it pertained to whatever she wanted to discuss with me, and why she had chosen to do something so drastic, knowing she could lose her friends' trust and possibly mine. What could have—

Gunshots sounded suddenly from outside my hotel room, and my thoughts halted as I listened in—muffled thuds, grunts, and combat that was too smooth and fast, enough to be missed if one didn't pay attention to the rise and fall of the sounds the atmosphere around them provided.

Suddenly, they stopped, and the sound of a door opening and closing reached my ears. I stilled but didn't turn.

My hand fisted around the flash drive in a vise grip, listening to the careful footsteps entering the bedroom—searching for me—a whiff of her perfume hit my nostrils, and I closed my eyes as her footsteps drew nearer, entering the small office-like space the hotel suite provided.

The footsteps stopped, and then what followed was the click of a gun leaving its safety.

I smiled.

"Turn around and get on your knees." Her scratchy voice, on edge, thick with emotions, had my jaw locked.

"Are we role-playing?"

"Do I sound like I'm fucking around?"

"Hard to tell," I spoke into the silence, listening to her unsteady breathing. "You do not sound quite like yourself at the moment."

I couldn't see her, but I knew she'd probably just shifted on her feet. I knew her heart was pounding—from the way she sounded, I knew she was hurt, though not physically—and from the way she talked, I knew something else had happened.

"Turn around, Elio."

Allowing another minute, I flexed the corded muscles around my neck and tentatively turned.

Her eyes were filled with . . . anger, swollen with tears she had probably cried before coming here, and I watched how fresh tears welled in her eyes as she looked down at my hand, which held the flash drive. "Get on your knees and hand over the drive." Her voice shook.

Concern tugged at a muscle in my chest, and I stepped closer. "What's wrong, Zahra?"

Her hands tightened on the gun, her index finger deadly close to the trigger. "Don't come any closer."

I frowned, taking another step, and she shifted on her feet, eyeing me carefully like she was genuinely scared of my next move, scared of me. "I'm warning you, Elio."

"Is this how you want to do this? Choose violence over cordiality?" I caught her swallowing as a tear slipped down her cheek. "What's wrong, querida?"

She sniffed, her hands flexing around the weapon's hilt as she flexed her shoulders. "I'm counting in my head. If you don't do as I say, I *will* shoot you."

"What happened?"

The anger flared in her eyes, and they hardened to slits. "Get on your fucking knees, Elio. Don't make me repeat myself."

She was going to do it. She would shoot me if I didn't comply; she was apparently too angry to see reason, and I was confused as to why this was happening. It couldn't be from the fact that I hadn't told her I had been to the underground before her or her team.

I had disarmed the building and dealt with unnoticeable traps that could have led to instant death for trespassers. I had been my usual self, always ten steps ahead . . . just like I had with the first two locations.

She took a threatening step forward. "Down. On your knees. Now."

I sighed. "All right, relax," I said, eyeing her and the gun before raising my hand a little to show her I meant no harm, neither did I intend to cause her harm, as I got on my knees before her. "You have me where you want me; now, can you please tell me what happened today and why you're crying?"

As if just noticing the tears on her cheeks, she rushed to wipe them off, still pointing the gun at me.

"Querida—"

"Don't call me that," she said without missing a beat. "Give me the flash drive."

"I will not," I told her, not letting my eyes fall from hers. "Not until you tell me what went wrong today."

She scoffed; her red-rimmed eyes, filled with tears, pierced me with the most cutting glare she had ever given me. Hate. There was so much hate in that glare. My thoughts faltered for a second, wondering why she would look at me like that. "I found your flash drive," she said, her chest rising and falling at an abnormal rate. "That's what went wrong."

I frowned. "That is impossible. I do not have one dedicated to me."

"Oh, but you do. The MCSS. Ring any bells?"

My brows shot up. "Oh, them."

Her expression twisted from hate to pure loathing, a snarl in her words as she said, "How did it feel, Elio? Listening to me talk about being violated by men old enough to have fathered me? How did it feel when I cried and you offered false comfort? How did it feel to make promises to me, telling me you would find the people responsible for the trafficking ring when you are the direct channel to where they originate from?"

I paused, watching her with my frown deepening as her words settled in my head. "That is a very heavy accusation to throw at me, Zahra."

"Accusation?" she asked, sounding indignant. "Accusation? You can still kneel here and lie to my fucking face in pretense?"

I blinked, unsure of what she was talking about. "I promise you; this isn't me in pretense; this is me watching you accuse me of something so diabolical after everything we've been through together."

"I saw it," she gritted out. "Your name, your fucking signature, Elio, on every file, every document for the MCSS, regarding shipping of children, illegal births, trafficking rings from various countries . . . Every authorization came from you; you want to tell me you don't know what I'm talking about?"

My mind was working a million miles per second. I was confused beyond comprehension.

The MCSS . . .

Trafficking rings . . .

Illegal births . . .

My authorization . . .

"Fine, I'll show you," she said, digging her free hand into the jacket she wore over a white tank top as she pulled out some papers. "This was from the year I was born. Check it out." She flung the papers at me.

Taking my eyes from her, I picked up the papers, looking through them. Frowning as I read.

What in the world . . .

My mind was drawing a blank, and my heart wasn't functioning correctly as my eyes went on, word after word. My signature was there, my name was there, on the page, with the MCSS dealings . . .

"Two hundred and sixty-six children were born into this business and trafficked that year. Alongside me. Two hundred and sixty-six out of thousands from the following years, the years before mine, up until now—all without identities because they were made for one thing and one thing only, to be used this way, to be sold. How could you, Elio?"

My head snapped upward as my eyes met hers, understanding the hate within them.

Her words . . . they were like consecutive slaps to my face.

Her accusation was cutting me more than the fact that this was what my father had needed my signature for when I was only eight.

She believed this. She believed I did this.

I tilted my head, watching her with disbelief as hurt made a home in the tightness beneath my chest.

It was that time all over again when my mother and siblings had burned in that church, my father had spread a rumor, I was accused, and no one had bothered to check the facts.

I dropped the papers, my gaze rising to the gun. I swallowed, letting the silence stretch as I looked back at her. "Well, what are you waiting for?"

She faltered at whatever she saw in my eyes.

"You have it all figured out. I hurt all those children and all those people . . . I am at the end of your gun. Kill me, get revenge once and for all, and end the MCSS and me. Then I won't hurt any more children, and I'll stop ordering my people to ensure all the trafficking is conducted perfectly."

"Your fucked-up sarcasm isn't really needed right now."

"Oh, it didn't sound like the truth? It didn't sound like something I would do? Did it sound absurd to you, Zahra?"

"You can't tell me you didn't know this was happening under your name, Elio, because that would be a lie. It's too huge to go under your nose."

"I don't know why you're still here fishing for answers when you've already made assumptions. You already think I'm capable of doing all that is written on this paper. You already look at me with hate; you've already pointed a gun at me."

I watched her throat work, her chest heaving.

We held our gazes for almost a minute, the doubt in her eyes filling the silence. The hurt I knew was in mine helped to accentuate the tension. I fought to control the dreadful heaviness on top of my heart. "You don't love me, Zahra," I said, my voice quiet as I swallowed. "You don't feel the same way I feel about you; you don't know what I'm capable of. You don't know me—and if I'm being honest, your accusation and your assumption without even deeming it fit to ask me? Hurts."

"How do you explain the signature—"

"Do I even have to explain anything to you?" The disbelief I felt made me wonder if this was really happening—if she was really asking me this. "Can't you see I would never be a part of something like this with everything you know about me? Isn't my—isn't my character enough to tell you that I would never do a thing like this? Isn't my love enough to show you that even if I knew about this happening under my name, I would tell you when you told me about your past?"

"Don't turn this around, what the fuck was I supposed to think? Your name was everywhere!"

"These people existed before I was even born. I have never been involved in the MCSS business, Zahra; neither did I care about what they were up to because when I decided to end my life, I was going to end this whole empire along with it. That was why I needed to find the flash drives. I didn't see one with my name, nor my empire's, nor my father's. The MCSS is sovereign. Do you know what 'sovereign' means?"

"I don't fucking care," she said, swallowing as tears welled in her eyes. "All I know is you are involved in the very thing responsible for this broken person that I am today."

I frowned. "Even if you know I didn't actively have anything to do with it?"

She didn't answer . . .

She didn't want to say something she couldn't take back.

What did she come here hoping to achieve?

I sighed. "You won't have to be at war with yourself if you just believe me—"

"I'll choose to believe whatever the hell I want to believe. I have been taught a lot of lessons in my life, and I cannot afford another one—not with you." Her voice shook. "Just give me the damn flash drive, Elio."

I looked at the drive in my hand. "Is this what you wanted? Is this drive the reason you needed the protection my name offered? You have a secret you don't want anyone to know? Or is this all for Manuel?"

She scoffed. "Manuel . . ." she mused aloud before she leveled me with a glare. "There's no Manuel, Elio."

I paused, watching her.

"There's just *me*. That flash drive belongs to me. I rule Sicily; I *own* Sicily. I've owned it for years."

I knew my soldiers would storm this place any minute, but the thought at the forefront of my mind was the information she had just let loose.

"You once asked me who I was," she said, her eyes and the tone of her voice promising malice. A different kind of composure—one that I saw and noted the first time she talked back to me—took over her features. "Manuel pushed me aside. He was done with me. Told me I could leave. He had used me, gotten all he wanted, and his obsession with me was slowly fading away . . ."

"You told me you left."

"I was naïve, tempted by the idea of freedom so I didn't see he had discarded me," she explained. "I left, yes. But I didn't tell you I went back. I went back, and slowly, gradually, I killed him. I made it hurt; I made it last a long time, made him suffer because nobody uses me, nobody *controls* me, I am the one who does the throwing away, I am the one in fucking control." She took a step forward. "I fought tooth and nail to become somebody in a world where I was made to be nobody.

"Manuel Conti has not been pronounced dead yet because I wanted it that way. Stopping this ring was my last mission before I settled down and tried to figure out what I wanted for myself and what I would do with the power I acquired after taking his life. I thought I had it all figured out. Bring down P. Deluxe Corp, stop the ring, and save a lot of people—and maybe I could get to keep Street, but then I found out that it is much, much more extensive than I thought, and the man that I—the man that I fell for, was the overseer of everything."

I could see the strength she'd used to hold the gun. The force of her hate. Her body shook with her words.

"I know the MCSS are sovereign," she bit out. "But without the Marino empire, they wouldn't exist; without your legal name as a backup, they wouldn't get away with this shit they're doing—trafficking and making children in the name of research facilities.

"I know you were maybe eight years old when I was born. But you're no longer eight, Elio. You're not a child; you know right from wrong and the consequences of ignorance, yet you chose never to check what these people were doing to earn you billions of dollars every damn month."

I clenched my jaw.

"What makes you think I would believe something so fucking unbelievable?" she asked.

"Because you're hurt, and you're not listening to me, and I understand—"

"You don't understand shit about me!"

"If you can just relax, sit down, and come to your senses

enough for you to think clearly, we wouldn't have to resort to being at odds with each other. We can figure something out."

"I don't want to figure anything out with you, Elio." She quickly looked toward the door and then back to me. "Give me the flash drive."

"Not until you listen to me. *Por favor*, Zahra, drop the gun. Any minute, my people will storm this room to find you pointing a gun at me. In this position, after your betrayal today, they will shoot first and ask questions later."

"Then give me the drive."

"I am not letting you leave. We can easily sort things out once you have a clearer mind."

The sound of footsteps reached us, and the moment she glanced back to the door, I charged. She gasped as I grabbed her wrist, raising her hand as a shot from the gun rang out, hitting the wall. I rose to my feet, and the weight of my body made her move backward as she fought me for the gun.

"Let go of the gun," I warned, but her grip was firm, even as I tried to pry her fingers from the weapon.

There was panic, anger, and hurt in her eyes, three dangerous emotions to be felt all at once. Three emotions that made me rethink our whole conversation. The tears that had been in her eyes, and her silence when I had asked her if she still hated me despite knowing I hadn't been actively fueling the MCSS's business.

"Zahra, we can talk about this."

"Let. Go. Of. Me," she said with grit, her voice strained as she tried to kick me, elbow me—anything to get me to let go of her and the gun, but I held firm, not wanting to hurt her.

"Why are you so scared of believing me? I know you know I have nothing to do with the MCSS, and I am ready to rectify my mistakes; why do you think I will hurt you when you know I do not judge you for your flaws and mistakes because we all make them? I love you regardless of your identity or anything you have done."

She supplied me with a humorless laugh. "Yeah?" she questioned, tears filling her eyes. "Even if I confess to being responsible for Casmiro's shooting?"

I held her wrist tighter as she tried to twist the gun until it was right at our sides, and my body pushed hers to the wall.

My eyes burned into hers as I said, "Even then, I love you."

Her lips trembled, her eyes softened, and her chest heaved, but she recovered from whatever thought had crossed her mind as her eyes hardened once more. "Well, I don't deserve it, and neither do I want it, so let me fucking go, Elio."

My heart squeezed. "Never. Not when I know that's not what you want."

"It's what I fucking want!" she lied, twisting her hand until the gun was between us. I felt it slipping from her grip as I fought with her to get ahold of it. I couldn't let my people see her with the gun. She was too stubborn, too hurt to see how dangerous that would be. "Let me go, Elio."

"Why!"

"I just want to leave, okay? I'm done here; give me the flash drive, and let me go. I *can't* be with you!"

I pinned her body to the wall, pressing against her, locking the weapon between us. "You want to leave me, Zahra? Do you think it'll be easy knowing all I know now? Did you think telling me all of this—hating me for something you know I wasn't responsible for, confessing to almost killing Casmiro, and making me think you didn't believe me when I told you I knew nothing about the MCSS—would make me let you go?"

Her façade faltered as my fingers worked on the gun between us while bringing my face closer to hers, her breathing mingling dangerously with mine. "You can run, Zahra; you can run like hell, go wherever the fuck you want to go, but know that I would never stop chasing after you. I will find you every damn time until you realize there is no point in running."

She closed her eyes, and tears ran down her cheeks as her body relaxed, trusting. "Why won't you just let me go, Elio?"

"Because I love you. Because whatever crime you commit is a crime I will forever be willing to forgive."

She shook her head. "No."

"Zahra—"

"I can't do this again."

"Listen to me—"

"No." She opened her eyes and pushed away from me, noticing her loss of control of the weapon. "I can't trust you. You and everyone in that fucking organization, you all are *monsters*, and I will not make the same mistake again. I will not trust the wrong person again."

"Zahra—" Her next move was fast; I didn't see it coming until I felt the pain exploding around my jaw from a hit caused by her head as she simultaneously slammed her leg against my shin, pushing me and regaining control of the weapon as she tried to reach for the flash drive.

I collected myself, swerved my hand, and threw the drive to another corner of the office. She charged toward it, but I blocked her path, my hand covering hers on the gun as she tried to push past me. This time, I didn't hold back on my strength. I tried prying her fingers off the weapon, leaning my weight over her.

"Zahra, listen!"

The sound of the hotel door slamming open made her jump in panic. She faltered, and as the weight of my body forcefully pushed hers to the wall, the gun went off between us at the impact.

She sucked in a sharp breath.

I froze.

Our struggles stopped as footsteps rushed into our space.

But they dulled out into background noise as the gun clattered to the ground.

Her breathing shuddered as she looked up at me, lips parted, eyes glistening. Slowly, ever so slowly, in my shocked stupor, I looked between us—at her chest. There was a rapidly spreading red stain on the white tank top she wore.

My heart stopped.

My mind stopped.

Everything stopped.

"El . . ." Her voice dropped faintly as she instinctively gripped the shirt around my bicep.

The last thing my sanity registered was the tiny sound of her breath stopping, the single tear that slipped from her drooping eyes, and her knees completely giving out right underneath me.

Acknowledgments

First things first, I want to thank my lord and savior for pulling me through.

To my wonderful agent, Thao Le, thank you for your constant support and cheers. To my amazing editor, Monique, the love you have for these characters never stops surprising me—thank you! And, of course, to the marvelous Mal, thank you for all you do! To the team at Bramble, you guys are awesome. Thank you for your continuous efforts in championing this series!

To my mom and dad, your prayers and your support for my passion will always be a blessing. Thank you! To my sisters and brothers, I wouldn't be here without your constant love and support, so thank you!

To my friends who have been with me from the start of this journey till now, thank you. I can't begin to start listing all the ways you made this process extra special!

To my inner circle at Maniero del Diavolo, your support will forever be the greatest thing this career has given me. Thank you Cat, Sofia, Lussy, Nono, Djama, Briar, Aleeza, Lea, Lisa, Rumy, Catherine, Dia, Directt, Mariam, and Maryam, I love you guys sooooo much!

To my wonderful PA, Salma, I thank the day you walked into my life and made this whole process smoother than I could have thought possible! Thank you!

And finally, to every reader, I appreciate you for spending time again with this series. I appreciate every support, every comment, shares and reviews—they mean the world to me!

Thank you, and see you in the next one!

About the Author

REBECCA JOHNPEE has been daydreaming epic, too-good-to-be-true scenarios since she discovered the magic in imagination. Once she found the art of putting those vivid scenarios on paper, she set out to make sure her characters found a home in the hearts of readers. Today, she writes romance across multiple genres, letting whichever story calls to her to lead the way. When she's not busy crafting new worlds, Johnpee is planning her next adventure to island countries, where she can indulge in her love for the ocean, meet new people, and immerse herself in different cultures.